MVFOL

Class

ALSO BY LUCINDA ROSENFELD

Class

A Novel

Lucinda
Rosenfeld

LITTLE, BROWN AND COMPANY
NEW YORK BOSTON LONDON.

Copyright © 2017 by Lucinda Rosenfeld

Little, Brown and Company
Hachette Book Group
1290 Avenue of the Americas, New York, NY 10104
littlebrown.com

First Edition: January 2017

Little, Brown and Company is a division of Hachette Book Group, Inc. The Little, Brown name and logo are trademarks of Hachette Book Group, Inc.

The Hachette Speakers Bureau provides a wide range of authors for speaking events. To find out more, go to hachettespeakersbureau.com or call (866) 376-6591.

ISBN 978-0-316-26541-6
LCCN 2016941820

10 9 8 7 6 5 4 3 2 1

LSC-C

Printed in the United States of America

To public schools everywhere

White people cannot, in the generality, be taken as models of how to live.

James Baldwin, *The Fire Next Time*

The poor are despised even by their neighbors, while the rich have many friends.

Proverbs 14:20

Class

K aren Kipple had always been an early riser. She relished the quiet, the calm, the way the light filtered
through the sycamore tree in front of her south-fac-
ing kitchen window, and the sensation of having the
house to herself, if only for an hour or two. Was it terrible to
admit that she never loved her daughter and husband so much
as when they were asleep? She also liked studying the forecast
while she drank her first cup of coffee of the day—checking
projected temperatures against monthly averages and feeling
appropriately blessed or outraged. As a child, Karen had made
fun of grown-ups who were always going on about the
weather; what could be duller? But as she'd gotten older, she'd
found herself endlessly diverted by the seeming randomness
and unpredictability of the sky overhead.

Karen had been married for ten years and, for the last five
of them, had been the director of development for a small
nonprofit devoted to tackling childhood hunger in the United
States. For the past two years, she'd also been trying to write
an op-ed, which she hoped one day to publish in a major news-

paper, about the relationship between nutrition and school readiness. Like many women, she struggled to balance the demands of motherhood and career, always convinced that she was shortchanging one or the other. But it was also true that, insofar as she'd long conflated leisure with laziness, her eight-year-old daughter, Ruby, provided her with a permanent alibi in the criminal case of Karen Kipple versus herself. Thanks to Ruby, Karen always felt busy and needed even when she wasn't officially working. And the permanent sense of obligation came by and large as a relief.

The only part of Karen's domestic routine that she consistently dreaded was getting her daughter up for school. Not only was Ruby a heavy sleeper who was almost always comatose when her alarm went off, but Constance C. Betts Elementary had recently moved up its start time to eight a.m. to accommodate the schedules of the teachers who lived in faraway suburbs and wanted to beat the traffic. Never mind that Betts was only three blocks away from the family's spacious two-bedroom condo in a converted nineteenth-century macaroni factory. Or that plenty of the students seemed to have no trouble arriving an hour early for the free breakfast, having commuted from parts of the city that, in some cases, Karen had never been to. Although Betts was a neighborhood school, it welcomed those from outside Cortland Hill as well, if only because it struggled to fill its seats with families who lived in zone. To Karen's shame and chagrin, Ruby often arrived late.

The morning in question, an unseasonably cold one in mid-March, began typically. Karen walked into Ruby's bedroom at 7:20 and found her daughter stock-still with her goldfish-motif quilt pulled over her head. Karen placed her hand on the lump below the quilt and gently rotated her from left to right. "Sweetie, it's time to get up."

There was no answer. Karen jostled and cajoled some more. Another three minutes went by, then four. Finally, there was movement, then a voice: "Leave me alone."

Karen had learned not to take Ruby's morning grumpiness personally. "I wish I could," she said. "But school is starting in exactly thirty-five minutes. And I've already given you an extra five. Plus, I made you eggs, and they're getting cold."

"Eggs are gross" came the reply. "They come out of chickens' butts."

"Well, then, you can just eat the toast," said Karen. There was more silence. Losing patience, Karen yanked the quilt off her daughter and said, "Get. Up. Now."

Finally, with a deep groan, Ruby rolled over, rubbed her eyes, and said, "What day is it?" Her flyaway brown hair looked like a bird's nest.

"Friday."

"I have gym today. I need to wear sneakers."

"Do you want me to get your sparkly ones?"

"Mr. Ronald is so strict," said Ruby, ignoring Karen's question. "He's always yelling at everyone, and he blows this whistle in your ear if you don't do what he says."

Karen sat down on the edge of the bed and leaned toward her daughter. "Don't tell anyone I told you this," she said, tucking a section of tangled hair around Ruby's ear. "But all the mean kids in school become gym teachers when they grow up."

Ruby seemed confused by the pronouncement. "*All* of them?" she asked, wrinkling her nose.

Karen considered the idea that, just maybe, she should have qualified her comments. What if Ruby repeated them to Mr.

Ronald? Or—God forbid—what if Ruby became a gym teacher when *she* grew up? "Well, not all of them, but many of them," she said. "Now, come on! It's the community-unit celebration this morning, so Mommy is actually coming to school with you."

This piece of news seemed instantly to alter Ruby's exhaustion level. "Yay!" she cried, bolting upright and throwing her legs over the side of her twin bed. In fact, Ruby's third-grade teacher had invited all the parents into the classroom that morning to view the breakfast-cereal boxes that, in keeping with a study unit on community, her students had decorated to look like civic buildings and storefronts.

It was 7:50 when Ruby and Karen finally put on their coats to leave. "Let's go wake up your lazybones father and say good-bye," said Karen, who never missed an opportunity to guilt her husband about his own struggles to remove himself from their bed. An incorrigible night owl, Matt often stayed up until two a.m. watching sports and reading left-wing political blogs. He could also sleep through a fire alarm. "Dad-ddddy, we're leaving," cried Ruby, half running down the hall, her knapsack flapping against her back.

"Rise and shine!" said Karen, following Ruby into the room and yanking on the shade cord to reveal a sharp-taloned sun.

"What time is it?" Matt muttered into his pillow.

"Time to get up," said Karen.

"Mommy says you're a lazybones!" said Ruby.

"Come here, you little whippersnapper," said Matt, reaching for Ruby's arm with his own impressively muscled one and pulling her into the bed, where he began to tickle and kiss her.

Ruby laughed and squealed. "Help! Daddy's keeping me captive."

"You actually have to let her go," said Karen. "Ruby's class is having its community-unit celebration this morning, and it's literally starting in six minutes."

"Shoot—why didn't you wake me up?" he said, reluctantly releasing Ruby and squinting at Karen. "I would have come."

"Oh, please," said Karen, making a superior face. "You were out cold."

The truth was that, although Matt's failure to help get Ruby up and out in the morning annoyed Karen in theory, in practice she found it easier to do it herself, without another tired and hungry body in the way—and doing everything the wrong way. The few times that school year that Matt had made lunch for Ruby, he'd put her sandwich loose in her lunch box and it had fallen apart. And then, according to Ruby, and even more traumatically, it had gotten soiled by an also-unwrapped pear.

Karen and Ruby arrived in the classroom with one minute to spare. There were just over a dozen parents in attendance, most but not all of them women. The majority of them were in jeans or sweats. A couple of them sported office attire. One mother, a smiley Yemeni woman whom Karen always exchanged warm hellos with, was wearing a long skirt and hijab. Karen had tried and failed to retain the woman's hard-to-pronounce name in her memory, and now it seemed too late, too insensitive, and too embarrassing to ask what it was again. Of course, what qualified as embarrassing was all a matter of perspective. At Ruby's eighth birthday party the year before, the woman's out-of-control daughter, Chahrazad, had gratuitously flashed her Hello Kitty underpants at a male classmate while belting out the pop-song lyric "'Heeeeeeyyyy, sexy lady,'" an awkward incident that Karen had still found less mortifying than the fact that, after the party, Chahrazad's mother had stood in front of Karen's building, forbidden, Karen had concluded, from entering another man's home.

While Ruby went to the closet to put away her coat and backpack, Karen made her way over to her best mom-friend in the class, Louise Bailey, who went by Lou. A freelance publicist and semi-stay-at-home mother of two—she had a daughter in fifth grade named DuBois and a son in Ruby's third-grade class named Zeke—Lou was also, hands down, the most stylish mother at Betts, if not the *only* stylish mother at Betts. "It's ridiculous how amazing you look," said Karen, who that morning, like every morning, was wearing nondescript basics in black and gray. Although she'd given up trying to be fashionable more than a decade ago, she still appreciated others who hadn't.

"Oh, please," said Lou, who was six years younger, three inches taller, ten pounds thinner, and wearing leather stovepipe jeans and a nubbly poncho she'd knit herself.

"Meanwhile, the excitement builds," said Karen.

"Can't you see me holding my breath?"

"I need more caffeine."

"Hands off, girl." Lou clutched her travel mug to her chest. "No fair."

"I bet you slept more than me last night."

"I bet you I didn't," said Karen, a chronic insomniac who had grown accustomed to getting by on five or six broken hours of sleep.

"Don't waste your money," said Lou. "DuBois threw up six times between midnight and five."

"Oh no. And okay, you win—"

"Welcome, parents of Room Three-oh-three!" Ruby's teacher, Tammy Hunt, shouted to be heard over the buzz of collected parents. A broad-shouldered, ruddy-faced triathlete of twenty-six, Miss Tammy had been an Outward Bound leader along the Canadian border before getting her master's in education. Her energy, dedication, and enthusiasm were still in evidence. So was her ability to command large groups of white-water rafters spread out across a quarter mile. "Over the past several weeks," she went on in a shockingly loud voice, "your *awesome* kids have been busy creating their own *amazing* community!"

"Ow," muttered Karen.

"And today we're inviting you to come explore it and to be the people in our neighborhood," Miss Tammy continued to trumpet.

"Where's Mr. Rogers?" Lou muttered back.

In suppressing a giggle—as a child, she'd belonged precisely to the *Mister Rogers*–watching public-television demographic—Karen accidentally released a noise that fell between a grunt and a snort. At the same moment, Ruby returned from the coat closet. "Mommy, come see!" she said, taking her mother by the wrist and leading her to the back of the classroom.

There, lined up atop a row of paint-splattered base cabinets, converted breakfast-cereal boxes formed a miniature skyline. A box of Frosted Flakes had been turned into a firehouse. A Life Cinnamon cereal had become a police station. A Nature's Path Organic Heritage Flakes box was now a grocery store. And a jumbo-size Cheerios, donated by Karen—Cheerios being the one mass-market cereal she was currently willing to buy—was a bank.

Or, at least, Karen assumed it was a bank, given the fact that her daughter had covered the box with royal-blue dollar signs. Unless it was supposed to be a pawnshop? Did her daughter know what a pawnshop was? Karen was contemplating the likely answer—to her knowledge, there was only one pawnshop still left in her actual neighborhood, no doubt soon to be shuttered and reborn as another luxury town-house development featuring oil-rubbed-bronze bath fixtures and radiant flooring—when Ruby lifted her gray-green eyes to her mother and said, "Do you like my Citibank?"

"Sweetie, Citibank is just the name of one particular bank," Karen said quickly. She was alarmed to think that her daughter had so thoroughly internalized a corporate brand that it had become interchangeable in her mind with the thing itself. Never mind the brand's contribution to the financial crisis of 2008. Though from what Karen had read, all the big banks were to blame. And besides, as a fund-raising professional, she relied on the largesse of financial-industry executives. "I think you just mean *bank*," she went on.

"Bank—whatever," said Ruby, clearly annoyed.

"I know that was all you meant," said Karen. "Anyway, you did a great job with the decorations!"

The sound of metal legs skidding across linoleum refocused her attention. It was followed by a piercing yowl. Karen turned toward the commotion and found Ruby's best-friend-of-the-moment, Maeve, cupping her face and wailing. Two feet away, Jayyden, a boy who had been in Ruby's class two years in a row, stood motionless, his arms crossed and his lower lip and jaw extended. Within seconds, it became clear that there was blood rushing out of Maeve's nose. Miss Tammy, who had no doubt honed her emergency management skills leading a dogsled team across the frozen tundra of

Boundary Waters, Minnesota, rushed to the scene. After expertly wrangling the girl into a chair and instructing her to tilt her head back, she turned to the parents and began issuing rapid-fire instructions: "Someone grab me a paper towel," "Call the school nurse," "Call the principal," "Have the main office contact Maeve's parents."

Wanting to be useful and feeling vaguely proprietary of Maeve, Karen offered herself up for the last task. But another parent had beat her to it. So Karen found herself standing helplessly with the others in a circle that had formed around the child and her immediate caretakers. This group soon included the school nurse, a squat-legged woman of indeterminate age, who quickly succeeded in stanching the blood flow.

Only then did Miss Tammy turn to the culprit. "Jayyden," she said. "Would you like to tell me what you had to do with this?"

It was several seconds before he spoke. "She told me my firehouse looked stupid," he mumbled plaintively. "Like me."

Tammy grimaced; cooperation and respect were her two big classroom themes. "That was not respectful of Maeve to say," she said. "But it also does not give you the right to punch her!" At that very moment, Karen could have sworn she heard Maeve ramp up the sniveling. "You're in *seriously* big trouble now, buddy," Miss Tammy went on with a quick laugh, her head waggling.

"Oooooh" went the more vocal members of the class, intuiting that this could only mean one thing for Jayyden: a visit to the office of Betts's longtime principal, Regina Chambers. An elegant African American woman in her midfifties, Principal Chambers had exceptionally good posture and a life-size cardboard cutout of President Obama next to her desk. Nearly everyone at the school was intimidated by her, Karen included, with the possible exception of a bunch of well-meaning Caucasian kindergarten mothers, new to the school and likely soon to depart it, who were constantly complaining about how the milk served in the cafeteria came from hormone-treated cows.

Of course, none of the same mothers would be caught dead letting little Henry or Tessa anywhere near the school lunch, instead packing aseptic eight-ounce cartons of organic vanilla milk in their children's bento lunch boxes, next to BPA-free Tupperware filled with fresh berries. Indeed, the only children at Betts who partook of Taco Tuesdays and Fish Finger Fridays were the ones getting it for free. But that was another matter…

In response to Miss Tammy's warning, Jayyden hung his head—so low that his chin was nearly touching his neck. All the better to hide his own tears, Karen suspected. As she stood watching the unfolding scene, her brain swirled with conflicting emotions. She couldn't help but feel that, to a certain extent, Maeve deserved it. In that moment, Maeve may have been the victim. But Karen hadn't forgotten how the child had come to her house for a playdate recently and peed in the bathroom trash can, or the time that Karen had taken her and Ruby out for overpriced whoopee pies at the "old-fashioned" bakeshop up the street, and Maeve had spit at the waitress.

Karen tried not to judge how other people raised their children, but in truth, she rarely missed an opportunity to do so. And in her opinion, Laura Collier and Evan Shaw, who co-owned a production company that specialized in TV and web commercials, were doing a fairly shitty job. They'd essentially farmed out the parenting to a rotating cast of Tibetan nannies who seemed to quit every three months because they were paid substandard wages yet were expected to do the grocery shopping and cook and clean as well as child-mind. Meanwhile, the amount of time Laura and Evan spent with Maeve and her younger brother seemed to be inversely proportional to the number of pictures they posted of them on Facebook and Instagram. They also ran an almost impossibly tight ship (from afar), insisting that their children wear sunscreen 365 days a year and abstain from all foods containing added sugar. Was it any wonder that, according to Ruby, Maeve hoarded Tootsie Rolls under her bed?

But then, was Karen any less neurotic or uptight than Laura about sun protection and sucrose?

And was it any surprise that Jayyden had hit Maeve? *Poor, unloved Jayyden.* From what Karen had heard around school, Jayyden's mother was in prison. And he'd never met his father, if such an individual could even be identified. As a result, he was reputed to live with someone named Aunt Carla and various cousins in a public housing project, Fairview Gardens, on the edge of the neighborhood. The project consisted of half a dozen mid-rise 1960s-era brick buildings with small barred windows. If there was any flora or fauna to be found around its concrete courtyards, Karen hadn't seen it. Friends in the neighborhood sometimes referred to the place ironically as the *pro-jay*—that is, as if it were fancy and French. (They called the big box store Target, *Tar-jay,* for the same reason.) Of course, it was just the opposite. That was the joke. Karen still hadn't determined if it was offensive or funny.

In all her time in Cortland Hill, Karen had entered Fairview Gardens only once—on a charity mission with Ruby's predominantly white Girl Scout troop, the year before.

(The residents of Fairview Gardens were almost entirely black.) The Daisies had been working on their Rose Petal, an embroidered uniform badge whose coordinating motto was "Make the world a better place," when a ferocious storm had cut off electricity to the buildings in the project for more than a week. It had been the troop leader's idea for the girls to make and deliver platters of peanut butter and jelly sandwiches to Fairview's community center. Karen had supported the plan wholeheartedly and offered to help. But entering the community center, a desolate affair featuring haphazardly arranged metal fold-up chairs, a Ping-Pong table with no net, and not a soul in sight, Karen had been simultaneously embarrassed and frightened. Reports of gang-related shootings at Fairview Gardens were not uncommon.

There was a personal angle to Karen's sympathy for Jayyden as well. In the beginning of second grade, he'd taken to imitating Ruby and, on those days when Karen picked Ruby up from school, and even though he hardly knew Karen, coming over to embrace her as if she were his own mother. As she'd patted his head and said, "Hello, sweetie," she'd felt proud and despondent in equal parts. He'd cut out the behavior after a month or two. Sometime the following spring, Karen heard rumors that an unnamed relative had been found to be abusing Jayyden. Children's Services had become involved. For a nanosecond, Karen imagined taking Jayyden into her home as a foster child, but then realized it was probably beyond her capabilities. Besides, who knew if Jayyden would even want to come? In any case, it had become clear in recent months that Jayyden had serious behavioral problems, if not an actual violent streak. Even before today, there had been reports of shoving and hair-pulling. A year older and larger than his third-grade classmates—he'd been left behind in kindergarten for not knowing his letters or colors yet—he'd also begun to cut a figure in the classroom that Karen imagined other children might find, as much as she hated to put it this way and as confident as she was that it had nothing to do with the color of his skin, physically intimidating.

But it was also the case that Karen aspired to a life spent making a difference and helping those less fortunate than herself. She tried to live in accordance with the politics and principles she believed in. These included the notion that public education was a force for good and that, without racially and economically integrated schools, equal opportunity couldn't exist. And so, the year Ruby turned five, Karen had happily enrolled her at Betts, aware that it lacked the reputation for academic excellence of other schools nearby but pleased that Ruby would be exposed to children who were less privileged than herself.

Yet over the previous three-plus years, a part of Karen had also come to feel thankful for any and all middle-class Caucasian or Asian children who attended Betts—and desirous that there should be more. (At present, the white population of the school hovered around 25 percent.) The truth was that she'd yet to grow entirely comfortable with being in the minority. Nor had she ever fully recovered from the shock of walking into Ruby's new classroom on her first day of kindergarten and finding herself gazing out on what appeared to her eyes to be a sea of beaded braids, buzz cuts, and neon backpacks with rubberized cartoon decals that ran counter to her finely honed bourgeois-bohemian aesthetic sensibility, which prized natural materials and a muted palette.

Karen had also failed to fully exorcise the deep-seated fear that a school having both an abundant population of brown and tan children and middling standardized test scores, as Betts did, must by definition offer an inferior educational experience.

But she also saw the school's diversity was an educational experience unto itself and, once or twice, had even felt teary-eyed at the spectacle and promise of so many beautiful children of so many different hues and hair types walking down the hall together.

And by any measure, Ruby had done well at Betts. A voracious reader, she was also proficient in adding, subtracting, and even early multiplication; sociable to the point of overbearing; and knowledgeable about many of the great figures of U.S. history, in particular Martin Luther King Jr. and Rosa Parks. In kindergarten, the white children in Ruby's class had had to sit in the back of the classroom for a period to see how it felt. And according to Ruby, her class had completed the same study unit on MLK four years in a row. Ruby could even recite the date he'd married Coretta (June 18, 1953). At Betts, it sometimes seemed to Karen that every month was Black History Month—except when it was Latino History Month. In keeping with the new Common Core curriculum, Ruby had recently written an "informative text," as essays were now known, on Cesar Chavez's advocacy on behalf of Latino migrant workers. Karen knew this because, out to dinner with her family one night, Ruby had asked the waitress if the Caesar salad was named after the aforementioned man, drawing a bemused look from the woman. Which Karen had found hilarious and embarrassing at the same time. "Sweetie, it's probably named after Julius Caesar," Karen had told her.

"Who's *that?*" Ruby asked—a question that Karen had found less charming.

Later, Karen learned that Caesar salad was actually named after the restaurateur Caesar Cardini—and felt foolish herself and a little more forgiving of her daughter and her school.

Yet during parent-teacher conferences, when Miss Tammy informed Karen that Ruby was the strongest reader in the class—or, in Miss Tammy's words, the "most *awesome* reader in Room Three-oh-three"—Karen's first thought was not pride but paranoia that Ruby's classmates must all be behind.

Moments after Nurse Smith led a still sniveling, now bandaged Maeve out of the classroom, Principal Chambers appeared in the doorway in a black pants suit and low heels, her expression stern. After a low-voiced conference with Miss Tammy in the corner, she took Jayyden by the back of his shirt collar and marched him out of the classroom. The other students looked on in stunned silence. The mood had shifted from celebration to sobriety.

"Fun morning," quipped Lou.

"What that kid needs is a serious whupping," muttered Sa'Ryah's mother, Desiree Johnston, an attractive single mother in her late twenties who worked in a Medicaid office.

"With all due respect, violence is not the answer to violence," demurred Ezra's mother, April Fishbach, a late-life PhD candidate in cultural anthropology as well as the president and sole active member of Betts's Parent Teacher Association.

Desiree rolled her eyes.

Marco Cicetti, who was the father of Maeve's other best friend, Amanda, seemed similarly unimpressed by April's argument. "Yeah, wait till it's your kid who ends up in the ER," he said.

"I completely agree—he needs to leave the school," said Bram's mother, Annika Van Den Berg, a five-foot-eleven Dutch architect who dressed in avant-garde fashions that resembled crumpled sleeping bags and who was clearly just slumming it for a few years before the family moved back to a canal house in Amsterdam filled with ultramodern molded-plastic furnishings.

"The whole Jayyden situation just makes me sad," muttered Karen. It was the only thing she felt it was permissible to say, striving as she always did for a tone of compassionate neutrality that would counteract any suspicions that she was just another white parent wishing the school would gentrify more quickly than it was.

"But where are these parents of Jayyden?" asked Annika in her stilted English.

"Mom in jail—dad, who knows," Lou said, shrugging.

"Trash begets trash," said Marco. "End of story."

Karen cringed at Marco's comment, while Mumia's father, Ralph Washington, who was the editor of a small hip-hop and black politics magazine, stepped into the fray. "Except you left out the beginning," he said hotly. "Where the legacy of slavery and the white hegemony begets the vicious cycle of black poverty."

There was an uncomfortable silence. Even April, who was never at a loss for sanctimonious words regarding social justice for poor minorities, seemed tongue-tied. Karen stared at her shoes.

Luckily, Miss Tammy chose that moment to return to the front of the classroom and say, at a marginally lower decibel level, "I'm sorry about the disruption, parents. But we're still *totally pumped* to have you here. And your children have worked *awesomely* hard on their buildings. So please continue to explore our community. But if you have to leave, don't forget to sign our guest book."

Suddenly conscious of time passing—and keen to escape the tension—Karen touched Ruby's arm and announced that she had to go.

"Maeve left early. Can I go home early too?" asked Ruby. As if the two children's disparate dismissal times were the real injustice.

"No, you cannot," said Karen, exasperated by the question.

But the sight of Ruby's wounded face undid Karen. Fearing she'd been too harsh, and even though both Ruby's pediatrician and dentist had urged her to cut back on the sweets, Karen said, "But I promise we'll go out for a treat after school—before gymnastics."

"What kind of treat?" asked Ruby, who was in the 25th percentile for height and the 80th for weight.

"Maybe ice cream."

"Awwww," Ruby moaned. "I'm tired of ice cream. Can't I have an icie?"

"No, you can't," said Karen, wondering if she had only herself to blame for her rising irritation.

In truth, Karen's complex and often contradictory relationship to eating had grown more so in recent years. This was due not only to her current job—to the truly hungry, all food was in some sense good food—but to the outsize importance that her particular demographic group had placed on the business of consuming calories. Along with weight, teeth, and marriage, food had somehow become a dividing line between the social classes, with the Earth Day–esque ideals of the 1960s having acquired snob appeal, and the well-off and well-educated increasingly buying "natural" and "fresh" and casting aspersions on those who didn't.

Karen herself had grown up in the 1970s and '80s eating Ring Dings and washing them down with cans of Tab, and so far, health-wise, she didn't seem any worse for it. But she also had a history of neurotic eating that dated back to late adolescence. It had never risen to the level of an eating disorder—she didn't have that kind of willpower—but it had left her overly preoccupied with every morsel she ate and, recently, what her husband and daughter ate. Unlike the majority of her female friends, Karen actually disliked cooking. Yet she took an almost maniacal level of pride in doing so and in presenting various fresh and healthy options that would provide her family with the nutrients they needed.

For all these reasons, Karen preferred to be financially extorted at the artisanal ice cream shop up the street that offered weird flavors like Rooibos Tea and Maple Fennel than to contemplate the number of chemical compounds that were entering her daughter's body via the neon-colored, artificially flavored, no doubt corn syrup–enhanced Italian ices that were sold outside her daughter's school for a dollar a pop by an older Hispanic lady in a gingham smock. The woman was clearly just trying to make a living. Karen nevertheless resented her for forcing parents like herself to engage in constant battles with their children over its purchase. The fact that a scoop of artisanal ice cream likely contained more calories in it than a small Italian ice didn't undermine her conviction.

"Why not?" the child moaned.

"You know I don't like all the chemicals in that stuff," said Karen.

"That's all you care about—chemicals," said Ruby.

"Don't be ridiculous."

"Then why don't you let me eat icies?"

"I'm not going to talk about this anymore."

A glint appeared in Ruby's eye. "Mommy—if you were stuck on a desert island and you had to eat at one chain restaurant for the rest of your life, would you choose Burger King, Taco Bell, KFC, or Wendy's?"

"Wendy's, because they have a salad bar," said Karen, who also recognized that her life was ripe for mockery. "Anyway, I *really* need to go."

"I thought you didn't have to work on Fridays."

"I have to work from home." With a quick kiss to Ruby's forehead, Karen walked out of the classroom and back down the hall. Typically, Friday mornings were among her favorite times of the week. But something about the Maeve-Jayyden melee had left her with a palpable sense of foreboding, as if she'd successfully fled a house fire but forgotten to close the door behind her.

Soon, she found herself back on the main floor of Betts, a tidy if depressingly low-ceilinged expanse of beige brick with a trophy case on one wall and the obligatory display of student-made tissue-paper collages decorating the other. As Karen passed the collages, her eyes scanned the names written on the bottom left corners. The newfangledness of the black ones with their apostrophes, dashes, purposeful misspellings, and randomly added letters (Queen-Zy, Beyonka, Yisabella, Jayyden) stood in stark contrast to the antiquation and preciosity of the white ones (Prudence, Violet, Silas, Leo). The disheartening thought suddenly struck Karen that Ruby fit snugly into the latter category. But she quickly pushed the idea away, assuring herself that it was a family name, since it had also been the name of her great-grandmother.

Just past the collages, the school's uniformed security guard sat at a wooden desk at a remove from the main entrance. Which had never made any sense to Karen. Wasn't the whole point of having a security guard to deter homicidal maniacs who might try to enter the building in possession of semiautomatic weaponry? Karen had considered scheduling a meeting with Principal Chambers to express her concern. But since she lived in fear of sounding like one of the rBGH crusaders— that is, another uptight white mother with a petty complaint—she'd decided against it, trusting fate, if barely, to deliver her daughter home safely each day.

On her way out of the building, Karen nearly collided with a late-arriving student. The girl probably wasn't much older than Ruby. But to Karen's eye, she appeared to be dangerously overweight, with early breast development and a prominent gut. She was also clutching a half-eaten jelly doughnut. In a series of flashes, Karen imagined the rest of the girl's tragic life. No doubt there would be a teen pregnancy, followed by a failure to graduate high school, a dead-end cashier job at a fast-food restaurant, more babies with unaccountable men, food stamps, diabetes type 2. She felt pity for the child on all fronts.

But at the sudden appearance of a woman who Karen assumed was the child's mother—she was walking behind the girl and ordering her to "Hurry your ass up!"—Karen felt her pity turning to disapproval. It wasn't just the woman's crude language or the fact that she was very large herself (her hips reminded Karen of the side hoops worn under dresses in Velázquez's paintings of seventeenth-century Spanish royals) yet was wearing skintight jeans with rhinestone studs down the sides, as if to call attention to her size. It was that she'd given her overweight child a doughnut for breakfast.

As if, seconds earlier, in order to win the affection of her own borderline chubby daughter, Karen hadn't promised Ruby a sugary treat as well. In that moment, Karen couldn't see that the doughnut might be an act of love on the part of this mother too, for whom it was quite possibly an affordable gift in an unaffordable world. She also managed to forget that sometimes, while in the car with Ruby, she f-worded other drivers—and that she owned a pair of skintight jeggings herself, which arguably looked no better on her own distressingly flat backside than on this woman's large and shapely one.

"If it gets any later," Karen heard the mother say as she passed her, "I'm gonna miss Education Partners orientation."

Karen blinked back her surprise. Education Partners was one of April Fishbach's pet projects, a volunteer program in which parents helped out in the classrooms, doing everything from putting away supplies to assisting children who were struggling to read. Karen herself was too busy/lazy/selfish, depending on your perspective, to donate her Friday mornings. But other heroic parents apparently had decided to do it—parents such as the Mother in the Rhinestone-Studded Jeans.

As Karen exited through the double doors and onto the street, she felt chastened by her apparently gross misreading of the family. That was the thing about clichés, she'd learned—

and yet somehow kept *not* learning. They were often true. Just as often, they weren't.

Six months earlier, the neighborhood's newest coffee shop, Laundry, had been an actual Laundromat with perpetually broken dryers, a peeling linoleum floor, and a tiny color TV installed near the ceiling and tuned to one or another daytime talk show catering to women. Now it featured exposed beams, dangling Edison bulbs in wire cages, recovered post-office cabinetry, free Wi-Fi, and whimsical line drawings of farm animals screen-printed onto reclaimed barn wood. Radiohead, Johnny Cash, and the Arctic Monkeys played in a loop on the sound system while the bespectacled patrons leaned stone-faced over their brushed-aluminum MacBook Airs. Karen considered Laundry to be overpriced and pretentious—and the coffee mediocre at best. But the choices were limited: a Dunkin' Donuts three blocks away or an even more expensive place up the street.

After ordering a five-dollar cup of single-origin organic coffee from Burundi and waiting ten minutes for a guy with a tattooed neck and hair that had been pulled back into a bun to pour hot water through what appeared to be a dirty sweat sock, Karen retreated to a honed-marble-and-wrought-iron table in back. There, she got out her laptop and assumed the facial expression of someone reviewing top secret plans to invade a nation in the Persian Gulf. In fact, she was searching for cut-glass boudoir lamps on eBay, and then for sea-grass throw rugs on Overstock.com, and then for girls' cardigans at Gap.com, as Ruby had recently lost her favorite bright pink one. Though that was really just an excuse to go to the website.

In truth, online shopping for clothes for her daughter and cheap crap for her home had become one of Karen's greatest pleasures in life. Lately, that pleasure had begun to resemble an addiction that she was deeply ashamed of and hid from her husband. If he found Karen on her laptop at night, she would always say she was reading the international edition of the *Guardian,* because it was hard to argue against someone's catching up on world events from a left-leaning perspective. And when packages arrived, which they did nearly every night—she and the UPS man, Larry, were on first-name terms—Karen would quickly open them, then flatten the cardboard boxes and put them outside in recycling before Matt came home and made comments.

Little wonder that, in recent months, Karen and Matt's joint checking account had fallen as low as it had. Though it hadn't helped that Karen had dropped her phone three times in one year, each time purchasing a replacement at full cost. There was also the not-so-small matter of her husband, who still had outstanding student loans, currently earning zero dollars per week. The previous fall, after working for twenty years as a housing lawyer fighting for tenants evicted by greedy landlords, Matt had felt burned out and quit his job. Now he and a few friends were building a one-stop realty website for low-income city dwellers, attaching those in need of housing to lists of everything from rent-stabilized apartments to subsidized-housing waiting lists and even market-rate-but-affordable apartments in lower-income suburbs. A nonprofit foundation had given Matt and his partners seed money to build the website and even provided them with temporary office space, but the funds were already starting to run low.

Secretly, Karen—who liked to refer to her husband's

project as Poor-coran, a joke that worked best with people who had familiarity with the New York and Florida real estate juggernaut Corcoran—thought the website was of dubious utility. In her experience, most poor people didn't have consistent access to the Internet. Some didn't even have e-mail addresses. Karen knew this because, as class parent the year before, she'd been asked to collect e-mail-contact info for all twenty-three students and had come up with only seventeen. But she wanted to be supportive of her husband, who was clearly excited about the project and had already put hundreds if not thousands of hours into it. Also, for the first five years after Ruby was born, and before Karen began working at Hungry Kids, Matt had earned far more than she had.

Karen and Matt were hardly indigent. According to Zillow.com, which Karen checked every so often when she needed cheering up about their finances, their apartment had nearly doubled in value in the three years since Karen and Matt had purchased it. As a down payment, they'd used a portion of the money Karen had inherited from her parents, who had died a few years before. In fact, their two-bedroom condo was now worth a cool million, possibly more. And Karen had money in the bank on top of that. But she hated the idea of dipping into her savings to pay for everyday purchases; God knew what college tuition would cost in ten years. Maybe that was why she felt even guiltier than usual that morning as she cardigan-shopped for Ruby. Karen was busily seeking out promo codes to plug into the Gap.com checkout page to mitigate that guilt when April Fishbach appeared in her face, flashing her Volunteer Hero smile. "Fancy running into you again!" she said.

April was dressed as if it were 1973: corduroy bell-bottoms, a frayed jean jacket covered with political buttons offering such dated slogans as NO NUKES, and lots of ugly silver-and-turquoise jewelry. Two slender bobby pins kept her frizzy hair off her lunar-size forehead. It seemed to Karen that, in a certain light, April Fishbach was actually quite pretty, or she might have been if she hadn't done everything possible to present the opposite impression. Objectively speaking, she and Karen had a good deal in common. In addition to both of them being white late-life mothers at Betts, their children (Ezra and Ruby) had been in class together since kindergarten. And both women had devoted their careers to bettering the lives of underprivileged populations. But Karen had never been able to stand April's company for more than two minutes at a time. "Oh, hey," she said, quickly closing Safari lest April see how Karen, in perusing Retailmenot.com, was failing to contribute to the Social Good.

"Well, that was quite a harrowing scene in there this morning," April continued.

"Yes, it was," said Karen.

"To be honest, I was shocked by how harsh Miss Tammy was with Jayyden. The child needs help, not punishing."

"Well, he did assault the girl."

"That's a bit of an exaggeration, don't you think?" April raised one overgrown eyebrow.

"Is it?" Something about April's presence had a way of turning Karen into an unfeeling reactionary.

"In any case, since I happen to have you cornered," said April, smiling again, "the volunteer committee could really use some manpower this month. Any chance you could take time out of your busy café schedule to give us a hand?"

Karen's entire body tensed with displeasure and defensiveness. "I really want to be helpful, April, but the truth is that I already work at a hunger-relief nonprofit full-time, except for Fridays mornings, when I basically have two hours to myself to answer e-mail and do laundry." She knew it was a slight exaggeration of her work schedule, but in this case it seemed merited.

"And drink slow-pour coffee!" declared April.

"Yes, I need caffeine in the morning like everyone else," said Karen.

"Well, how about just an hour every other Friday?"

An escape route from April's altruistic web seeming less and less feasible, Karen released a long sigh. "If I can find the time, sure," she said. "What are my options?"

"Let's see," April said. "Well, the arts committee needs volunteers to sit at a table in the lobby on Visiting Artists Day, which happens to land on the second Friday of April, if that works for you, and register our arriving artists. The garden committee needs someone to rake out dead leaves. The fundraising committee needs someone to organize a penny harvest. The after-school committee needs someone to help with bookkeeping. The talent show needs a pianist, if you happen to play. Mr. Thad from the science room needs someone to take care of his white rat and boa constrictor over spring break. And last but by no means least, my Education Partners program could *always* use more hands in the classroom. What do you say?"

Karen guiltily flashed back to her silent encounter with the Mother in the Rhinestone-Studded Jeans. But her shame on that count did nothing to dissuade her from mentally vetting the options that April had laid out in an attempt to gauge which one would be the least taxing. Snakes and rodents were off the table: Karen had a long-standing phobia of both. And she'd quit piano lessons in the fourth grade. As for organizing a penny harvest, she already spent Monday through Thursday of every week soliciting money, if in slightly larger denominations; the thought of doing so a fifth day a week was almost too much to bear. Meanwhile, volunteering for April's signature program seemed above and beyond the call of duty. "How about I register artists on Visiting Arts Day?" offered Karen.

"It's not Visiting Arts Day. It's Visiting Ar-*tists* Day," said April.

"Fine, Visiting Ar-*tists* Day," said Karen.

"Excellent!" said April. "But we actually need you to do more than just check names off a list and point people in the right direction. We need interviews too. I have a printout with five questions for each of them. The artists can fill them out themselves—we'll have pencils on hand—or you can read them the questions and write down their answers."

"In the middle of the lobby?" asked Karen.

"Yes, in the middle of the lobby. Is that a problem?"

"Well, the lobby seems like a hard place to do interviews. I mean, depending on when they arrive, it can be really loud. Plus, they're going to be standing there wanting to get to whichever classroom they've been assigned to. Can't we e-mail them questions in advance?"

"That's a terrible idea," April shot back.

"It is?"

"Yes. It is."

Karen felt heat on her forehead. "Because I thought of it, April, and you didn't?" she said sarcastically.

"Look," said April, flaring her nostrils. "If volunteering

for Visiting Artists Day is too large of a commitment for you right now, I can find someone else. These are working artists who are taking time out of their busy schedules to visit the school—"

"Exactly," said Karen, "which is why I was suggesting we save everyone time and let them answer the questions at their leisure."

"Well, it wasn't a helpful suggestion," April said sharply.

Karen could feel blood rushing to her cheeks. *April, did anyone ever tell you what a self-righteous little twat you are?* she imagined saying out loud. But she knew it wasn't worth the subsequent fallout. There were still three months of third grade left. Also, it was still early in the morning, and Karen had drunk only half her sock coffee. "April, if you want my help on Visiting Artists Day, e-mail me," she said in a leaden voice. "But I've got work to do right now."

"Fine," said April. Chin raised, she stomped off.

Karen happily resumed her top secret Gap.com shopping. Although it was generally true that she was thankful for any and all Caucasian or Asian parents who sent their children to Betts, there were exceptions that proved the rule. First among them was April Fishbach.

Twenty minutes later, Karen collected her belongings, returned her mug to the counter, and walked out. A block from home, she bumped into a former mom-acquaintance from the Elm Tree Center for Early Childhood Development, the play-based private nursery school that Ruby had attended before matriculating at Betts. The woman was dressed in high-tech running gear and carrying a cardboard box filled with gnarled-looking fresh vegetables with scrotal-like hairs growing off them—no doubt her weekly community-supported agriculture allotment. Karen never knew what to do with root vegetables when she brought them home; they tended to sit in the produce drawer of her fridge until they began to leak green juice, at which point she threw them out. "Karen! Oh my God!" said Leslie. *"How are you?"*

"We're good!" said Karen, trying to match Leslie's excited tone. "How about you guys? How's Clare? How are the kids?" Back when Karen seemed to spend half her life at playgrounds—she was working only part-time then, freelancing—she and Leslie would sometimes share a bench while their children climbed the play structures. They'd chat about nap schedules, breast-feeding schedules, the pros and cons of thumb-sucking versus pacifiers, and whether grapes were safe for toddlers to eat or if they presented a compelling choking risk unless sliced in half. Karen had found that the minutiae of early-year parenting was fascinating for the exact moment you were living it, after which it became, quite possibly, the most boring subject on earth.

"We're hanging in there." Leslie laughed and sighed. "You know, the usual impossible juggling act."

Was the comment an oblique dig at Karen for having only one child and therefore having it easy while Leslie and her wife toiled away at raising two? Or was Karen projecting? "I know it well," Karen replied in an arch voice.

"So, what's going on with Ruby? Where is she in school again?" Leslie narrowed her eyes and cocked her head.

"She goes to Betts," said Karen, defensive before she'd even gotten the words out.

"Really? Wow!" said Leslie, blinking and nodding in slow motion.

"Don't act so surprised," said Karen.

"I'm not at all! We almost sent Willa there. I mean, we're actually zoned for the school. Have you guys been happy there?" Leslie blinked again.

Karen's heart had begun to pound. Defending her daughter's school to college-educated white liberals in the neighborhood who were zoned for Betts but who didn't send their children there on account, Karen assumed, of the number of black and brown faces they saw in the schoolyard had become her second obsession, after online shopping. "*So* happy. Honestly, it's an *amazing* place—the teachers are beyond dedicated, and the kids are literally from all over the world," she said. "It's like a Benetton ad from the eighties come to life." Karen always exaggerated her fondness for the school in reaction to those who shunned it. She had two goals: to foster guilt and shame, and to instill doubt about whatever alternative had been secured.

"Wow, that sounds amazing," said Leslie. "I'm so happy for you guys."

"And where's Willa?" Karen couldn't help herself.

"She's actually in a brilliant-and-exceptional program." Leslie grinned sheepishly.

"Oh. How's that going?" said Karen, feeling even more embattled as she recalled the 71 out of 100 that Ruby, then age four, had scored on the so-called B-and-E test. Karen later concluded that Ruby had been more interested in the fish tank in the testing lady's office than in counting the number of triangles and circles. Or was that just an excuse to ease the pain of acknowledging that her daughter was merely average? Then again, it had been widely rumored at Elm Tree that Leslie and Clare had had their then-four-year-old daughter tutored for the test by a Harvard grad who charged two hundred and fifty dollars an hour.

"It's okaayyyy," Leslie answered in a singsongy voice. "I mean, the commute is a *total* pain in the ass." Karen didn't answer. Was she supposed to express sympathy? "But we just felt Willa was one of those kids who needed to be around other really motivated kids or she'd kind of drift off. And I guess we were also worried about sending her to Betts because it seemed a little—I don't know—*crazy* over there. And, like, maybe the kids didn't all seem that *inspired*." She lifted her shoulders and pressed her teeth together as if she were stepping on hot coals.

Every fiber of Karen's being wanted to answer, *You mean, because so many of them are black?* (The city's B-and-E programs were made up almost entirely of white and Asian students.) But she didn't. She was a member of polite society, and people in polite society didn't mention skin color.

"Also, we just felt Willa would do better in a more nurturing environment," Leslie went on. "She's kind of a sensitive kid."

"Oh, is the B-and-E class really small?" asked Karen.

"Well, not anymore—unfortunately," Leslie said with a bitter laugh. "She's got thirty-two kids in her class this year."

"Wow, that's big!"

"But her teacher is great. I mean, if anyone can handle that many little smarty-pants, it's her. So that's something."

"Right—well, Ruby's class has only twenty-five kids in it this year," said Karen, simultaneously bristling and gloating.

"Wow! Lucky you—that's really small!" said Leslie.

"But of course, the vast majority of them are incredibly stupid." Where had that come from?

Leslie laughed nervously. "I'm sure they're not *stupid*."

"Oh, I'm sure they are! My daughter in particular," Karen went on. "She got, like, a two on that B-and-E test. I doubt she'll even get into community college. She'll be lucky to get a job as a cashier at CVS. Maybe your daughter will take pity on her some day and hire her as the receptionist at her quant fund or something." Had she really just said that?

"You're so funny," said Leslie, but she wasn't laughing or even smiling. And it was suddenly clear that she couldn't wait to get away from Karen. "Well, it was great running into you," she said, readjusting her box of scrotal-haired vegetables in her arms and taking a step backward.

"Yeah, you too!" said Karen, half mortified, half elated by her outburst.

As she continued down the block, she entertained the perversely affirming notion that, far from being a racist, she might well be its diametric opposite, insofar as it tended to be white people who irked her the most.

Karen hadn't always seen the world through the lens of race or class. Growing up in an affluent suburb, she'd actually paid scant attention to the subject. This was not so much because she had a naturally open mind or had been raised with good values but because pretty much everyone in her town was white and middle to upper-middle class. That included Karen's own family. Her father, Herb, was a tax lawyer who made a good salary. Her mother was a housewife who sometimes helped in his office. Pretty much all the kids Karen knew attended the same legendarily rigorous public school, which sent as many of their graduates to Ivy League schools as the privates nearby did. To the extent that there was a pecking order—and there was, of course, by high school—it had mainly to do with whether or not you were having sex. Karen wasn't.

Yet from an early age, she'd been hypercognizant of others' suffering, beginning with her own family's. When Karen was still a small child, her mother, Ruth, had started taking to her bed for days at a time. "Mom has a migraine" was always the official explanation. But eventually it became clear that the pain was more pervasive than that. Karen's father had done his best to take care of her, driving her to endless doctors who never seemed able to find a cause or offer a solution. But despite his intelligence, he'd had a helpless quality when it came to interpersonal relations, especially those involving himself and his wife. He was by nature reserved—by Karen's count, he'd spoken a total of three hundred sentences to her during his lifetime—and his wife's depression seemed especially designed to make him shrink further into himself.

Meanwhile, Karen's older brother, Rob, began doing bong hits in his bedroom while he was still in middle school. He was also a boy, and boys weren't expected to help around the house. It therefore fell to Karen to keep Ruth Kipple happy and in the world. At least, that was how it had always felt to Karen. And her mother would reinforce the notion by saying terrible things that Karen realized were terrible only when she was older—things like "I would have ended my life long ago if it wasn't for you" and "You're all I have to live for." At the time, Karen had considered them compliments.

At some point in her early teens, Karen felt compelled to take on certain aspects of the traditional-mother role herself—making meals for the family, doing laundry, keeping the house going and everyone's morale up. But even before then, she'd internalized the notion that she'd been put on this earth to solve others' problems. In early childhood, Karen had found an outlet for the sentiment by taking care of animals, especially sick and orphaned ones. Deprived of a pet—her mother refused to take responsibility for one while Karen was at school—Karen had a vast collection of miniature glass animals that she would sometimes break on purpose, forcing her to conduct "surgery" and glue them back together, an activity she found deeply satisfying. On occasion, she got to practice her craft on live beings. When she was around nine, a sparrow with a broken wing appeared on the front steps of her family's home. Clueless, Karen tried to splint the bird's wing with a toothpick and a piece of masking tape. Finding him dead the next morning, she wept and blamed herself.

Around the age of ten, Karen abandoned the cause of sick animals in favor of Third World children with cleft palates. She would spend hours staring at their photos and imagining their embarrassment and pain. Soon, she began donating half her allowance to the Smile Train. She was also drawn to tales of pioneer girls of early America, girls who had made do with so little. For all of her mid- to late childhood, her favorite book was *Little Women*. But whereas other girls she knew identified with Jo, the sprightly and unruly tomboy, Karen related best to the kind, obedient oldest sister, Meg, the one who wanted most of all to do the right thing and to please her parents. Indeed, it was as much for her mother as for herself that, after high school, Karen, the ultimate good student, had landed at an Ivy League university. Karen still remembered how Ruth had cried with happiness when she'd heard that Karen had been accepted.

But it was there, in the hallowed, neo-Gothic halls of that elite institution, that Karen's desire to be good mutated into a powerful desire to right the wrongs of an unequal and unjust society. A significant number of her classmates had, like Karen, gone to public high schools located in the upscale suburbs of major metropolises. But the most glamorous kids, Karen soon realized, were legacies and other well-connected types who had attended various prep schools, some boarding, some not, up and down the Eastern or Western Seaboard. Some were Southern debutantes, others were Park Avenue Jews, Persian ex-pats, or the progeny of Hollywood royalty. No doubt these well-off students had their own internecine tensions. But to Karen, they occupied a single fortress of privilege, impenetrable to the outside world. They also seemed to possess a shared body of esoteric knowledge. They knew about cocktails and catamarans, ski resorts and stepmothers. Life experience was only half the equation; confidence was the other. None of them seemed ever to have spent a moment questioning his or her place in the world, or even his or her place at an elite institution of higher education. And why should they? It seemed increasingly clear to Karen that the random luck of birth accounted for most of what people called success in life. Far Left politics, which she'd embraced around the same time, lent heft to the hunch. Then Karen became indignant on a whole other level.

If Karen had been entirely honest with herself, she would have acknowledged that the quasi-Marxist worldview she'd adopted around that time, with the help of several tenured radicals in the political philosophy department, had also provided her with an exit ramp off the aspiration highway. Being political meant you didn't have to be pretty or popular. Karen's new belief system even came with its own lifestyle—cafés at which to drink black coffee, film societies to belong to (in four years of college, Karen never missed a Mike Leigh or Ousmane Sembène screening), clothes to wear (vintage black leather jackets from thrift stores were a particular favorite). With her newly discovered political consciousness, Karen became a full-fledged campus activist, joining the local chapter of ACT UP and attending Take Back the Night rallies. She also got involved in the anti–South African–apartheid effort, for which she spent more than a few nights camping out in a makeshift shanty in the quad, one sleeping bag away, if she could arrange it, from Mike Grovesnor, a graduate student in political science who was obsessed with long-distance running and punk bands, particularly the Dead Kennedys. It was to him that she finally lost her virginity, the summer before her junior year, though nothing more came of their relationship after their one awkward night.

That same summer, Karen went to Guatemala to learn Spanish and help refurbish a rural school attended by the children of poverty-stricken peasants. At least, that was the plan. In practice, she and the other volunteers spent most of the time in an un-air-conditioned classroom conjugating verbs. *Yo podría, tú podrías, usted/él/ella podría, nosotros podríamos…* Though on occasion there were interactions with actual Spanish-speaking people. Karen still recalled the tiny little Guatemalan boy who, during a school visit and with what appeared to be complete sincerity, had asked Karen, who was partial to black clothing and admittedly had a pointy nose, thin face, and pale skin, if she was a *bruja real*—that is, a "real witch." Apparently, a rumor was circulating. At the time, Karen had laughed off the question. But somehow the very notion had embarrassed her.

When Karen returned to college, she found that her position as a do-gooder Lefty gave her a kind of reverse status among the prep-school types, who had been groomed since birth to get dressed up and raise money. Indeed, her first foray into fund-raising, on behalf of low-income AIDS patients, took place during her junior year of college. By senior year, she actually managed to become friendly with some of the people she'd once considered adversaries, perhaps explaining why she grew ever more ashamed of her own merely bourgeois origins. The Kipples, Karen came to realize, were neither affluent enough to be impressive (there were no compounds on private islands, no great-grandfathers who'd helped found X or Y, not even trust funds passed down to the children) nor remotely poor and/or bohemian enough to qualify as exotic or authentic. Rather, Karen's childhood, despite her mother's problems, had been privileged in all the most conventionally upper-middle-class ways. There had been piano, ballet, and tennis lessons, winter trips to Disneyland, summer camp in Maine, even an SAT tutor when it came time for that in high school. Or maybe Karen's shame had as much to do with the aura of melancholy that permeated her family's four-bedroom center-hall Colonial with beige wall-to-wall carpeting. In any case, when people asked where she was from, she took to answering "the beautiful suburbs" in an arch tone of voice.

At 2:50 p.m., Karen returned to Betts to pick up Ruby. Not in the mood for a fight, she relented on the Italian ice front. But the sight of Ruby's blue-stained tongue distressed Karen in ways she couldn't begin to explain, calling to mind the defected Russian spy who, a few years earlier, had been slowly poisoned by radioactive polonium in his tea. Meanwhile, Ruby herself seemed to be energized to the point of mania. She was running in circles and doing cartwheels across the blacktop. Karen barely got her to gymnastics class on time, even though the Little Gym was only a few blocks away.

Matt got home at seven. "Hey, KK," he said, appearing in the door. "What's the news in Macaroni-Land?"

KK and Macaroni-Land were his affectionate nicknames for his wife and home, respectively. Karen thought Macaroni-Land was cute, but her own nickname always sounded to her ears a little too much like the acronym for the Ku Klux Klan. "Hey, you're home early," she said.

"Am I?" he said.

As he took off his coat, the last button on his button-down strained against his belly and revealed a tiny triangle of hair. With his compact build and swarthy complexion, Matt had never fit Karen's ideal of male beauty, which tended toward the lean and fair. But she'd always regarded her husband as manly in a winning way. And although he worked out irregularly—basketball was his main source of exercise—he hadn't grown flabby and double-chinned like so many of her friends' husbands. He'd also kept his head of hair, which was still shiny and, for the most part, dark. "We aim to please," he muttered. "You aim too, please." Then he started chuckling.

"What in *God's* name are you talking about?" said Karen.

"Did I ever tell you about that sign I saw in the men's room of that Greyhound station in Eugene?" said Matt. "Damn, that was funny. I have no idea why it came to me just now." He went over and put his hands on Karen's waist.

"Maybe you had to be there," she said, though she secretly found it funny too. Like her father, Karen was a lover of bad puns.

"Maybe."

"Well, did you aim?"

"I did my best." He kissed her on the mouth, then pressed his groin into her crotch.

"Don't be disgusting," she murmured as she kissed him back. It pleased her to think that after ten years of marriage, her husband was still attracted to her. She was still attracted to him too. Though in keeping with male fashion trends, Matt had recently grown a patchy beard, and Karen had yet to grow accustomed to the scratchy feel of it against her cheek and chin.

Just then, Ruby ran into the living room in her pajamas with her stuffed octopus, Octi, filling her arms. "Daddy!" she cried.

Matt abruptly withdrew from Karen. "Hey, Scooby Doo-bie!" he said, lifting Ruby into his arms. "How was school today?"

"Fine," she said in the babyish voice she sometimes adopted in the evenings. "But Octi had a bad day. So can you say something nice to her?"

"Sure I can," said Matt, draping two of the doll's tentacles over his shoulders. "Listen, Octi—there are more fish in the sea than have ever been caught…"

"My mother used to say that," said Karen.

"You mean after you brought me home for the first time."

"Ha-ha."

Ruby extended her neck. "Mommy, what are my magnet dolls doing over there in that big bag by the door?" she asked, back to her regular voice.

"You never play with them anymore, sweetie," said Karen. "And we don't have that much room in the apartment. I'm taking them to the Salvation Army so kids who can't afford new toys can play with them."

"But I *do* play with them!" cried Ruby, squinching up her face.

"The Salvation Army? Seriously? You know they try to convert people over there," said Matt, a committed atheist whose parents attended a Methodist church.

"Okay. But they also do a lot of food assistance," said Karen, who was ethnically Jewish but who described herself as an agnostic. "HK even contracts with them."

"I just think the Homeless Solutions Thrift Store will make better use of Ruby's old toys," said Matt, his tone turning serious, "without bringing in all that salvation BS."

"But why can't I keep my own toys?" moaned Ruby.

"Maybe they will," said Karen, ignoring her daughter's lament. "But the Homeless Solutions donation center is two miles away, and there's a Salvation Army on our corner. So I can actually drop stuff there on my way to the train instead of having to get in the car to take it somewhere—or instead of asking you to get in the car to take it somewhere, which we both know will mean that bag will be sitting in the hall getting tripped over for the next two years."

"Touché," said Matt, conceding the fight and, in doing so, pleasing Karen, who smiled triumphantly.

After Ruby went to bed, Karen and Matt sat on the sofa and shared frustrations from their workdays. Matt told Karen about what a hard time the staff was having getting the city's housing authority to cooperate with his website. Karen told Matt about how the grant she was writing was taking forever—and also about what had happened at the community-unit party. "Which one is Maeve again?" asked Matt.

Karen didn't understand how her husband couldn't keep straight their only child's few friends, but she chalked it up to a failure of vision above all else. By nature, Matt wasn't very observant. Karen could get a new pillow for the sofa, and two months would go by before he noticed—if he ever did. "The blond one who looks like JonBenét Ramsey who comes over to our house, like, every weekend?" said Karen.

"She wears heavy makeup and cowgirl outfits?" asked Matt.

"No! I just mean she looks like her. Blond and blue-eyed with a turned-up nose."

"Oh, right—I know who she is."

"Or at least it was turned-up until Jayyden got there," joked Karen.

"So he broke her nose?" asked Matt.

"I haven't heard," said Karen, shrugging. "I mean, I assume her mom, Laura, would have e-mailed me if it was that bad. But who knows. She and Maeve's dad, Evan, are probably out of town shooting an important GlaxoSmithKline commercial and haven't heard the news about their daughter yet. Seriously, those two are never around. I honestly don't know why they had kids."

"Did you know pharmaceutical companies are banned from directly advertising to consumers in every country in the world except the U.S., New Zealand, and Brazil?" said Matt.

"Why am I not surprised?" said Karen, shaking her head. Then she launched into a harsh description of her run-in with Leslie Pfeiffer. "She might as well have said, 'We couldn't deal with all the black people at your school so we decided to send our precious firstborn to an apartheid-like all-white B-and-E program in the middle of a poor black school, where she won't actually have to interact with any dark children because they keep them in their own holding pens.'"

"That sounds charming," said Matt.

"Yeah, really charming," said Karen.

"People think Republicans are racists," said Matt, who had grown up in Tacoma, Washington, where his not particularly warm but refreshingly sane parents toiled as a college secretary and a building contractor. "But I've always thought college-educated liberals are actually the worst."

"I totally agree." To Karen's mind, it was her and Matt's shared political outlook and commitment to social justice, combined with their willingness to impugn those who didn't share it, that had kept them more or less happily partnered for ten years. Also, they still had fairly decent if infrequent sex.

After their chat, Matt and Karen went back to their computers, as they tended to do in the evenings after Ruby went to bed. Since there was no word from Laura, Karen briefly considered sending her a *hope everything is okay*–type e-mail. Like other mothers thrown together on account of their children's affection for one another, and even though it was quite possible that Laura secretly disapproved of Karen as much as Karen secretly disapproved of Laura, they went through the motions of being happy to see each other on the rare occasions when they did. They also regularly Liked each other's Facebook photos of their children doing cute things, though Karen posted far fewer than Laura did. For no discernible reason, they also occasionally shared incredibly intimate details about their personal lives. The previous December, while at a birthday party for a classmate of Ruby and Maeve's, Laura had revealed to Karen that for a year or more after giving birth to Maeve's younger brother, Indy, she'd lost control of her bladder, regularly peed in her pants, and had at least once accidentally done so on her husband while they were having sex. It had been a detail too much for Karen, who hadn't quite been able to get the image out of her head.

But in the end, Karen decided to hold off on sending anything. She wasn't sure what tone to strike and was concerned about coming across as either nosy or inappropriately blasé. There was something about Laura that made Karen feel like she was one of those overinvolved, overprotective mothers who had no lives outside of their children—or like she was totally negligent. There was no in-between. Besides, Karen was fairly certain that despite her tears, Maeve was *just fine*.

On Saturday morning, Matt announced he had to go back to the office. Keen to work on her essay about nutrition and educational outcomes, Karen gave herself a temporary dispensation to remove all limits on screen time enjoyed by her daughter. As it happened, Karen ended up reading the paper and falling asleep. But the three of them went on a family outing to the zoo on Sunday morning, which Karen didn't exactly enjoy, since it was still freezing outside and, at that point in her life, animals were not of particular interest to her. But returning to their warm home, she was happy to have gone, if only because, for once, the whole family was together and because it seemed like the kind of thing families did on weekends. And there was still a side of Karen that wanted to do things right, even though she felt haunted and repulsed by the sight of the baboons, whose bulbous red anuses suggested to her in a dispiriting way that we were all just animals whose sole purpose on the planet was to create offspring and then die.

On Monday, Karen met an old college acquaintance named

Clay Phipps for lunch. Having tagged him as a potential Hungry Kids donor and possibly even a candidate for its board of directors, she'd e-mailed him cold and asked to meet. From what she'd read in the financial press, he'd founded his hedge fund, which used a new quantitative trading strategy, while he was still in business school. He was now worth hundreds of millions of dollars, if not a cool billion, and had homes in Jackson Hole, Bermuda, and probably three other places. Though he'd hardly started out in life poor. His father had been high up at Morgan Stanley and his mother—Karen remembered someone in college telling her—was related to the Vanderbilts. Or maybe it was the Astors.

It had never been among Karen's life goals to suck up to rich guys and cajole them into parting with fractions of their fortunes—far from it. After college, she'd actually considered becoming a social worker. But a hands-on job leading arts-and-crafts workshops at a battered-women's shelter had convinced her that her talents, such as they were, lay elsewhere. She'd felt awkward around the women, and they didn't seem to connect with her either. Though a few did ask for money, which made her feel even more uncomfortable. As a result, Karen changed direction and lent her passion for social action to various left-leaning advocacy groups in Washington, DC, where she became expert at press releases.

But after Bill Clinton more or less killed welfare in '96, Karen realized that the groups she worked for had pretty much *no* influence whatsoever. She pivoted yet again, pursuing a master's degree in public health, which also led nowhere. It was mostly by default that she wound up in the world of philanthropy. A job offer to help raise money for a national reproductive-health and -rights organization came through a friend of a friend. Needing employment in any case, Karen decided it was better to help by some means than not to help at all. She also came to believe, contrary to the mantra of the hippie era, that everything important was predicated on money. Love and good health could not always be purchased, it was true. Nearly everything else could be.

During Karen's first two years at Hungry Kids, she'd concentrated her efforts on grant writing, submitting elaborate proposals to faceless and secretive nonprofit organizations as well as the charitable wings of multinational corporations. But in the past few years, it had become clear to her that members of the .01 percent with autonomy over their own fortunes and family foundations were a far more expedient source of cash. In an ideal world, the IRS would be collecting enough taxes from these very people to feed the nation's poor. But to Karen's mind, the U.S. government had long ago stopped taking responsibility for the needy, so it was left to people like her, and organizations like Hungry Kids, to lead the effort.

But direct fund-raising had changed her. Despite Karen's innate discomfort with the idea of so much money being concentrated in so few hands, a part of her had come, if not to idolize, then certainly to find fascinating the very demographic from whom she solicited funds. She studied their clothes, their mannerisms, their speech patterns, and their lifestyles. The most curious of her findings? The .01 percent didn't decorate their own Christmas trees; rather, experts were called in to distribute the baubles evenly and drape the skirts *just so*. They purchased wine at auctions, not stores. And each child got his or her own nanny, all the better if the caregivers spoke to their charges exclusively in Mandarin before the kids entered their foreign-language immersion programs at their exclusive private schools.

As Karen made her way to the restaurant, she tried to remember how she and Clay had actually met, but she couldn't. All she recalled was his undying crush on her beautiful lesbian roommate from Toronto, Lydia Glenn. To the extent that Karen and Clay had bonded at all, it had been over his unrequited love for Lydia. In fact, when Karen had e-mailed two weeks earlier, she hadn't been entirely sure he'd remember who she was and had actually signed off *Karen, former roommate of Lovely Lydia :-)*. But his e-mail back had been immediate and enthusiastic, which had surprised and flattered her. He'd insisted on making the lunch reservation himself— at some seafood place near his office. Concerned about being late, Karen had arrived early, and first.

Elegant but antiseptic, it was the kind of establishment that owed its existence to corporate expense accounts. Everything about it, from the napkins to the waiters to the kayak-shaped dishes filled with glistening Italian olives, was a shade of off white. It was also eerily quiet but for the occasional high-pitched laugh that floated over the tables like a harmonic overtone. "I'm meeting Clay Phipps," Karen murmured to the hostess, who murmured in response, "Follow me, please," then led Karen to a corner table in back.

Clay arrived shortly after her. Up close, he looked surprisingly similar to the way he had in college, his dark blond hair still wavy and windswept, if somewhat wispier, his good looks still boyish. Though he was significantly shorter than Karen remembered. The most visible indicators of time's passage were the knife cuts on the outer corners of his light blue eyes and the strands of silver that were now threaded through his hair in the manner of an Indian textile. He was dressed like a college student also, in faded Levi's, white sneakers, and a ratty gray fleece pullover with a zipper at the neck. Against trend, he looked thinner than he had at age twenty-one, even verging on gaunt. The thought crossed Karen's mind that he was probably on one of those strange diets involving raw kale or whatnot that the rich sometimes went on at the advice of their personal trainers. "Karen!" he said with a big smile.

"Clay!" she said, hugging him hello.

"So, how are you after all these years?" he said, sitting down. He propped his elbows on the table, just as Karen's mother had always warned her not to, leaned forward, and gazed at her intently.

Embarrassed by the attention and also feeling overdressed in her black skirt suit, Karen looked away. "I'm good!" she said. "What has it been—like, twenty-five years?" Regaining her composure, she turned her gaze back to him.

"Probably," he said.

"To be honest, when I e-mailed you, I wasn't even sure you'd remember who I was."

"Of course I remember!"

"Are you still in touch with Lydia?"

"God, no. Are you?"

"I haven't seen her since graduation, but we're Facebook friends. Unless I'm mistaken, she's the director of a women's theater collective. I get announcements about her shows."

"That's so perfect," said Clay, rolling his eyes. "And let me guess—she lives in Portland, or something."

"That sounds about right," said Karen, smiling. "Or maybe it's Vancouver. I can't remember."

"I don't know what I was thinking," he went on. "She was the biggest dyke on the whole planet. And yet, in my great naïveté, I somehow imagined that my charms would be enough to convert her." He smiled back.

"From what I recall, it was a valiant effort."

"—that failed miserably."

They both laughed.

"I assume you eventually found love elsewhere," Karen said.

"Don't assume so much," Clay replied. "But first, I want to hear about you. What have you been doing since college?"

"That's a very good question—let's see," said Karen. "Well, the nineties are kind of a blur at this point. I worked in DC for a while."

"Such a boring fucking place."

"Tell me about it. Then, at around thirty, I got a master's degree, which I never use. For a split second after that, I worked at Planned Parenthood."

"Giving abortions?" asked Clay.

"Excuse me?"

"Just kidding."

"I was actually in the communications department, but whatever," Karen said with a quick laugh as she tried to gauge whether or not she should be mortally offended. Her whole life, she'd had a tendency toward delayed reactions.

"For the record, I fully support Planned Parenthood," said Clay, as if he could tell she was still deciding. "I think I even give them money."

"Oh—cool," said Karen, trying to smile.

"And then what?" asked Clay.

"Well, at some point, I began fund-raising for the causes

I care about. And at another point, I got married and had a kid. My husband and I actually met at the Republican National Convention, if you can believe it. Or, really, *outside* the Republican National Convention. If I remember correctly, we were both chanting, 'Hey, ho, the GOP must go.'" Somehow, Karen sensed that Clay, whatever his current political persuasion, would appreciate that last detail.

And he did. "Of course you were," he said, seeming inordinately pleased, if only because the anecdote fit so neatly into his picture of the world. "I love it."

"And our daughter is about to turn nine," Karen went on. "And I don't have to tell you what I'm doing right now, because you already know! What about you?"

"What *about* me?" he said, popping an olive into his mouth as if there weren't much to say.

"I don't know! Tell me anything."

"Well, I'm permanently jet-lagged. And I have four kids. How's that?"

"Four! Yikes," said Karen, who had noticed in her travels that only the very rich and the very poor had families that large anymore. "I can barely manage one."

"Yeah, well, we have a lot of help." Clay unfolded his napkin and placed it in his lap. "But to be honest, it's been kind of stressful lately. My wife basically hates my guts."

"Oh no!" said Karen, surprised at how forthcoming he was being and titillated to have such personal information in her possession but also feeling that she somehow needed to even the score. "Well, my husband and I barely see each other," she told him. "He used to work as a housing lawyer, but now he's building this website and app, and he's never home. But why am I telling you this?" She laughed again, this time nervously. Now that she'd said so much, she felt guilty and keen to bring the conversation back to its original impetus in case Clay had forgotten why she'd invited him to lunch. "Anyway, I hope you don't mind me e-mailing you out of nowhere. I'm sure you're incredibly busy. But I heard you were involved in philanthropy, and I just wanted to let you know that Hungry Kids is an amazing cause. People think starving children exist only in Africa. But it's a big issue right here in our own backyards. It's even worse for these kids on weekends and in the summertime when schools are out and not providing free breakfast and lunch. By our estimates, there are currently one point seven million people living in food-insecure households here in the city and surrounding areas, one million of whom are children and three hundred thousand of whom are grownups who are eligible for food stamps but who don't have them. So part of what we do is help parents file for the benefits their families are entitled to. We also help stock food pantries and soup kitchens—"

"It all sounds very admirable," said Clay, interrupting. "In fact, I had my assistant look up your GuideStar rating this morning and apparently you guys get five stars. But first I have a question." He laid a hand on Karen's forearm. "Do you think we could order before we talk any more about your good cause? To be honest, I'm fucking starving…speaking of starving."

"Of course!" said Karen, embarrassed. Had she come on too strong, too early? You had to time these things for maximum impact. Following Clay's lead, she picked up her menu and quickly announced, "I think I'm going to get the wild salmon."

"Always a solid choice," said Clay, motioning for the waiter.

He ordered for them both—oysters on the half shell for himself, along with some pasta dish involving scallops, a large bottle of sparkling water, and a half a dozen exotic-sounding appetizers that Karen doubted they'd be able to finish, which struck her as ironic considering they were there to address food scarcity. But no matter.

After the waiter left, Clay said, "So, back to your thing...I have a *real* question for you. I hope you're not offended by my asking it. But the poor children one sees around the city don't always look exactly, well—how do I put this nicely?—*starving*. Sometimes the opposite."

Karen had heard the question before. "Actually, childhood obesity has a lot to do with food scarcity. When they have no access to nutritious food, children are more likely to fill up on empty calories that taste good while they're eating them but don't make them feel full or provide them with adequate nutrients. You can be obese *and* malnourished. That's the irony. And that's where Hungry Kids' education program comes in. We have this amazing troupe of young actors who visit the public schools and perform skits that teach young children about healthy eating habits. They're actually hilarious. They all dress up as fruits and vegetables."

"Sounds amusing," said Clay.

Was he mocking her? Karen couldn't tell. "Anyway," she continued, "we'd be totally thrilled if you wanted to get involved. Eighty percent of donations go directly to feeding the poor and related programs. I should add that we also have this fantastic new outreach program, Keep It Fresh, which increases access to affordable and nutritious fresh food in low-income neighborhoods and enables economic development through creating or expanding food-related jobs and—"

"I'm happy to help," said Clay, again cutting her off and also sounding the tiniest bit impatient.

Or was Karen overinterpreting? "Thank you so much, Clay," she said, relieved to have gotten the ask part of the conversation over with, even as she wished she'd waited.

"It's my pleasure," said Clay. Then he narrowed his eyes at her, smiled, and said, "It's good to see you, Karen Kipple from College."

"It's good to see you too!" said Karen, deciding that, in all likelihood, he was just feeling nostalgic for his Sigma Chi days and mistakenly thinking she'd been a part of them.

"Don't take this the wrong way," he went on while fishing an olive pit out of his mouth, "but you're one of the few people I know who looks better than they did when we were young."

"Oh, thanks!" she said, not sure whether to be flattered or hurt. It struck her as the ultimate left-handed compliment. "Was I really ugly then?"

"Not at all, but you wore some kind of ring thingy in your nose, which I hope you don't mind me saying I'm glad to see gone."

"Why would I mind?" Karen said. Though, in truth, she *did* mind. The hole had eventually become infected, and she'd had to let it close up. But there had been a time and place when that tiny gold ring had made her feel subversive, which was the attribute to which everyone in Karen's social circle had aspired back then.

"You also had a baby face, and now you're kind of chiseled and hot," said Clay.

"Tell that to my husband!" Karen laughed, shocked by the direction in which the conversation had turned.

"Tell me his name, and I will."

"It's Matt. He's a great guy. But you know how it goes after you've been married for a while. People basically stop seeing each other." Was she being disloyal? "I could seriously be wearing two different shoes, and I don't think he'd notice." What Karen didn't tell Clay was that one of the things that had initially attracted her to Matt was his self-reliance—a reliance so evolved that it sometimes bordered on benign neglect of the people around him. Matt didn't seem to need or want anyone's help, and that realization had come as a huge relief to Karen—at least in the early days of their marriage.

Clay took a sip of his sparkling water and wiped his mouth. Then he looked straight at her—straight through her, it seemed to Karen—and said, "I'd notice."

Was Clay Phipps just one of those people who used flattery the way others used humor—to put others at ease? Or was he flirting with her? Was that even possible? And if he was, why? "Is that right?" was all Karen could think to say back. It had been so long since she'd been complimented on her appearance that she'd forgotten how gratifying it was. With her mop of unruly hair, small breasts, and proportionally wide hips, she'd never conformed to any American ideal of femininity. But there had been a very brief window in her midtwenties—after she'd finally slimmed down, thanks to a strict if unhealthy diet of salads and nonfat frozen yogurt, and learned how to defrizz her hair—when she'd attracted a certain amount of attention from the opposite sex, which she'd rewarded with short-term flings. At its most intoxicating, being a sex object had felt like an escape route from the mundane and from the burden of her upbringing. At its worst, it had felt like a full-time job. There had been endless hairs to pluck, StairMasters to master, scales to stand on and lament the previous evening's caloric intake, and lotions and potions to rub in and rinse off again. But to have experienced even a taste of the strange kind of power that accompanied youthful beauty was, to some extent, to mourn its passing for the rest of your life.

Karen and Clay filled the rest of the hour with discussions of long-lost friends from college—mostly his fraternity brothers, the majority of whom Karen barely recalled but, for Clay's benefit and, by extension, the benefit of Hungry Kids, pretended to have vivid memories of...

"I assume you remember Scooter, my roommate in the house—the dickhead with the American flag bong?"

"Of course I remember!"

"Well, after Lehman folded and his marriage blew up, the guy hightailed it to Tortola for a breather and apparently never left. Rumor has it he now rides around in a fucking pizza boat, if you can believe it, offering pepperoni slices to passing yachtsmen."

"You're kidding."

All of the old brothers apparently worked in tech or finance, or used to do so until their midlife crises, and were about to remarry or were busy disentangling themselves from their old marriages and going through messy divorces. When the bill came, Clay reached into his coat pocket and Karen didn't bother objecting. After laying out his Am Ex black card on the tray, he pulled a rumpled paper check out of his pocket with the name of his family's LLC at the top. "How much does Starving Children or whatever it's called need?" he said. "Sorry—I'm terrible with names. Though I'd never forget yours."

"It's *Hungry Kids,*" said Karen, embarrassed and also surprised he was opening his wallet this quickly. It usually took a few weeks to get money out of anyone. At the very least, there were accounting teams to consult. Besides, who carried around paper checks anymore? "But—oh my God, Clay, you don't have to do it right here! I mean, unless you want to…"

"Why wait? As you said, the kids in my backyard are hungry. Though maybe not the kids in my *actual* backyard, since those are my own greedy little bastards."

"Point taken," said Karen, feeling bold. "Well, how's seventy-five grand, and you win my eternal devotion?"

"Let's make it a hundred," he said, writing down the number and then signing his name at the bottom with what looked like a single horizontal line.

"I don't know what to say."

"You don't have to say anything."

"Well, thank you so much, Clay. *Really*."

"My pleasure. Hey, next summer, you and Mark—"

"It's Matt."

"Matt—that's right. Well, you and Matt should come visit us out at the beach. We've got lots of room. And my youngest daughter, Quinn, just turned eight. She and your kid—"

"Ruby."

"*Ruby*—that's my niece's name too."

"Funny," said Karen. "Where does she live?"

"San Fran."

"Of course," said Karen, grimacing. While pregnant, she'd spent countless nights lying awake trying to dream up a name that sounded original without being odd, dignified while still cute. She didn't want it to overwhelm her husband's last name either; to her mind, McClelland was already a mouthful. Karen had always considered her own first name to be dispiritingly bland and was determined not to stigmatize her own daughter in a similar fashion. She'd always hated her last name too, if only because it rhymed with *nipple* and had therefore inspired endless schoolyard taunts. According to family lore, Kipple had once been Kiplowitz, but the bureaucrats at Ellis Island couldn't be bothered to spell it out. Matt hadn't seemed to care all that much *what* they named the baby, though he'd boycotted one suggestion of Karen's (Eden), insisting that it sounded like a stripper. Ruby had been Karen's second choice, and Matt had been fine with it. But now she wished he hadn't been. There seemed to be Rubys everywhere. Or, at least, they were everywhere in a certain milieu. There had been two others in Ruby's pre-K class at Elm Tree alone. And there were three in her gymnastics class. Though there seemed to be considerably fewer at Betts.

"Well, your Ruby and my Quinn can play in the pool while the grown-ups keep themselves in refreshments," said Clay.

"That sounds like a dream," said Karen, knowing it would never happen. There was no way Matt would ever agree to show up at the home of some hedge-fund zillionaire acquaintance of his wife's and partake of the guy's munificence, never mind spend the night in his mansion. Matt had had the same friends since high school and showed few signs of being interested in making new ones.

"Great. I'll have my assistant call you to book a weekend. In the meantime, I should really run. I'm actually going to Hong Kong this afternoon."

"You're kidding."

"Wish I was. Long fucking flight. But it was great to see you." Clay stood up. So did Karen. They embraced again. "Seriously, you look amazing."

"So do you," said Karen. "The fleece is very flattering."

"Are you kidding? I put on this jacket especially for you."
He lifted his pullover by the zippered collar and grinned at
her.

"Well, it's a winning look."

"Not as winning as yours."

"You're a total liar. But thanks."

"Not in this case." He kissed Karen on the cheek and
walked out.

Karen stayed behind to finish her sparkling water and, for
a few more minutes, to bask in the afterglow of what, on all
counts, had to be called a successful lunch.

On Mondays, Wednesdays, and Thursdays, Ruby stayed late
for Betts's after-school program, which was known simply
as After School. Ruby's first two years at the school, Karen
had secretly dismissed the program as subsidized daycare
for low-income students. Instead, she'd had Ashley, a white
twenty-year-old psychology major at a local college, pick
Ruby up at three o'clock three days a week. Karen couldn't
deal with the racial politics of employing a woman with
darker skin than her own to help raise her child. Or was
her prohibition on doing so even more problematic? Was
she denying jobs to the people who needed them most? In
any case, mostly for financial reasons, she'd decided to give
After School a chance this year and had been pleasantly surprised by the results. Ruby seemed fine about staying late a
few afternoons a week. And at fifteen bucks for the whole
afternoon, it was certainly cheaper, and arguably more educational, than having Ashley bring Ruby home at three
o'clock to do glitter tattoos.

Still giddy from her lunch with Clay when she entered the

building later that afternoon, Karen also felt uncharacteristically sanguine about the school. At the sight of a fifth-grader sitting in the hall sipping a Pepsi, Karen, rather than experiencing the usual tsunami of disapproval regarding the empty calories, told herself that her daughter was receiving an invaluable, once-in-a-lifetime education in multiculturalism and class difference. It was the same when, on her way into the gymnasium, she passed two mothers talking and overheard one of them say to the other, "I pulled off all my gels this morning, but I ain't be getting them redone till payday," her fingernails raised for inspection. Rather than cringe at the woman's grammar—never mind Karen's feelings about nail extensions—Karen imagined how stressful it would be to live paycheck to paycheck and reminded herself how lucky she was. Moreover, at the sight of her own rosy-cheeked progeny sitting in the corner of the gymnasium awaiting pickup, Karen felt as if she were the luckiest woman in the world. "Ruby Doobie!" she cried.

"Mommy!" cried Ruby, matching Karen's exuberant tone as she jumped up and ran toward her. Mother and daughter embraced as closely as flesh allowed. The word *miracle* got thrown around a lot when it came to children. But Ruby's existence often struck Karen as that very thing—not only because Karen had spent two frustrating years trying to get pregnant, but because Karen had put all her own unrealized dreams of changing the world into her daughter's not-quite-four-foot frame.

But Karen's sense of well-being lasted only so long. On the walk home late that afternoon, their fingers entwined and arms swinging in unison, Ruby informed her mother that Maeve was still out. Somehow, Karen found the news disturbing and kept returning to it throughout the evening, wondering if she'd underestimated the severity of Maeve's injuries. Having resolved to send Maeve's mother, Laura, a carefully worded e-mail inquiring about her daughter's condition, Karen then struggled to get Ruby to bed. Ruby claimed not to be tired and fought all of Karen's attempts to convince her otherwise until Karen's entire body was in a tangle of frustration.

She'd only just gotten Ruby down for the night—nearly an hour later than normal—when Matt waltzed through the door. He was late, as usual, but even later than usual. And Karen was as irritated as ever, but even more so. Sometimes it seemed as if Matt considered raising Ruby to be Karen's project rather than a joint one. Or was that unfair? Maybe she was just mad at him for not being as complimentary as Clay Phipps. "What's up?" he said, taking off his coat.

"What's up?" she answered, her voice rising on the *up*. "It just took me, like, two hours to get Ruby to sleep. That's what's up. She only quieted down, like, five minutes ago. And I'm completely fried."

"So go to bed," said Matt.

"That's not the point."

"I'm sorry I'm late," he said, seeming finally to comprehend. "But you won't believe this story."

"What story?" said Karen, softening slightly.

"You know the old Dominican guy down the block who's always sitting on the stoop—Miguel?"

"Yeah."

"He's getting kicked out of his ground-floor apartment after forty fucking years. I mean, the guy fucking grew up there! But his mom died a few years ago, and she was the only family he had. And now this scumbag developer has come in and is planning to turn it into a single-family, state-of-the-art 'passive house'"—Matt made quote marks in the air—"whatever the fuck that is. Anyway, I offered to represent him for free in housing court. We were out on his stoop talking strategy."

"Well, that was nice of you," said Karen, feeling torn. On the one hand, she admired her husband for taking up cases he didn't need to take up. She also felt sorry for Miguel, who had always been friendly to her and Ruby, sometimes making funny noises with his cheek and thumb for Ruby's amusement as they walked by. Moreover, the loss of Miguel would undoubtedly make the neighborhood a tiny bit less diverse and a tiny bit more like a community with invisible gates. It wasn't hard to imagine the guy ending up on the street either.

On the other hand, she couldn't help but feel that Matt's time might be just as well spent paying attention to his wife and daughter as it was helping out a neighbor. There was also the fact that Karen was terrified of Miguel's pit bull, who had a thick black ring around one eye, giving him the appearance of a canine pirate. Then there was the deafening salsa he played at all hours of the day and night, apparently unaware that others might not enjoy his music as much as he did. Karen also secretly considered the building as it existed now to be a blight on the block, with its plastic-sheathed windows and chipping stucco. The fetid garbage smell that emanated from the front yard was another matter, as was the Dominican flag that Miguel flew out his window, the sight of which Karen found difficult to reconcile with her interior-decorating taste. Not that she was prepared to admit any of this to her husband. "But if the building is already sold," she said, "I doubt there's much you or anyone else can do. I'm sure Miguel didn't have a lease."

"He didn't have a lease, but he's always paid his rent," said Matt. "And—most important—he's a human being who deserves a roof over his head."

"Well, I feel bad for the guy," said Karen. "But in all honesty, I won't miss his dog. I actually cross the street when it comes near me."

"Jesus! Whose side are you on?" cried Matt.

"I'm on Miguel's side!" replied Karen. "But I also think pit bulls are scary. They're illegal in England, you know."

"Pit bulls aren't even a real breed of dog—look it up. It's just a blanket term. But whatever." Matt grimaced. "So, what did you do today?"

As generic and open-ended as the question was, it still irked Karen. "You mean in addition to getting our daughter fed, bathed, and to sleep? Well, I made a hundred grand for the organization at lunch."

"Wow, good job."

"Yeah, I had lunch with a college acquaintance—this preppy guy named Clay Phipps who's made a gazillion dollars running some hedge fund. He actually wrote a check on the spot."

"Nice tax write-off, I guess. Or at least it would be if he paid taxes, which he probably doesn't, being a hedgie and all."

"Do you have to be so cynical?"

"You probably wouldn't like me if I wasn't." Matt smiled.

"Whatever you say." Karen smiled back. "Anyway, he invited the three of us out to visit him and his family next summer at his waterfront mansion." Karen didn't actually know for a fact that the island house was on the waterfront, but she assumed so. She also assumed her husband would reject the invitation outright. But she needed to go through the motions of asking him so she could feel frustrated and resentful but also admire his steadfastness to his principles.

"Sorry—I'll leave the social climbing to you," said Matt, right on cue.

"So you'd rather spend the entire summer stuck in the city," said Karen, "sweltering to death and going to 'family swim' at the overchlorinated YMCA pool than get wined and dined in some gorgeous house with ocean breezes while Ruby plays in an actual pool that doesn't require shower shoes when you walk around it because there aren't pubic hairs everywhere you look?"

"I thought your whole thing was that you hated vacations."

"Maybe I do, and maybe I don't."

"Karen, I don't know this guy from Adam," Matt continued. "What am I going to do there? Lie in a lounger humming to myself while the two of you talk about what happened to everyone in your freshman dorm?"

"Fine," she said, still playing the martyr even though she had to admit that her husband had a point. "You're not invited. Okay? Forget I ever said anything. It's better to be hot and bothered and have integrity than to actually enjoy the summer. Because life is long."

Matt rolled his eyes and sighed. "Speaking of shower shoes, I'm going to shower, if you don't mind."

"Why would I mind?"

After he disappeared, Karen sat down on the sofa with her laptop and began composing a message to Maeve's mother, Laura. Just as she was typing the sentence *I hope Maeve is doing okay,* an e-mail from Laura herself uncannily flashed across Karen's screen. On further inspection, she determined it was a group e-mail sent to all the parents in Ruby's third-grade class. Karen quickly scanned the message. It read:

Dear Room 303 Parents,

As some of you know, our daughter, Maeve, was injured Friday morning during the community-unit celebration. Evan and I had an early-morning work commitment and were unable to attend. But we've pieced together what happened by speaking to various people who were there at the time. We also saw firsthand the injuries suffered by our daughter, who has a fractured septum, had to spend a full day in the hospital, and is now suffering from PTSD.

This is not the first time that Jayyden Price has bullied our daughter. What happened on Friday was part of a longstanding pattern that began in second grade and that includes verbal taunts and, in at least one case prior to Friday's incident, physical violence. During recess last spring, he kicked Maeve in the shin, causing severe bruising.

We have felt privileged to be part of a school community that prioritizes diversity. But our daughter's physical safety trumps all else. Principal Chambers does not seem to agree. Here is a transcript of our meeting with her yesterday, which my husband, Evan, recorded:

Evan: We don't feel safe having our daughter in the same class as this child [Jayyden Price].
Ms. Chambers: I can assure you that [Jayyden] is receiving all the special services this school offers. He meets

with our school psychologist three days a week, and
since the incident, he has been banned from recess.
There is no excuse for what he did to your daughter,
but I ask you to appreciate that he has an unstable
family situation. And I understand that your daughter
can be provocative.

Evan: So you're blaming our daughter for having her
nose broken? Unbelievable—

Ms. Chambers (interrupting): I'm not saying that.

Laura: We feel sorry for Jayyden. But our first priority is
keeping our own daughter safe. How can it be that, as
principal, your first priority is not guaranteeing the
safety of the children at this school?

Ms. Chambers: I can do my best to create a supportive
and accountable environment, but I cannot guarantee
the safety of any child. I wish I could. [Laughs.]

Evan: Well, you can guarantee that our daughter will
not be bullied by Jayyden by removing him from the
school and sending him somewhere for troubled chil-
dren.

Ms. Chambers: I cannot make Jayyden leave this school.
Nor is there anywhere I can legally send him. This is a
public school, and he has just as much of a right to be
here as Maeve does.

Evan: Well, then we're taking Maeve out.

Ms. Chambers: We'll be sorry to see your family go—and
we hope you change your minds.

In short, she offered nothing—and we will not, alas, be
changing our minds. Maeve will miss all her friends at
Betts, just as we will miss being part of the Betts commu-

nity. But we feel we have no other choice but to remove her from the school. We've appealed to the board of education this week for a safety transfer to another elementary school in the district.

Thank you for your support and understanding,
Laura Collier and Evan Shaw
(parents of Maeve Collier-Shaw)

Karen's first emotion, before she realized what the e-mail actually amounted to—namely, a kiss-off to the parent body of Betts—was hurt. In Laura's attempt to piece together what happened, why had she not reached out to Karen? Had Laura developed a stealth friendship with one of the other mothers in the class? Karen's second emotion was embarrassment and discomfort on behalf of Jayyden and his family. Then she recalled that there was no e-mail contact info on the class list for Jayyden, so it was unlikely that Aunt Carla or any of Jayyden's cousins would ever see Laura's letter. Karen's third thought was that Ruby would be upset when she heard Maeve was leaving Betts.

But the reality—which was only now beginning to dawn on Karen—was that she was just as upset as her daughter was likely to be, if not more so, by Maeve's departure. It was not the loss of Maeve, per se, but the loss of her representative status. By Karen's calculations, Ruby would now be one of only three Caucasian girls in the class—possibly four, depending on whether you counted the Cuban girl, Sofia. Maeve had also been Room 303's only blonde—a superficial detail, of course. And yet, somehow, it mattered. Somehow, the existence of that golden hair in that kaleidoscopic setting held the promise of a more beautiful and more unified world.

Hoping there might still be time to talk Maeve's parents out of their decision, Karen quickly crafted a response, the goal of which was to strike a seemingly supportive tone that simultaneously challenged Laura's assumptions and transferred Karen's shame at her own census-taking onto the other woman. It read as follows:

L, I cannot believe what you have all been through! What a nightmare. Poor you. And poor Maeve. I hope she makes a speedy recovery…As for school stuff, I totally understand where you're coming from. You must have been beyond freaked when you got that call from school yesterday morning—I know I would have been. But I have to admit I'm sad at the prospect of losing you guys and wonder if it's too late to talk you out of it. I ask selfishly, of course. But R is going to miss M so much—and Matt and I will miss you guys too!

I also think you are going to find there are problem kids at every school—no matter the student body's color or creed—and that the diversity at Betts is not easily replicated. Plus, in a country with almost no gun-control laws, it's true that no one person can actually guarantee the safety of anyone else. Maybe that was all Principal Chambers meant in her tone-deaf way? At the same time, I understand you need to do what's best for your family. And I totally respect that. I just thought I'd put my two cents in. I'm also more than happy to chat about any of this any time you want to, though no pressure.

In any case, when Maeve is up to it, let's definitely schedule another playdate for the girls...

xx Karen

It took Karen a full hour to compose the e-mail. In an earlier draft, she'd ended with *Let's schedule a playdate when Maeve is back in fighting shape.* But she'd been concerned that Laura would think she was implying that Maeve was the one who'd started up with Jayyden. The e-mail left Karen's computer at quarter to ten that evening. There was no immediate reply.

There was no response from Laura the next morning either, or the next afternoon, which Karen found surprising. To her knowledge, Laura was a compulsive texter and e-mailer and rarely if ever went off the grid.

That same afternoon, there was a staff outing to one of Hungry Kids' contracted food pantries that included a photo op with the deputy mayor. Karen smiled for the cameras, shook hands with various low-level politicians, and made small talk with the pantry employees and volunteers. But her head was elsewhere—namely, on the Collier-Shaw clan. And it stayed there throughout the evening too. She couldn't entirely explain why Maeve's disappearance from Betts bothered her as much as it did, but something about it felt like a repudiation of Karen's own choices.

What's more, at the dinner table that evening, Ruby reported that, while Maeve still wasn't back, there was a new student in her class—a girl from Egypt named Fatima. A few days ago, Karen might have found this an interesting and potentially enriching development for Ruby and for Room 303.

Now, Karen calculated in her head that, with Maeve gone and Fatima having just arrived, the percentage of Caucasian students in the class had suddenly fallen below the critical 20 percent mark.

Or, at least, it felt critical to Karen. As she stood at the sink loading the dishwasher, she felt resentful of both the Collier-Shaw family for abandoning ship and Jayyden Price and his absentee parents for driving them away. But she was also utterly disgusted with herself for having made such a crude numerical calculation. Why couldn't she simply be proud of the fact that her daughter went to the rare integrated (or semi-integrated) public school where white people were the minority? Besides, wasn't that the future of America?

To Karen's surprise, Ruby seemed more or less Zen about Maeve's absence. It was a girl named Mia Hernandez whom she suddenly wanted to have playdates with anyway—Ruby came home the next afternoon calling Mia her NBF. While Karen was still unsettled by the loss of Maeve, she was also proud and surprised to hear that her daughter had apparently reached out across what Karen imagined to be both cultural and economic divides to befriend the girl, though maybe the latter presumption was presumptuous. All Karen really knew was that Mia's family hailed from Puerto Rico, a fact that Ruby had learned during Room 303's immigration unit the previous month and relayed in passing to Karen. But in Karen's experience, the children of native-born, college-educated parents tended to find one another and then stick together, somehow sniffing out the other adults' class credentials before they even knew the right questions to ask. To Karen's amazement, the first friend Ruby ever made at Betts—a boy who had subsequently moved out of the city—just happened to be the son of a guy Matt had briefly roomed with at law school. And it didn't seem like an accident that, at least until the week before, Ruby's best friend at the school was one of the other four white girls in her class.

That said, Karen had come to believe that the parents played a role in the children's self-segregation. Every year, she threw Ruby a birthday party, and every year she was puzzled to find that, with a few exceptions, the white, Asian, and interracial children whom Ruby invited showed up, while the black and Hispanic children with parents of lesser means didn't. Their mothers either sent their regrets or simply didn't respond. In a few cases, they never opened the invitation at all. Was it because they didn't recognize the Evite format? Lived too far away? Didn't feel comfortable? Had complicated work schedules and child-care arrangements that made dropping off and picking up a child in the middle of a Saturday afternoon too difficult? Karen knew there were a million possible explanations, all of them valid. But she always felt the tiniest bit hurt that her attempts at a magnanimous gesture toward One World–ness were met with silence—even when she'd used extra Evite "coins" to send the invitations again.

At work the next day, there was a planning meeting to discuss Hungry Kids' annual spring gala/benefit. Naturally, Karen had already added Clay's name to the guest list. She'd also mailed him an old-fashioned note on thick card stock, thanking him for his generous contribution. She didn't expect to hear back, since no one really replied to paper letters anymore, much less wrote them. But for murky reasons—the desire to be complimented on her appearance again? Excitement at the prospect of a luxury mini-vacation at the beach next summer?—she found herself wishing he'd get back in touch and scanning her in-box in search of his name.

She also found herself scanning it for Laura's. It had been three days since Karen had written her an e-mail, and Laura still hadn't responded, which Karen found both curious and pointed. Meanwhile, at school drop-off on Friday—a week to the day since Jayyden had pummeled Maeve—Karen spotted the culprit shuffling down the hall. He'd had the outline of a race car shaved into his buzz cut. And his backpack was falling so low on his shoulders that it bounced against the back of his legs.

Recalling their embraces from the year before and possessed for a moment by the self-aggrandizing notion that the extension of friendship by a nice lady like herself could somehow benefit him in life, Karen called out, "Hi, Jayyden!" in a buoyant voice.

At the sound of his name, he quickly turned around. But seeing it was Karen, he immediately lost interest. "Hey, Ruby's mom," he mumbled before he turned back around and continued shuffling down the hall.

Karen *finally* received a reply from Laura that evening. It read as follows:

Hey, Karen,

Thanks for your note. I, too, wish there was a way for us to stay. But Maeve literally begged us not to make her go to school on Monday. And neither Evan nor I had the heart to force her. Also, to be completely honest, we really don't feel comfortable sending her there anymore.

We've enjoyed getting to know your family over the past

*few years. And Maeve is going to miss Ruby, for sure. We'll
have to keep in touch.*

Best, Laura

Karen had to admit that, at least on the surface, Laura's e-mail was perfectly nice and certainly polite. But considering Maeve and Ruby were best friends, it also struck Karen as insultingly laconic in addition to being dismissive. Laura seemed barely to have considered Karen's arguments. As a result, Karen couldn't help but feel as if she'd been blown off like so many pencil shavings after a standardized math test. Nonetheless, she couldn't stop herself from writing back to ask where Maeve would be attending third grade instead.

The next morning, Laura relayed the answer in one word, which she didn't bother to capitalize, as if the leap were that insignificant. She wrote, simply,

mather

Karen did realize there were atrocities being committed around the globe at that very moment that were far worse than the one of which Laura Collier and Evan Shaw now appeared to be guilty. Even so, Laura's answer made Karen feel almost physically ill. The school known as Mather—official name: Edward G. Mather Elementary—was the esteemed public elementary five blocks east of Betts where the majority of Ruby's friends from pre-K at Elm Tree, with their heirloom names, sparkly headbands, Mini Boden anoraks, and seaweed snacks, had matriculated. Karen had heard of families lying about their addresses or cramming their families into tiny apartments in order to gain entry into the school, but this was the first time she'd heard about anyone seeking a safety transfer as a way in. Suddenly, Laura and Evan's response to Jayyden's punch seemed less like a defensive posture or overreaction than a cynical ploy to game the system.

It also seemed clear to Karen that Laura and Evan, whom she'd once taken for art-school types who'd sold out only because there were bills that needed to be paid, were actually shameless and conniving opportunists, no better than Clay Phipps, if significantly less wealthy. But at least he was up-front about his motives. Drunk on a heady brew of jealousy and resentment, Karen wrote back:

Wow—lucky you guys! And nice way to work the system. ☺

Had her response been that nakedly passive aggressive? Whatever the case, Laura didn't reply. This time, Karen wasn't entirely surprised.

It happened that Karen's closest mom-friend at Betts, Lou, was also dark-skinned. Second-generation Jamaican, she'd been raised in New Hampshire, of all unlikely places, and was now married to an Icelandic guy who worked in graphic design. Karen prized Lou for being warm and witty. But she was also aware of taking an inordinate amount of pride in the existence of their friendship, which seemed to prove that she was the kind of person she liked to think of herself as—that is, a person with friends from all walks of life. Because of this, she was aware of putting more effort into the relationship's maintenance than she put into friendships with her old (mainly white) friends, whose e-mails she often didn't answer for days and on whom she canceled dinners, coffees, and drinks as frequently as she scheduled them.

But it was also true that, in that particular moment, Karen felt more comfortable with Lou than she did with many of the old gang from her twenties and early thirties, all of whom had subsequently paired up and produced two children per couple, spaced two years and ten months apart. Because the majority of these old friends sent their children to segregated schools that were populated entirely by professional-class families like themselves, Karen felt she could no longer entirely relate to them, whereas she and Lou, despite the difference in their skin colors and backgrounds, were *in it together*.

Except never entirely.

The one thing Karen struggled to talk about with Lou was the racial composition of Betts. To Karen, Lou's children, with their caramel-colored skin, frizzy gold hair, and hazel eyes, reminded her of nothing so much as beautiful glowing lanterns. At the same time, Karen recognized that, according to the peculiar logic of the country in which they both lived, Lou and her kids, though not her husband, were understood to be black. Therefore, Karen was constantly on guard about saying the wrong thing and broached the race issue carefully, if at all. Though it felt equally weird to pretend there wasn't one. "So, could you believe that e-mail from Maeve's mom last night?" Karen began at pickup late the next day as she and Lou walked out of the building together, their children three paces ahead.

"Yeah, well, I can't say I'm surprised by any of it," said Lou, shrugging and sounding unbothered. Or was that just an act? "They were never a good fit at this school."

"I agree. Though Ruby is really upset about Maeve leaving," Karen found herself lying—maybe as cover for her own distress. "And I kind of think Principal Chambers could have handled the whole thing better too." What Karen didn't say was that it was a common point of agreement among the white parents at the school that Regina Chambers always prioritized the needs of the parents of color over those of their paler counterparts. Though Karen had no factual evidence of this, being too timid ever to have approached the woman with concerns of her own.

"She can be inflexible," agreed Lou. "But in the case of Jayyden, there's nothing she can do. You can't suspend kids till fourth grade. And as far as I know, they don't have reform schools for kids Jayyden's age anymore. The last administration phased them out. They were seen as 'pipelines to prison.'" Lou made quotes in the air. "And Jayyden is plenty smart, so they can't put him in special ed. Maybe Regina didn't properly explain all that to Maeve's parents." Lou was one of a few parents who was on first-name terms with the principal, a fact that filled Karen with quiet awe.

"Or maybe they didn't want to hear it," said Karen, hesitating before she spoke again. "To be honest, I think Laura and Evan are racists, and they're just using this incident as an excuse to take Maeve out of the school."

"Karen, honey," Lou said, half laughing, as she touched Karen's arm. "All white people are racists."

"Ugh, is that true?" said Karen, squinching up her face and somehow hurt at the suggestion. She'd always assumed that Lou didn't think she was like that—and, moreover, that her friendship with Lou meant she *wasn't* like that.

"My husband is the worst," Lou went on.

"Oh, stop! That can't be true," Karen said, shocked at the very suggestion. Or was Lou joking?

"Of course it is," she said. "But I don't care. I'm his wife. He has no choice but to love me. I'll kill him if he doesn't."

Both of them had started laughing—maybe to take the pressure off. "You're so hard on Gunnar," said Karen.

When Matt got home that evening, neither early nor late, Karen told him that Ruby's friend Maeve was transferring to Mather—and that, as ridiculous as it might sound, the whole thing had put her in a bad mood all day.

"Wait—which school is that again?" he asked as he leafed through the pile of bills that Karen had conspicuously left on the kitchen counter, secretly hoping it would inspire him to go back to a paying job.

Karen squinted at her husband. "You just don't care about this stuff," she said. "Do you?"

"I do care. I just think you're getting overinvolved in the whole thing."

"Thanks."

"Also, you said the parents were total douche bags, so what do you care what they do?"

"They are, but Maeve was Ruby's best friend."

"So she'll make a new best friend. Besides, it's elementary school. They don't actually learn anything."

"Except reading, writing, math, how to speak in complete sentences, and how to get along with other kids."

"Karen," said Matt, lowering his chin and making eye contact for the first time. "Rubes comes from a middle-class home. Or, really, let's be honest, upper middle class. We may not make very much salary-wise, but we own a valuable piece of real estate, we've got some money in the bank, both of us have degrees from elite colleges. Which means that Ruby will probably end up at some elite college too. Did you know the major determinant of a child's future position on the socioeconomic ladder is the education level attained by the mother? They've done studies. And since you have two degrees, one of which is from a frigging Ivy League university, I'm really not that worried! Plus, I think it's good for her to be interacting with poor kids. Maybe she'll gain some perspective on how privileged she is."

"I guess," said Karen, glancing at their galley kitchen with its off-the-shelf Home Depot cabinetry and secretly wishing she and Matt were a little bit *more* privileged.

"Plus, the way the world works," Matt went on, "it's unlikely she'll ever again end up in such close proximity to the kind of kids she's meeting now. They start tracking them by middle school."

"If she gets *into* a decent middle school," Karen said ruefully. "Anyway, in case you were curious, Mather is the school where all of Ruby's friends from Elm Tree went."

"Oh—right," he said as he made his way over to the fridge and pulled out a locally brewed ale. Once, Matt had drunk Corona Extra. But Karen had seen an article on the Internet about how it contained corn syrup, a foodstuff that she'd come to understand was a thousand times worse than sugar. Though she wasn't entirely sure why, as corn itself had never struck her as a particularly venal product. In any case, Karen had urged him to stop buying it, and eventually, begrudgingly, he'd complied.

Bread had been subjected to a similar pressurized winnowing in the Kipple-McClelland household. Once, Arnold's multigrain had been good enough for lunch. Now Karen shopped at the bakery with the French name up the street, frequently splurging on the blended rye and wheat *miche* that, according to its museum label, had been subjected to sixty-eight hours of fermentation. In a different life, Karen would have heard the word *fermentation* and run in the other direction. But that was then. Even Ruby thought the *miche* was delicious. But was it five-dollars-a-loaf better than Arnold's? "Is that all you have to say?" she asked him.

"Look, Karen," Matt replied in a weary tone. "Rubes is happy. That's all that matters."

"How do you know she's happy?" Karen shot back. The moment she said it, she knew she shouldn't have. But it was too late.

Now it was Matt's turn to get defensive. Slack-jawed, he stared at Karen. Then he said, "Excuse me?"

"I mean, have you asked her lately if she's happy at school?"

Clearly angered by the implication that he wasn't around enough to know what was going on in his daughter's life, Matt didn't even deign to answer Karen's last question. Instead, he narrowed his eyes, shook his head, took a swig of his beer, and walked out of the room while Karen stood there motionless, not entirely sure how they'd arrived at the place they'd arrived or whether she should apologize or dig in but feeling suddenly alone and adrift.

Her thoughts turned to her dead parents. The truth was that, while Karen was fine in a day-to-day sense, she still hadn't found relief from the rudderless feeling that her mother's death in particular had engendered. In some ways, it had only gotten harder. In the first few days and even weeks after she died, Karen's memories of her were so vivid that she almost felt as if Ruth Kipple were still out there somewhere. And they'd buoyed her through the shock.

It wasn't until recently, when Karen found herself struggling to remember how her mother looked and sounded, to recall her thinning auburn hair, light brown eyes, and throaty voice, that time seemed to stretch out indefinitely ahead of her, with every new calendar day bringing Karen further away from the last time she'd seen her alive. Only then did the magnitude of what had happened finally set in. So did the mundaneness.

One day, Herb Kipple, who'd never drunk or smoked, had gotten a stomachache. A week later, he'd been diagnosed with terminal pancreatic cancer. He was gone in under three months. And then, just like that, Karen's mother, not wanting to be left out or left behind, or maybe because she was brokenhearted—or maybe it was all just random chance—had received a cancer diagnosis of her own. For a brief window of time, when she was still cogent but clearly dying, she'd seemed almost relieved and even liberated—possibly because the illness had lent a certain concreteness to her discontent. But then, just as quickly as in Karen's father, the disease took charge. Her mother's naps grew longer, then even longer. Finally, she too shriveled up and slipped into the abyss. And that was that. The world went on as before.

Except it hadn't for Karen.

For one thing, her parents' deaths had removed a psychic barrier between Karen and her own mortality. Once a comfortably abstract notion, her own demise now seemed to be, if not imminent, then waving in the near distance. Karen was especially terrified of dropping dead before Ruby was fully grown and out of the house. She worried how Matt would manage and also that Ruby would end up subsisting entirely on junk food because Matt would fail to notice or care. For another thing, Karen felt bitter both that her parents were missing out on Ruby's childhood and that Ruby was missing out on knowing them. Or was the real loss on Karen's side— the loss of a mirror to reflect back her own choices and confirm once and for all that she was a good daughter and, by extension, a good person?

In truth, when Ruth Kipple was still alive, Karen had considered her to be an endless burden. Karen had felt guilty for not visiting enough, not doing enough, as if there were anything anyone could have done about her mother's depression and, later, her dying. To an extent, her death had come as a relief to Karen. It also felt like a terrible waste. All that suffering; what had been the purpose? It had produced no great poetry or scientific breakthroughs, only more suffering—for her family members, for herself.

In any case, Karen had no one to talk about it with anymore. Her friends had long since ceased inquiring how she was doing. And even at the time, there had been an assumption that Karen must have been happy that the whole ordeal was over. Matt had been supportive in the immediate aftermath, but Karen sensed his patience had run out too. And Karen's brother, Rob, who sold surf equipment in Orange County and whom Karen spoke to twice a year, if that, had seemed relatively unmoved by the events, having separated himself from the family psychodrama decades earlier. Or maybe it was just that he wasn't willing to share his grief with Karen. After all this time, he still seemed resentful that she'd been their mother's favorite and had played the dutiful-child role that he'd never wanted for himself. On the phone, he answered Karen's questions monosyllabically, then made up excuses about why he needed to hang up.

Suddenly desperate to reconnect with Matt, Karen followed him into their bedroom. She found him typing on his phone. "I'm sorry I implied you were a bad father," she said. "I don't think that, and I shouldn't have said it. And I know you're working really hard on this project, and it means a lot to you."

It was another five seconds before he stopped typing. "It doesn't matter what it means to me," he finally answered, his tone flat and his eyes still cast south. "It's about connecting people in need with affordable housing."

"Matt, I'm sorry."

"Fine," he said. "Apology accepted." But he didn't smile or show other physical signs of having forgiven her. Even so, Karen walked over to him and leaned her head against his burly chest. In response, he laid a hand on her hair. But seconds later, he pulled it away. "I have to take out the garbage," he said.

He and Karen hadn't had sex in two weeks. When a dry spell lasted more than two weeks, Karen always began to feel antsy. Partly, it was physical. But it was also that not having sex seemed like a prime indicator of marital distress. The complicating factor was that, even as Karen craved relief on both counts, she dreaded its fulfillment, if only because the sex act seemed to require a level of energy she could no longer summon at will.

That weekend, Mia came over for a playdate, accompanied by her mother, Michelle. Aside from exchanging a few friendly smiles and partaking in a handful of three-sentence conversations about classroom-related matters, the two women barely knew each other. But Karen was determined to establish an atmosphere where both mother and daughter would feel comfortable. "Hi, you guys!" She greeted them at the door—and found herself strangely nervous. "So glad you could make it!"

"Please—Mia would not have missed it," said Michelle, leaning in to hug and kiss Karen on both cheeks, a move whose intimacy surprised and flattered Karen.

"Well, Ruby has been excited all morning too," she said, before turning around and calling into the distance, "Rubes—your friend is here." Then she turned back. "Come in—please!" she said. As Karen surreptitiously scanned Michelle's face, she was reminded of how pretty she was, with her high cheekbones and saucer-like brown eyes.

"You have such a nice place," said Michelle, looking around the living room.

"Oh, thanks. It's amazing what you can do with Ikea furniture!" said Karen, even though no more than two things in the whole condo—a lamp and a bookcase—hailed from the big box store. But she didn't want Michelle to think that, just because she and Ruby might be better *off* than Michelle and Mia, Karen thought she was also in some way *better*. That said, Karen had seen Michelle and Mia coming out of an attractive, brick-fronted, newly constructed mid-rise in the morning. Given that Karen understood Michelle to have a clerical job at the bureau of sanitation, she assumed that the family lived in one of the building's hard-to-come-by, low-income, set-aside apartments. So at least Karen didn't have to feel guilty about having a proper home.

"Yeah, but damn, that furniture is hard to put together," said Michelle.

"Tell me about it," said Karen, laughing. "Would you guys like something to drink?" She leaned down. "What about you, Mia? I was thinking of making hot chocolate."

The child didn't answer; she just stood there, clutching her mother's sleeve and staring at Karen.

Karen stared back, fascinated not only by Mia's shiny and perfectly executed black braids, which were so tight that her eyes appeared to be capable of peripheral vision, but also by Mia's clothes. Karen couldn't help but notice that they were adorned with tiny polo players. Nor did the garments appear to be designer knockoffs. The stitching was flawless, the cotton luxuriously thick and soft. Which meant that Michelle had likely spent a small fortune on the outfit, which further confused Karen. How could she afford to spend that kind of dough on her daughter's clothing? Or was it simply that Michelle took pride in her daughter looking cute and, like all mothers, splurged on occasion, putting the charges on Visa?

But if the latter was true, was there an aspirational element to the selection? Or had the polo-player logo long since ceased to signify a desire to hang out with the kind of people who actually played polo? And how did that relate to the fact that Mia's current best friend (Ruby) was Caucasian? Or did Michelle not think about these things?

"Mia, answer Ruby's mom," said Michelle.

"No, thank you," the child mumbled.

"Well, maybe you guys can have something later on," offered Karen.

"Can I see the Barbies?" asked Mia.

"Say 'please,'" said Michelle, turning from Mia to Karen. "Sorry, my daughter has the worst manners."

"Oh, she's fine," said Karen, waving the suggestion away.

"Can I please see the Barbies?" said Mia.

"Of course!" said Karen, suddenly regretting her accommodation of Ruby's insistence that all her Barbie dolls have blond hair. For Christmas the year before, Karen had bought her City Shopper Barbie, who was a brunette, but Ruby had promptly cut all her hair off with Matt's toenail clippers, giving the doll the appearance of an impossibly sexy chemo patient. "Ruby!" Karen called into the other room. "What are you doing? Your friend is here, waiting for you."

Just then, Ruby appeared—in a rainbow-striped wig, feather boa, and leotard, her convex tummy stretching the nylon fabric to its limits. "Surprise!" she yelled while striking a showgirl pose, one leg in front of the other and hands on her nonexistent hips.

"Hi, Ruby," Mia said, giggling.

"Sweetie—can we tone it down a tiny bit?" said Karen, embarrassed both by Ruby's pose and by the fact of her daughter's distended stomach. Karen feared that Michelle would think she was one of those rich, laissez-faire parents who never disciplined their children, mistakenly believing that they needed to express themselves, even when they were acting like entitled little brats.

"But I'm a celebrity," Ruby explained.

"Funny," said Karen, "because last time I checked, you were a third-grader." Undaunted, Ruby began to gyrate. Desperate to interrupt the proceedings, Karen took hold of Ruby's arm mid-swivel and said, "Mia really wants to see your Barbies. Can you take her to your room and show her? *Now?*"

"Come with me," said Ruby, grabbing Mia's wrist and yanking her away—summoning in Karen both relief and a new cause for alarm: What if Michelle thought Ruby was bossing her daughter around?

"Ruby reminds me of me at that age," announced Michelle.

"You mean bossy and a huge pain in the butt?" said Karen. "I don't believe it."

"Oh, stop," said Michelle, laughing. "Your daughter's got character!"

"That's very sweet," said Karen, who found herself feeling unexpectedly warm toward her visitor. After the girls vanished, she turned to Michelle, let out a heavy sigh meant to allude to the exhausting job known as motherhood, and said, "Maybe this is crazy, but how about a glass of something? I know it's early in the afternoon. But I'm ready if you are."

"Why not?" said Michelle. "To be honest, I could use one."

"I could *always* use one."

Michelle grinned back at her and said, "That makes two of us," further pleasing Karen, who hoped to be perceived by her guest as sophisticated—after all, she was easily fifteen years Michelle's senior—without being superior.

As Karen took two wineglasses down from the shelf and emptied a recently opened bottle of New Zealand sauvignon blanc into them, the women commiserated about how ridiculously cold it still was outside. Then Karen pulled up a stool across from Michelle, who was already seated at Karen's butcher-block kitchen island, and said, "So, what's new in your life?"

"Seriously?" said Michelle, one eyebrow lifted as she raised her glass to her lips.

"Seriously," said Karen.

"My husband, Benny, Mia, and me? We're fine," said Michelle. "But can I tell you"—she extended her neck forward—"Benny's ex, Gisela? She's literally *killing* me right now. Like, she and my stepdaughter, Juliana, just got evicted again."

"Oh my God, are you serious?" said Karen, amazed at how forthcoming Michelle was being—it was almost as if she'd forgotten that she and Karen didn't actually know each other—but also flattered to be entrusted with such personal information and happy for the distraction from her own problems. In truth, it alarmed and excited her to think that her daughter was only two degrees of separation away from the kind of people who got evicted.

"Totally serious," said Michelle.

"What a nightmare," said Karen. "So where are they living now?"

"Probably someone's floor. Or a shelter. I don't even ask anymore!"

"That's terrible," said Karen, shaking her head.

"I just feel bad for my stepdaughter, Juliana," Michelle continued. "She's, like, a sweet kid. But when she comes over to our house, she cries when it's time to leave 'cause Mia's got all these games to play with and her own room and stuff. And Juliana's got, like, nothing." She shrugged.

"Who can blame her?" said Karen, shrugging herself.

"But what can I do?" said Michelle. "I don't have room for her. And I sure as hell don't have room for Gisela."

"Well, she can't really expect you to put them all up."

"I don't know what she expects. But seriously, Karen?" Michelle pulled her stool in even closer. "Benny and I *worked* to get where we are. Like, we worked our butts off. So did my *mami* and *papi*—they always paid the rent on time. But Benny's *papi* left his *mami* when she was eight months pregnant with Benny. Then he got AIDS and, like, died on the street, but that's a whole other story."

"Oh my God, that's *awful!*" said Karen, even as a part of her wondered if Michelle was playing up her and Benny's hard-knocks background for Karen's own edification.

"Anyway, Benny knows that I will chop his you-know-what off if he leaves me for another girl. And he's not going to, because he's not like that. He's working the night shift right now."

"What does he do? I mean, where does he work?" said Karen, correcting herself. To her mind, the first question implied that the subject had selected one or another specialized field that provided, along with money, some sense of personal fulfillment, whereas one couldn't presume that working-class people did their jobs for any reason other than that they had to. Or was that patronizing?

"He's a security guard," said Michelle. "It's not ideal hours, but it's steady money. And that's where our priority is right now. We want to do what's best for our family."

"That's why your life is good, and hers isn't," said Karen.

"Exactly. And Gisela—she wants to get high and buy stuff she doesn't need. Hello? What about food for your children?" Michelle gestured elaborately with her long, perfectly manicured red nails, making Karen suddenly self-conscious about her own unadorned, vaguely filthy, and partially chewed-off ones.

"God, that is so depressing. I feel so sorry for Juliana," said Karen, hiding her hands under the table.

"I feel sorry for her too. But I'm sorry—I have *no* sympathy for Gisela."

"And why should you?"

"Seriously, Karen? I want to take her by the shoulders and shake her and say, 'You know what? You need to get your shit together. No one is going to bail you out anymore.'"

"Gisela has to learn that," Karen heard herself agreeing, even as she realized that the faith in self-reliance that Michelle was preaching and that Karen was now seconding was right out of the Republican Party playbook that Karen had spent a lifetime claiming to abhor because it placed all the blame for being poor *on* the poor.

"Oh! I completely forgot," said Michelle, reaching into her bag and, to Karen's secret horror, pulling out a large package of Chips Ahoy! chocolate chip cookies. On closer inspection, they appeared to have Reese's Pieces candy embedded in them. "I bought a treat for the girls," Michelle went on.

"That was so sweet of you!" said Karen, dark visions of polyunsaturated cooking oil filling her head. As she took the package out of Michelle's hand, she racked her brain for an excuse why it shouldn't be opened just then. "Will you forgive me if we save them for later?" she spluttered. "The truth is that we had a super-late lunch, and I let Ruby have this huge cupcake for dessert. And to be honest, she goes a little insane when she gets too much sugar! I mean, even more insane than she already is." Karen laughed to hide her discomfort with lying.

"Of course!" said Michelle, shrugging and seeming unbothered.

But Karen couldn't tell if it was an act or not. And really, why should Michelle believe her? Hadn't Karen just offered the girls hot chocolate and, when that was turned down, promised to give Mia another sweet treat later? Also, who had lunch at four o'clock? "Anyway, back to Juliana's mom," Karen said shakily. "Doesn't she have any other family she could live with?"

"I wish," muttered Michelle.

Was it Karen's paranoia or had Michelle's voice grown suddenly chilly? Ten more minutes passed, during which time the two women wound up discussing the hell of pregnancy-related nausea—likely one of few common threads in their life histories. Then Michelle stood up and announced she had to run an errand, if that was okay.

"Go ahead!" said Karen.

"I shouldn't be more than twenty minutes," said Michelle.

"Please, take your time," said Karen, hoping it was more like an *hour* and twenty minutes, not because she didn't like Michelle—really, she felt the opposite—but because she was now convinced that Michelle could see right through her. That is, see her for the neurotic elitist she really was. "The girls will be fine," she continued.

"Well, if you're sure..."

"Totally."

Closing the door behind Michelle, Karen felt her chest expand as if with fresh oxygen. She sat down on her linen-upholstered, feather-down sofa, which she'd purchased on sale at Restoration Hardware—not Ikea—and closed her eyes.

Hungry Kids was participating in a national hunger-relief conference in Kansas City, Missouri, and on Friday afternoon, at the request of the Hungry Kids' executive director, Karen flew there and sat in on panel discussions with titles like "Moving Beyond the Soup Kitchen: Sustainable Nutrition in the New Century" and "Filling the Pantry: New Approaches to Hunger-Relief Development." It was nice to get a break from the normal domestic routines. But Karen ultimately found the weekend a waste of time and resources, both the organization's and her own. She also felt bad about abandoning Ruby for three whole days. Even when she wasn't traveling, Karen never felt she was spending enough time with her daughter. Though when they were together, Karen was often counting the minutes until she could be by herself again.

By Sunday morning, she was counting the minutes until they could be reunited.

On Sunday evening, she unlocked the door to the apartment and found Ruby and Matt seated catty-corner from each other at the dining-room table. "Hey, guys!" said Karen.

"Hello, weary traveler," said Matt.

"Mommy!" cried Ruby, eyes wide with excitement as she jumped out of her seat and ran to her mother.

"Hello, my sweet pumpkin—I missed you terribly," said Karen, enveloping her body with her own and luxuriating in the velvety suppleness of Ruby's cheeks. "But I need to use the bathroom. You go finish your dinner." She carried her daughter back to the table and deposited her in her chair. Then she kissed her husband hello. His breath was redolent of garlic and pork. As she pulled away, her eyes fell on the greasy Chinese food that he and Ruby were in the process of devouring. "Good job holding down the fort," she said, relief now tinged with dismay. "But, oh my God, what kind of crap are you two eating?" Karen knew that, for the good of her marriage, she ought to refrain from criticizing Matt the moment she walked in the door. It would make her sound unappreciative of the time he'd just spent watching Ruby while Karen was gone, especially considering the tiff they'd had the week before. Judging from the fact that she and Matt still hadn't had sex, they hadn't fully made up from it either. But wasn't Ruby's health important too?

"Mommy said a bad word!" cried Ruby.

"*Crap* isn't that bad a word," said Karen. "But even if it was, grown-ups are allowed to use bad words."

"Thank you for your opinion of both my parental skills and my menu selection," said Matt.

"Sorry, and you're welcome," said Karen. "But"—she couldn't stop herself—"didn't we agree that, on the pediatrician's orders, Ruby wasn't going to eat food like that anymore?"

"Mmm, isn't this delicious?" said Matt, turning defiantly to Ruby, another forkful of slop lifted to his mouth. Of all the injustices of the modern world that he got worked up about, chemical additives in his food didn't even make the top one hundred.

Ruby seemed to share his indifference. "Yummy!" she declared while sucking a piece of dripping broccoli into her mouth.

At least she's eating vegetables, Karen thought. But who knew what evils lurked in the brown sauce? "I'm going to use the bathroom," she said again, turning away.

"Have a good trip?" Matt called after her in a sarcastic tone.

"It was fine, thanks," she called back. But she didn't feel fine. Everything seemed to be slipping out of her control.

On Thursday evening, Karen had dinner with her friend Allison Berger. The two women had met in the mid-1990s at a meeting for a short-lived feminist activist group that modeled itself after ACT UP. Now a financial journalist who wrote about inequality and wage stagnation for a legendary left-wing magazine, Allison was married with two children, lived in a five-story town house on the best block in the neighborhood, and spent her leisure time playing tennis and perusing the Scalamandré wall-coverings catalog in search of the right Chinoise Exotique for her guest bathroom. She also sent her two children to the Eastbrook Lab, an elite prep school with a progressive approach to education where the tuition was equivalent to the average annual household income in America for a family of four. Allison's husband, who made the extravagance possible, was a litigation partner at a white-shoe law firm. In addition to defending Fortune 500 companies, he did just enough pro bono work to dispel allegations that he was a corporate tool.

Karen wouldn't necessarily have objected to any part of the picture, except for the fact that, in recent years, Allison's columns had assumed a strident and didactic tone that seemed, if not hypocritical, then certainly at odds with her lifestyle. She was always just returning from some exclusive eco-resort in Costa Rica or snowcapped mountain in Idaho that was accessible only by helicopter with this or that wealthy and connected new friend. It was as if there were two Allisons, and one was always trying to shame the other, except it was the first one who showed up in print, constantly taking the other to task for her sense of entitlement. A recent column about how the wealthy preserved class privilege via connections, internships, and estate tax law and how it was nearly impossible for someone in the bottom quadrant of the socioeconomic ladder to climb to the top was headlined "All in the Family: How the Filthy Rich Keep Getting Filthier." Nonetheless, she and Karen had a rich history. And Allison had always been a loyal friend.

Barn Yard, the farm-to-table restaurant at which the two met that evening, had long, carefully distressed communal tables running the length of its unfinished-wood floor. Karen found Allison sitting at the end of one of them and somewhat squeamishly took a seat across from her. Communal tables never failed to remind Karen of the church-basement soup kitchens that Hungry Kids oversaw. Partly owing to acne scars left over from high school, Allison had never been beautiful.

But with her platinum-dyed pixie cut and slim figure, which she played up with oversize jewelry and formfitting clothes, she was chic in a way that seemed to exist outside of aging. "Anna Karenina!" she cried at the sight of Karen. It was an old joke, harking back to the days when both of them had had personal lives that could be described as dramatic. In truth, Karen could hardly remember hers. "It's insane how long we haven't seen each other," Allison went on. "Tell me everything."

"I wish I had something to tell you," said Karen. "My life is so boring, it might fall asleep."

"I don't believe that for a minute," said Allison. "What's his name?"

"Whose name?"

"The Swedish UNICEF executive you're sneaking off to the Mandarin Oriental with every Wednesday at three."

"Ha-ha. What I think you mean is 'How was the Comfort Inn in Kansas City that you spent last weekend in—alone—while attending a nonprofit development conference?'"

"Okay, you win."

"In the plus column, a hedge-fund guy I went to college with recently told me I was hot while I was asking for a donation."

"You see! I told you that you were this close to having an affair."

"He also told me I was really ugly in college and I looked better without a nose ring."

"Screw him. I bet you looked adorable. But please tell me there wasn't a skull dangling off the ring or something."

"No skull, I promise—just a graceful gold hoop."

"What do you say we order something to drink?"

"Excellent idea."

Just then, the waiter arrived. After taking their drink orders, he gave them menus that appeared to be printed on pieces of birch bark. Karen and Allison began to read them. After a few moments, Allison said, "Oh Jesus, did you see the special today? 'Pan-seared locally sourced pigeon.' Seriously, this may be the moment when the urban-farming movement went a step too far."

"Are you f-ing serious?" said Karen, scanning the entrées in search of the offending listing. "That is *so* disgusting."

Allison pursed her lips for a moment. Then she burst forth with "Just kidding!"

"You're so full of it tonight!" Karen cried and tsked before she swatted Allison's arm across the table.

The waiter came back with their wine, then delivered a four-minute disquisition on the specials. While he rambled on, Karen found her mind wandering. The only words that reached her ears were *horseradish crème fraîche* and *pickled raisins.* But when he finally finished, she felt guilty, considering how long it had probably taken him to memorize all the ingredients.

After the waiter had gone, Allison said, "So, what's the news on your end? How's Ruby Tuesday?"

"The usual," said Karen. "You know, needy, demanding, and overbearing, but basically fine. What about yours?"

"Driving me insane," said Allison. "All I can say is, thank God for the invention of ADHD. Or I guess I should be praising the Lord for Big Pharm. Thanks to Adderall, my kids are actually doing their homework this year, which is more than they did last year. Though what I really wish the pharmaceutical industry would invent is a drug to prevent middle-class white boys from imagining they're gangster rappers. They could call it You're-Not-Black-at-All or something."

For a split second, Karen considered pointing out that Allison's children were not actually middle class. She decided to let it go in favor of laughing and saying, "Stop! You're killing me." Besides, it wasn't entirely clear that Karen's child was middle class either.

"Seriously, Lucien goes around saying 'Yo-yo-yo' to everyone and telling them they've got *swag*," said Allison. "To be honest, I don't even know what swag is—except that I feel fairly sure I don't have any. Meanwhile, Esme is obsessed with that horrible Australian rapper Iggy Azalea and wants to be a makeup artist when she grows up. For this, we spend a kajillion dollars in tuition per year." She shook her head and rolled her eyes.

"Hey, there's always public school!" said Karen.

"Believe me, I'm thinking about it," said Allison, even though both of them knew she wasn't doing anything of the kind.

"Not only is it free," Karen continued, with a perverse desire to bolster Allison's position, as if trying it on for size, "but you get to send your children to school with tragic 'ghetto' kids who are being abused at home and take out their rage issues in the classroom, where they break other kids' noses for calling them stupid, which is basically what happened in Ruby's third-grade class last week." For white liberals like Karen, it had somehow become okay to throw around the g word as an adjective, at least among other white liberals. Surely they'd understand that you were using the word ironically and in quotes; that you were being self-consciously provocative, not condemnatory; and that you were still fully aware of the unspeakable historical precedents, beginning with slavery, that had led to the development of the underclass you were referencing. Besides, calling something ghetto wasn't racist, went the thinking, because it alluded to a condition, not a people.

Except no sooner had Karen used the word than she felt ashamed. Would she have used the term with a black friend? Probably not.

"Are you serious?" said Allison. Eyes bugging, she lowered her chin and leaned in.

"Dead serious," said Karen, who sometimes felt as if she were providing Allison with material for her columns that, as a journalist, she should have gone searching for herself. Karen was also aware of playing up her access to the poor, just as Michelle may well have been exaggerating the dysfunction in her own extended family for Karen's benefit. Just as easily, Karen could have told Allison about how the fifth-grade chess team at Betts had made it to the state championships. But what was the fun in that? "Oh, and the girl who got socked in the face, who was one of the four white girls in the class—and also Ruby's best friend—just transferred out of the school," Karen went on. "Which is kind of a bummer. But, whatever." She shrugged, trying to downplay her investment.

"Wow," said Allison, eyebrows now up near her hairline. "Well, I wish Eastbrook Lab had a few *more* disadvantaged minorities. Seriously, the only kids of color in the whole school are adopted ones from Ethiopia with white parents who thought it would be really cool to go to Africa and buy a child like Madonna did. Oh, and there's one half-black girl in Esme's class whose dad is one of the top guys at Bank of America, but that so doesn't count. I think there's one *actual* impoverished scholarship student in the other seventh-grade

class, the one that Lucien's not in. Maybe it's the school jan-
itor's son or something? But really, everyone else is either a
banker's or a lawyer's kid, including my own little brats. It's so
disgusting. A kid in Lucien's class literally just hired Kanye to
perform at his bar mitzvah. And Esme's fourth grade is almost
as bad. I was picking her up the other day, and I heard this little missy saying"—Allison assumed a high-pitched voice—"'I
spent spring break at the Four Seasons in Nevis. Where did
your family go?'"

"Sounds awesome," said Karen, who couldn't always tell
the difference between Allison bragging and Allison complaining. "How do I get myself invited?"

"You and me both." Allison laughed. "We just got back
from ten days with David's parents in Florida. Shoot me now."

"Don't his parents have a house on the Gulf Coast?"

"Yeah, in Naples. The infinity pool was nice, I admit. But
they're honest-to-God Rush Limbaugh fans. It's really hard
being around them, to tell you the truth. They think Obama
is a communist agitator—as if. I honestly couldn't wait for
school to start again. Though of course, Eastbrook being Eastbrook, they were off for practically the entire month of March.
It's like, the more you pay in tuition, the fewer days of school
there are."

"That's crazy," said Karen, feeling marginally better about
her own life again. In Karen's experience, as much as she
adored Ruby, *school holidays* was an oxymoron.

"And it's only been two months since the four weeks they
had off for Christmas and New Year's," said Allison. "Also,
can I tell you? I just found out that, for snack at Eastbrook's
after-school program, they hand out Oreos. *Real* Oreos. Like,
the Nabisco version with the trans fats, not even the Paul

Newman kind. As if the school doesn't bring in enough tuition dollars to buy non-crap cookies." Allison shook her head and scoffed.

Growing the tiniest bit weary of Allison's tirade, Karen downed half the wine in her glass and began to sing a commercial jingle from her own youth: "'Do you know exactly how to eat an Oreo'—"

But Allison didn't get the hint and apparently wasn't finished. "And don't even get me started about the math program," she went on, and on. "I swear, the fourth-graders haven't learned multiplication yet. Or at least my fourth-grader hasn't. They're still adding, like, twenty plus forty. It's pathetic…"

To be fair, Allison and Karen had a long-standing tradition of ragging on everyone and everything in their lives. Some of it was serious; some clearly for sport. But at that moment, Karen had the distinct impression that Allison was playing up her discontent for Karen's benefit. As if the education Karen was providing her only child was so inadequate that she needed to hear that private school wasn't perfect either. "Allison," she said, grabbing her friend's wrist and leaning forward. "If you hate the school that much, why do you send your kids there? I'm serious."

Allison let out a whimpery little moan, as if she were a teenager who'd been caught at the front door breaking curfew. "I know. You're right. It's just—it's complicated. David never went to public school, so he doesn't even consider it an option. And I guess I've bought into that whole BS about progressive education, even though I'm not sure what it really means, although I think it has something to do with school not just being about memorization and test prep and the kids getting to dress up in fairy costumes and write their own plays or something. But mostly, once your kids are in private school, it's really hard to go backward. Or forward. Or whatever you want to call it. Not that we can actually afford to send them to Eastbrook—this ridiculous basement-pool dig-out is literally eating up every last dollar we own—but whatever. I just have to say, I really admire you for sticking it out in public school, and not even one of the famous or selective ones." She smiled apologetically at Karen, just as Leslie Pfeiffer had done on the street.

"Sticking it out?" scoffed Karen, because it was the easiest point to argue. "Ruby is only in third grade. I wouldn't really call that sticking it out. But whatever! Compliment taken."

"What do you say we order?" said Allison, adjusting her chair. "I'm suddenly starving."

"Sounds good to me," said Karen.

"To be honest, I get so bored talking about my kids," Allison added while perusing her menu a final time. As if *she*'d been the one monologuing Karen with a jeremiad against Betts.

Karen bristled, irritated on multiple fronts. Not only did Allison's declaration seem like a cop-out, but it also implied that Karen, not Allison, had been the one who'd forced them to talk about their children at the expense of more interesting topics. "I'm not bored," she demurred. "But sure. Let's talk about something else."

"There must be something on this menu that isn't pigeon."

"Locally sourced rat?" said Karen.

"Ha," said Allison.

The joke was less funny the second time around.

*　　*　　*

When Karen got home from dinner, she found Matt sprawled on the living-room sofa watching a basketball game. His dirty socks were in balls beneath the coffee table. His dirty dinner plate was on the coffee table alongside a saucer holding a morass of crumbs and melting butter. "Hey," she said, wishing he would put the laundry, dirty dishes, and perishables where they belonged—that is, in the hamper, dishwasher, and re-frigerator, respectively. Karen worked hard at keeping a com-fortable and orderly home, and Matt seemed always to be thwarting her efforts with his indifference, his slovenliness, his failure even to notice when things were amiss. Then again, she was the one who'd just been out to dinner while Matt had stayed home and watched Ruby. And what if Karen was turn-ing into one of those fussy old ladies she'd been so frightened of as a child—the type who'd reprimand you in gift shops and antique stores for touching the merchandise?

"Hey, what's up?" he said with a brief glance in her direc-tion. "How was your dinner?"

"Fun," she said, pointedly carrying Matt's dirty dishes to the sink. Not that he seemed to notice. "Though Allison was do-ing her usual complaining about how much her fabulous life sucks."

"That sounds familiar," he said.

Was he trying to imply that he'd heard all of Karen's stories before or agreeing that Allison was always complaining? Karen couldn't tell. Matt had never registered any particular objection to Allison. But he seemed to regard all of Karen's old friends as types rather than actual people. "Come on, Kev!" he shouted at the TV screen.

Feeling suddenly frustrated, Karen found herself blurting out, "I feel like we've hardly spoken lately."

"Aren't we speaking right now?" asked Matt.

"Yeah, but I feel like you're always a million miles away all the time."

"Hey, *you* were the one out with friends tonight, not me."

"I know. It's just—I don't know."

"Sorry if I've seemed distracted. Work has been really intense lately."

"Do you want to plan a date night?"

"Sure."

"Also, if you want to come to the HK benefit, we have to get a sitter."

"Of course I'll come. What night is it again?"

"The eighteenth."

"Oh, shiiitttt." Matt hit his forehead with his palm.

"What?" said Karen.

"That's the night of our dinner with the foundation people," he said. "They want updating. And I guess we're also hoping to talk them into replenishing the coffers, so to speak." Karen didn't answer. He was telling her this now? "I'm really sorry about that," Matt continued, sounding genuinely remorseful. But a millisecond later, he was leaning toward the TV, arms outstretched, yelling, *"Where's the fucking defense?"* As if the matter of his nonattendance at her biggest work event of the year had already been settled and forgotten about.

Except it hadn't.

"I also feel like you don't take what I do seriously," said Karen. It was less that she believed this to be true than that she didn't feel like letting Matt off the hook. Not yet. She also wanted his attention.

Finally, he turned away from the screen and squinted at her. "Kar—*what* in Yahweh's name are you talking about?"

"I think you think housing is more important than hunger," she went on, half knowing that her argument verged on the absurd. "Like, you think people can live without enough food but not without roofs over their heads, whereas to me, it actually seems like the other way around."

"That is *such* a ridiculous thing to say that I'm not even going to honor it with a response," he said. "Though I will say this: I'm not the one who came up with the 'hilarious'"—Matt made quotes in the air—"nickname for the project I've devoted the last twelve months of my life to. Honestly, it was funny the first time you called it Poor-coran, but less so the four hundredth."

Matt's offense took Karen by surprise. "I was just trying to make you laugh," she said. "Sorry if it didn't work."

"It's okay," he said, backing down. "Luckily, I have a thick skin."

But unlike Matt's team, Karen wasn't ready to cede the offense. "If you had a big event, I'd come," she said.

Matt released a long sigh. "If you really want me to try and reschedule the dinner, I will. But I can't promise it'll work. They set it up months ago, and it took like a week to find a date that worked for everyone."

"I don't want you to do it unless you *want* to do it," said Karen, aware that she sounded juvenile and petulant but feeling that it was somehow merited.

"You know, it's kind of a big night for me too," he said.

"What a coincidence."

Matt grimaced, looked away. Then he turned back to her and said, "Honestly, Karen, you sound like your mother right now. The whole world is allied against you, and you're going to make everyone feel bad about it. Is that the idea?"

The accusation made Karen recoil in shame; was he right? "Yes, that's exactly the idea," she muttered on her way out of the room.

"Come onnnnnn," said Matt. But he wasn't talking to her. The other team must have gotten a basket.

There were two e-mails of note waiting in Karen's in-box. The first was from Laura, saying that Maeve was starting to settle in at Mather but that she definitely missed her old friends, like Ruby. To that end, she wrote, *Would Ruby like to come over for a playdate on Saturday afternoon? Unfortunately, Evan and I will be traveling for work, but our new nanny, Jangchup, will be here with the kids, and I know Maeve would love it if Ruby could join them.*

Karen read the e-mail with a certain amount of relish and feeling partially vindicated. It seemed as if, without her having done anything, the power had somehow shifted back into her hands. And she had every intention of exercising it—that is, of punishing Laura and her husband for taking Maeve out of Betts by withholding Ruby's company. Karen knew she was being petty. It was also arguable that she was being unfair to Ruby, who would surely have jumped at the chance to bake cookies and rainbow-loom with her old friend the following weekend—and who, in truth, had no plans whatsoever on Saturday. But Karen also knew that her daughter could live happily without having done so. With an absurd level of satisfaction, Karen replied:

Hi, Laura. Unfortunately, Ruby already has plans with another friend that afternoon, so I'm afraid she's not going to be able to make it. But thanks for the invite. Best, Karen

The second e-mail that came in was a Listserv announcement from Principal Chambers explaining that, due to the school's underenrollment—Betts was at only 75 percent capacity that year—the city's board of education was planning to move a new K-through-5 Winners Circle charter school into the top floor of the building.

Karen found the news disheartening on multiple fronts. First, she was dismayed to hear that enrollment was flagging at Betts. All the other schools in the area were bursting at the seams; why not Betts? And what did it say about the education she was providing her daughter if the school couldn't fill its own classrooms? Second, Karen was upset at the prospect of the school having to share facilities with a new one. She'd read stories in the local papers about public-school children in co-located buildings having to eat lunch at nine in the morning and play dodgeball in the hallway while the charter students enjoyed free run of the cafeteria and the gym when they weren't learning Java on their spanking-new iPads or building robots with the help of their 3-D printers.

Karen objected to Winners Circle on ideological grounds as well. It wasn't just that the schools were famously run like military-training camps with punishments meted out for every set of hands not folded neatly in a lap, or that they received taxpayer funds but were accountable to no one in the government. It was that WC's consistently good test scores seemed at first glance to prove that poverty wasn't a factor in children's outcomes without acknowledging that WC's student body was self-selecting and that problem children were regularly "counseled out"—that is, sent back to neighborhood public schools, which inevitably suffered the consequences.

And yet, families of color in disadvantaged neighborhoods generally seemed to welcome the arrival of new WC schools, which confused Karen and made her wonder if it was elitist of her to object to them.

She was vaguely aware that some of Hungry Kids' main donors also supported charter schools, though until just then, she'd never given the crossover much thought. Suddenly curious, she opened Winners Circle's website and clicked on the tab marked *Board of Directors*. There were twelve names listed. The first, second, third, and fourth were the usual chief executive officers or managing directors of companies whose names consisted of a predatory bird or a multisyllabic term invoking the beauty of nature followed by the word *Capital* or *Fund*. The fifth guy was the former governor of Massachusetts. The sixth was a timber-company executive. The seventh was a cellular-communications titan.

The eighth was—was it possible?—Clay.

Karen's eyes blinked then widened at the sight of her new-old friend's name typed out in an elegant Garamond. It seemed impossible, but there he was. The description beneath his name read:

Clayton R. Phipps III

Prior to forming Buzzard Capital, a private investment firm, in May 2010, Clay Phipps was a partner at Babbling Brook LLC, where he had portfolio and general-management responsibilities and chaired the firm's advisory committee.

Fascinated by the coincidence and horrified by the connection, Karen quickly banged out an e-mail to him.

Hi, Clay,

Hope all is well and I'm looking forward to seeing you at the gala!

I'm actually writing about a non-HK-related matter. I just got an e-mail from Betts Elementary, a public school in Cortland Hill that my daughter attends. Apparently there are plans to move a new K-through-5 Winners Circle charter school into the building in September. I see that you are on the board of directors. If you have any influence in this area, can you please attempt to put a stop to it? If the WC network has such deep pockets, I really don't see why it can't build its own schools instead of poaching existing ones at the taxpayers' expense. What's more, my daughter's school building is already close to capacity, and I would hate to see her and her friends getting squeezed.

I would also hate to see the student body of Betts—which includes children who come halfway across the city every morning to get there—begin to feel bad about themselves because the new charter kids get to sit in freshly painted classrooms with new computers while the regular public-school kids don't, since the governor never stops cutting funding.

In case you couldn't guess, I'm not a fan of the discipline-and-test-prep model of WC either. That's not my idea of a well-rounded education, and I suspect it's not yours either.

Thank you, Clay. I appreciate anything you can do. I wouldn't be bothering you about this, but it affects my family directly.

Yours,
Karen

Karen knew she should probably sleep on the e-mail before she sent it. What if it antagonized Clay, and he withdrew his support from HK? Then what would she have accomplished? Here, she'd recently roped in an important new source of funds for the organization. And there were children who would eat a hot meal that very night because of his contribution from the week before. But unable to turn off the blasting radio in her brain—and half convinced that every second counted—Karen clicked Send.

To her surprise, Clay wrote back almost immediately:

Ah, the leftist firebrand I remember from college returns with an even sharper set of claws! Nice to hear from you again, Karen Kipple. But back to your question…If I wheedle WC's CEO into finding another location, will you dance with me at the benefit next week? I can rumba and fox-trot, courtesy of the National League of Junior Cotillions of Charleston, circa 1986. But seriously, if the computers are going to be that much nicer across the hall, why don't you just transfer your daughter?

Was he kidding about Karen transferring Ruby? Had he not read her e-mail, registered her objections? Or was everything a joke to him? The jocular tone of Clay's e-mail infuriated Karen in its apparent refusal to take her argument seriously. Nonetheless, she found herself tickled by his invitation to dance. She was also pleased and relieved by his quick response and seemingly genuine offer to help thwart the co-location and wrote back:

CP, Many thanks for offering to help—and also for the "helpful" suggestion to have Ruby change schools. One more ques-

tion: Would you send your children to a Winners Circle school? Bet not. Your friend the firebrand, KK

As Karen waited for a reply, she opened Facebook. The first item in her newsfeed was a picture of a scraggly cockapoo with its tongue out standing in a field of grass. Karen's elementary-school friend Sue Borneo had posted it. Karen hadn't seen Sue in nearly thirty years and it seemed unlikely that she would see her in the *next* thirty either. Their lives had taken completely different paths. Sue had never left the town they'd grown up in, had three teenage children, and worked at her family's jewelry store. If she and Karen were put in the same room, it was doubtful they'd have found anything to say to each other after they'd finished reminiscing about their fourth-grade classmate who'd later gone to jail for pederasty. But through the arguably pointless alchemy of social media, they were back in touch—at least in a fashion. Beneath the photograph, Sue had written, *RIP, Meatball.* And now Karen felt like she had to comment, mostly because *not* to do so seemed thoughtless. But how? She didn't feel right about clicking *Like*, since wouldn't that imply she liked Meatball's death? So she wrote, *Very sorry for your loss, Sue,* then felt like a fraud, since, in truth, she wasn't all that sorry.

The next post came courtesy of Laura Collier. It was a photo of Maeve holding up a skateboard covered with tiny skulls. Her long hair was poking out of a straw fedora, and her upper body was encased in a tiny black leather motorcycle jacket. *First board,* read the caption. The comments below ranged from *Amaaazzzing* to *Such a hipster!* to *So beautiful and chic, like her mama.* Even though the whole setup seemed staged to induce envy and made Karen feel vaguely like throwing up, she felt somehow compelled to click on the thumbs-up icon, if only to be a good sport. In doing so, she elevated the number of Likes from 203 to 204, then wished she hadn't. But un-Liking the photo seemed even more pathetic. So she moved on.

Maeve's father, Evan, was responsible for the third post in Karen's newsfeed. He'd linked to a news story about Trayvon Martin, the seventeen-year-old African American boy who was gunned down by a citizen vigilante in Florida. According to the article, the perpetrator was apparently never going to be charged with anything, not even a civil rights violation. Evan had added his own caption beneath the story: *Disgusting—#blacklivesmatter.* Karen felt disgusted as well—not just at the obvious injustice of Trayvon's killer going free but also just as viscerally at Laura and Evan. It seemed to Karen that they pretended to care about the fate of African Americans yet had taken their daughter out of a school precisely because of the existence of one of them, if not all of them. And wasn't that the real reason the Collier-Shaws had left Betts—that there were too many of *them* for Evan and Laura's taste? It was easy to get worked up about racism when you didn't have to engage with any *actual black people.* Not that Karen, aside from her friendship with Lou, led an integrated life. But at least she tried.

For a brief moment, Karen imagined commenting beneath Evan's caption, *Disgusting—so long as there aren't too many boys with his shade of skin in your daughter's classroom?* But she knew she was a hypocrite too and that if she'd been walking down a quiet street after sundown, and Trayvon Martin had come up it in a hoodie with the hood pulled tight, she might well have let her imagination run wild with pictures and incidents culled from tabloid newspapers and late-night cop shows, and, if it was possible to do so without causing offense, she would have crossed the street. (College-educated white liberals were nearly as terrified of being seen as racists as they were of encountering black male teenagers on an empty street after dark.)

Karen was closing out of Facebook when, once again, Clay's name flashed onto her desktop. He'd replied.

Of course not. My kids go to private school. But then, I'm really rich. xox

At least he's being honest, she thought. But the response aggravated her as well. It seemed so smug, so facile. Karen knew that if she didn't answer, she would come away with the upper hand. Only, she couldn't quite bear not to get the last word—and wrote back:

Lucky you.

Her flipness masked defensiveness. In that moment, Karen had the distinct impression that her daughter's school—and, by extension, Karen's entire way of being—was under attack. Moreover, battle lines having been drawn, it was time to choose a side. It was also time she put her professional skills to use. Swallowing her pride, Karen opened a new window and quickly drafted an e-mail to April Fishbach, reiterating her pledge to man the front table at Visiting Artists Day and also offering both to chair the PTA's fund-raising committee and to help elevate the profile of the school. Betts might not have been a clothing or cosmetics brand, but in a public-school system where parents had choices about where to send their kids, even elementary schools had to market themselves.

A reply arrived just ten minutes later.

Dear Karen,

On behalf of the PTA of Constance C. Betts Elementary, I'm delighted to hear that you've finally decided to volunteer your time, and I accept your offer to fund-raise! But you make one mistake: the fund-raising committee already has a chairperson. It's me. In this case, however, I'm happy to share the honors and responsibilities with you as cochairs. Perhaps we can meet for coffee tomorrow or the next day to talk strategy. I look forward to hearing from you.

April Fishbach
The best way to find yourself is to lose yourself in the service of others.—Mahatma Gandhi

Karen had grown so accustomed to April's power-mongering that her response failed to evoke anything in Karen but resignation. April was simply the price one paid for trying to help out. Though Karen had found that the woman did serve one useful purpose: her very unbearableness provided endless opportunities for bonding among those who found her similarly hard to stomach. Before answering April's e-mail, Karen forwarded it to Lou with the subject heading *Classic April.*

To Karen's delight, Lou immediately wrote back:

She is such a shrew. How does her husband stand her? And those poor kids. Also, who knew she was responsible for the Indian independence movement? Not I. hahaha

Karen wrote back:

If Gandhi were a parent at Betts, do you think she'd even let him run his own bake sale?

Lou wrote back:

Not a chance.

Karen was still giggling to herself as she replied to April:

That's fine. How's tomorrow morning at Laundry at 8:30?

April replied:

At 8:25 would be better, as I'm conducting an important Education Partners workshop at 8:50.

April's e-mail was followed by yet another one from Clay:

But when will I get lucky with you?

Karen felt as if a sticky mass had spontaneously formed in the back of her throat, preventing her from swallowing. Did he mean what she thought he meant? Or was he only joking around? And wasn't he married? Karen's heart pounded with confusion and excitement as she typed out the words:

We shall see.

To Karen's mind, her response was noncommittal enough to be safe, but open-ended enough not to discourage his efforts. Because the truth was that it felt good to be flirted with—better than good. It felt as if the shapes in the room were just coming into focus, revealing their angles and contours after a long, deep sleep...

The next morning, after dropping Ruby off at school—only five minutes late, which was earlier than usual—Karen set out for her first fund-raising meeting with April. It was already a few days into the month (of April), but there weren't many visible signs of spring. The trees were still bare, the crocus buds shut tight, the chill formidable. Spring had not sprung.

En route to Laundry, Karen found herself hunching her shoulders against the wind, pulling her jacket collar tight around her neck, and secretly wishing that global warming, or climate change, or whatever you were supposed to call it now, would happen sooner rather than later so she would no longer have to suffer through the winter. Was that selfish of her? Probably, yes; if she really cared about the planet, she would just bundle up and deal with it, the way her daughter seemed to do. In fact, Ruby seemed completely oblivious to the elements, putting on T-shirts, shorts, and sundresses in winter and failing ever to see the point of wearing a hat.

The same Tattoo Guy with the man-bun from last time was behind the counter, but Karen actually managed to get a "Hey" and a half smile out of him before she ordered. Seconds later, April appeared at her side, clipboard in one hand, masala chai tea in the other. "Morning, Cochair!" she said brightly to Karen.

"Hey," said Karen, already regretting her offer from the night before. "I'm just ordering."

"I'm at the table in back."

"Be right there," said Karen.

But her slow-pour coffee took even longer than usual to pour, and April looked irritable by the time Karen finally joined her. "Sorry about that," she said. "My coffee took forever."

"It's fine. I'm used to having my time wasted," snapped April.

"April—how about cutting me some slack this morning?" said Karen, sighing. "It's still early."

"Fine, but only if you answer my question." She leaned in, her gaze laserlike, her giant forehead gleaming beneath the dangling Edison bulbs. "Have you been in touch with Maeve's parents?"

"Not really..." said Karen, who couldn't bear to get into it with April but didn't want her to think she'd lost any social capital. "I mean, just some e-mails," she added, shrugging. "Why?"

"I understand they've switched her to the private public school known as Edward G. Mather."

"Yeah, I heard the same," said Karen, surprised to learn that April, too, cared about and must have been irked by Maeve's transfer. They had that in common as well.

"I have to say, I was slightly appalled by the way the family handled it," April went on. "Sending out that group e-mail reproducing their conversation with Principal Chambers? I thought it was very insensitive to Jayyden's situation and also a violation of all parties' privacy, including Principal Chambers's."

Karen secretly agreed with April, but under no circumstances was she willing to admit that. "Yeah, well, I guess they were pretty upset," she said, attempting a tone of neutrality.

"That's no excuse," said April.

"Maybe not—anyway." Karen cleared her throat in a way that was meant to signal their mutual need to get on with it and then out of there. "Since we don't have much time, here are my thoughts on fund-raising for Betts. In the bigger picture, I think we need to raise the profile of the school so it attracts more families with money from the neighborhood. That's a long-term goal. More immediately, I think we should do a direct appeal to the families we already have. The postage will probably cost a few hundred bucks. But assuming we can get all the home addresses of our families from the main office, I think it'll be worth it. I'm happy to attempt a letter explaining that the school is basically under siege—not just from the statehouse, which cuts the public education budget every year, but from private entities like Winners Circle, who now want our classrooms too.

"I thought I could do a bullet-style list of all the extras that PTA money *could* be paying for if everyone got together and gave something. I have a feeling that we have quite a few families at the school, especially in kindergarten, who are actually in a position to give real money but who haven't done so because, essentially, no one has ever pressured them into giving. Honestly, in all my years at Betts, I've never gotten a single letter asking for money, whereas my understanding is that other schools in the area basically *bombard* the parents with requests. I've heard that at Mather they send incoming kindergartners' parents a letter in July, before their kids even arrive, demanding a thousand bucks from each family. Obviously, we're not going to get anything close to that kind of money out of the average Betts household. But I don't see why we can't ask for something."

For a few beats after Karen finished, April sat glaring at her and saying nothing. Then, overenunciating every syllable, her delivery glacial, she asked, "You want to send a letter by regular mail to our students' *homes* asking their parents to give us *money?*"

"Yes," said Karen, ignoring whatever point April was trying to make. "Direct appeals are really the beginning for every campaign. And as I said, since I'm under no illusions that we have a particularly wealthy student body, I'll mention in my letter that no amount is too small. The important part is that everyone give what they can, whether it's ten dollars, a hundred, or—hard to imagine, but you never know—a thousand. Participation is key. Later in the spring or early next fall, maybe we can start looking outside the school for matching grants and whatnot."

April pursed her lips and looked away, her eyes appearing to home in on an etching of a donkey. Finally, she turned back to Karen and declared in a rapid clip, "I'm sorry, but I think it's aggressive, and it's not who we are as a school."

"You think asking for money is aggressive?" asked Karen, incredulous.

"Yes. I do," said April.

Karen leaned forward. "But April, how are we going to raise money if we don't ask for it?"

"Our families contribute in other ways."

"Yes, some contribute in other ways. And a few have devoted their lives to bettering the school, like you have. And I really admire you for it. But many families at the school basically use the place as a free daycare center and can't even be bothered to walk their children into the building, let alone attend any events in the classroom, because they don't give a fuck, or they're overwhelmed and can't deal, or it's a cultural difference, or whatever. So let's not mythologize-slash-romanticize poverty here. But I'm fairly sure there are a bunch of families in the lower grades who are pretty financially comfortable, like those women who are always complaining about the hormones in the milk in the cafeteria. And obviously those are the people we'd be targeting. Because I'm sure their kids all went to private preschools and now these children are attending kindergarten for free. So their families probably have some money to spare."

"I don't care if they eat gold bricks for breakfast," April shot back. "I think it's invasive, and I think it's alienating for those families who aren't in a position to give. If you want to do a penny or nickel or even dime harvest in the school lobby and encourage everyone to drop their spare change into a giant jar, that's one thing. But sending personal letters? I'm sorry, I'm just not comfortable with that at all." She shook her head.

"Okay, so we can put the letters in their backpack folders," said Karen. "Or, if the main office is willing to share the e-mail addresses they have on file, we can do it that way."

"However you send it, we're still fostering an inequitable system in which schools with wealthier student bodies have more perks than those without," countered April. "This is supposed to be a public school, not a private one."

Exasperated, Karen felt her eyelids beginning to droop. "April, I agree with everything you're saying," she said slowly. "But for the moment, the system is what it is. And if you don't believe in fund-raising, *why* be cochair of the fund-raising committee? For that matter, why do we even *have* a fund-raising committee? Also, do you ever stop to wonder why you feel compelled to argue with everything everyone says? What if, for once, just as an experiment, you tried agreeing with someone? You might find that people would actually be willing to join some of the committees you ran and even become active members of the PTA. Or do you prefer to reign over a kingdom of one?"

April apparently could think of no answers to any of Karen's questions—at least, not ones she was willing to share. For a good half a minute, the two of them sat in silence, avoiding each other's gazes, April flaring her nostrils and Karen grimacing. Finally, April pushed back her chair, stood up, and said, "Fine—do what you want. I have an important Education Partners workshop to run."

"Thank you," said Karen.

"There's no need to thank me—I just do what I can to help," said April. Chin raised and in full martyr mode, she stomped off.

That year, HK's annual gala was being held in the banquet hall of a beaux arts building downtown. As in the past, the organization had hired a hyperorganized, headset-wearing event planner named Barbara to mastermind the festivities, so Karen was free to come as just one of the guests. Wearing her only decent black dress—the same knee-length shift she wore to all work-related parties—she arrived at seven sharp and made her way to the bar. At seven fifteen, there was no one there, which seemed slightly ominous. Then, suddenly, at seven thirty, a mass of people showed up, and a mob scene ensued.

Guests crowded into an anteroom, where silent auction items had been laid out on long rental tables covered with white cloths. As Karen sipped from a glass of pinot grigio, she did a cursory review of the offerings. There were cashmere baby hats, private tours of art museums, front-row tickets to Broadway shows, interior-decorating consultations, seven-night luxury beachfront resort accommodations in the Turks and Caicos Islands, spa services involving heated rocks, and giant baskets of beauty products wrapped in crinkly cellophane and tied with giant bows. *The finest South American botanical ingredients,* read one description, *combine with cutting-edge science to boost the skin's inner strength and revitalize its outer beauty. This his-and-hers gift basket even comes with a handy red carrying case—value $450.*

Gazing out at the crowd, Karen saw a mass of wraithlike women bedecked in sparkly jewelry interspersed with pasty fat men with bald pates who understood that thinness was ultimately aspirational and that they required no such leverage. First among them was Lew Cantor, a private-equity honcho who sat on the board of directors of Hungry Kids. Lew had given a hundred grand last year. Karen had inherited him from the previous development director, Deb Lennon, which made it all the more essential that Karen go over and greet him. "Lew! It's wonderful to see you!" she said.

"Hello there," he said. "It's Carol. Right?"

"Karen, but don't worry about it! You're looking very festive tonight."

"Eh? You like the bow tie?"

"I do like bow ties. How is your lovely wife?"

"She's vanished to Aspen. I haven't seen her in weeks!" He chuckled.

"Oh, well, when you next see her, give her my regards. You know, this organization couldn't do its work without you two…"

Karen was still pissed at Matt for blowing off the event, but mostly in principle. In truth, his absence gave her the freedom to conduct the necessary business of glad-handing the guests without feeling self-conscious or judged. It also gave her the freedom to socialize as she pleased. Although Karen had no close friends in the office, she got along with most everyone there, from Letitia Gutierrez, the sultry benefits associate, to Cary Ann Kreamer, the Southern sorority-sister-ish nutrition coordinator. But she was most fond of the outreach director, Troy Gafferty, whom she wished she saw more of; unfortunately for Karen, he was usually busy "reaching out" in a remote part of the city.

The estranged son of Jehovah's Witnesses, Troy, who was now in his forties, had lost his lover to AIDS fifteen years before. Miraculously, he himself hadn't contracted the virus. But for unclear reasons, he hadn't had a real relationship since. At present, he lived alone in a bare-bones studio over a deli and liked to joke that the families he assisted sometimes had nicer apartments than he did. That evening, Karen and Troy made the rounds together, shaking donors' hands (Karen would introduce him as "our heroic man in the field, Troy") and whispering about who had and hadn't shown up.

To Karen's relief, one of the Krugs, of the Krug real estate empire, was at that very moment kicking back gin and tonics beneath a gilt-framed portrait of a long-forgotten elder statesman. But to her disappointment, a certain first-generation Googler was so far a no-show. There was still no sign of Clay Phipps either. Karen found herself checking every few minutes. But since he'd not just RSVP'd but purchased an entire table, Karen was confident that he'd eventually arrive. And then he did.

At the first glimpse of him—he was wearing a slightly rumpled white button-down and a pin-striped navy-blue suit—Karen felt as if her stomach were a pincushion pierced with hundreds of tiny holes. He was accompanied by a coterie of slightly younger, square-jawed Asian and Caucasian men (maybe his employees at Buzzard?), as well as a sleek, tawny-skinned woman of unclear age and ethnicity to whom he was walking close enough to suggest a spousal relationship. The woman was wearing a red dress with a scooped-out neck and a simple gold choker. Karen knew she shouldn't be surprised to find that Clay was married to a woman of color. Why shouldn't he have been? But she *was* surprised—surprised and impressed and somehow even more nervous. Countering fear with alacrity and leaving Troy in conversation with Cary Ann about next week's menu, Karen bounded over to where Clay and his wife stood. "Hello there," she chirped, addressing them both.

"Well, hello there, Karen Kipple," Clay replied in his endlessly cheeky way.

"So glad you could come," said Karen, leaning in for an air kiss. He smelled of citrus and cedarwood.

"The pleasure is mine."

Since no introduction was immediately forthcoming, Karen extended a hand to the woman at his side and said, "I'm Karen, the development director of Hungry Kids."

"Hello," she said, with the faintest of smiles.

"My bad manners—this is my wife, Verdun," said Clay, laying his hand on her shoulder.

Was it Karen's imagination or did she shrink slightly at the gesture? "Verdun, it's so nice to meet you," she said, wondering how the woman had ended up with the same name as a famous battlefield in World War I. "And what a beautiful name."

"Thank you," said Verdun. But again she offered no conversational opening.

"Well, I'll let you guys mingle," said Karen. Feeling suddenly uncomfortable in her skin, she turned away and scurried back toward Troy.

"What was that about?" he said, one eyebrow raised.

"Don't ask," she answered.

Troy never missed anything.

At seven forty-five, Barbara the Event Planner ushered the crowd into the main hall. Beneath a coffered ceiling inlaid with intricate mosaics were scores of circular tables laid with crisp white cloths. At eight, guests began to take their seats. Karen smiled gamely as she sat down at a table with the Jesse James Foundation people—they were Hungry Kids' largest source of funding—even as she dreaded the thought of spending the next hour and a half making small talk with them. Jesse James modeled itself after a corporation, using metrics to analyze the efficacy of the programs it sponsored, and its employees tended to have all the spontaneity of spreadsheets. "I hope you all found something to drink!" said Karen, lifting a second glass of pinot to her lips.

"We did, thank you," replied a man in a light blue button-down. After consulting his fitness watch, he reached for his seltzer.

"Great," said Karen, realizing she'd already run out of conversation.

Every year at the gala, Karen was aware of a disconnect

between the rich people who got dressed up in fancy clothes and ate salmon tartare and pumpkin soup with sage cream and the cause she and her colleagues were promoting. That evening, the divide felt especially vast. At table 1 sat the film actress Nava Gresham and at table 2, the everyman comic Dan Greene alongside TV chef Francoise Roy, who was famous for making huge messes in the kitchen and calling everything "Supreme!" Every now and then, Karen would glance over at table 12, where Clay and Verdun were seated with their entourage, but he had his back to her. And Verdun's impassive facial expression remained unaltered.

Between dinner and dessert, the film actress glided to the podium, her head held high. She was wearing a short-sleeved black turtleneck and sequined miniskirt that showcased her insect-like legs. "I'm Nava Gresham," she began—as if everyone in the audience didn't already know. "And I want to talk to you about the important issue of child hunger." Her hair was skinned back into a tight bun clearly meant to connote a seriousness of purpose, and she spoke in a dramatic and impassioned way about the shame of the city's starving children, which she claimed to take personally. "I mean, here we are in one of the great cities of the world. And there are children in it who are going to bed hungry at night. It's just plain wrong, and it breaks my heart, as I know it breaks yours. I've never been very religious but there is one phrase I learned in Sunday school as a child that has stayed with me all these years: *There but for the grace of God go I.* Because these children who go to bed hungry—they are part of our family too, the *human family.*

"In the past year and a half," Nava continued, "in order to prepare for my next film role, I had the opportunity to accompany Molly and the other amazing staff at Hungry Kids as they visited families for whom hunger is a daily reality. In the film, I play a single mother named Clara who can't afford to feed her son, who suffers from gigantism. In desperation, Clara turns to prostitution. The film won't change the world, but with any luck, it will bring attention to an issue that it's in our power to solve. The film is called *Feast and Famine*. Earlier this year, it was at the Berlin Film Festival, where I'm humbled to say it received the Alfred Bauer Prize, which is given to a feature that opens new perspectives. It's being released in the U.S. next month, and I would be honored if you went to see it. I also hope you will continue to support Hungry Kids, a heroic organization doing heroic things."

When Nava finished speaking, Karen found herself clapping politely—and marveling at the ingenious way in which the woman had managed to promote her own career while ostensibly promoting the cause of child hunger. Also, why did actresses always have to call them films while the rest of the world referred to them as movies? What's more, the plot of *Feast and Famine* sounded completely absurd.

Next up was Dan Greene, the comic relief for the evening, who began by imploring the assembled guests to be sure to finish their dinner: "Just for tonight, I'm your mom, reminding you that there are starving kids in the world and that if you don't finish your spinach, there's no Jell-O for dessert…" Karen found the monologue pedestrian and cringe-worthy, but again she joined in the applause.

Finally, HK's executive director—and Karen's boss—Molly Gluck glided out to the podium. Her emaciated frame was cloaked in what appeared to be a burlap sack, lending her the appearance of a medieval monk. It had been noted by many that Molly seemed to have an easier time feeding others than herself. Or maybe it was just that she starved herself in solidarity with the poor. Whatever the case, it seemed likely that Molly had never noted the irony of her anorexia, her earnestness being pervasive—except when it came to celebrities, for whom she seemed to harbor limitless reserves of adoration. "Thank you all for being here and for feeding the poor children of this city," she began in a wobbly voice that threatened to become weepy when she turned to the film actress and said, "And thank you, Nava, for inspiring us all. You are *my* hero." Her eyes flickered before she turned to the other guests of honor and added, "I also want to thank Francoise and Dan, both of whom have done *so* much for this organization in the past few years, as well as our media sponsor, *Fine Food* magazine, and also our title sponsors, Nabisco products and Tommy Hilfiger USA…"

The acknowledgments list went on and on and included a perfunctory shout-out to Karen. At the end of it, Molly summoned from the wings two adorable seven-year-old African American identical twins with elaborately beaded hair as examples of those who had benefited from the organization's largesse. She introduced them as "Zaniyah and Saniyah, the closeness of whose names mirror their closeness as sisters."

This time, the guests clapped thunderously and for so long that the applause turned into a standing ovation. Though it was unclear to Karen who or what the crowd was cheering for. Zaniyah and Saniyah, for being brave in the face of their poverty, or at least brave enough to show up and face a roomful of gawking 1 Percenters? Or was the crowd cheering itself and its own generosity in helping these two fill their bellies? Also, what kind of clueless mother thought it was a great idea to give her identical twins rhyming names? Surely, Zaniyah and Saniyah would spend their entire lives trying to differentiate themselves. Or was that very assumption—and Karen's faith in individualism—itself hopelessly bourgeois?

In any event, the response made Karen uncomfortable. And she felt her chest contracting and shoulders rounding as she rose with the crowd. She had to remind herself that everybody was there for a good cause. And if the donors wanted to congratulate themselves while reducing their mainly ill-gotten gains, who was she to say they shouldn't?

After the flourless chocolate-mousse cake had been served and cleared, the band—a bunch of middle-aged white guys in jeans and high-tops doing covers of pop and soft-rock hits from the 1970s and '80s—began to play. Karen had recently fled to Troy's table, not only because the Jesse James people had been boring her to tears but because Troy's table afforded a better view of Clay's. Two songs in, the man himself sauntered over and asked Karen if she'd care to dance.

"Uh, I guess," said Karen, apprehensive in light of Verdun's presence. "But—um—doesn't your wife want to?"

"Karen, sweetie," Clay said, lowering his chin as he laid a hand on her arm. "I'm not suggesting we have sex."

Mortified by the way he'd spelled out the subtext, reducing their flirtation to its crude essence, Karen felt blood rushing to her cheeks. "I wasn't saying that!" she cried, as embarrassed by the suggestion as she was somehow wounded by its refutation. He must have been kidding in his e-mail about wanting to get lucky.

"So what's your answer, lady?" Clay pressed on.

"Sure—why not?" said Karen, feeling she couldn't turn

him down now. Besides, she had no desire to. In truth, she rarely got the opportunity to slow-dance. She and Matt hadn't done so since their wedding night, ten years ago.

"Good answer," said Clay, taking her hand and leading her to the makeshift dance floor. There, he rested his other hand on her waist while Karen hesitantly placed her own on his shoulder. The band had just launched into a tinny cover of Steely Dan's "Babylon Sisters." As the two of them began to move to the music in tentative circles, Clay belted out the lyrics without any hint of self-consciousness. "'This is no one night stand,'" he sang while drawing her toward him. "'It's a real occasion.'" When he got to the line about "the end of a perfect day," he suddenly dipped Karen backward.

"Help!" Karen cried and laughed in protest. But it was too late. Her head was already by the floor, the world upside down. And Clay kept it that way for longer than she would have liked and until she was compelled to cry out, "Seriously! Clay! Lift me up."

Finally, he did. But when she returned to an upright position, equilibrium had not been restored. All the colors around her seemed brighter, including Clay's blue eyes, which appeared to her like two little swimming pools. Karen longed to dive in. The music seemed sharper too, and as if it were playing inside her chest. What's more, she found some kind of electrical charge passing between her and Clay. And Karen could tell by the way he was looking at her—probingly, curiously, suddenly half smiling as his chest rose and fell—that Clay felt it too. He had also stopped singing. They were only inches apart now—so close that tiny beads of sweat were visible in the hair follicles between his nose and mouth. But for reasons Karen couldn't explain, their sudden intimacy felt entirely natural, so much so that she longed to lean her head against his chest.

She didn't dare. Clay's wife, Verdun, was just on the other side of the dance floor, her head turned away but conceivably watching them out of the corner of her eye.

And Clay wasn't just a man who wasn't Karen's husband. He was an unrepentant capitalist—a Moneyman with a capital *M*. If that objection made Karen sound like a college sophomore, so be it. Clay didn't occupy merely another rung of the economic ladder; he occupied a wholly separate ladder than the one on which Karen and Matt currently rested their feet. His politics were another matter, if he even had any. "Did you like that?" he muttered suggestively in her ear.

Karen had just mumbled, "Maybe," when the spell was suddenly broken for her. As the bandleader sang "'So fine, so young—tell me I'm the only one,'" the unwelcome thought popped into her head that she was neither young nor the only one. Rather, it seemed suddenly and painfully clear to her that what she was experiencing was no more than a ridiculous, alcohol-fueled dance-floor flirtation between two old married friends. "I'm going to get something to drink," she said, slipping away.

Troy caught up with her at the bar. "Well, hello there, dancing queen," he began.

"Oh God, I was making a complete fool of myself out there, wasn't I?" said Karen, horrified to think that he too might have been watching.

"Hardly! You looked smart and chic! Especially upside down," he added with a smile.

"Ha," said Karen.

"But last time I checked"—Troy leaned toward Karen's ear,

so his words were only barely audible—"that was not your husband out there on the dance floor with you. Though far be it from me to get all Moral Majority on you."

Karen shut her eyes. "I actually wish you *would* get Moral Majority–ish on me. I think I'm having a midlife crisis."

"He *is* sort of handsome in a windswept, captain-of-the-Sail-America-syndicate sort of way," offered Troy.

"The *what?*" said Karen.

"Don't ask me how I know this, but I believe they won the America's Cup a few years ago."

"How do you know that?" asked Karen just as Clay reappeared, a toothpick in one corner of his mouth. At the sight of him, Karen experienced another swell of attraction and misgivings.

"Drink?" he said.

"Sure," said Karen, breaking her own two-glass policy.

When he returned with a sweet Bellini for each of them, Karen said, "Clay, this is Hungry Kids' outreach director, Troy Gafferty."

"Hello, man of good deeds," said Clay, extending a hand. "I myself am a man of worthless numerical manipulation. Though I do try and donate a few of the proceeds to deserving causes. And I pay my staff well."

"Well, good for you," said Troy in a vaguely mocking voice. "So, are you having fun tonight?"

"A boatload," he said. "Though I can't say the same for my wife."

Karen's heart raced at the mere mention of her existence.

"I'm sorry to hear that," said Troy.

"Unfortunately, she left early with a migraine," Clay went on. "So I'm on my own for the rest of the night."

Was he saying this for Karen's benefit? And was it even true? Karen glanced across the room and confirmed that, in fact, Verdun was no longer seated at table 12. Had she seen her husband flirting with another woman and stomped off in a rage? If so, Karen didn't blame her. Matt would have been infuriated by the sight of her and Clay on the dance floor. Or had Verdun really had a headache? As Karen considered the possibilities, dread and excitement commingled in her chest. It had been ages since she'd been the possible center of any drama.

"Oh, dear—benefit parties give me migraines too," offered Troy. "Maybe it's because everyone is so pleased with themselves—present company excluded, of course."

Clay laughed. "Maybe that's it."

"Well, I hope she feels better," piped in Karen, realizing it was the most generic possible thing she could have said but feeling she needed to display concern.

"I'm sure she'll be fine after a night without me," said Clay.

"My husband is on his own tonight too—at some dinner," offered Karen. "No doubt enjoying himself on account of my not being there to nag him about his disgusting table manners." Had she really just said that?

"Well, I'll leave you two married people to discuss the infinite joys of conjugal relations," said Troy, stepping away. "I'm going to see how Molly is doing—a woman for whom, it must be said, joy does not come easily."

"And it has been said many times before," added Karen, turning to Clay to explain. "We're talking about the woman in the burlap sack who got weepy at the podium while thanking the movie star."

"Ah," said Clay, chuckling.

Troy laughed too. Then he took off in search of their boss.

"Finish your drink and come with me," said Clay, taking Karen's free hand.

"There's no way I'm dancing to 'Footloose'!" she cried.

"Oh yes you are," he said, dragging her back to the dance floor, though admittedly with Karen's tacit consent.

More dancing led to more refreshments, which led to more dancing and more alcohol. By ten, Karen was on the precipice of being wasted. "It's a marvelous night," Clay murmured in her ear while they slow-danced to Van Morrison's "Moondance." Karen had to agree. At the same time, she wasn't so wasted that she could escape the conviction that she was betraying both her husband and Clay's wife. That Verdun wasn't white somehow made the perfidy even more inexcusable.

Karen was also neglecting her work.

Still, didn't she deserve some fun? In truth, there had been a paucity of it in her life over the past few years—really, a paucity of it throughout Karen's lifetime. She had no one to blame but herself. Friends of hers had devoted long periods of their youth and even their thirties to nothing more than the privileges of their age—that is, to altering their brain chemistry via drink and drugs, skydiving and having sex with strangers, all with the single goal of amplifying the experience of being alive. They'd traveled too—far and wide and back again—while Karen had always had a tendency to shy away from experience. Ever conscious of what she perceived to be wasting time, she also struggled to be in the moment, to stop eyeing the clock and wondering and worrying about what came next and thinking she really ought to get home.

But that night, she had no desire to leave. Apparently, neither did Troy or Clay. The band had packed up; the bartender was loading dirty glasses into plastic crates. But the three of them were still there. They were the last to walk through the front entrance when, at eleven, the lights in the ballroom were switched off.

It was drizzling and still unseasonably cold. Usually obsessed with the weather, Karen hardly noticed. It was enough that Clay was near. What's more, the blur of streaky lights and whizzing traffic made her nostalgic for her youth, when the very idea of urban living, with its heady mix of grit and glamour, had been compelling to her—at least in theory. In recent years, Karen's romance with danger, to the extent that it had ever even existed, had been replaced by the desire for comfort above all. But what if that impulse, too, was on its way out?

A part of Karen wished that Troy had left earlier and on his own. Another part was relieved by his presence, since it removed any potential question marks or awkwardness regarding what happened next with Clay. In any case, all three were headed to different neighborhoods, so there was no possibility of any of them sharing a taxi or Uber. When the first cab pulled up, chivalry prevailed, with both men offering it to Karen. With as much subtlety as she could manage, she tried to put them off, pointing out that Troy had to wake up earlier than the rest of them.

"Don't worry, I'll be fine," he said, ignoring her cue, whether by accident or intent. "You go ahead."

"Okay—well—good night, everyone," she said. What else could she say? Besides, it was clearly for the best. She hugged one, then the other. Though her embrace of Clay had a wholly different, more languid feel. "I'm going home to sleep this off," she told them both.

"Night-night," said Troy.

"Sleep tight," said Clay.

Karen pulled the door closed, and the car pulled away.

Out the back window, she watched the two men watching her until they shrank to the size of matchsticks, then disappeared from view, just like they all would someday.

On most nights, Karen fell asleep reviewing the to-do list she kept on her computer and in her head and, despite her fatigue, half wishing it were morning already so she could begin checking things off, from amending the data plan on her phone, to purchasing more individual organic applesauces to put in Ruby's lunch box, to calling the plumber about the dripping showerhead. Her dreams typically followed suit, the majority of them so prosaic that she sometimes felt embarrassed when she woke up. They also made her wonder if the myriad mundane responsibilities of motherhood had shut off some invisible valve that controlled the imagination until all that was left was the directive to purchase more paper towels. But that night, as she lay in bed—thankfully, Matt wasn't home yet—all thoughts of household products gave way to thoughts of Clay: the way he stood, the way he danced, the way he murmured in her ear.

Too drunk and aroused to sleep, Karen replayed each of the seemingly magical moments that they'd shared, already half convinced that they would never be repeated. Clay belonged to another world than hers, as well as another marriage. And Karen was under no illusion that there was any vehicle that could successfully transport her between the two. Though it was also true that, at times, Karen felt as if her own husband belonged to another universe. Once, she'd found his lower-middle-class origins to be winningly authentic. She admired the fact that he was the first one in his family to have gone to college and that he wasn't impressed by wealth. But as she'd gotten older, she sometimes found herself wishing he'd come from a family that was a little more landed, a little more bourgeois, if only so he could appreciate her own occasional longings for luxury and comfort. Matt was always keeping it real, whereas Karen increasingly longed to escape reality. It also drove her crazy the way he mispronounced words and names. She still hadn't forgotten the time he'd referred to her college-era hero, the French Marxist social theorist Michel Foucault, as *Michael Foo-colt*.

As if he were some kind of Chinese pony.

When Matt finally came to bed, Karen pretended to be asleep. It must have been three in the morning before she nodded off. She dreamed she was skiing down a Swiss Alp with a Russian spy after her who turned out to be Sue Borneo from fourth grade. Which somehow made sense.

The next morning, she tiptoed out of the house with Ruby, leaving Matt splayed on the bed.

Arriving at work later that morning, Karen felt elated despite her exhaustion. In the office kitchen, she came across Molly placing a Tupperware filled with dry lettuce in the fridge. "God, I have the worst headache," said Karen, reaching for the Mr. Coffee pot.

"Really? Why?" said Molly, forehead knit.

"Because of the benefit last night?"

"Oh." Molly looked mystified.

Shaking her head, Karen sat down at her computer and checked her in-box. There were the usual press releases from various social service agencies and nonprofits interspersed with LOSE WEIGHT FAST and YOU MAY STILL FIND A DIVORCE ATTORNEY and DEAR MADAM I AM MR UGOCHUKWO FROM NIGERIA 8 MILLION U.S. DOLLARS HAS BEEN LEFT TO YOU BY A DISTANT RELATIVE–style spam. There was also a personal e-mail from Stuart Levy, the executive director of the Jesse James Foundation, which seemed odd and possibly ominous. Karen clicked on it.

What appeared next was an apologetic letter explaining that the foundation was removing its support from Hungry Kids in favor of a new satellite program in urban farming that had been launched by HK's main—and far better endowed—rival, City Feeds. The news was a blow on several levels. Not only did the withdrawal mean a greatly reduced financial profile for Hungry Kids, but Karen's continued employment was predicated on her earning a multiple of her salary. Without Jesse James on board, that multiple would be far harder to achieve. Which made Clay's new patronage that much more important to her— even as she blamed him, at least in part, for the withdrawal.

She blamed herself as well. *Maybe if I'd spent less time dancing to "Footloose" and more time buttering up the Jesse James automatons,* Karen thought, *disaster could have been averted.* She also thought the key to solving the obesity epidemic in inner cities was not growing tomato plants in abandoned lots. What were people supposed to eat the other three seasons of the year? To her mind, it was one of those misguided help-people-help-themselves ideas that actually helped no one. But that was beside the point now…

To Karen's further disappointment, there was no morning follow-up e-mail from Clay. Though there was a personal e-mail from Mia's mother, Michelle. The subject heading was *Ruby*. Karen immediately assumed it was a reciprocal playdate invitation. Keen for a distraction from her work woes, she clicked on it. It read,

Karen, good morning. I'm sorry to have to bring this up with you, but Ruby has been pointing at Mia's private parts in the schoolyard and yelling, "Mia has a wiener." This has made Mia extremely uncomfortable. I would appreciate it if you would please discuss your daughter's inappropriate behavior with her and ask her to stop. Thank you, Michelle

On first reading, Karen felt a giggle rise in her windpipe. Surely it was some kind of joke. Except it didn't seem to be. Irritation followed—not only on her daughter's behalf but also on her own. Didn't all children find the topic of wieners and wee-wees endlessly fascinating? Didn't all adults too? And why shouldn't they? It was natural to be curious. And who was to say that the purported behavior had even occurred? Though even if Ruby really had pointed at Mia's crotch and accused her of having male genitals, did it merit such a stern e-mail? They were still too young to understand *why* society insisted some parts be kept covered and others not. And if Michelle was that upset, she could have spoken to Karen in person rather than lodging the complaint as she had—formally, in writing, as if Ruby had committed a sex crime. It seemed suddenly clear that an ocean separated Karen and Michelle after all and that the intimacy they'd shared during Mia and Ruby's playdate the week before—at least until the Chips Ahoy! had appeared—had been no more than a mirage.

It was also clear that Karen's workday was off to an epically bad start.

Just then, her phone pinged with a text from Matt. *How was the event last night?*

Apparently a fiasco, Karen wrote back. *Jesse James pulling funds from HK. Also, Ruby's friend's mother accusing Ruby of be-ing sexual predator. Not kidding. Details tk.*

Oh no and whhaaaaat? he replied.

And how was your dinner? she wrote back, reminded that her husband was the one adult in her life who really cared about her.

Inconclusive, he answered.

Even so, Karen was still hoping to hear from Clay and found herself checking her in-box at five-minute intervals throughout the day. When six o'clock arrived and he still hadn't written, it confirmed her suspicion that their flirtation was a pointless distraction. It also shored up her resolve to keep their relationship professional.

That evening, over a dinner of buttered bow ties, organic chicken tenders sautéed with panko bread crumbs, and peeled slices of McIntosh apple—to date, Karen had chosen to ignore the implications of her daughter's preference for all-white and beige dinner food—she attempted to address the Mia business with her. "So, you and Mia are still friends, right?" she said.

"Why?" asked Ruby.

"Because her mom says you've been saying stuff to her in the playground that she doesn't like."

"I was just kidding!"

"Sweetie, people call them private parts because they're pri-vate. You can't talk about other people's. You know that, right? Or touch them."

"We were just kidding around! I told her she had a penis, and she told me I had a vagina."

Karen winced. She had never liked the word *vagina* and did her best to avoid all mention of it, especially with her husband and even, when possible, with her gynecologist. In college, the preferred term had been *pussy*. But now that word too seemed embarrassing and like a relic from the days when being a "bad girl" was considered a good thing, which had never made that much sense to Karen. "Well, even if it's all just a joke, her mom doesn't want you to do it anymore," she said. "Mia feels embarrassed when you accuse her of having boy parts."

"She didn't seem embarrassed," said Ruby.

"Well, her mom says she was."

"I'm the one who should be embarrassed. I'm, like, the only person in my entire class who doesn't have their own electronic device!"

"What?" said Karen.

"Yisabella and Destiny have their own iPhones. And a bunch of other kids have iPads. Even Mia has a Kindle. And I have nothing. It's not fair."

"Ruby—that can't be true," said Karen, mystified as to how the same children who received free lunch could possibly own expensive Apple products. What was she missing?

"It *is* true," said Ruby.

"Well, I'm sorry, but those things cost a lot, and Daddy and I are not made of money," said Karen, noting the irony of her making this argument when their family likely had sixteen times as much as the average Betts one. "Anyway," she went on, keen to change the topic. "Tell me about school. Has the new visiting drama coach started?"

"We're doing a play about slavery," answered Ruby.

"Oh! Cool!" said Karen. "Who do you play?"

"I'm Sa'Ryah's slave, but it's *so* backward. Like, if this was the olden days, Sa'Ryah would be *my* slave and I would have been *her* master, 'cause I have light skin and she has dark. I told her that."

"You told her that?" said Karen, aghast.

"Well, it's true!" cried Ruby.

Not for the first time that day, Karen found herself at a loss for words.

She was clearing the plates when Matt came through the door. "Hey, stranger," she said, struck by how handsome her husband looked in his royal-blue-and-white checked shirt. It was her favorite shirt on him, even if she preferred it tucked to untucked.

"Hey—what's going on in Macaroni-Land?" said Matt. He came over and kissed Karen hello on the lips. Was it possible that, just as she'd become attracted to another man, they'd finally made up?

"Not much," said Karen. He wasn't just loyal, she thought. He was cute too.

And Ruby adored him. At the sight of him, she rushed into his arms, crying, "Daddddddyyyyyy."

"Hello, Scooby Doobie the Ruby," he said. Sometimes it seemed as if the less the fathers did, the more their offspring received them as heroes.

While Matt read Ruby a page from *The Guinness Book of World Records*—Ruby never tired of hearing about the tallest man, a record currently held by an eight-foot-three-inch Turk with prominent ears—Karen crafted a response to Michelle with the aim of respectfully addressing Michelle's concerns while subtly pointing out that (a) Mia was not necessarily an innocent party in the whole thing, and (b) the whole kerfuffle was essentially over nothing.

Hi, Michelle. I'm very sorry if Ruby upset Mia and, by extension, you. I talked to her about it tonight, and she said it was

*just a joke between friends—and that Mia also sometimes
teases her about having a vagina. That said, I've reminded
Ruby that other people's private parts are not to be discussed,
not even as part of a game, and I think she understood. I hope
we can get the girls together for a (G-rated) playdate soon!
LOL, Karen*

Ordinarily, Karen might have waited up to see if Michelle
responded. But that night, she went to bed at the same hour as
Ruby. She was unable to keep her eyes open a moment longer.
She'd also reluctantly agreed to give up her Friday morning to
chaperone Ruby's class trip to a nearby botanical garden, and
the school buses were leaving shortly after dawn.

As if the day ahead weren't daunting enough, Karen woke
to a bone-chilling drizzle falling from a charcoal sky. But a
promise was a promise. And so, she caffeinated herself into
compliance, dressed in four layers, then went to rouse Ruby.

Forty minutes later, as she headed up the bus's narrow aisle,
Karen found herself unexpectedly claustrophobic and eyeing
the emergency exits. Her thoughts alighted on the field trips
of her youth with their frantic scrambling for a willing but socially acceptable seatmate. To her recollection, the odd kid out
(often Karen) always got paired with the teacher, bestowing
on him or her instant pariah status. But that morning, Miss
Tammy had already made arrangements to share her bench
seat with Jayyden, no doubt with the motive of keeping a close
eye on him. The two sat in the first row, just behind the driver
and several rows ahead of the next student in the class.

To Karen's surprise, Ruby wanted to share a seat with her
mother. The two wound up in the third row from the back,

across from Mia, who was perfectly turned out that morning in purple rain boots and a matching purple polka-dotted raincoat with a tie belt. At the sight of the girl, Karen experienced a twinge of hostility on her daughter's behalf. It was Mia, after all, who had tattled to her mother about Ruby's X-rated playground shenanigans. Then again, Mia was a child and Karen was an adult. "Hi, Mia!" she forced herself to say in a chirpy voice. "I like your raincoat!"

"Thank you," Mia answered, then turned back to her seatmate, a stocky girl with pigtails, a heavy jaw, and half-moon shadows under her liquid eyes. Karen had seen the girl many times before but hadn't yet attached a name to the face. Mia began whispering in the girl's ear, causing Karen to worry that Ruby would feel excluded. Yet Ruby didn't seem particularly bothered. Or maybe she hadn't even noticed, preoccupied as she was with Karen's phone, which she'd brazenly taken out of Karen's bag and begun to play Candy Crush on. So Karen tried not to care either. And when Mia and the other girl stopped whispering, Karen leaned into the aisle and said, "I'm Ruby's mom. What's your name?"

"Empriss," the girl replied.

"Hi, Empriss!" said Karen, mentally scrolling through the class list that had been distributed at the beginning of the year and recalling with sudden fascination that Empriss Jones was the girl who lived in a family shelter for victims of domestic abuse. Karen knew this because, for fun—if that was the right word—she would occasionally, secretly Google-Earth her daughter's classmates' street addresses. That was how she knew the shelter was located in a five-story salmon stucco building with filthy windows draped with white sheets and nary a tree in sight on the street out front. It faced a highway on one side and a bus depot enclosed by a chain-link fence on the other. Stealing another glance across the aisle, Karen noted with curiosity that Empriss was dressed in clean leggings and a hoodie and what appeared to be a pair of brand-new Nike sneakers with bright white laces. The only detail that was amiss was that her *Frozen* T-shirt was several sizes too small. When she raised her arms, a substantial subsection of tummy spilled out over the gap.

Finally, the bus pulled up in front of the botanical gardens, and the class disembarked. The tour guide was a fashionably butch young Korean woman dressed in a baseball cap, a vintage windbreaker, and ripped jeans. In a booming voice, she introduced herself as Meghan, then began to apologize. Owing to the exceptionally cold winter and late arrival of spring, it turned out that nothing was blooming that was supposed to be blooming, including the cherry blossoms that the class had specifically come to see. (The third-grade science curriculum was all about the life cycle of flowering trees.) Not surprisingly, after twenty minutes of traipsing through fields of wet leaves, the kids began asking when they could eat lunch. But Miss Tammy told them they were being disrespectful to Meghan, who continued to apologize as she took them through the gardens.

Finally, Meghan led them to a basement area beneath the administrative building. Wet, cold, and now ravenous, the children sat down at metal tables and tore into the brown bags that Miss Tammy had asked them to bring from home. Ruby and Karen sat across from Mia and Empriss. As Ruby peeled open her YoKids organic yogurt, and Karen dug into her quinoa, feta, and heirloom tomato salad (she had also brought blueberries), Empriss unpacked a thin white-bread sandwich with a fluorescent orange interior, a vending machine–size bag of Cheetos, and a sugar-sweetened "grape drink."

"Ew—your lunch looks disgusting," Ruby blurted out while unwrapping the organic Applegate turkey sandwich on European rye that Karen had made her earlier that morning.

"Ruby! Don't be rude," cried Karen, fearing that, in her quest to preserve both the health of her daughter and that of the planet, she'd inadvertently turned the former into a hideous food snob. Never mind that Karen's own stomach had rolled over at the sight of Empriss's neon lunch.

"It's just ham and cheese," said Empriss, shrugging.

"Just ignore her," said Karen to Empriss, trying to make amends. "My daughter is a totally fussy eater."

"I'm not fussy," Empriss said proudly.

"Well, good for you," said Karen, pleased to have finally engaged her.

"The only thing I don't like is vegetables," Empriss went on.

"Not even carrots?" asked Karen, feigning surprise.

"I hate carrots. Once, my mom and me went to Super Wings, and she said, 'If you eat a carrot, I'll give you a hundred dollars.'"

"I hope you ate it! That's a pretty good deal."

"Nah, I felt like puking when I tried to eat that thing. But I should have."

"Well, I think carrots are crunchy and delicious," said Karen, attempting to strike a playful tone lest Empriss think she was lecturing her. "Do you like fruit? Fruit is healthy too."

"Yeah, I like fruit," said Empriss. "Especially bananas—like Nicki Minaj." She smiled toothily.

"Bananas are healthy," said Karen, ignoring the pop-culture reference, which she didn't understand in any case.

"I like fruit juice too," declared Empriss.

"Well, that's not as good for you as fruit," said Karen.

"Well, you gotta drink something!" said Empriss.

"Mom, do we have to talk about healthy eating all the time?" asked Ruby, rolling her eyes.

"What about water?" asked Karen, ignoring her daughter.

"We don't have water in our apartment," said Empriss.

"What?" cried Karen. "But what if you're thirsty?" Despite a decade working in poverty relief, she never ceased to be shocked by tales of privation in the developed world.

"Then you gotta buy something to drink," explained Empriss.

"But how do you take a bath or a shower?"

"That water works. But the water in the sink—it don't come out."

Now genuinely outraged on Empriss's family's behalf, Karen went into problem-solving mode, thinking maybe she could draw on her contacts at the Mission for the Homeless— a sister organization of Hungry Kids—and have them file a complaint against the facility in which Empriss's family lived. "Do you have a super or someone who oversees the—place you live? Because you know your mom has the right to demand repairs."

"My stepdad said he's gonna get it fixed," said Empriss, shrugging again.

"Oh! Well, that's good," said Karen, startled to hear that Empriss was being raised in a two-parent household. She'd assumed that the child would only have a mother. "Your stepdad sounds like a nice guy," she offered.

"Yeah, he's pretty nice," she said. "He's nicer than my real dad. My mom had to leave him because he hit her. And then he had this friend who's a cop and he gave my dad a gun. That's when we moved to the shelter. Also, my uncle got shot at the project, and my mom said we weren't safe there no more."

"Wow! Well, that's good your mom did that," said Karen, nearly choking on her quinoa, even though the news seemed to make no impression on Ruby. She sat quietly munching on her sandwich, apparently indifferent to the problems of the world—or at least Empriss's family's problems.

"Hey, no fair," she said, lifting her chin so she could see into Karen's Tupperware, "you didn't pack *me* any blueberries."

On the bus going back to school, the Dutch architect's red-headed son, Bram, and the black editor/activist's son, Mumia, began to kick the seat in front of them, causing a fight with the girls who were sitting there (Jayla and Yisabella), which somehow set off a bus-wide, girls-against-boys battle involving spitballs. Chahrazad, the raucous Yemeni child, was of course the leader of the girls' brigade, while Mumia commanded the boys' batallion. By the time Karen got home— the kids had returned to the classroom for the last part of the day—she was so exhausted and stressed out by being around twenty-five eight- and nine-year-olds screaming about butts and ear wax that she had to take a nap. When she woke up, she discovered it was nearly time to go back to Betts to pick up Ruby. Readying herself to return, Karen experienced new levels of respect for Miss Tammy.

At two forty-five, she was passing through the gate that led to the schoolyard when she nearly collided with Mia's mother, Michelle, who was approaching from the other direction. "Oh—hey!" said Karen, keen to establish that she had no hard feelings toward Michelle, just as she hoped Michelle had none toward her. But Michelle glared at her, said nothing, and marched on. Rattled by the rebuff and eager to avoid walking in lockstep with Michelle, Karen stopped walking and pretended to search for something in her bag. She pulled out her phone and discovered a recently arrived text from Clay Phipps. Her heart leaping—where had he even gotten her phone number?—she read:

Hey, dancing queen, made inquiries for u re WC's move to your kid's PS, but afraid my hands r tied. Apologies. Dinner Tuesday night? Say yes.

More bad news for the school, Karen thought. But this time her frustration and disappointment were mixed with tingling excitement at having heard from Clay again and, what's more, at him having asked her out to dinner. On a date. Because wasn't that what it was? It wasn't as if they had any Hungry Kids business to discuss. And knowing that he'd made inquiries on her behalf while she wasn't there—and while she was going about the business of her life, unaware—made her even more excited.

And yet, ever since the gala, Karen had felt a little like a middle-aged Cinderella, returned to a life of hearth sweeping the day after the royal ball. Moreover, while the families of the students at Constance C. Betts trundled by in various states of bedragglement and hopelessness—including a grandma with what appeared to be a burned face holding a cane in one hand and a cigarette in the other—Clay seemed so many miles away as to be almost fantastical. Karen also suspected that Clay's efforts to veto Winners Circle's co-location had been halfhearted at best. But this was the wrong time to start doubting him.

Hungry Kids needed his money—and Karen, for whatever combination of reasons, needed his attentions. Even so, dinner was out of the question. How would she ever justify such a thing to Matt? How could she justify it to herself?

In any case, she needed to pick up Ruby. After enough time had passed that Karen could reasonably assume Michelle and Mia had left the building, she followed the thinning crowd into the gymnasium. By then, everyone in Ruby's class was gone except for Ruby and Jayyden. The latter sat with his head bowed and his legs extended in front of him, scratching at something on his jeans. According to Ruby, Jayyden was retrieved every day by an older cousin who arrived at least an hour after school had been dismissed, forcing Jayyden to kill endless amounts of time in the hall outside the principal's office. Although the after-school program offered financial aid to students whose families couldn't afford the fifteen bucks a day, no one had ever turned in an application on his behalf, so the school couldn't legally send him to it. And so he sat—and sat. "Hi, sweetie," said Karen, glancing helplessly over at Jayyden as she reached down to pull Ruby off the floor.

"Thanks for forgetting about me," she announced.

"Sorry, but I'm only two minutes late," said Karen, steering her away. "And I just spent half the day with you already. What did you do when you got back to school?"

"Nothing," Ruby replied with a shrug.

"Nothing?" asked Karen.

"Just boring stuff."

"Why was it boring?"

"Because it's too easy," said Ruby, "and we never learn anything."

"What's too easy?" asked Karen, attempting to quiet her own distress at this revelation. "I don't understand."

"Every part, but especially math. We always have to *show our work* even if it's just, like, twenty-five plus twenty-five. It's so stupid. Like, we can't just say, 'It's fifty.' Also, we did the same unit in second grade."

"That does sound frustrating. But I thought you were doing fractions now. That's what Miss Tammy's newsletter said."

"Well, we *were* going to start fractions," said Ruby. "But this afternoon, while Miss Tammy was trying to teach us, Empriss started calling out and making fart noises like she does every day now."

"And what did Miss Tammy do?" asked Karen, further dismayed but also surprised. The picture that Ruby was painting of Empriss didn't mesh with the outspoken but overall cooperative child Karen had met on the class trip to the botanical gardens.

"She told her to stop," said Ruby.

"Did she?"

"She stopped calling out, but she was still making fart noises. It was *so* annoying. Finally, Miss Tammy called the principal, and she took Empriss out of class. But by then, it was time to pack up."

Sympathetic to both sides, Karen wondered if there was some way to turn the anecdote into a teachable moment—that is, an opportunity to instruct her daughter about socioeconomic difference and unequally distributed resources. "That must be frustrating," she said, choosing her words carefully. "But you know Empriss is probably trying to get attention because she doesn't get enough at home—because her parents are probably busy and preoccupied just trying to put food on the table. Being very poor, like her family is, can be very stressful for grown-ups."

"How do you know she's poor?" asked Ruby.

"I just do," said Karen, embarrassed to admit the truth even to her daughter.

"Well, then, why does she have her own iPhone Five?"

"I don't know the answer to that. But you realize that Empriss's family doesn't live in a nice house like we do."

"We don't live in a house—we live in an apartment," Ruby pointed out.

"Well, a nice *apartment,*" Karen went on. "Empriss's family lives in a homeless shelter because they can't afford a real apartment with separate bedrooms and everything. So next time Empriss is annoying you, will you try to think about that before you feel critical?"

"If they're so poor, why doesn't her mom get a job?" said Ruby.

"It's not that easy," said Karen.

"Can we go home now?" asked Ruby, showing no signs of having registered the intended message.

"We're going, we're going!" said Karen, leading her daughter out of the gym and feeling frustrated not for the first time by what she felt to be a lack of empathy on Ruby's part. What was Karen doing wrong? She feared the only thing she'd accomplished by sending her child to a mixed-income school was to make Ruby feel venomous toward at-risk children. Or was she expecting too much from an eight-year-old?

That weekend, Karen and Matt finally had sex. It was neither great nor terrible, neither loving nor angry. All parts functioned as designed, and afterward Karen felt relieved and refreshed. But the high lasted only so long. By morning, she was back to fretting and obsessing over what to do with regard to both Clay and Betts. Needless to say, she couldn't very well discuss the former with Matt. But in light of their recent tiff, she was also reluctant to raise the latter. Instead, on Sunday night, she vented to Miss Tammy in an e-mail.

> *Hi, Tammy. So sorry to bother you on the weekend, but Ruby has been complaining that the math program isn't quite challenging enough. Is there any way you could throw some harder worksheets her way? My husband and I would really appreciate it. Also, I hate to bring this up, but I understand that a certain girl (Empriss) has been regularly disrupting the classroom. I'm aware that she has a challenging situation at home, but I'm wondering whether there are services available at the school that could be utilized to help her control her impulses so she doesn't jeopardize her classmates' ability to learn. Thank you, Karen*

But as soon as she clicked Send, she felt uneasy. She feared that she sounded like one of those brilliant-and-exceptional parents who seemed genuinely to believe that, by random chance that had nothing to do with their socioeconomic status, God had granted them the stewardship of a certifiable Einstein (or two). She also worried that, by tattling on Empriss, she was only adding to the girl's troubles.

Tammy replied almost immediately.

> *Hey, Karen,*
>
> *I've offered to give your daughter supplemental math worksheets. But she always tells me she hates math. As for Empriss,*

yes, the school psychologists have been working with her. But thanks for your "concern."

Tammy
   P.S. Speaking of interrupting learning, Ruby has been arriving late to school almost every day. It would be way more awesome if you got her here on time. Thank you.

If Miss Tammy was unmoved by Karen's pleas, then so be it. But she didn't see why the teacher had to be a complete and utter *bitch* about it. With a shudder, Karen hit Delete and tried to pretend the e-mail exchange had never happened.

For the next week, she busied herself writing a grant proposal to the Walmart Foundation. She heard nothing else from Clay or Michelle. Nor did she answer Clay's text. With varying degrees of success, she attempted to put both of them out of her mind.

Then Ruby came home from school and glumly announced that in the cafeteria that day, Mia had told Ruby that she wouldn't be friends with her anymore unless Ruby threw out the remains of Mia's lunch.

"*What?* Tell her to throw out her own frigging lunch!" cried Karen, shocked and outraged—possibly too much so. Karen had never been good at separating her own history of social rejections from those of her young daughter's.

"I told her I didn't want to," Ruby continued. "So she got up and went to sit with Empriss and then she didn't talk to me for the rest of the day." Ruby made a sad-clown face.

"Well, that was a very mean thing for her to do," said Karen, her upset now metastasizing into full-blown resentment at the entire Hernandez family—minus Mia's tragic half sister, Juliana—even as a part of Karen wondered how Michelle would greet the news that Mia's NBF, similar to Gisela and Juliana, lived in a shelter. With compassion? Further condemnation? "I don't want you to talk to her anymore," Karen went on. "Tomorrow I want you to play with someone else at recess and sit with someone else at lunch."

"But there's no one else to sit with," said Ruby.

"What about Happy?" Karen heard herself invoke the name of one of the only other white girls in the class—a skinny thing with flyaway hair and buckteeth whose parents seemed strange and vacant-eyed and dressed as if they were in a movie or a play about nineteenth-century pioneers on the American frontier, or possibly a polygamous cult, the mother in long prairie skirts and high-necked lace blouses, the father in trousers with suspenders. Or maybe they were just hipsters. Karen had reached an age where she struggled to discern what was considered cool. But Ruby had mentioned in passing that Happy had reached the dizzying alphabetical heights of S-T on the leveled scale that all the teachers at Betts used to judge their students' reading abilities. Or maybe it was T-U. Not that Happy was unique in the achievement. There was a sweet and taciturn African American girl named Essence who shared in the distinction. According to Ruby, Essence lived an hour and a half away from Betts and woke at five each morning so she wouldn't be late for school. But given the physical distance between Ruby's and Essence's homes, Karen assumed that an outside-of-school friendship between the two would prove challenging. Or was that just an excuse? Was it the cultural distance between them that Karen assumed would present the largest obstacle?

Ruby scrunched up her face as if she'd just smelled something rotten and said, "Happy's into girlie stuff like anime and My Little Pony."

"My Little Pony is girlie," said Karen, confused. "But Barbies aren't?"

"Barbies are different."

"Well, then, why don't you sit with Zeke? You've been friends since kindergarten."

"Mommy, I'm not going to eat lunch at the *boys'* table!" Ruby rolled her eyes and shook her head as if her mother's ignorance were almost beyond comment. Maybe it was.

Karen had always thought elementary-school scissors, with their rounded blades, were too dull to cut anything sturdier than a piece of construction paper. Until she learned otherwise, she'd also thought that Jayyden Price was just a boy who got mad when kids teased him; that is, a boy like any other boy, just a little madder and a little more troubled—and a lot more tragic. But that evening, Ruby reported in a tone that was more reportorial than frantic that Jayyden had tried to choke a boy in her class named Dashiell, then stabbed him with a scissors. And now Karen wasn't so sure anymore. All of this had apparently happened in art class. "*What?* I don't understand," she said, hungry for a reason, or at least evidence of a provocation so outrageous that it would explain, if not justify, Jayyden's anger. If there was no valid excuse, then Laura Collier and Evan Shaw weren't conniving racists but overprotective realists, and it was possible that Karen's daughter's safety was at risk as well. "Why would Jayyden have done that?" she went on.

"Well, Dashiell accused Jayyden of stealing his Starburst," said Ruby. "And Jayyden said he didn't. And then Dashiell told him he didn't believe him. And then Jayyden got mad and made fun of Dashiell for wearing boxer shorts, and Dashiell pushed him. Then they started fighting, and Jayyden put his arm around Dashiell's neck and stuck the scissors into his arm."

"Oh my God, that's terrible! What did the teacher do?"

"She was screaming at them. They both had to go to the principal. Well, actually, Dashiell had to go to the nurse first because he was bleeding all over."

Karen gripped Ruby's arm and looked straight into her eyes. "Ruby, tell me the truth—has Jayyden ever bothered you?"

"Well, he's usually pretty nice to me," said Ruby. "But yesterday he *did* use the f-word." She lowered her head and rounded her back. Though whether the stance was born of fear or embarrassment at having referenced a swearword, it was hard to know.

"How did he use it?" said Karen, alarm bells ringing. "What did he say?"

"He asked me what I was doing at recess. Because he said"—Ruby leaned in, so she could whisper—"he wanted to f-word with me."

Karen felt her head grow light. Ruby was only a child—not exactly a trustworthy source or a reliable narrator. But the language was so specific, it was hard not to believe that she was repeating exactly what she'd heard. *I want to fuck with you.* Karen understood it to be some variation of the phrase *I want to fuck you up.* That is, mess with her, harm her. "But what do you think he meant?" she asked.

Ruby shrugged as if Karen had asked her to predict the weather on Friday and said, "I don't know."

"Well, did he seem like he was just kidding around? Was he mad at you about something?"

"Well, second period, I did tell him to leave Empriss alone, because he was making fun of her for not having her own bed."

"That was sweet of you," said Karen, her pride in her daughter's defense of her impoverished classmate momentarily trumping her distress at Jayyden's threat. Never mind Karen's disbelief that someone in Jayyden's situation would be teasing another classmate about her lowly status on the socioeconomic ladder. "But I thought you didn't like Empriss," she went on.

"I don't like her," explained Ruby. "But I felt sorry for her."

"Well, good for you," said Karen. But the song and dance that Ruby then began spontaneously to perform in front of Karen's closet mirror only exacerbated her misgivings about the school. "'When you're ready, come and get it, na-na-na,'" she sang while wiggling her behind.

"Ruby, stop that. It's inappropriate," said Karen, dismayed by both the lyrics and the sexual nature of Ruby's movements. Or was it not sexual if there was no knowledge of sex? From what Karen could tell, Ruby had no idea how babies were made, and Karen hadn't yet offered to explain.

"But all the sassy girls in school twerk," said Ruby. "Like Janiyah, Khloee, and Jasleen."

"I don't care what all the girls are doing," said Karen, for whom the t-word seemed like an omen of civilization's final descent. Though what in particular was so terrible about a bunch of eight- and nine-year-olds shaking their backsides was hard to say. What if they simply found it funny? And wasn't the area of the body from which waste matter was expelled inherently amusing? Even so, Karen couldn't ignore the growing conviction that invisible forces of corruption, dissolution, and danger were growing ever closer to her daughter, turning her head in the wrong direction and pulling her farther away from Karen's reach—a conviction that only grew stronger after Ruby leaned forward and said, "Can I tell you something else?"

"What?" said Karen.

"Jasleen and Janiyah both wear *bras!*"

"Well, I think that's ridiculous," said Karen. "I don't see why girls your age need to wear bras when they don't have boobs."

Ruby shrugged, then lay down.

After Karen tucked her in, she went back into the living room where Matt sat reading sports scores on his phone and told him what Jayyden had said to Ruby.

"Boys just say stuff," he said. He sounded as unconcerned as Ruby. "Besides, he didn't say he wanted to fuck her *up*—or, God forbid, *fuck her*. He said he wanted to fuck *with* her. Honestly, it doesn't sound that bad to me. Having said that, I wouldn't be that psyched if I were Dashboard's parents right now, or whatever that kid's name is."

"It's Dashiell, not Dashboard," said Karen, not in the mood for Matt's punning. "His parents own the artisanal sausage place up the street."

"Isn't that kind of an oxymoron?" said Matt. "I mean, isn't the whole point of sausages that they're highly processed and really bad for you?"

"The artisanal ones are probably bad but not *as* bad for you, because they don't have as many additives in them. But I'm trying to talk to you about something else!"

"Oh, right."

"So you'd rather wait until Ruby is Jayyden's next victim than try to do something about it now?"

"He's not going to go after Ruby. He only goes after the kids who start up with him. And Ruby's not like that. Also, they're eight years old. Can we please not lose sight of that fact?"

"That's not even true—Jayyden is nine going on ten," said Karen.

"Whatever," said Matt.

"I'm thinking of talking to the principal about it."

"You sound like Maeve's parents."

The accusation made Karen wince. In her mind, Laura and Evan had become the apotheosis of liberal hypocrisy. "That's not fair," she said.

But wasn't the child's removal her unspoken goal too? And what if Laura and Evan had had a valid point about Principal Chambers protecting Jayyden at the expense of the others? Or had skin color distorted Karen's perception to the point of blindness? If some troubled white boy had told Ruby he wanted to *fuck with her* at recess, surely Karen would have been concerned as well. But *how* concerned? And what would happen to Jayyden? Maybe April Fishbach was right, and the child needed succor, not censor. But did he have to get that help in the same building, the same room, as Ruby was in?

"Honestly, Karen, I really think you're overreacting," said Matt.

"Am I?" She could no longer tell.

Maybe not surprisingly, Karen and Ruby were late for school the next day. But Karen's chronic insomnia was only partly to blame. Her head awhirl with visions of Jayyden inserting various sharp implements into her daughter's flesh, Karen felt uneasy even entering the school building. And having finally done so, she was reluctant to let her daughter walk down the now-deserted hall. "I love you," she said—twice.

"Mommy, you're embarrassing me," said Ruby.

"Sorry, sweetie—sometimes moms are really embarrassing," said Karen.

For the rest of the day, every time the phone rang at work—before Karen picked it up and found it was a robo-call from a politician or HK's charming but lazy truck driver Gregor calling in sick with a bad back, as he constantly did—Karen imagined it was the main office of Betts Elementary phoning to say that her daughter had been taken away in an ambulance. She even pictured herself in reaction, trembling and hyperventilating as she fled her office, the image superimposed over stock photos of slumped bodies from the latest school shooting, the latest terrorist attack. There was a new one seemingly every day. Was it any wonder she felt as if she were being thrown from the stern of a small boat to the bow and back again? Nausea was a not-unexpected by-product.

Yet Karen had always prided herself on being strong, reasonable, tolerant, and tempered—not a hysteric shivering and cowering in the corner at the very suggestion of ghosts. What was happening to her? How had she allowed her dreams to supplant reality? And what was fear, after all, but a projection into a future that no one could predict?

Only, for Karen, the future felt like right now. That Ruby apparently had a perfectly fine day at school that day did nothing to diminish her paranoia. "I need to talk to you," she told Matt that night. "And it's important."

"*Again?*" he said.

"Can you please mute the game?" Legs splayed on the sofa, he begrudgingly hit the remote. "I want to take Ruby out of Betts," she said.

Matt unleashed a long sigh. "Is this about that kid again?"

"Yes, it's about *that kid,* who is endangering the welfare of not just Ruby but all the other kids in his class. But it's also about the fact that Ruby is bored and coming home singing really inappropriate songs she picks up in the schoolyard."

"You mean, songs courtesy of the black girls with their morally bankrupt hip-hop culture?" countered Matt.

"I didn't say anything about race," Karen shot back.

"Well, I did. Besides, since when have you been a puritan?"

"Since today."

"Whatever you say, Miss My Favorite Song in Fourth Grade Was 'My Sharona' by the Knack."

"Okay, forget about music," said Karen, already exasperated. "There's also the fact that Ruby's only friend at school turned on her, and the mother turned on me. And now it's really uncomfortable for both of us."

"So she'll make new friends."

"With who?"

Matt shrugged. "I don't know. Aren't there twenty-four other kids in her class?"

"Twenty-two of whom she has nothing in common with."

"So, *that's* what this is about," said Matt with a leading smile that Karen didn't appreciate. So often, Karen felt as if her husband was trying to out her as a reactionary or—even worse—a racist. "I don't know what you're talking about," she said.

"There aren't enough white kids," said Matt, spelling it out for her. "Isn't that the real issue here?"

"I never said that. *You* did," said Karen.

"But that's what you were thinking."

Was Matt right, and was that why Karen wanted to take Ruby out of Betts? Karen refused to believe that about herself. It went against all her ideals and, really, everything she'd spent her life working toward. "It has nothing to do with race," she told him. "I just don't feel comfortable leaving her there in the morning anymore."

"Well, I do," said Matt. "Maybe she'll learn the meaning of compassion, something you seem to have forgotten the definition of."

"And maybe you'll stop being so self-righteous," said Karen, "and admit there are serious behavioral and discipline issues over there and also that it's basically impossible for one teacher with twenty-five students to simultaneously teach kids who've had every advantage, like Ruby, and kids who live in homeless shelters and housing projects and barely have parents and are almost always behind in school."

"So you want to send her to private school?" asked Matt. "Because money is the new IQ, and all rich kids are smart and want to learn. Is that how it works?"

"It has nothing to do with money," scoffed Karen. "It has to do with coming from a functional family where people care about their kids getting an education and encourage them. In any case, we can't afford private. And you know I don't believe in it anyway."

"So you want to move to the all-white half of Cortland Hill? Is that the idea? Or—even better—to a house in the suburbs with a picket fence and a green lawn?"

"I don't particularly *want* to. But I'm not a hundred percent opposed to the idea," said Karen.

"Well, I am," said Matt. "This is my home, and I have no intention of leaving it."

"It's my home too," said Karen. "And please don't make me point out who actually put down the money for it."

Matt's jaw visibly tensed. For a few seconds, he didn't speak. Then he said, "Are you *seriously* going there?"

"Sorry, that was unnecessary," said Karen, already regretting the gambit.

"Thank you for your apology," said Matt.

"So we'll stay here. Are you happy now?"

"Happy enough."

Well, you're the only one who is, Karen was tempted to reply, but this time she stopped herself. "I'm going to shower," she said instead and walked out of the room.

Undressing in the bedroom, she caught sight of her reflection in the full-length mirror. Although she was forty-five, it still came as a surprise and a disappointment to find that her body no longer resembled her youthful image of herself, which she continued to cling to despite all evidence to the contrary. Instead, she appeared in the mirror that evening as bulky in all the wrong places and hollow in the others, like a banana split that had been left out in the sun for too long. A part of Karen understood that it no longer mattered what she looked like without her clothes on, since she was (a) already married and (b) at the end of her childbearing years and therefore not expected to resemble a totem of fertility.

But in that moment, it *did* matter. She felt old and irrelevant and, as with many women in moments of insecurity, began to mentally flagellate herself for her lack of self-control—for her failure to go to the gym often enough and eat sparingly at all times. Her diet may have been largely organic, but it was also frequently excessive. The problem was that the salads never filled her up. And the smoothies only left her craving something smoother, like ice cream.

Once in the shower, the simple joy of hot water streaming down her scalp and back soothed and distracted her. But when she emerged from the downpour, her dissatisfaction both with herself and with the world returned. For Karen, negativity was like a wisteria vine that, if left to its own devices, would creep into every last crevice of her conscience and wind itself around every last limb until she felt strangled by her own discontent and desperate to escape. "I'm going out for milk," she called out over the voice of the sportscaster.

"Don't we have some?" Matt called back.

"Not enough," she answered. It seemed like the easiest explanation.

Karen locked the door behind her and headed to the elevator.

It was far from warm outside, but the dampness had lifted. And the air felt cool and fresh on Karen's face. Pausing outside the front door of her building, she looked around her. The doggie-day-care center next door was dark. So was the Vietnamese sandwich shop that had recently taken over from a bail bondsman. Only the Korean deli and the bistro on the corner appeared to be open for business. The latter business was so cool it didn't even have a name. What it did have was greasy comfort food with a gourmet flair, like cheeseburgers made of dry-aged beef with cave-aged cheddar. In the new culinary economy, it seemed, everybody wanted food that had been sitting around for a long time. Karen marveled that it wasn't the other way around. Out of habit more than anything else, she began walking toward it.

Peering into the bistro's handsomely canopied windows, she saw tables of white people in their twenties and thirties, their faces elastic with the effects of alcohol, their clothes just the tiniest bit rumpled, their hair unkempt, their heads thrown back in laughter. Every Wednesday—Karen had seen the posters in the window—the bistro hosted a bingo night, which was clearly meant to be ironic. Karen had always hated board games, even as a child, finding them dull and fundamentally pointless. She had a far more ambivalent relationship with the bistro itself.

When Karen first moved to the neighborhood, there had been a decrepit bodega in the same spot. Karen had almost never shopped there, choosing to buy her staples at the more upscale Korean-owned deli nearby or to order them online. But once in a while, when the deli had run out of milk or orange juice, she'd find herself walking on the bodega's broken black-and-white-vinyl-tiled floor while a tabby cat with green-gold eyes darted in and out of the aisles. The Tunisian immigrant family who owned the place must have been trying to capitalize on the first wave of gentrification to hit the neighborhood when, one day, they erected a new marquee promising ORGANUK FOOD. The misspelling had made Karen cringe. Not surprisingly, a year or so later, the bodega was shuttered. For six months, the store sat empty. Then the bistro guys arrived in their black leather motorcycle jackets. While they stood out front smoking American Spirit cigarettes and talking on their phones, a crew of Central American construction workers began yanking out the vinyl tiles and chucking them into a dumpster, exposing the original wide-plank subfloor—

and ultimately increasing the property value of Karen and Matt's condo.

And now, next to the Bistro with No Name, where there had previously been an African American barbershop—until the barber was shot dead in what the local papers called a personal dispute—there was a store that sold macaroons and nothing more. It was closed for the night, but the display window was still lit, revealing Easter egg–colored disks laid out in rows in an old-fashioned oak-and-glass case with cabriole legs. Beneath the sweets were handwritten note cards advertising exotic flavors like passion fruit and champagne. Karen thought of jewels in a jewelry store. She also thought that, whatever it was the macaroon people were selling, it had very little to do with eating. But then, for people in a certain milieu, a milieu that surely included Karen, this was what food had increasingly become—a luxury item, rather than a means to stay alive.

The sound of clinking glass turned Karen's attention away from the macaroons and toward the curb, where a homeless man with a filthy dreadlocked beard and a bum leg scrounged through a blue trash bag, presumably in search of redeemable bottles. Tuesday evening was when residents of the neighborhood put out their recyclables for Wednesday-morning pickup. At the sight of the man, Karen felt competing desires: to reach out and to run far away, to sympathize but also to condemn. As if there were no history, no mitigating circumstances that had led to his situation in life. When had she grown so callous, she wondered—in life, in her marriage? As the man began to hobble away with his giant clanging bag of recyclables slung Santa-style over his rounded back, Karen guiltily thrust a five-dollar bill into his hand. "May God bless you," he muttered after her.

"Good luck," she told him.

As if luck had anything to do with it.

After crossing the neighborhood's main commercial thoroughfare, Karen started down a leafy street lined with handsomely proportioned, history-rich nineteenth-century brick row houses with brass hardware on the doors. She'd crossed the line that separated the Betts school district from the one zoned for Edward G. Mather. Here, the homes featured plaques claiming to have been the birthplaces of important but now obscure figures from the Civil War, from literature, and from architecture. Staring covetously through their elongated windows, she could make out chandeliers of various vintages, beginning with the introduction of the gas lamp and continuing into the present, with sleek steel, brass, and glass versions from Design Within Reach. Karen's wealthy friends, like Allison, called it Design Out of Reach, even though they readily dove their hands into their wallets in order to purchase home furnishings from the place. (They also referred to Whole Foods as Whole Paycheck, even as they continued to buy their heirloom tomatoes there.) But then, in the city in which they all lived, feeling poor was apparently intrinsic to the experience of being rich, unless you were *incredibly* rich. Allison and her family actually lived just around the corner. It was another of the ironies of the area that the real estate had gotten so expensive, and the people moving into it so moneyed, that they didn't necessarily even use the public school that had made the neighborhood so sought after just a few years before.

The block was deserted except for a Caucasian man with a shaved head, walking a French bulldog. The man was dressed in the casual uniform of the Euro elite: dark-wash jeans, a black suit jacket, a crisp white dress shirt, and black loafers with a silver horse bit on each toe. Karen guessed he was a private banker, or maybe an art consultant who advised bankers. In any case, he exuded a compelling type of confidence. And as the two passed each other, she smiled what she imagined to be her most beguiling smile. But the man stared blankly back at her—really, through her. Reminded again of her reduced desirability, being a woman over forty, Karen felt ashamed and embarrassed and turned her eyes toward the curb, where clear plastic bags filled with paper trash formed high-class hillocks beneath the streetlamp.

Through the plastic, she could make out back issues of *Bon Appétit* magazine and various official-looking envelopes that bore the insignias of financial institutions like PricewaterhouseCoopers and Fidelity. It was *that* kind of neighborhood, filled with *those* kind of people, she thought—the kind she'd spent her life both shunning for their sense of entitlement and trying to keep up with, in roughly equivalent proportions. But in that moment, the latter impulse was in ascendance. Although Karen was aware that, compared to the vast majority of city dwellers, she and Matt were greatly privileged, she also saw her own family as being at a distinct disadvantage. Why should the children on this block get to walk the hallowed halls of Mather instead of the higgledy-piggledy ones of Betts? It seemed as unfair as—well—cancer. Also as random.

Of course, the disparity in privilege between Karen and Clay Phipps was surely many times greater than it was between her and the public-school parents in the neighborhood who sent their children to Mather. But Clay's wealth was so beyond the realm of imaginable that it somehow didn't merit comparison, whereas walking down Pendleton Street, which was only four blocks from Karen's home, she had the uneasy feeling that she'd taken a wrong turn a hundred miles back, and now it was too late to turn around. She'd never find the exit in time, never catch the train. It had already left the station without her. And there wasn't another one coming any time soon. Karen had never considered herself to be a particularly competitive person. But even if winning wasn't her life's goal, it was also true that she hated to lose.

As she continued down the block, her eye caught the familiar periwinkle-colored font of the local gas company, then the word NONE printed in large caps. Probably a utility bill tossed out by a resident who owed nothing, Karen figured. It seemed like the perfect metaphor for the people who lived there. She kept walking. She walked all the way to the corner. Then she paused, an idea unspooling in her head: Why couldn't that utility bill be hers and, by extension, why couldn't she pretend to be a resident of Pendleton Street, in which case she'd be legally entitled to send her daughter to Mather?

In truth, it wasn't the first time Karen had contemplated lying about her address to secure a better school. Once or twice, it had even crossed her mind to ask Allison if she could borrow hers. Allison probably wouldn't have minded. But the loss of pride to Karen had seemed potentially detrimental to their friendship. Despite their intimacy, she relished the ability to quietly dangle her woman-of-the-people credentials in Allison's face. What's more, Karen had never stolen anything in her life other than a towel from the Yucatán resort where she and Matt had spent their honeymoon. And even that breach, the pettiest of crimes, had caused her heart to palpitate. She could still recall how, while checking out, she'd been half convinced that the man behind the front desk could see into her luggage. She'd also half expected the police suddenly to appear.

And yet, rationally speaking, just as in the case of the filched towel, Karen didn't see how anyone stood to suffer from her walking away with a stranger's already-paid gas bill. Besides, she wasn't committing to any actions, only giving herself options. Pivoting right, then left, she surveyed the now-empty streetscape. The private banker/art consultant and his bulldog had vanished, and no one had taken their place. Or at least no one Karen could see. In the time since she'd left her house, the sky had turned a rich shade of Prussian blue. In the far distance came the muted ululating of an emergency vehicle.

Walking at a brisk pace, Karen reapproached the trash bag. After coming to a stop two feet away, she stood eyeing the bill through the plastic, coveting it like she occasionally craved brownies and cupcakes. But what good had abstention ever done? Karen found that if she said no to a late-afternoon pastry, she would end up eating bread and butter at dinner and feeling equally gluttonous.

The word NONE seemed to be staring back at her, offering itself up as both warning and invitation, but more the latter.

Karen suddenly untwisted the twisty tie that was holding the bag together, thrust her hand into the pile, grabbed hold of the bill, and stuck it in her purse. Her heart was beating madly as she skedaddled back down the block—not so fast as to seem suspicious if anyone should appear, but rapidly enough to discourage questions.

Five minutes after that, she was standing in line at the Korean grocer on her corner, waiting to pay for an exorbitantly priced half gallon of organic 2 percent milk. The carton featured a pastoral scene that seemed to have been lifted out of a nineteenth-century children's book, with brown-and-white-dappled cows grazing on a rolling green hill next to a red barn. Matt was convinced that the entire organic movement was a scam and that all you were really paying for was the pretty picture on the side of the carton and, by extension, nostalgia for the fantasy of a simpler era. But Karen wasn't so sure. A few years earlier, she'd read an article in the *Huffington Post* linking the hormones in nonorganic milk to early puberty. Now she lived in fear of Ruby getting her period while still in elementary school and regularly snuck surreptitious glances at both her daughter's pubis in search of darkening follicles and her chest in search of buds. It seemed so unfair for a child to be burdened that way at such an early age. But it was also that early menses seemed to portend other undesirable early firsts—for example, teenage pregnancy. Then again, most of the ugly, plastic picture-less milk cartons promised *no hormones* as well, and Karen couldn't bring herself to buy them. So maybe she really was a fool.

A fool and also now a thief.

"Where have *you* been?" Matt asked as Karen closed the door behind her. But to her relief, his voice was more inquisitive than angry.

"Sorry, I ran into a friend on the street," she said, amazed at how easily the lie spilled from her lips.

"I thought you'd gotten mugged," he went on. "I was actually worried about you. I called your cell and you didn't answer."

"Oh, sorry—I must not have heard it ring," said Karen. She went into the kitchen to put away the milk they didn't need.

"Anyway, I'm going to hit the sack early," said Matt. "I didn't sleep well last night."

Karen was surprised and relieved by this small stroke of fortune. When did Matt ever go to bed early? It also felt like fate—that she should be left to her own devices that night. "Okay, good night," she told him.

"Nighty-night," he replied.

Karen couldn't tell whether or not he was still mad at her for mentioning who had made the down payment on their apartment. But in truth, a good portion of her marriage in the past year or two had been conducted in a gray space between *fine* and *annoyed*, with the two of them operating at a temperature that fell between temperate and chilly. After Matt disappeared into the bedroom, she sat down at her desk and pulled the stolen bill out of her bag. Under the lamp, it revealed new attributes. A greasy brown-black smear on the top left corner suggested recent contact with a banana peel. Or at least, Karen hoped it was a banana. The sight sent a brief spasm of disgust shooting up her spine.

Recovering, Karen noted for the first time that the bill was addressed to Nathaniel Bordwell at 321 Pendleton Street, no apartment number, suggesting that Bordwell and his family lived on all four floors of their extra-wide town house. *Lucky them,* she thought. Feeling marginally less guilty, she smoothed the creases, wiped the stain off as best she could with a tissue, and placed the paper beneath a well-thumbed hardback of Barbara Ehrenreich's *Nickel and Dimed*. At one time, it had been her favorite book. But that evening, its greatest value to her was as a paperweight.

Next, Karen opened her laptop, located a realty website that offered a free lease template, and downloaded it onto her desktop. Then she drew up a lease for herself and her family for an apartment she designated as 321 Pendleton Street, no. 2. She identified Nathaniel Bordwell as her landlord and set the rental price at a multiple of a thousand that wasn't quite market rate but was by no means cheap, suggesting a long-term arrangement. When she'd finished, she printed out two copies that she signed and dated with two distinct signatures using two different pens, a blue one for her, a black one for her imaginary landlord, whom she somehow envisioned as having tiny, precise handwriting. Then she paused to admire her work. To Karen's eye, it was an impressive piece of forgery. Whether she dared to share it with the outside world was another matter. Thankfully, she didn't have to decide just then. She slid the document into a manila envelope along with the stolen bill and a copy of Ruby's birth certificate, then placed the envelope in her handbag.

It was now well past midnight. Karen knew she ought to go to bed. But she was too stimulated by visions of the future that her deception had rendered feasible. She pictured Maeve and Ruby jumping rope together in the schoolyard of Mather, their pigtails flying, then in a sunny classroom filled with well-behaved, majority-white children from similar backgrounds, all of them sitting crisscross-applesauce-style as they read classics of children's literature like *Charlotte's Web* and *Stuart Little,* and none of them twerking, punching, or calling out. But the movie kept getting interrupted. Karen's conscience wasn't the only obstacle. There were logistical issues as well; how would Karen explain to the school administrators why her utility bill was not in her name? And what if they demanded secondary proof of residence?

Also, what if Karen and Nathaniel Bordwell turned out to

be connected in ways that she didn't yet realize? Karen opened Facebook and typed his name into the search box. To her surprise, nothing came up. But a subsequent Google search revealed a person with his name participating in a half marathon to raise money for paraplegia and motor-neuron disease research. Assuming it was the same Nathaniel Bordwell, it had the effect of rendering him a real person and, what's more, a person who, like Karen, was trying to do good in the world, a person whom she could potentially relate to. It also made her want to know more—if he was young or old (probably not that old if he'd recently run a half marathon) and whether he preferred lakes or oceans, blondes or brunettes, sweet or savory breakfasts. And were his cholesterol numbers low or high? His parents still alive?

More urgently, how would Karen account for Ruby's midyear school switch when she ran into the Betts mothers at the supermarket? She could pretend that her family had moved. But what if they should find out she'd done no such thing? For that matter, how would she explain Ruby's sudden appearance at Mather to Evan and Laura? Would it sound farfetched to say that Ruby had gotten a safety transfer there too? Karen also worried about what kind of message she'd be sending her daughter by lying about where they lived—unless, of course, she lied to Ruby too. But she couldn't lie to Matt. And Karen knew without having to ask him that he'd disapprove. But then, wasn't it a mother's job to do the very best she could by her children? Wasn't that her primary mission on this earth? And Edward G. Mather Elementary was widely regarded as a *great school.*

At two in the morning, Karen climbed into bed, threw an arm around Matt's middle, and pressed her breasts against his back. Her frustration with him of a few hours earlier had morphed into fear of his contempt. But it seemed to Karen that her husband could be ethical to a fault: What good was probity when everyone else was lying through their teeth? Karen recalled the Israeli mother down the street who had conveniently split up with her husband just in time for him to secure a lease in the Mather school district—and for their daughter to begin kindergarten there. Yet a few months later, when Karen had run into her in a nearby toy shop, Irit had been visibly pregnant. "Wow! Congratulations!" Karen had said, confused.

"Thank you," Irit had answered in her staccato English. "We decided to have a second after all." She smiled.

"Oh, right," said Karen, doubting that Irit's husband had ever moved out in the first place. At the time, Karen had been just short of scandalized.

It turned out she was no better.

That night, Karen dreamed she was attempting to enroll Ruby at Mather, except she'd left the necessary documents at home and then, when she'd retraced her steps and retrieved them, she couldn't find a pencil, then couldn't find the door to the administrative office—kept opening the wrong one, walking in circles... She woke up, consulted the clock, found it was still the middle of the night, and fell asleep again, only to have another version of the same dream twenty minutes later. It must have happened six times. When Karen's alarm finally went off in the morning, she felt leaden with exhaustion. Armed with the rationale that Ruby would likely be changing schools in a matter of days anyway, she allowed herself to press the Off button and went back to sleep.

It was Ruby who woke her the next time. "Mommy! Get up!" she cried. "It's the realistic-fiction celebration. And it's five after eight." Ruby was already dressed, putting Karen to shame. Matt was still asleep, just like he always was.

"I'm *so* sorry, sweetie," mumbled Karen, lurching toward the kitchen. "Mommy didn't sleep very well last night." She dressed as quickly as she could.

When she and Ruby finally opened the door to the classroom, the celebration appeared to be well under way, if not almost over. Lou looked over with a raised eyebrow and a half smile, which Karen responded to with a sheepish grin. She could have sworn that Miss Tammy, noting her and Ruby's late arrival, shot her a dirty look, but maybe Karen was projecting. In any case, Miss Tammy appeared to be deep in conversation with Michelle on the other side of the room.

The children's stories were laid out on the tables where they regularly sat, which were really just bunches of metal desks pushed together. Next to the stories were Comments sheets and No. 2 pencils. Parents were supposed to walk around the classroom, read the children's stories, and write encouraging words about them. "Come see mine first," said Ruby. To Karen's relief, Ruby led her to a table at the opposite end of the room from where Michelle and Tammy were standing. Karen put on her glasses and began to read.

Ruby's story was about a girl who goes to a sleepover party and can't sleep because the mom is snoring in the next room. The girl gets so tired of the sound of the mom snoring that she puts a pillow over the mom's face, accidentally killing her. Karen found it vaguely disturbing. Did Ruby entertain violent thoughts of smothering her friends' parents? Her own parents? Or was it just a story? Maybe Karen was reading too much into it, just like she seemed to read too much into everything. "Did you like it?" Ruby asked in an excited tone.

"You'll have to read my comment," said Karen. Then she wrote, *Nice job, but are you trying to send me a message?! Love, Mommy* on the accompanying sheet. Concerned that Ruby would be offended, Karen was busy drawing a smiley face next to her comment when she realized that Jayyden was standing diagonally behind her. "Oh, hey, Jayyden," she said, flinching ever so slightly as she whipped around to greet him.

"Hey, Ruby's mom," he mumbled.

He was wearing a plaid shirt and jeans. His cheeks looked fuller than she remembered. And the race-car design that had been shaved into his hair had already started to grow out; now it just looked patchy. Was Karen really taking Ruby out of Betts on account of this…child?

As usual, it was clear that no one in Jayyden's family had shown up for the celebration. With a swirling brew of sympathy, trepidation, and—if it was possible—preemptive nostalgia, Karen asked, "Which one is your story?"

"That one," he said, pointing to a sheet of lined paper next to Ruby's.

"Oh, cool," said Karen, lifting it up.

The story was only one page long and featured poor grammar and spelling. But in its own way, it was well paced and kept the reader wanting to know more. Or maybe it was just that Karen could never hear enough about how the other half lived. Jayyden's story was about a boy who gets into a fistfight on the playground with another boy because of a misunderstanding; one gives the other a black eye, but they eventually become friends. By the end of the story, the two are close enough to call each other the n-word, have their own special handshake, and share a pizza together at the park. In the narrative, Karen found both confirmation of Jayyden's disposition toward violence and a challenge to her assumption that he was beyond redemption. There was one comment on the Comments sheet—*Good job,* signed *Jasleen's mom.* Seeking to inspire the author, not patronize him—or, God forbid, antagonize him—Karen wrote: *Very well-told story! I felt like I was there. I'm glad Aquille and DeShawn make up in the end. I wish I could hear more about what happens to them. You're a talented writer. Ruby's mom.* Then she set her pencil back down on the table and glanced over at the author. Jayyden looked at her inquisitively. Or was it suspiciously? Or maybe he wasn't seeing her at all. "Cool story!" Karen told him.

"Thanks," he said. But he didn't immediately pick up the Comments sheet to see what she'd written.

Karen moved on to the next story at the table, which was by April Fishbach's son, Ezra. It was called "The Story of Cheese," and it was about a boy who gets mad at his mom at the food co-op they belong to because she won't buy him his favorite kind of "fedda"; his mom explains that armies from the country where the cheese is made are occupying another country and killing innocent people, so they have to buy cheese from somewhere else. *Very realistic,* Karen wrote. She was tempted to add, *I could see your mom denying you nutrition for geopolitical reasons,* but refrained. April herself was standing only a few feet away, dinning in Mumia's dad's ear about a sit-down to protest police brutality that she was apparently organizing. Ralph was smiling but appeared skeptical.

Karen would have liked to read Chahrazad's story, but the girl's writing was tiny, and Karen needed stronger glasses. All she could make out was the title: "The Girl Who Didn't Want to Go Back to Yemen." So she skipped ahead to the last one at the table, which had been written by Empriss. At first glance, the story appeared to be quite long. But after opening it, Karen discovered that Empriss had written only one sentence per page and that the book was mostly composed of illustrations done with a purple marker. It was called "The Present." On the cover Empriss had drawn a picture of a girl holding hands with a stick figure wearing sunglasses. The story was about a girl named E. who hadn't seen her dad since she was four years old. She asks her mom why her dad went away. But her mother won't say why. Then he shows up, and he has a present for her—a locket in the shape of a heart—and he tells her he loves her and he's sorry he had to go, but now he's back. On the last page of the story there was a disclaimer. Empriss had written: *If this sounds realistic, that's because, if I saw my dad, I'd be so happy too. I'd throw my arms around him and tell him I loved him. Because I only saw him once since I was four.*

Wow—powerful story, wrote Karen as an achy feeling enveloped her chest, and her eyes grew shiny with tears. Though whether or not her upset was due to Empriss's storytelling skills was hard to say.

"You okay?" said Lou, suddenly appearing at Karen's side.

"Oh, thanks. Just having a hard day," said Karen, dabbing her eyes with her knuckles.

"Hey, I'm here if you need me."

"Thank you—really," said Karen, spontaneously reaching over and hugging Lou even as she saw before her the limits of their friendship. Karen feared that, if Lou knew where she was headed later that morning, she'd judge Karen in the same way that Karen had once judged Laura Collier. Karen also doubted that Lou would still be hugging her. "I'm just losing it for no apparent reason," she went on. "Though I did have a horrible fight with my husband last night."

"Find me a couple who doesn't fight," said Lou. "I've never met any. Gunnar and I? We try to stick to physical violence only, especially when it involves dirty dishes left in the sink for ten straight hours while he's lying on the sofa playing Shadow of Mordor."

"Okay, that makes me feel better," said Karen, chuckling through her tears. "By the way, if you need a good laugh yourself, check out"—she leaned into Lou's ear—"you-know-who's son's story. It's a classic of the genre. Set in a food co-op, of course."

"Naturally," said Lou.

"Though if you're in the mood for heartbreak, that one will slay you." Karen discreetly pointed at Empriss's paper.

"Oh, yeah. I read that," said Lou. "I believe that genre is called So Realistic It's Actually Memoir."

"Exactly," said Karen.

"People screw up their kids so badly." Lou shook her head.

"I hope I'm not one of them," said Karen.

"Please," said Lou, making a wry face. "You mean by providing Ruby with too many after-school enrichment classes in one week?"

"Are you telling me I'm a horrible cliché?"

"The worst," said Lou, smiling.

Lou's words were still reverberating in Karen's head when, five minutes later, she said good-bye to her, then to Ruby, and headed back out of the building. At the corner of Cortland, rather than continue walking to the train station, she turned left—in the direction of Edward G. Mather Elementary.

* * *

The building itself was nothing much to look at: a low-lying white-brick structure dating back to the 1960s. But the landscaping was pristine. Clusters of purple and white early-spring crocuses decorated the flowerbeds. And there was nary a Skittles or Snickers wrapper in sight. What's more, the glass-enclosed bulletin board by the entrance featured an announcement for an upcoming wine tasting for parents. OUR BIGGEST SPRING FUND-RAISER! it read. Beneath the headline was a black-on-white ink drawing of a hand wrapped around an angled goblet, its elongated fingers adorned with cocktail rings. By comparison, the outdoor message board at Betts was caked in grime, splattered with bird shit, and still featured an announcement from the previous fall about registering for pre-K.

Also unlike at Ruby's current school, the security guard at Mather sat in the lobby directly facing the front doors, a fact that Karen noted with relief and approval as she walked into the building. "Excuse me, I'm here to register," she told the man.

"You'll have to speak up, ma'am," he answered.

Karen suddenly realized that she was whispering. "The main office?" she tried again, a little louder this time.

"It's down the hall to the left," he said. "Can I see some ID?"

Karen showed him her driver's license. Then she entered her name in the arrivals' log in an only partly decipherable script, reluctant to be recognized. What the two schools *did* seem to have in common, Karen noted on her way down the hall, was their art curricula. Just as at Betts, student-made tissue-paper collages decorated the walls. But to Karen's untrained eye, the ones at Mather were a little more sophisticated, the shapes positioned a little less haphazardly. Or was she projecting? Maybe they were exactly the same, the defining difference being the names inscribed on the bottom right-hand corners of the construction paper: *Daisy, Lincoln, Sadie, Gemma, Oliver*. You could imagine all of them a hundred years ago in their Sunday best, wearing hats and carrying handkerchiefs. There was not a Zaniyah or a Janiyah in sight.

"Can I help you?" asked an older white lady behind the front desk, the soufflé-like appearance of her frosted hair suggesting it had been set in a beauty parlor with an astronaut-helmet-style bubble dryer.

"Oh, hi!" said Karen, smiling and trying to sound casual. "We just moved to the neighborhood. I'm here to sign my daughter up for third grade. I hope I'm in the right place!"

"That's not for me to say," snapped the woman, immediately putting Karen on edge.

"Well, I *think* we're zoned for the school," Karen continued with a lighthearted laugh while her heart went pitter-patter. "Here's our lease, my daughter's birth certificate, and our gas and electric bill." She laid the documents on the counter.

"Fill this out first," said the woman, handing Karen a form that asked for her child's name, address, birth date, and other basic information and leaving the documents she'd brought lying unattended on the counter. Karen wished she could take them back. What if a parent should walk in and spot them—a parent like Nathaniel Bordwell?

"Of course," she said, reaching her hand into her bag for a pen, only to come up with nothing. "I'm *so* sorry," she went on while trying to quell the panic that was now seizing her throat—panic built partly of the fact that her dream from the previous night appeared to be coming true. How soon before the doors began to vanish, followed by the floor and the ceiling, until Karen was suspended in midair? "But is there any way I could borrow a pen?"

Looking mildly peeved, the Woman with the Frosted Hair handed over a ballpoint featuring the name of a local plumbing company.

"Thank you so much," said Karen, gripping the pen in her fist so tightly that after she'd finished filling out the required information (she listed her address as 321 Pendleton Street, no. 2), her hand ached.

Frosted Hair took the form from Karen, finally (to Karen's relief) scooped up the documents that Karen had left on the counter, and typed something into her desktop computer. Then she looked up and said, "Why is the name on the bill different from your family's name?"

Karen had predicted the question—and planned her answer. "I know, it's ridiculous," she replied with a conspiratorial roll of her eyes, as if they were all in this absurd charade known as urban life together. But the woman stared blankly back at her. "Our landlord likes to have all the bills in his name," Karen went on. "And then we pay him what we owe. Don't ask me why!" She laughed again, this time to hide her terror, while Frosted Hair reexamined her documentation, her head moving from side to side. Karen stood there, waiting. It might only have been for twenty seconds but to Karen, it felt like twenty minutes. Her entire future, as well as that of her daughter, seemed to hang in the balance of this stranger's mood—and whether she'd awoken that morning to the sound of birds chirping or an obnoxious car alarm.

Finally, without explanation, Frosted Hair ambled over to a copy machine, placed the document that Karen had filled out beneath its cover, and pressed START. Then she handed Karen a short stack of papers to sign, including one verifying that the information she'd provided was true under penalty of law. Refusing to ponder the implications of that threat, Karen signed them all in her best cursive and then pushed them toward the woman with a cheerful "Here you go! Oh, and here's your pen!" She laid the plumbing-company ballpoint on top of the documents she'd signed.

Frosted Hair slid the pile off the counter without a thank-you. Then she announced, "School starts at eight thirty. Your daughter can come tomorrow. I'll inform the principal today so she can make a class assignment."

"Great—thanks very much," chirped Karen, trying to sound upbeat but not so appreciative that her enthusiasm would seem suspect. After all, wasn't it her daughter's right to attend the public school that her family's home was zoned for?

"You're welcome," Frosted Hair muttered ungraciously before she turned her back.

Could that really be it? Karen wondered as she made her way out of the office, then back down the hall. She couldn't believe how easy it had all been.

She couldn't believe what she'd just done either. But when she pushed open the double doors to the street and an undulating ribbon of crystalline sunlight appeared over the clouds, it didn't seem like a coincidence. It seemed as if spring had been merely waiting for Karen to solicit it herself.

Almost giddy with relief and feeling newly energized, she lifted her face to the sun and let the rays warm her cheeks and lids. Then she headed up the block, past the Mather school-yard, where recess was now in progress. On the other side of the fence, ahead of where she walked, a group of girls about the same age as Ruby were drawing with sticks in the

dirt border around the blacktop and whispering conspiratori-
ally. Instead of the jeans, sweatshirts, and sneakers that Karen
had grown accustomed to seeing at Betts, they were wearing
puffer vests, patterned tights, corduroy minis, suede boots, and
sparkly headbands in their shiny blond and light brown bobs.
As Karen got closer, she realized that the blonde with the
longest stick was Maeve.

A whiff of hurt regarding the apparent ease with which her
daughter's onetime best friend had apparently found a new one
(or two, or three) momentarily ate into the relief that Karen had
experienced when she left the school building. But she pushed
the feeling away, telling herself that, for once, Maeve had done
nothing wrong. Besides, in due time, Ruby might be palling
around with the same gaggle. As Karen passed her, she lowered
her head so Maeve wouldn't recognize her.

In her peripheral vision, she couldn't help but note that
Maeve's nose looked *just fine*.

Karen had a busy day at work with meetings and conference
calls. HK was launching a new healthy-eating initiative for
young children, called What I Ate, which promised to simultaneously improve early writing skills and get kids to think
about what they were eating by having them keep daily food
logs. Which was exactly what Karen had done in her late
teens, at the height of her neurotic-eating years, registering the
calorie count in parentheses next to each food item she'd consumed. To her mind, it was a slippery slope from there to a
full-fledged eating disorder. But no matter. What I Ate was
the brainchild of HK's nutritionist, Cary Ann, and everyone
else at the organization, including Molly, was excited about it.

At six o'clock, Karen returned to Betts to pick up Ruby

from what Karen envisioned would be Ruby's final after-school session—and found her daughter in an unexpectedly and somewhat confusingly buoyant mood. "Mama Kajama!" cried Ruby, running into her mother's arms. It was one of their jokey phrases.

"Hi there, sweetie!" said Karen, kissing her head and weighing the possibility that Ruby was simply happy to see her and be heading home. "What do you say we get out of here?" She took Ruby's hand and led her away from the second-floor classroom in which she was supposedly learning the art of puppetry.

"What's for dinner?" said Ruby. "I'm starving."

"I'm not sure yet," said Karen, who secretly wished her daughter didn't enjoy eating as much as she seemed to.

In the stairwell that led down to the front entrance, Ruby and Karen encountered a young couple changing a newborn's diaper on the windowsill of the second-floor landing. The man was holding up the baby's dimpled legs while the mother wiped its rear. Karen felt vaguely repulsed. *Couldn't they have found a more secluded setting?* she thought. Then again, where were these people, who quite possibly lived far from the school, supposed to change their baby? There were no adults allowed in the girls' and boys' bathrooms. And in truth Karen had seen a couple doing the same thing in the open back of their Passat station wagon directly in front of the Bistro with No Name the weekend before.

"Hey, Ruby," came a voice.

"Hey," Ruby, who was farther down the staircase, answered flatly.

"What after-school class are you in?"

"Puppetry."

"I'm in karate."

"Oh."

Karen glanced down and saw Empriss leaning against the banister, one flight below, a lollipop in her mouth. It occurred to Karen suddenly that the baby-changers must have been Empriss's mother and stepfather. Guilt washed over Karen— not just that her daughter was being so unfriendly, but that Karen herself had been silently passing judgment on the way these people lived when their lives were so much harder than hers.

At the same time, Karen couldn't help but question why people in financial straits as dire as theirs were bringing more babies into the world. Or was Karen an awful person for even thinking that way? The desire to reproduce was biological, universal, and arguably irrational in all of us, and there was no reason to believe that the same fantasies and ambitions that inspired the rich to make tiny versions of themselves who promised to outlive them would fail to motivate the poor. And it was Matt who had pointed out one night that, far from poor children being a burden on any system, capitalism depended on them, insofar as it required an endless supply of future laborers. Besides, the only area of the labor market predicted to expand over the coming century was the service industry. Before he became a housing lawyer, Matt had been an assistant attorney for the hotel employees' union. "She's adorable," said Karen, trying to compensate for her daughter's standoffishness. "How old?"

"Three months," the mother said, smiling back.

"What's her name?" The baby had a giant pink bow on top of its bald head, so Karen assumed it was a girl.

"Kimora."

"What a beautiful name!" said Karen, who probably would have answered the same way even if the child had been called Adolf.

"Thank you."

"Well, have a good evening."

"Same to you," said the woman.

"You weren't very friendly," Karen groused to her daughter as they stepped outside.

"Mommy, Empriss is a bully!" said Ruby.

"Ruby, do you even *know* what bullying is?" said Karen, doubtful.

"Yes! We had an assembly and a workshop on it."

"Well, she seemed perfectly nice just then."

"That's because her mom was standing right there. She's always nice around grown-ups."

"Does this have to do with her being best friends with Mia now?"

"No! I don't care who she's friends with!" Ruby insisted. "And I'm not even friends with Mia anymore." This was not unwelcome news to Karen. "I just don't like Empriss. Okay?" Ruby went on.

"You don't have to be friends with her," said Karen. "But can't you be nice?"

"Why should I be nice? Yesterday she called me a tattletale just because I told Miss Tammy that she was hiding in the girls' room when we had a fire drill. And she's always saying I get in everyone's business and try to boss people around."

"Well, *do* you?" asked Karen.

"Mommmmm!" cried Ruby, clearly exasperated.

"Okay, okay." As Karen pulled back, she pondered Ruby's question: Why *was* it so important to Karen that her daughter make an effort with Empriss at the very moment when she was taking her daughter out of the girl's school? In all likelihood, they would never see each other again. Was Karen trying to reassure herself that Ruby's imminent departure from Betts had nothing to do with the school's inclusion of students like Empriss? And why was it so difficult for Karen to accept the idea that a girl who lived in a homeless shelter might also occasionally be obnoxious? To have faced extreme adversity didn't guarantee a winning personality or strong moral fiber—possibly just the opposite. "I believe you," said Karen. "I just—well, we've talked about it before. Empriss has a way harder life than you. I'm not excusing the way she acts. I just want you to remember that. In any case, you probably won't be seeing that much of Empriss in the future"—Karen figured she might as well tell her now—"because you're changing schools."

Ruby stopped walking. They were two blocks from home. *"What?"* she said, turning to her mother, her thin eyebrows lifted nearly to her hairline. "Why?"

"Because Mommy thinks you'll get a better education elsewhere," Karen said quickly.

Ruby looked stricken. "But where am I going?"

"To Mather, where Maeve goes now."

"But I'm not even friends with her anymore."

Karen suddenly regretted the abruptness with which she'd turned down Laura's playdate invitation a few weeks back. "Well, that's just because you haven't seen her for a while," she said. "You will be again, I'm sure. Besides, there will be a hundred new girls to be friends with there." Karen put her arm around her daughter.

But Ruby shrugged it off. "I'm not going," she announced.

"Sweetie," said Karen, trying to disguise her own alarm at Ruby's alarm. She hadn't expected so much resistance. "You were the one who told me a few days ago that school was too easy and that you weren't being challenged and also that you had no one to sit with at lunch."

"Well, it wasn't too easy today," she said. "And Amanda and I sit together at lunch."

"Amanda? Who was friends with Maeve?"

"Yes."

Karen was baffled. When had all this happened? "Well, we can discuss it at home, with Daddy, but to do that you need to keep walking." Karen was already thinking ahead to the far more agonizing task of telling Matt.

"Fine," said Ruby. "But I'm not leaving Betts."

But at least she was walking in the direction of home again.

Ordinarily, Karen was irritated when Matt got home after eight. But to her relief that evening, Ruby was already in bed when Karen heard the key in the lock—at a quarter to nine. Not that she was willing to acknowledge the relief. It seemed more important that she continue to keep score in the never-ending tennis match known as her marriage. "Where have *you* been?" was her opening question. Maybe it was aggressive, but wasn't his chronic lateness a form of aggression? Fifteen–love, Karen.

"Sorry, I got caught up in work stuff," he said. "And then Mike and I went to get something to eat."

"Right," said Karen, who suspected he was also trying to avoid her—and that he still hadn't forgiven her for pointing out who had put up the money for the down payment on their condo.

"How was your day?" he asked.

"Fine," she answered. Then she took a deep breath and said, "I registered Ruby at Mather."

"What?" said Matt.

"I enrolled her at Mather Elementary," Karen told him again. "She's going to start tomorrow."

"You signed Ruby up for a new school?"

"I'm sorry I didn't tell you earlier."

"Isn't that a zoned school?"

"I called over there, and they happened to have a space."

"And when did you do this?"

"This morning."

"Really? So, you just randomly called, and they said, 'Sure.'"

"Sort of."

"Or you lied to them," said Matt. "Just like you're lying to me right now."

"I'm telling you the truth," said Karen, apparently unconvincingly.

"But you told *them* that we live somewhere we don't," he countered. "Which is also why you didn't tell me until just now, because you knew I'd disapprove of you *breaking the law*. You also made the decision to transfer Ruby without me agreeing to it."

Matt was right, of course, but Karen still felt unfairly maligned. "Well, you weren't going to do anything about anything," she said. "So I took action myself. If that's a crime, so be it!"

"I matter, Karen," said Matt, taking a step closer and beating his chest with his fists, as if he were Tarzan calling for Jane. "My opinions matter. And Ruby is *our* child—not *your* child.

But you chose to make a unilateral decision concerning her without consulting me first."

Karen could no longer tell who was right—the voice in her head or the voice in her ears. In that moment all she knew was that the understanding that she and Matt were two like-minded souls wading through the muck had begun to falter. "Fine—you win," Karen told him. "We'll keep her at Betts through fifth grade, knife wounds and all."

Matt's eyes popped. "What knife wounds?"

Karen couldn't come up with an answer.

"You're really losing it," he said, shaking his head.

Was sanity slipping from Karen's grasp? Even if it was, she wasn't willing to concede—not just then, maybe never. "And you just want to be able to brag to all your friends that your daughter attends a minority-white school," she went on. "Isn't that what this is really about?" If Matt was going to hurl insults at her, Karen didn't see why she shouldn't do some flinging herself. Maybe her dirtiest secret of all was that she loved a good fight.

"How dare you," he said.

"Well, I see no other reason why you won't let me take her out of a school where, literally, her *safety* is endangered."

"Says who?"

"Says me," said Karen. "And I'm her mother." It was a last-resort argument, she knew. But she'd run out of better ones.

Falling momentarily silent, Matt narrowed his eyes at her.

Karen stared back, feeling angry and ashamed and also inexplicably blank toward the man she'd promised to love and cherish a decade ago.

Finally, he spoke. "You've changed," he began in a lower register. "What's happened to you?"

"Nothing's happened to me," she said.

"You used to care about the world."

But Karen was thinking something similar—that her husband had changed; that he used to care about her, and now he cared only about the people out there. "And you used to care about your family," she said.

"Karen, you're the one trying to write me *out* of this family," said Matt. "And to be honest, it's making me question our whole marriage."

"So, go ahead and question!" cried Karen, outwardly defiant but inwardly trembling—less at the prospect of losing Matt than at the thought of being alone. However unhappily, Karen's parents had managed to stay married for forty years, and Karen had always assumed she'd do the same. And if she wasn't particularly happy herself, she wasn't particularly *un*happy. Was that such a terrible thing to be? In truth, intimacy had never been her strongest suit. In a strange way, she was most comfortable near but apart from loved ones—say, working on her laptop in the bedroom while Ruby slept in the next room over and Matt watched basketball in the room next to that.

"Okay, I will," Matt went on, his face twisting into an unrecognizable mask. "What else are you lying about? Are you fucking someone else also?"

"Fuck you," said Karen, her heart now pounding.

"I've had enough," Matt said on his way out of the room. Though not before he'd shot Karen a look of absolute disgust. He hated her. At least, that was how it seemed. The realization was devastating, but also, in some way, fascinating. At moments of crisis, Karen had always had the strange ability to remove herself from the drama, as if it were happening on a stage and she was sitting in the back row of the theater, watching.

She and Matt went to sleep not speaking and on opposite sides of the bed. But as upset as Karen was about their fight, she was equally concerned about Ruby making a good impression on her first day at her new school. Mather was four blocks farther away than Betts, but their school day began ten minutes later, so Karen didn't technically need to reset the alarm. Just to be safe, though, she set it five minutes ahead.

When Karen woke up the next morning, dawn was just breaking. Against the still-dark walls, the light that filtered through the shades had the hazy quality of smoke from a campfire that hadn't quite burned itself out. It would probably be a beautiful day. Next to her but facing the other direction, Matt lay motionless and in a deep sleep. Pondering the randomness of marriage—how had this man of all the men in the world's population become her husband?—Karen tiptoed out of bed to go make coffee. An hour later, she went to wake Ruby and found her in an inexplicably compliant mood.

But forty minutes after that, when Karen took a right, not a left, on the corner of Cortland Avenue, Ruby accused Karen of lying, just as Matt had done the night before. "Sweetie, I never lied to you," Karen said shakily. "I told you that you were starting your new school this morning. You must have forgotten."

"You didn't tell me I was starting *today!*" said Ruby.

"Will you just do me this favor and try it for one day? If you don't like it, you can go back to Betts tomorrow." Just then, that false promise seemed like Karen's only hope.

"Fine," Ruby said contemptuously as she followed her mother down the block.

What Karen couldn't have guessed was how anxious she herself would feel on the way to Mather Elementary. Not only was she wary of seeing Betts parents on the street, who would wonder why she and Ruby were headed in the wrong direction, but she was fearful of running into Mather parents she knew from Elm Tree and the playground who would know where Karen's family *really* lived.

What she couldn't have predicted was that the most immediate threat would come from an absolute stranger. After waiting patiently for the light to change at the corner of Cortland and Donohue and for the red hand signal to turn into the outline of a walking man, Karen and Ruby stepped into the crosswalk. At the same moment, a thirty-something white male on a bicycle appeared out of nowhere and nearly mowed them both down. Jumping out of the way, Karen screamed, "Watch where you're going, you *fucking asshole!*"

While the biker lifted his left hand off the handlebars and extended his middle finger, Ruby muttered with apparent fascination, "Mommy, you just used two *really* bad words."

Karen felt ashamed of her behavior. What kind of example was she setting for her daughter? Even so, she couldn't stop herself from calling after him, "I hope you get hit by a bus!" Then she turned back to Ruby, her heart still in her throat, and said, "Sorry, sweetie—on special occasions, like when someone almost kills them, grown-ups are allowed to curse."

"But do you really hope that man dies?" asked Ruby.

"No," said Karen. "But there's nothing worse than bikers who believe they belong to a superior race because of their reduced carbon emissions."

Ruby looked at her mother like she was crazy and said, "Huh?"

"I mean, I don't hope he *dies,*" she said, "but I don't hope he has a good life either."

"Do you want me to have a good life?" asked Ruby. They had arrived at the other side of the street.

Karen drew her daughter near and kissed her forehead. "That's my greatest wish in the world," she said. And it was true. Wasn't that why she'd done everything she'd done—and did everything she did?

Five minutes later they arrived at the school and joined the throng of parents and children amassed in the courtyard outside the front entrance, saying their good-byes. Understandably apprehensive, Ruby came to a sudden stop. So did Karen. Her eyes traveling from left to right and back again, she scanned the crowd. To her amazement, there was not a single dark-skinned child in the mix. There wasn't a tan-skinned one either. There were hardly even any brunettes. It was as if Karen had fallen asleep and woken up in Norway. All around her were blonds—dark blonds, light blonds, strawberry blonds, and sandy blonds. Karen found the sight both disorienting and distressing.

Meanwhile, all the parents seemed to be going gray, owing to the fact that they all appeared to be Karen's age and in some cases even older. Yet they were dressed like teenagers. Despite their silver-flecked beards and soft stomachs, the dads wore holey jeans, faded T-shirts with stretched-out necks advertising colleges and film festivals, and navy-blue ski hats, even though it was now spring. And despite their crow's-feet and drooping backsides, the moms wore little-girl barrettes on their side-parted hair, embroidered Indian tunics with deep

Vs, white cotton jeans that ended at the calf, simple gold or silver jewelry, and clogs of all colors and varieties: high-heeled clogs, boot clogs, closed-heel clogs, open-heel clogs, platform clogs, and clogs with ankle straps. Karen had never seen so many wooden heels in her life. Moreover, the dress code maintained by the Mather parents was so casual as to suggest that few were keeping traditional office hours or reporting to any kind of boss, raising the question of who paid for the real estate that had won their children access to the school in the first place.

Karen also found herself bemused by a new poster that had been hung on the outdoor bulletin board. JOIN THE MULTICULTURAL COMMITTEE! it read. NEXT MEETING—APRIL 17.

The sneaking if unwelcome thought occurred to Karen that when people said Mather was a great school, what they really meant was not that the teachers were so amazing or that the PTA was so strong or that the arts program was so extensive but that the housing in its catchment area was prohibitively expensive for poor minorities. It followed that an "up-and-coming" school—Karen had heard neighbors describe Betts this way—was one that was getting whiter but was still majority black and brown.

"We're *so* behind on the camp-sign-up front," Karen heard one Embroidered Tunic Mom say to another. "All we have Otis down for is, like, one week of Engineering Elves in July."

"I was going to get the Number Sixes," another voice cut in, "but I just felt like the Hasbeens were more forgiving around the toes. And the heel was, like, a tiny bit lower…"

And then a third: "Of course! Just have your nanny text our nanny."

Just then, from a few yards down the block, came a piercing

cry: "Winslow! You need to *slow down*. There are *other people* on the sidewalk." Karen looked up just as a short, wiry boy in a black helmet rode his Razor scooter directly into her ankle.

"Ow," she said, reaching down to rub it.

"Are you okay?" asked Ruby.

"I'm fine," said Karen, irritated by the failure of supervision that the collision implied.

Just then, a woman whom Karen presumed to be Winslow's mother appeared before her. She had her hair back in a pony-tail and no makeup on. "I'm *so* sorry," she said before turning to her son and saying, "Winslow, say you're sorry!"

"Sorry," the kid mumbled.

"I'm seriously *so* embarrassed," said the woman, turning back to Karen. Although she was now standing right in front of her, she continued to speak in an unnecessarily projected voice, as if other people might be interested in hearing what she was saying. "My son is, like, a *complete* maniac on that thing," she went on. "I can't even keep up with him."

"It's fine—really," said Karen. She tried to smile in appreci-ation of the apology. But she had the distinct impression that, for Winslow's mother, the child's speed and carelessness was meant to be understood as a metaphor for his fast learning, his quick wit, brash creativity, and intellectual chance-taking.

Or did the woman simply feel bad that her son had ridden into Karen?

"Watch where you're going next time," Ruby suddenly piped up. "You could have hurt my mom."

"Rubes, it's fine—really," said Karen, embarrassed and touched in equal parts. "It was an accident."

Just across the courtyard, Karen caught sight of a mother she'd briefly known when they both had kids at Elm Tree.

From what Karen recalled, the woman made baby slings out of vintage calicos and sold them on Etsy under the name of her older daughter (Clover). She was also visibly pregnant. Karen recalled that her younger daughter, who was Ruby's year, was named Ivy. Would her third child be called Pachysandra—or maybe just Ground Cover? As Karen followed the mob into the school building, she lowered her eyes to avoid having to say hello.

A minute later, Karen found herself back in Mather's main office. "She's in Ms. Millburn's class," said the woman with the frosted hair.

"Oh, terrific!" said Karen, as if Ms. Millburn's reputation preceded her.

"Third floor, room three-eleven."

The morning bell was ringing. Karen and Ruby returned to the hall. The crowd of arriving students and parents had begun to thin. As the two of them ascended the stairs to the third floor, Karen tried to silence their mutual anxiety with meaningless chatter. "Hm, I wonder if this is the right staircase. Well, I guess we'll soon find out! Wow, there are a lot of steps!" She rambled on, and on, while Ruby stared stonily ahead and said not a word. Finally, at the end of the hall, Karen located a door marked 311. Ruby took a step backward while Karen tentatively pushed it open, craned her neck into the resulting space, and said, "Excuse me?"

It was a classroom like any other public school's: crowded and colorful, with fluorescent lights attached to the ceiling, linoleum tiles on the floor, and a hodgepodge of lists, charts, maps, calendars, and inane inspirational posters pinned to the walls. One read TODAY IS A GREAT DAY TO LEARN SOMETHING NEW! But here the walls were freshly painted mint green, the children's chairs had gleaming chrome legs, the desks were not covered with the brown residue of partially peeled-off stickers, and there was a seemingly brand-new multicolor rug depicting the United States up near the whiteboard. The three-pronged cactus representing Arizona immediately called to Karen's mind a devil's pitchfork.

The only adult in the room—presumably Ms. Millburn—glanced over from where she was standing near the board. To Karen's amazement, she looked uncannily like Miss Tammy, only about five years into the future and with a ring on her fourth finger. "Can I help you?" she said.

"Sorry—my daughter is new," said Karen. "And we were told to come here."

The students, who until then had been busy putting their backpacks and coats away in the closet, turned to gawk.

With a grimace and a waggle of her large head, Ms. Millburn walked brusquely over to where Karen and, behind her, Ruby stood. "No one told me we were getting a new student," she said. It was unclear to whom the comment was addressed, but it struck Karen as unnecessarily harsh. Then again, there must have been thirty students in the class already, if not more, which meant that Ruby would be number thirty-something. No wonder the teacher didn't look pleased about the arrival of a new student, Karen thought guiltily. She also wondered if Ruby would be able to learn anything in such a large class. "Hello there," Ms. Millburn went on, sounding slightly more genial as she leaned her head around Karen and into the hallway to address Ruby, who was now hiding directly behind her mother. "What's your name?" she asked.

"Ruby," she replied in a barely audible voice.

"Why don't you come in," said Ms. Millburn.

"Go!" said Karen, attempting to pry her daughter's hand off her jacket sleeve.

But Ruby clung to her, wouldn't budge. As so often happened these days, Karen felt her frustration growing into franticness. It was Ms. Millburn who finally coaxed Ruby away. "Why don't you follow me, and I'll show you where to put your coat," she said, taking her hand and leading her into the classroom. Relieved, Karen ducked away.

As luck—or, really, the lack thereof—would have it, Karen nearly collided at the front entrance with Maeve and her father, Evan. Maeve looked predictably trendy in a leopard-print top with dolman sleeves and capri leggings. So did Evan in his black T-shirt with the mathematical symbol pi on it and black track pants with a white stripe down the side. Since Karen had last seen him, he'd grown a rectangular-shaped mustache that made him look the tiniest bit like Hitler. "Evan!" said Karen, hoping this encounter would go smoother than the others she'd had that morning.

"Hey—what are you doing here?" he said in his faux mellow drawl. Karen could never tell if he was stoned or just acting that way.

"Ruby just started here," Karen said simply. No apology, no explanation. It seemed like the safest approach. Besides, it wasn't as if Maeve's family lived in the right zone either.

But, then, why did Karen feel so uncomfortable and so out of place? Or would she always feel that way, wherever she went in life? "Oh—cool," he said. But he was looking at Karen—in her dowdy office separates—as if she were anything but.

"Ruby goes to Mather?" asked Maeve.

"This is her first day!" said Karen.

"Who does she have?"

"Ms. Millburn."

"I'm in Ms. Carter's class."

"Oh, too bad," said Karen, disappointed. "But can you do me a favor and find her at recess? She doesn't know anyone here."

"All right," said Maeve, with a distinct lack of enthusiasm that Karen pretended she hadn't detected.

"Well, it was nice to see you," said Evan. "But I'm actually running late. And so is Maeve. So we really should get a move on."

"Same here," said Karen, childishly wishing she'd been the first to express the need to flee.

As she walked back out into the brisk morning air, she made a mental note to e-mail Laura that night, before Laura started drawing her own conclusions.

In the first years of Karen and Matt's romance and then domestic partnership and even marriage, they'd spoken on the phone up to four times a day and e-mailed at least twice daily. But in recent years, entire weeks went by without either one of them trying to get in touch with the other one while they were at work. Familiarity was the most generous explanation. But on that day, anger and pride were clearly to blame for the silence.

It seemed only fair that Karen pick Ruby up from her first day at her new school. As such, she worked through lunch and slipped out shortly after. Which is to say, she fretted all morning and got nothing done. She had lunch at her desk. Then it was time to go. At five minutes to three, Karen found herself on the Mather playground surrounded by a mixture of Ski Hat Dads, Embroidered Tunic Moms, and slow-moving, middle-aged women mainly of Caribbean descent sporting gold teeth and pushing expensive strollers containing the baby brothers and sisters of the Mather students. To Karen's relief, she didn't recognize any of the parents or even nannies. Finally, the students from Ms. Millburn's class appeared. Ruby was last in line. "Ruby!" Karen cried and waved, an exaggerated smile plastered on her face.

Her expression grim, the child said nothing as she followed her mother out of the schoolyard and through the gate. But once on the street, she said, "Can we go home now?"

"Of course," said Karen, fearing the worst.

"In case you were wondering, I hated school," Ruby went on.

"Oh, sweetie, I'm sorry," said Karen, her heart heavy. "But the first day is always rough. Can you at least give it a week before you decide you don't want to go back?"

"You said I only had to go one day."

"How about two?"

Ruby didn't answer.

"Well, was the teacher nice at least?" asked Karen.

"She was way too strict," said Ruby, "and the kids were mean."

"Oh no."

"And I had no one to sit with at lunch."

"But that's because you don't know anyone yet. I'm sure you'll make friends by the end of the week. You're so good at that... Did you see Maeve?"

"She's not in my class."

"You didn't even see her at lunch or at recess?"

"She said hi. And then she ran away to play with her friends."

Karen took this last dispatch especially hard. "I promise it will get easier," she told her.

But how could she be sure?

When they got home, rather than insist Ruby do her homework first, Karen let her play on the iPad for an hour. She knew she was setting a bad precedent, but at that moment she needed an ally most of all. She heard the key in the lock at seven fifteen and, fearing a reprise of the night before, went into the bedroom to hide from her husband. *This is what our marriage has become,* she thought as she pressed her ear to the door.

Karen overheard Ruby addressing the same complaints to her father that she'd already addressed to Karen. But to her surprise, Matt didn't immediately say yes when Ruby asked him if she could return to Betts the next day. It was the way he referred to Karen that wounded her. "That's not a decision I can make alone," he said. "Your mother and I both have to agree to it." Karen appreciated the deference, but *your mother* rather than just *Mommy,* or even *Mom?* To Karen, it was reminiscent of the way divorced parents spoke about their former spouses to their children. Was that where this was headed? Was that where Matt *wanted* things to be headed?

Angry and hurt, Karen lifted her cell phone off her bed and idly scrolled through her messages. She'd never replied to Clay's dinner invitation from the week before. But maybe there was still time, she thought. And it was just dinner— it was just one night in a long life. And she could always back out at the last minute. She could tell Matt she had a work event. Though considering they were barely speaking, it might not even be necessary to come up with an excuse. *Sorry for the delay. Problems on the home front...Sounds fun—time?*

Location? Karen typed, then stood staring at what she'd written, daring herself to catapult it across the length of the city and into Clay's pocket in far less time than it took to blink. Both the immediacy and the intimacy of digital communications still astounded her when she stopped to think about it.

But she couldn't do it, wouldn't let herself. Karen knew that, far from making dinner plans with another man, this was the time to turn to her husband, apologize for having angered him, and promise to mend her ways in the future. Then she remembered the look on Matt's face when he'd walked out of the room the night before. It seemed suddenly possible that he'd never loved her, never would...

After Karen pressed Send, her heart broke into a gallop.

Not even thirty seconds later, a response appeared on the screen of her phone: *I thought you'd never write back.* The text was followed by another one listing the name and address of an Italian restaurant that Karen had never heard of. There was a third message after that: *How's 7:30 tomorrow night sweet special k?*

She felt as if oxygen was suddenly in short supply, causing her heart to pump harder and faster, while her head threatened to float up to the ceiling. Did Clay really find her *special?* And if so, why did she care as much as she did? *See u there sweet c,* Karen found herself writing back and then pressing Send.

xoxo, Clay wrote back, causing her whole body to tremble.

For Karen, the exchange, as brief as it was, had all the mesmerizing power of a dark secret whispered in the ear of one schoolgirl by another.

But immediately afterward, the practical and efficient side of her returned. Thinking ahead, she texted Ashley to see if she could stay late the next day. (She could.) So when Karen and Matt walked by each other in the hall a few minutes later, she told him only "Ashley is sitting tomorrow night—I have dinner plans."

"Fine," he said, his voice ice-cold approaching cryogenic.

"If you get home before me, please pay her."

"How much am I supposed to pay her?"

"However long she stays times her hourly rate."

"What's our hourly rate again?"

"How can you not know that?"

"Can you just *tell* me her hourly rate?"

"Forget it, I'll pay her myself."

"Fine."

Ever more convinced of Matt's failure to do his fair share on the domestic front—even as she secretly preferred to do most of it herself—Karen returned to her computer and began typing a new e-mail.

Hey, Laura, I don't know if Evan told you that we ran into each other this morning, but Ruby just started at Mather! Yes, it's true. (Long story, not unrelated to yours.) Anyway, I wanted to see if we could make a plan for the girls for one day after school next week? Sadly, I don't think they're in the same class. But I'm hoping/assuming they will get to see each other at recess, lunch, etc.... Anyway, let me know your and M's schedule when you have a chance. Our old sitter, Ashley the Queen of Nail Art, is back to Monday, Wednesday, and Thursday pickups, and I know she'd be happy to bring Maeve home with Ruby any of those days for a playdate. I also know R would love to hang with M! Hope all is well on your end. Karen

Laura's response arrived only five minutes later:

Wow, I had no idea Ruby had transferred. That's so unexpected. I thought you guys were so committed to the whole diversity thing...Anyway, it would be nice to get the girls together. But to be honest, Maeve is totally overscheduled right now, with Mathnasium on Mondays, Beyblades on Tuesdays, hip-hop on Wednesdays, rock climbing on Thursdays, and coding on Fridays. And weekends are kind of reserved for family time these days because Evan and I have been so slammed with work. But I'm sure the girls will get a chance to hang at school, and hopefully you and I will see each other one of these weeks too. Best, LC

Karen knew she shouldn't have been surprised that Laura's response, its superficially congenial tone notwithstanding, amounted to a wholesale rejection. After all, Karen had done the same to her the month before. But she *was* surprised. She also felt unexpectedly wounded that Laura apparently no longer wished for Maeve and Ruby's friendship to go on at their new school—at least that seemed to be the subtext of her e-mail. Since there were a hundred other third-graders at Mather who looked like Maeve, Karen told herself it was no great loss.

If only she could have believed it.

How Karen got Ruby to school the next morning—in a downpour, no less—was a long story. But it involved the promise of unlimited screen time for a set period of days, as well as certain chemically enhanced and teeth-rotting sweets that Karen normally disapproved of and Ruby naturally loved. Several times during the negotiations, the compromises seemed too steep, and Karen was prepared to walk away and return Ruby to Betts and the status quo that seemed to satisfy everyone but herself. But by some miracle, the two of them made it inside Mather before the second bell had rung.

Five minutes after that, Karen was outside again, alone on the street with her umbrella and bags, walking toward the train station and contemplating an entire day and night with neither angry daughter nor angry husband telling her what she'd done wrong. Karen knew she should have felt relieved. And she did. But she also found herself apprehensive and on edge, as if an earthquake had been recorded out at sea, and a tsunami was predicted to make landfall that evening, but the exact location was still unclear. In the meantime, all was still and serene. The rain had tapered off, and the streets seemed unusually empty of traffic. In search of reassurance that she wouldn't be among those swept away by the deluge, Karen found herself dialing Troy. Not the type to judge, he was also the only one of her friends who'd met Clay.

"Is everything okay?" he asked, sounding alarmed.

"Why?" said Karen.

"I can't believe you called me. Who uses the telephone anymore?"

Karen laughed. "Fair point. I guess everything isn't okay."

"I charge two twenty-five an hour."

"I'll pay you back in sugarless gum."

"Fine—go ahead."

"My husband wants to divorce me because I enrolled Ruby at a new school without telling him, and I'm having dinner with Clay Phipps tonight and it has nothing to do with fundraising."

"Hmmmm," said Troy. "Well, make sure you order the most expensive bottle of wine on the menu. I'm thinking a Château Lafite-Rothschild Bordeaux from the early nineties."

"You're no help," said Karen.

"Kar—if you were raised by the Witnesses, you'd understand that Jehovah generously and willingly forgives even serious sins if you have a properly repentant attitude."

"But what if I'm not a Jehovah's Witness?"

"Then you're screwed. Speaking of getting screwed."

"We're just having dinner!" cried Karen.

But were they? And what did Clay understand that Karen didn't?

At 7:28 that evening, she found herself in a funky, old-school Italian restaurant. There were red-and-white-gingham vinyl tablecloths on all the tables and vintage black-and-white photos of famous boxers on the walls. Clay was already seated at the bar, drinking what appeared to be an orange juice on ice and staring at his phone. Excited but nervous, Karen approached and said, "Hey."

Clay looked up and, at the sight of her, smiled and said, "Hey, what's up?"

But he didn't immediately rise from his stool or tell her how happy he was to see her or how beautiful she looked. Which surprised and further unnerved Karen, who was left to lean over, kiss him hello on the cheek, and say, "Not a lot," then stand there awkwardly, shifting her weight from one foot to the other, not sure if she should sit down or, if so, where. The whole exchange was so informal that, for a brief moment, Karen wondered if she'd invented their entire flirtation. But after she collected herself, Clay's nonchalance, by taking the pressure off whatever would follow, came as a relief.

"Sorry," he said, glancing at his phone one more time before he grabbed a salted peanut from a complimentary bowl and popped it in his mouth. "This jackass who works for me lost us a lot of money today."

"How?" said Karen, taking a seat on the stool next to his.

"The model he was using blew up."

"Should I flatter myself by thinking I would actually understand if you tried to explain?"

Clay laughed. "I wouldn't bother. But the guy should have known better."

"Can I ask you another question?"

"Sure."

"Does *anyone* understand what you do for a living?"

"Not really. Sometimes not even me. But let's not talk about work. It's too depressing."

"I can pretty much guarantee that how I spend my days is eleven times more depressing than how you spend yours," said Karen.

"Fair enough. What can I get you to drink?"

"I don't know—surprise me."

"One Bill Cosby Special coming right up. Waiter!" Clay motioned for the man behind the bar.

"You're a terrible person," Karen said, chuckling and punching Clay's arm.

"Ow," he said, grinning back.

"Also, did I ever tell you that you basically lost me my biggest donor at the benefit that night? They e-mailed the next morning to say they were switching allegiances to our main rival. All that time you and I were dancing to those cheesy songs from the eighties, I could have been chatting them up."

"Yeah, but admit it, you had more fun than you've had in a year shaking your booty to 'Footloose,'" said Clay.

How did he know? "Maybe I did," Karen said coyly, "and maybe I didn't."

"Besides, you have me on board now, and—you never know—I might pony up a few more rubles at Christmastime."

"I can't wait," she said, reaching for a peanut herself. Under ordinary circumstances, the blatant mixing of business and pleasure that Clay was engaging in would have discomfited Karen. But somehow—maybe because the circumstances weren't ordinary, or maybe because the pleasure was so immediate—it didn't. Or maybe it was that his fortune was so large that it rendered money, even if he'd lost a little bit of it today, almost beside the point.

Just then, Clay took Karen's hand in his own, leaned forward slightly, gazed at her intently, and said, "Me neither—how about we get out of here?"

"And go where?" said Karen, taken aback. Hadn't they just arrived?

"I have a room booked at the Mandarin Oriental and a car waiting out front. Sorry if that's presumptuous." He smiled sheepishly.

"Excuse me?" cried Karen, laughing again and pulling her hand away, because it was all so sudden and suddenly so real. And what kind of fool reaches middle age and still thinks her fantasies will come true? "We haven't even had dinner," she told him.

"We can eat later—or order room service," said Clay. "Come on. Say yes. What do you have to lose?"

"My marriage, for one thing!" answered Karen.

"Mark will never find out."

"It's Matt."

"Matt. Whatever. Don't you ever just want to escape your life for a few hours—or is your life pure, unfettered joy?"

"At the moment, it's pure hell."

"Funny—so is mine. But we can pretend we're happy. We can get in bed and watch sitcoms. You don't even have to kiss me."

"I just have to sleep with you."

"Who said anything about sleeping?"

"I did," said Karen.

"Well, that's your problem, then," said Clay, shrugging, but not unkindly.

"And the fact that you're married too isn't an issue?"

Clay sighed as he reached for his drink. "The way I see it, we're both going to be dead soon anyway. What do we have left—thirty years, thirty-five, forty if we're lucky? Except maybe it wouldn't be *that* lucky. Have you ever met an eighty-five-year-old who's honestly enjoying his life? I haven't. And forget about ninety. Unless you think it's fun being slumped in a chair reminiscing about the good old days while slowly losing your mind. After that, welcome to the junkyard of human existence. Sure, after we're gone, our kids will cry for a few weeks and pretend to miss us. But they'll get over it—they always do—while the rest of the world will soon forget we were ever born, unless by some fluke one of us discovers the cure for cancer in the next ten years. Then again, can you name the guy who eradicated smallpox? Me neither. So, I guess my feeling is, why not grab a little happiness where you find it? Maybe that makes me an asshole, but that's kind of the position I've settled on at this point in my life. Have I had affairs? Yes. Have I had one recently? No. Do I find myself at this particular moment in time strangely besotted with you, Karen Kipple from College? Yes." Clay stared lustily at Karen. Then he lifted his highball glass off the bar and had a final chug, which made his Adam's apple bob up and down like a pinball in a machine. Setting the empty glass on the bar, he let out a contented "Ahhh" and added, "I love orange juice—one of the great inventions."

"Second only to the lightbulb," offered Karen, swallowing hard.

"Don't forget the drum machine."

Karen found herself grinning at Clay, who grinned back. Maybe he's right, she thought, and none of it matters—not the charity we believe ennobles us or the temptations we punish ourselves for succumbing to. We're all going to be gone soon anyway.

And Karen was flattered and aroused. And it seemed like her last chance to act like a drunken fool and be the object of someone's desire before she shriveled up and ceased to be the object of anything but pity. And as bad as her body looked now, it was bound to look worse in five years.

And maybe monogamy was nothing more than a middle-class convention.

And Karen had grown so tired of trying to be good all the time—once the Good Daughter and the Good Student; now the Good Mother, the Good Citizen, the Good Wife.

And since her husband had already accused her of being unfaithful, Karen felt somehow compelled to fulfill his paranoid prophecy and pay him back for always being mad at her. And if he never learned the truth, and if it was only this one time, would she still be hurting him? If a woman falls in a forest—or a five-star hotel room—and no one hears her moan, or at least no one but an acquaintance from college whom she hasn't seen in twenty-four years, does she still make a sound?

And although it went against all her closest-held convictions, Karen had to admit that Clay's phenomenal wealth was part of his appeal. It divorced him from the mundane concerns of everyday life—made him seem lofty by association, even if he was really only perched atop a mountain of paper. Indeed, Clay was so rich that he didn't have to worry about the things that other people, other couples, worried and fought about, like living in the right school district or running up too large a bill at Gap Kids.

While in Clay's company, Karen didn't feel as if she were being judged on whether or not she held the correct position either. In fact, he seemed completely uninterested in her politics, her values, her commitment to anything but the here and now.

Even so, doubt snuck in. "I just—" she began.

"You just *what?*" said Clay, again taking her hand and massaging it.

"I guess I just don't understand why you...I mean, we don't even know each other anymore. Not that we ever really did."

"Speak for yourself, Kipple. In case you never noticed, I had a total thing for you in college."

"For *me?* I thought you were in love with Lydia."

"Well, that was where you were wrong."

Was he telling the truth? Did it even matter? For once, Karen was in the moment, and the moment beckoned. "Well, how about you order me a non-laced-with-anything, non–Bill Cosby glass of wine," Karen told him, "and I'll see how I feel after I drink it?"

"At your service," said Clay, flagging down the bartender.

At some point soon after, their knees brushed against each other, their breath grew warm on each other's cheeks. Before long, Clay was whispering in her ear, whispering in a low voice, "I want to kiss you so badly right now," and then, "I want to be inside you."

By then, it was too late—too late for resolve, too late to ask Chahrazad's mom her name again...

At the hotel, they shared a bottle of 1996 Krug Clos d'Ambonnay—Karen made a mental note of the vintage so she could tell Troy—toasting their lack of a future as they drank. Then they watched an Animal Planet rerun of a show called *Puppy Bowl,* in which dogs played football. At some point after that, they fell backward. As their bodies came together, Karen felt as if the two of them were in a giant snow globe with sparkly silver bits swirling all around them, enveloping them in a dizzy dream. For as long as the sky kept falling, they lay safe inside, hidden from view, removed from time and space. "Karen Kipple," Clay kept whispering as he ran his hands down her, then pushed himself inside her until she couldn't see straight, couldn't tell the walls from the ceiling, or the ceiling from the floor. It was only after the last of the sparkly silver bits had settled, and she and Clay lay collapsed on the bed, that reality began to reassert itself. The image of Ruby's rosy cheeks springing to mind, Karen glanced at the clock on the bedside table, then bolted upright. "Shit— I have to go," she said, throwing her legs over the side of the bed.

"Why?" said Clay, his lids half closed as he reached out an arm to pull her back.

"Because," she said, sliding out from under him. She felt as if her mouth were filled with paste.

"Kiss me one more time."

She kissed him one more time, but her head was already elsewhere. A swirling mix of panic, satiety, shame, and delirium now filled it, propelling her homeward.

In the elevator down to the lobby, Karen closed her eyes and imagined the snow globe splitting and herself falling through the bottom. Down and down and down she fell until she reached the red-hot magma at the earth's core and was instantly burned into oblivion. But when the elevator doors opened, she found the ground still cold and firm beneath her feet and her flesh unscathed. She hurried through the lobby and exited onto the street, her eyes scanning the curb in search of a taxi. She found one idling in front of an Indian restaurant nearby and climbed in.

Karen arrived home to find Ashley sitting on the sofa watching the *Real Housewives of Somewhere-or-Other* without the sound. To her surprise and relief, there was no sign of Matt. "Hi! Sorry I'm late," she said, waving her arms around. "Dinner went on forever." When had she become such a good liar?

Or maybe she wasn't as good as she thought. "No problem," said Ashley, but she was looking at her employer funny. Did Karen look suspiciously disheveled? Or was she projecting? Maybe twenty-year-old Ashley couldn't have cared less where the geriatric mother of her evening charge had been. When Karen was Ashley's age, she'd barely noticed the existence of people over forty. They might as well have been furniture, which she also hadn't noticed. These days, when Karen walked into a room, the first thing she checked out was the decor.

The other difference between Karen at twenty-five and Karen at forty-five was that, in her youthful prime, she'd been dogged by self-consciousness. As a result, sex had felt more like a performance than a source of pleasure. She'd been close to thirty when she'd had her first real orgasm. And it had come as a revelation. But even then, it had seemed apart from her—a thing that happened to her rather than a thing she embodied. It was only now that Karen was in middle age, her hair silvering and the veins protruding behind her knees, that she found herself capable of feeling as if her entire being had been doused with gasoline in preparation for a match. It all seemed backward; wasn't sex for the young?

After Karen thanked Ashley for her service and sent her home with an extra-large wad of cash commensurate with Karen's guilt, she went to check on Ruby. She found her daughter lying on her side with her arms wrapped around her stuffed octopus, Octi. Her lips were parted, her lashes fluttering ever so slightly, her cheeks flushed. Lying there, Ruby looked like a picture of innocence. Karen wondered how soon she'd learn the truth about the world—not just about rape, murder, torture, and war, but about the ways in which people who claimed to love each other tore each other apart for no obvious reason. She also wondered if and when Ruby—not just Empriss—would begin writing "realistic fiction" about her fractured family.

Suddenly, Karen couldn't believe what she'd done or how she could have risked so much for the temporary cessation of an animal urge. Or did Karen and Clay's connection run deeper than biology? It had certainly felt that way. But then, Karen had never understood the concept of casual sex. It was never casual to her. In any event, Karen was determined to keep her infidelity a secret. After burying her soiled clothes in the bottom of the hamper, she stepped into a scalding shower and attempted to wash away every last trace of Clay. She was toweling off when she heard Matt come through the door. "Hey," she said, walking out in a robe and half expecting to be condemned on the spot.

But he didn't even look up. "Hey," he replied blankly as he went through the mail on the kitchen counter. "How was your dinner?"

"Fine," she answered. "What have you been up to?"

"Nothing much."

"Well, I'm going to sleep."

"Okay," he said. Apparently, he had no more questions.

As Karen walked out of the room, she realized that Matt suspected nothing. What's more, it was likely to stay that way unless Clay reached out to him, which seemed unlikely. The burden of her betrayal, she realized, fell on her. Cheating had proved so easy. Keeping it to herself would be the hard part. The desire to confess stood *right there,* like a meter reader waiting at the front door.

Entering her bedroom, Karen glimpsed a sheet of bubble wrap poking out from under her bed—evidence of her latest online purchase, whatever it had been. In truth, she could no longer remember. By the time one of her many purchases arrived, Karen often didn't even want whatever it was, or it failed to live up to her expectations, or it didn't look like it had in the picture, or she'd find herself focusing all her energy and regret on the unnecessary amount of packing materials that had been used or the amount of money she'd spent that she shouldn't have. Although she was capable of paying hundreds of dollars for a single-boiler espresso machine from Italy,

Karen had a deeply ingrained cheap streak as well, which caused her to do things like go to the library and photocopy the crossword puzzle from the Sunday paper rather than pay for a subscription.

Karen lifted the bubble wrap off the floor, then sat down on her bed and began systematically to squish, row by row by row, every last pocket of air, as if, with the eradication of oxygen from that particular sheet of plastic, she would finally gain control over herself and the world. For several minutes, she fell into a mental state where no cogent thoughts entered her head, only the sound of *pop-pop-pop*. While the feeling lasted, it was nearly as blissful as her time in the hotel with Clay had been. But when she finished and the sheet lay flat—and then so did Karen—she felt as if the planet were careening off its axis, spinning wildly toward the sun. It was Karen's impossible job to redirect its path before it crashed and burned. She went to the bathroom for a drink of water and an aspirin and came back. But the room kept spinning; the gods kept laughing. Matt didn't come to bed till two a.m. Karen pretended to be asleep.

It was just another lie.

But in the morning, there was a small gift awaiting Karen. To her shock, Ruby didn't complain about going to her new school. Mostly, she just seemed excited about seeing her mother again after a daylong absence. "Mommy Kajami!" she cried at the sight of Karen leaning over her bed.

"Hello, sweetheart—Mommy missed you so much yesterday," said Karen. Her heart flush with an emotion that fell between love and regret, she brushed the hair off Ruby's face.

"Me too," said Ruby.

And after arriving at school, she scurried down the hall

toward the staircase that led to her new classroom without further comment.

It was on Karen's way to work, just as she was approaching the entrance to the train station, that her luck ran out. Walking by at the same moment was Lou. Unable to deal with the disapproval and disappointment that Karen assumed Lou would experience after learning that Karen had taken Ruby out of Betts, Karen had more or less shut out all thoughts of her in the previous week. But there was no avoiding them now. "Lou!" said Karen, for a brief moment entertaining the idea that she could tell her about Clay instead.

"Hey, stranger," said Lou. "Long time no see."

"I know—"

"Off to the office?"

"Unfortunately, I am—what about you?"

"I'm going to the dentist, if you must know."

"I hope it's nothing bad."

"Just my lousy mouth with its many cavities."

"If it makes you feel any better, I have the same lousy mouth."

"I do feel better," said Lou. "But what's going on with Ruby? Zeke says she's been out all week. Everything okay?"

"Everything's fine," said Karen. "Well, it's actually not fine. My marriage is literally on death row."

"Whose isn't?" Lou said with a laugh.

Karen knew she couldn't keep up the banter indefinitely. "Lou, there's something I have to tell you," she began with a scrunched face. "I took Ruby out of Betts."

"You *what?*" cried Lou, her eyebrows up near her hairline.

"I just—" Whatever remorse Karen had felt the previous

night about sleeping with Clay was easily matched by the contrition she felt standing there. Maybe it was because her marital betrayal was an all-white affair, whereas her school betrayal contained a racial component.

"You just *what?*" she said again.

"I just got freaked out about Jayyden. That was part of it. He sort of made a threat against Ruby."

"What kind of threat?"

"He told her he was going to—*fuck with her.*"

Lou paused to grimace before she spoke. Then she said, "Perhaps you're unfamiliar with African American vernacular? *Fucking with someone* means you want to spend time with them."

"I didn't know that," said Karen, staring at her shoes.

"And where is Ruby now?" asked Lou.

Karen motioned behind her. "She's over there at"—Karen swallowed the final word of her sentence—"Mather."

"Ah, the school Maeve fled to," said Lou, reminding them both.

"Yes—except Maeve doesn't actually talk to Ruby anymore." But if Karen had thought she could enlist Lou's sympathies by telling her about how Ruby had been blown off by her former best friend, she was mistaken.

"I'm sorry to hear that," Lou said after a while. But she didn't sound sorry at all.

Karen couldn't very well blame her. The silence that followed was as thick as concrete, and it ended only when Karen told Lou, "I'm sorry too—about not telling you sooner."

"Well, I don't know what to say," said Lou. But she thought of one thing: "I guess I thought you were different from them."

Lou didn't have to explain who *them* were. The words were

like a fist through Karen's stomach. "I hope we can still be friends," she said helplessly.

"Sure, we can still be friends," said Lou. But in that moment, Karen saw that her and Lou's friendship, however richly textured, was ultimately one of association. With Betts out of the picture, they no longer had enough in common. They were suddenly two women on a street, one with light skin and one with dark. Since Ruby had decided boys had cooties, Karen didn't even have the excuse of their kids being close anymore. "Anyway, as I was saying, I have cavities to fill," Lou went on. But her tone had already changed; now it sounded distant and matter-of-fact.

"Of course," said Karen. "Bye, Lou."

"See you," said Lou. She didn't even say Karen's name.

As Karen walked away, she wondered if there was anyone in her life other than Ruby whom she wasn't in the process of alienating.

By chance, Troy had business in the office that morning. "Oh no," he said as he passed by her desk.

"How did you know?" she asked.

"One look at those liquid eyes and that quivering lower lip told me everything," he answered.

"Can I buy you a coffee?"

"Do I have a choice?"

"Not really."

"What do I do now?" Karen asked him in line at the Starbucks in the lobby. "Do I tell my husband?"

"If you want to be a single mother, yes," said Troy. "Otherwise, I advise keeping your mouth shut."

"But what if I can't stop thinking about him?"

"Write bad poetry and never show it to anyone. Or listen to Coldplay—that should cure you of feelings...The only thing that guy is good for in the long term is a fat donation to HK before the end of the tax year."

"Why are you always right?"

"Please. If I had all the answers, I wouldn't be having a fling with a man whose supposedly affectionate moniker for me is Fatso and who makes me feel bad about myself for not going to the gym every day."

"Troy, that sounds horrible! You have to get rid of the guy."

"Just as you must get rid of yours," he replied.

Karen resolved to do as Troy had said.

But breaking free of Clay became that much harder to conceive of after a bike messenger arrived at the office that afternoon with a package for her. Inside was a palm-size pale blue box containing a pair of diamond studs the size of shirt buttons. While there was no accompanying card, Karen didn't need one to know who they were from. For a few moments, she sat staring at the earrings and reveling in their scintillating splendor, which made her feel brilliant and desirable by association—and even more desirous of Clay. (The most recent piece of jewelry that Matt had bought her was her wedding ring, a simple gold band that owed its existence to a small-scale mining cooperative in central Peru.) At the same time, she couldn't get past the notion that the earrings were, in some sense, payment for sex, which in turn made her feel like a prostitute. Disgusted with both herself and Clay, Karen closed the box and stuck it in the top drawer of her desk behind a three-pack of Post-it notes.

And that evening, gathering courage, she made a first attempt at repairing her marriage. "I'm sorry I didn't ask your opinion before I enrolled Ruby at Mather," she told Matt. "It was wrong of me."

"Thank you for your apology," he replied.

While hardly effusive, Matt's response seemed like a positive indicator. And for a brief window that evening, Karen allowed herself to be encouraged about her chances for a peaceful old age. But when a message came in from Clay at eleven, just as she was climbing into bed, her heart thumped with such ferocity that she thought it might come catapulting out of her body. He'd written:

Already missing the puppies—and you. Animal Planet redo next week, same time? Xoxo—p.s. Forgot to ask if you had pierced ears...

For several seconds, Karen stood frozen and with her fingers poised over the screen of her phone. Every part of her wanted to write back, *Me too, and yes.* She felt so aroused, but also embarrassed to feel that way. Lust was such a crude emotion—so primal and unsophisticated, really. So selfish too—not unlike Clay. It was true that he wrote checks for good causes. But what social value was there in taking high-risk bets on obscure financial products? Matt, by contrast, might have been unromantic, but he was also impressive. And he was committed to improving the lives of others, not just improving the bottom lines of his already fabulously wealthy clients. Besides, there was no evidence that Clay was prepared to make any changes to his personal life. Though even if he was, Karen couldn't see herself as the second wife of a billionaire, ordering around the staff. She felt guilty even asking Ashley to load the dishwasher. If Karen left Matt, it would be just her and Ruby, their voices echoing through the apartment. Before Karen had a chance to change her mind, she wrote back:

Wish I could, but I can't. Hope you understand...
Thank you for the beautiful earrings—they will always remind me of you (and the puppies). Karen

Then she proceeded to check her phone every two minutes for the next half hour to see if Clay would write back. He didn't.

When Karen checked again in the morning, there was still no response. To her disappointment, he seemed to have understood only too well—and fallen silent. Then she felt as lonely and invisible as a speck of debris floating in outer space.

The following night, Karen received her first group e-mail as a Mather parent. It was from the Gladiola Street Block Association, and it bore the alarming headline *Urgent—All Mather Parents, Please Read.* Admittedly, there was a certain frisson in finding herself among the lucky few who'd played the game well enough to be receiving such an e-mail. But the feeling quickly gave way to something more uncomfortable. The e-mail read:

Dear Mather Parents:

As residents of the neighborhood, we want to make you aware of a project that will have a significant impact on your school community. The Department of Corrections (DOC) is opening a parole center on Gladiola Street, just three blocks from your school. The DOC made the decision to combine two existing facilities into one location, which will service all six thousand parolees in the city. The center is scheduled to start operations early next year.

While those of us who live on the block recognize the important role that the DOC plays in the city, we feel that the location of a parole center in our neighborhood is unjustified. First, the lack of public-transportation options near the proposed site means that parolees will be a constant presence on our streets, potentially impacting both the surrounding retail landscape and the quality of life enjoyed by neighborhood residents. Second, the existence of such a facility near an elementary school raises serious safety concerns.

If you share our concerns, please join us for a strategy meeting next Tuesday night. Details are below.

Thank you,
Gladiola Street Block Association Executive Board

Karen supposed you could argue that parolees, insofar as they were already mixed up with the criminal justice system, were inherently dangerous no matter their skin color. Conversely, you could protest that the criminal justice system was hopelessly racist and therefore indicative of nothing. Whatever the case, Karen suspected that, more than safety concerns, what the Gladiola Street Block Association really objected to was an influx of poor black and brown men into the neighborhood. But who was she to pass judgment when this was the very community she'd taken desperate and even duplicitous measures to become part of? After clicking Delete, she did her best to forget she'd ever read the e-mail.

She did her best to forget about Clay too. But it wasn't nearly as easy. At various intervals throughout the day, Karen imagined him pulling her toward him, bending her over, as she heard in her head the low murmurs he'd made while he was inside her. She'd lost her appetite too. Even so, she kept cooking, kept trying to impose order and regimen on the chaos. But the hole in her heart wouldn't stop oozing raw matter or insisting on body over mind. On Friday night, while preparing dinner for Ruby, Karen nearly gagged at the sight and feel of raw chicken breasts in her hands, as slippery as they were dense. She pictured a row of bulbous white maggots crawling along the skin.

But dinner brought relief as well. Seated across from her, Ruby told Karen about a girl in her class named Lulu who was in love with Justin Bieber, then about another girl named Charlotte who had given Ruby an extremely desirable Shopkin called Milly Mushroom in exchange for Ruby's D'lish Donut. It seemed that Ruby was actually starting to make friends at Mather. Karen could have wept with relief.

And later that evening, Ruby received her first playdate invitation from a certain susanb8@gmail.com:

Hi, Karen. I got your e-mail from Ms. Millburn. Would your daughter, Ruby, like to come over for a playdate with my daughter, Charlotte, one day after school next week? Tuesdays and Thursdays are best. We live right near the school. I can pick her up and take her home with Charlotte. Let me know when you have a chance. All best, Susan

Karen immediately wrote back.

Susan, thanks so much for writing! I'm sure Ruby would love to have a playdate with Charlotte. Next Tuesday is perfect for

*us. I will let Ms. Millburn know that you are bringing home
both girls. What time should I or my sitter pick Ruby up from
your house, and what is your address? Thanks and regards,
Karen*

Susan replied.

How's five o'clock? We're at 321 Pendleton. See you then!

At first reading, *321 Pendleton* failed to register with Karen
as anything more than an address. A split second later, to her
horror and fascination, she realized it was Nathaniel Bordwell's address. *That* Nathaniel Bordwell. Which meant that
Charlotte was most likely Nathaniel's daughter (or grand-
daughter) and Susan his wife (or daughter, or daughter-in-
law). What were the chances of Ruby befriending the one
child in a school of seven hundred whom Karen would have
wished her to stay away from? She supposed the odds were
one in seven hundred. But now that Ruby had beaten them,
what was she supposed to do?

Karen knew it would be prudent for her to write back and
say she'd forgotten about a prior engagement and needed to
reschedule and then fail to do so—and hope that, in the in-
tervening weeks, the two girls lost interest in each other. But
the truth was that it also pained her to have to contemplate
canceling. She'd been so tickled on Ruby's behalf to receive
the invitation, which had somehow confirmed for Karen that
she'd made the right decision in taking her daughter out of
Betts. (What mother doesn't want her child to be popular and
have lots of friends?) Plus, Karen knew Ruby would be tickled
too. And what were the chances that the Bordwells would go

to the school administrative office and discover that the address that Ruby's family had registered her with at Mather was, in fact, their own? Moreover, if the discrepancy between Ruby's real and fake addresses should ever come to light, Karen could always claim it was a mistake on the part of the school.

"Guess what—your new friend Charlotte invited you on a playdate!" Karen couldn't resist telling Ruby that evening.

"Really?" said Ruby.

"Really."

"Yay! I wonder if her mom will let us play Minecraft. Charlotte loves Minecraft so much she's going to be an Enderman for Halloween. She already has her costume picked out."

"Wow—that far in advance?" said Karen, who had lost the ability to differentiate between her daughter's excitement and her own.

Hungry Kids was such a small organization that, at times, everyone's job bled into everyone else's. Because of this, Molly had asked Karen to coordinate an Easter Sunday feast and egg hunt at a soup kitchen run out of a Baptist church that was practically in Karen's backyard—or, really, the backyard of the Fairview Gardens public housing project.

Karen's first decision as organizer was to fill the plastic eggs that the children would hunt for with tiny boxes of raisins rather than the usual milk chocolate morsels in colored tinfoil. In the back of her mind, she worried that the switch was a patronizing and Scrooge-like gesture, akin to the no-candy e-mail that Laura Collier had sent out to her daughter's class the autumn before. But then, part of Hungry Kids' mission was to encourage healthy eating habits in a population at high risk for diabetes. Ever keen to instill a sense of social responsibility in her only child, Karen had decided to bring Ruby along to the event, explaining that they'd be "serving a fancy lunch to people who can't afford to do anything fancy."

"I have to serve?" cried Ruby. "I'm just a kid!"

"You don't have to serve," said Karen. "But maybe you can help carry a few things to the table. Is that too much to ask?"

"But what if they're heavy?"

"Then you don't have to carry them," said Karen, sighing. "You just have to be nice. Okay?"

"Fine."

"Plus, there's going to be an Easter egg hunt."

"Really?" Ruby sounded suddenly more enthusiastic.

"Yes," said Karen, who didn't have the heart to tell her about the raisins, not least because Ruby had always detested them. Secretly, so did Karen.

On the Sunday in question, Karen woke inexplicably late to find a cold rain beating on the windows. Distressed, she reminded herself that the feast was scheduled to take place in the church's basement, not outside, and that the Easter egg hunt was easily moved into the church proper. There were plenty of hiding opportunities in the pews. Keen to keep up morale, Karen texted these sentiments to her two-person volunteer corps, who were due to arrive at the church in advance of her and set up. Then she went to make breakfast.

Ruby was in the living room Netflixing a salacious tween sitcom that, in all likelihood, she'd been watching for an hour already. It was one of the mysteries of the universe why her daughter, who struggled to wake up for school, voluntarily woke at dawn on weekend mornings, seemingly fresh and rested. The situation with her husband wasn't all that different: Matt had a standing Sunday-morning basketball game that he was religious about attending, but during the week he seemed unable to get out of bed before ten. Was it unfair to expect consistency in others?

"Sweetie," Karen announced at quarter to eleven, "it's time to get dressed for the Easter lunch. Now."

"Can I just watch the end of the show?" asked Ruby. "There's only five more minutes." There were always five more minutes.

"I'd really rather you turned off the TV," said Karen. "You've been watching for almost three hours already, because Mommy was being Bad Mommy and felt like doing her own thing this morning."

"Pretty pleeeease?" moaned Ruby.

"Fine, but only if you promise to get dressed up," said Karen, who, when it came to parenting, didn't see any harm in bargaining.

"I promise," said Ruby, who not only honored her pledge but who felt compelled to try on every dress in her closet, the majority of which she'd outgrown two years before.

By the time Ruby and Karen got out the door—Ruby in a purple-flowered sundress that wouldn't zip all the way up— they were not just late but horribly so. Karen was on the verge of a panic attack. Still, it seemed crazy to drive to the church and then have to look for parking when it was only four blocks away. So the two of them set out on foot and, at Karen's directive, never stopped moving, not even when there was a red light or vehicles in their path. Karen knew that by crossing against the lights, she was taking risks. But despite being a nonbeliever, she childishly imagined that no God would allow her and Ruby to perish while en route to a church basement to deliver Easter lunch to the poor.

Karen had passed by the church probably twenty times in the past ten years, but until that morning she'd never taken a good look at it. On closer inspection, it was a boxy and charmless affair, its beige brick façade interrupted only by two sliver windows that seemed designed to keep *out* the sun. A large black metal cross hung over a set of steel double doors. Next to the doors, a white nylon banner announced THE FIRST BAPTIST CHURCH OF CHRIST ALMIGHTY and implored congregants to FOLLOW CHRIST'S WORD. Someone had incongruously draped a pair of Air Jordans with the laces tied together over the rusted chain-link fence that separated the front yard from the sidewalk. On one side of the fence was crabgrass. On the other was a concrete sidewalk that had been broken and distended by the roots of a nearby ginkgo tree. Karen pulled open the door to the church, Ruby's hand in her free one, and found herself face to face with an elderly African American lady in a robin's egg–blue hat decorated with ribbons. The woman was sitting at a folding table covered with photocopied brochures. "Welcome to First Baptist," she said.

"Thank you!" said Karen. "I'm from Hungry Kids, and my daughter and I are here to help with the Easter luncheon."

"May the Lord bless you," said the lady, beaming. "And may the Lord bless your daughter."

"Oh, that's very kind," said Karen, smiling as broadly as she felt she could without seeming patronizing. "I hope we're not too late."

"They're just getting started, I believe."

"Fantastic! Where do I go?"

"Right that way," said the lady, pointing down a short staircase with frayed rubber treads.

"Thank you very much," said Karen. "And happy Easter!"

Did people wish each other a happy Easter? Or did that sound *weird*? Karen suddenly couldn't remember. By then, she was at the bottom of the stairs, gazing into a windowless room with brick walls painted a dirty shade of yellow and a half a dozen long metal tables covered with pale blue nylon cloths. On the far wall, a few citizen volunteers dished out beef and gravy, honey-glazed carrots, and potatoes au gratin from large metal vats. A line of about thirty-five, with an equal number of grown-ups and children, stretched from the vats to the wall. Karen was thanking the citizen volunteers for their service and apologizing for being late when Ruby pointed at the far end of the food line and cried, "Look, Mommy! It's Jayyden!"

Karen looked up with a start and confirmed what her daughter had already discovered. A baseball hat casting a shadow over his already deep-set eyes, Jayyden stood surrounded by five other children ranging in age from four to fourteen. The lot of them, with their vastly different heights, formed a mini-skyline of their own. Behind the children was a very large woman with a somber expression. She was wearing sweatpants and shower shoes, and her hair was pulled back and enclosed in some kind of net. Was this Aunt Carla? As Karen connected the dots, she realized that her fear of Jayyden's potential for violence, however justifiable, was a cover for something deeper, more nefarious, and less easy to rationalize—namely, contempt for the version of poverty Jayyden's hodgepodge family embodied. *Poor blacks.* That was how Karen's mother had referred to people like them. The two words had been inseparable and almost interchangeable to her, possibly because Ruth Kipple didn't really know any middle- or upper-class African Americans, but also because it had been an easy way of dismissing an entire subset of society that she didn't understand—a way that Karen herself had not entirely escaped. That was clear to her now as never before, and she cringed in recognition.

Nor had the irony of the present situation escaped her. Here she'd gone to near-criminal lengths to get Ruby away from the boy, only to voluntarily bring them together on Easter morning to teach Ruby about social responsibility. "What a funny coincidence," murmured Karen—really, to herself—as she watched her daughter walk over and say, "Hey, Jayyden."

"Hey, Ruby," she heard him reply in a neutral voice. "How come you don't come to school no more?" If he was embarrassed to be there, waiting in line with his aunt for a free meal in a church basement, he didn't show it.

"I go to a new school," Ruby told him.

"Why'd you leave ours?"

"My mom wanted me to."

"Oh."

"What are you guys doing in math?" was Ruby's next question.

"I don't know." He shrugged. "Just stuff. Like fractions."

"Oh. At my new school, we're doing multiplication."

Just then, Jayyden's baby cousin fell onto his bottom and began crying. Not untenderly, Jayyden turned around, picked him up, and dusted him off—and for the moment lost interest in Ruby.

But the two joined forces a half an hour later for the egg hunt. Karen watched as Ruby and Jayyden playfully tussled over a purple plastic one that had been hidden under the church pews. In the end, it was Ruby who claimed it. But after she separated the two halves and discovered the raisins inside, she made a face and handed the reassembled egg back to Jayy-den, who opened it and popped a raisin in his mouth. And hadn't that been Karen's goal all along—to get poor children to eat fruit and vegetables? It was true that Ruby's dentist had recommended staying off the dried versions. Even so, Karen hadn't stopped believing that raisins were nutritionally superior to Milky Ways.

"Mommy, why were there raisins in the Easter eggs?" was Ruby's first question on their way home.

"Because they're healthier than candy," Karen told her.

"So the Easter Bunny wants poor people to be healthier?"

Karen had forgotten about the Easter Bunny. "Something like that," she said, already uncomfortable with where the conversation was going.

"But then, why do other people get chocolate? The Easter Bunny doesn't care if rich kids eat healthy?"

"I think he wants everyone to be healthy. But a little chocolate isn't that bad," Karen said unsteadily.

"Mommy, can I ask another question?" asked Ruby.

"Of course!"

"Why did all the people getting free food have dark skin? And also, the people you see on the street who are asking for money, they always have dark skin too."

"Well, that's a complicated question," said Karen, struggling to come up with an explanation that would be intelligible to an eight-year-old. "You see, in the olden days, even after slavery was outlawed, people with white skin wouldn't give people with dark skin jobs or let them buy houses or, in some places, even let them vote. So, even though things are a little better now, thanks to Martin Luther King and others, a lot of people with dark skin are still very poor, because they don't inherit anything. And it's hard to join the middle class when you start off with nothing."

"What does *inherit* mean?"

"It means that when someone dies, they leave you money."

"Like Grandma and Grandpa left us money?"

"Exactly."

"But the president has dark skin."

"Yes, but that's the first time a president ever has."

"I have one more question."

"What's that?"

"Why does everyone at my new school have light skin?"

"That's a complicated question too," said Karen. "Unfortunately, most schools are very *segregated*. That means that they are all one kind of people or all the other."

"But Betts wasn't like that," Ruby pointed out.

"No, it wasn't, that's true," said Karen, who could do nothing but agree.

And then there was Clay. Now that she'd asked him to go away, and it appeared that he had, Karen couldn't stop wishing he'd get back in touch. She couldn't stop dreaming of their next encounter either, even as she regretted the one they'd already had and forbade herself from initiating a new meeting. Karen's emotions were so confusing to her—his silence felt like another death in the family—and also so consuming that they left little room for thinking about how she could improve her marriage.

And yet, confoundingly, Matt didn't seem entirely unhappy with their current marital détente. Karen had always suspected that he had intimacy problems that were as bad if not worse than her own. Now she wondered if their fight had given him an excuse to further retreat into himself and indulge his antisocial tendencies. On those rare occasions when they were at home together and interacting, he'd answer Karen's questions monosyllabically, a blank expression on his face, after which point the two of them would retreat back to their respective electronic devices. Or was she projecting? Maybe Matt was as discontented with the status quo as Karen currently was.

On Monday morning, while eating a croissant at her desk—every now and then, Karen couldn't help herself and indulged in refined flour—she happened on an article in a local newspaper about the Winners Circle charter school chain's co-location in Betts Elementary. According to the article, which described the co-location as "controversial," parents there were protesting on the grounds that it would deprive general-education students of their music studio and special-ed kids of their physical therapy room. In paragraph three, it was noted that Winners Circle had the backing of many prominent figures in finance, especially in the hedge-fund world, including Clayton Phipps III. At the sight of his name, spelled out in all its establishmentarian glory, Karen found herself startled and disoriented. It seemed almost impossible that the person she was reading about should be the same one she spent her days and nights dreaming about—and she quickly closed the article, telling herself that neither Clay nor Betts qualified as her problem anymore.

For the rest of the day at work, Karen comforted herself with visions of Ruby and Charlotte Bordwell on their playdate. She imagined them sitting on a floral wool area rug, in shades of hot pink and celery, playing Connect4 or making fishtail braids on Charlotte's extensive collection of American

Girl dolls. She also e-mailed Ms. Millburn to tell her that Charlotte's mother, Susan, not Ashley, would be picking Ruby up from school. As for retrieving Ruby from Susan's house after the playdate was over, Karen had decided to do so herself. It seemed safer that way. What if Ashley accidentally revealed where Karen lived? Plus, it hardly seemed worth Ashley's time for her to arrive so late in the day. And what if this was Karen's one chance to meet her unwitting patron saint?

When Karen hadn't been paying attention, the weather had grown positively balmy. As she exited the train station late that afternoon, a fluttery breeze blew the hair off her face and tickled her nose. For a brief moment, life offered itself up not as a cauldron of conflict but as a delightful comedy of manners, its myriad intrigues to be reveled in rather than reviled. But the sight of the same private banker/art dealer whom Karen had crossed paths with the night she'd stolen Nathaniel Bordwell's utility bill interrupted the reverie. Somehow, he seemed at least partly to blame for everything that had happened. If only he'd smiled back, maybe she wouldn't have sought love and validation elsewhere, Karen thought. As before, the man had a cigarette between his lips and a phone tucked between his shoulder and his cheek. In the daylight, he looked more dissolute than distinguished. This time, as he drew near, she glowered. It was unclear if he noticed.

Turning onto Pendleton, she found the cherry trees just past blooming season. Even so, or maybe because of it, the streetscape had never looked so magical. The sidewalk blanketed in tiny pink petals, it resembled a real-life Candy Land or the end of a wedding reception after the confetti had been tossed over the happy couple.

When Karen arrived at the Bordwells' stately brick manse,

she paused to collect herself and take in her surroundings. Someone had filled the flower boxes beneath the second-floor windows with silken pansies, only adding to the aura of genteel charm. Karen took a deep breath, opened the gate, and started up the short path that led to the Bordwells' forest-green front door. Standing before it, she found no doorbell, only a brass knocker with a lion's head at the top. The lion had its mouth opened, as if in a silent roar. Karen could relate. She knocked twice and waited.

Soon, a trim but large-boned white woman of probably forty or forty-two, wearing black stretchy pants that flared at the ankle and a pristine white tank top, her dirty-blond hair pulled back in a ponytail, appeared in the portico. She was far from beautiful, but she had bright eyes and perfect teeth. "Welcome!" she said. "You must be Ruby's mom."

"Yes! Hi! I'm Karen," she said, putting out her hand.

"And I'm Susan," said the woman. "It's nice to meet you. Please—come in."

"Thank you," said Karen, following her into a high-ceilinged living room that, while fashionably minimalist in its way, had an unfurnished quality that surprised her. There was no coffee table in front of the sofa and no rug on the floor. Even more incongruous, considering that Susan clearly liked to exercise, there was what appeared to be an elevator in back. To Karen's disappointment, there was also no sign of anyone named Nathaniel, and Karen didn't feel right about asking who or where he was. "And thanks also for picking up Ruby," she went on.

"It was my pleasure!" said Susan. "The girls had a great time."

"I'm so glad," said Karen.

"Not that I was even allowed in Char's room. Every time I went to check on them, she told me to go away."

"Oh no!"

"Can I take your coat?"

"That's okay," said Karen, raising her palm. "We should probably get going."

"Well, the girls are still sequestered upstairs." Susan walked over to a white-painted staircase with a glossy black banister and a navy-blue wool runner that appeared to be in need of vacuuming and called up it, "Charlotte! Ruby's mom is here." There was no immediate answer, but that didn't prevent Susan Bordwell from turning back to Karen. "So, I understand Ruby is new to Mather," she said.

"It's true!" Karen told her in as airy a tone as she could manage. "Ruby just started a few weeks ago."

"Did you just move to the neighborhood?" asked Susan, head cocked.

Karen could have guessed that the question was coming. Even so, its articulation made her wince. "Well, not really—it's kind of a long story," she answered with a flourish of her hand that she hoped would discourage the woman from asking her to elaborate. "We were at another school."

"Really?" said Susan. "Which one?"

"Betts," said Karen.

"Which one is that again?" asked Susan, squinting. "Truth be told, there are so many schools around here, I get confused."

Considering that the school was only four blocks away, the question astonished Karen. Was Betts so down-market that it didn't even register on the radar of Cortland Hill's professional class? "It's on Groveland, just off Magnolia?" she said.

"Oh, of course."

"One of her classmates transferred to Mather as well," offered Karen, hoping that a second example would make her *long complicated story* sound that much more legitimate—and even less interesting.

"Really?" said Susan.

"A girl named Maeve—also in third grade."

"That name sounds familiar."

There was a brief pause, during which time Karen prayed that Susan wasn't going to ask her what street her family lived on. Instead, to Karen's relief, she asked, "And do you—work outside the home?" For a certain subset of mothers, it was the preferred phrasing of what had become a delicate question. This way, went the thinking, even a woman who answered in the negative would have no need to get defensive, since her work *in the home* would already have been acknowledged.

"I do," Karen was happy to tell her and to change topics. "I actually work in the nonprofit sector, for a hunger-relief charity. Doing fund-raising. Or development, as it's known in the business."

Susan's eyes opened wider. "*Really?* How wonderful of you."

"It's just a job." Flattered despite herself, Karen laughed and shrugged. "What about you?"

She shook her head. "Stay-at-home mom for the moment! I used to be a corporate lawyer. But after my son, Xander, was born, I gave up. The hours were impossible."

"I'm sure," said Karen.

"So I just volunteer now."

"How great."

"And my husband, Nate, works from home." Karen's heart skipped a beat. "So we're basically the parents who are always around. I'm sure it drives our kids crazy!" She laughed lightly.

"Oh, I'm sure they secretly love it," said Karen, who, despite her raging curiosity, didn't feel it was polite to ask what Susan's husband, Nate, did for a living.

"I'm not sure about that!" said Susan. "Anyway, you probably don't know this, but I'm actually the president of the PTA this year."

"Oh—wow!" Karen said unhappily, dread flooding her chest at the thought that Susan Bordwell potentially had access to the school's administrative files.

"And on that note," Susan continued, "I hate to ask you this, because I'm sure you're as busy as the next working mother. But the school lost its longtime treasurer last June— her youngest child graduated from fifth grade. And she doubled as our fund-raising chair. So, of course, now I'm wondering if there's *any* chance you'd be willing to lend your expertise to the school. Even if it's just in the short term."

"Oh—my goodness—I'm flattered," said Karen, feeling trapped. She'd gone into charity work to help the disadvantaged, not the already thriving. Except at that moment, saying no seemed next to impossible. She already felt so indebted to the Bordwell family. And joining the Mather PTA seemed like the surest method of erasing any suggestion or suspicion of Karen's being an interloper. "Well, it's true I don't have much time. But I'd be happy to do what I can," she said. "I understand the school has been really successful at fund-raising in the past. Is that right?"

Susan smiled graciously. "Yes, well, we've been very fortunate in that way. In recent years, we've ranked in the top five public schools in the city in terms of fund-raising muscle. Of course, I'd like to see that rise to number one! But maybe that's unrealistic. All the *really big* money is across the river." She shrugged and smiled at the same time as if to say, *What can anyone do?* "But we do have one claim to fame—we're the only elementary school in the city whose PTA has financed its own organic rooftop garden."

"Wow, I didn't know that," said Karen, who hated gardening even more than she hated cooking.

Susan went on: "Unfortunately, some people in the neighborhood—even some people at the school—resent us for constantly hitting up the parents. But the way I see it, we really don't have a choice. Not only does the statehouse continue to cut the education budget every year, but the very poor schools—by which I mean the ones where most of the children are receiving free lunch—get a ton of money from the federal government under the Title One statute. I have no problem with that—at least, not in theory—except it leaves middle-class kids out in the cold. If our PTA didn't fund-raise, we'd be talking about a bare-bones operation with no arts education, no strings program, no fifth-grade overnight trip, no computers, no library even! We'd also have no assistants in our jam-packed kindergarten classrooms. And our rooftop garden would be a pipe dream.

"So, yes, we pay for a lot of extras. But if we want to provide our children with a well-rounded education, this is really the only way to do it. Besides, not all our families are wealthy. The maintenance and kitchen staffs send their kids here. That's ten families right there. And we also have families in the community who spend way more than they can afford on rent so they can send their kids to Mather, but who literally have three dollars at the end of the month for groceries."

Maybe they should stop shopping at Whole Foods, Karen was

tempted to cut in, but she refrained, instead opting for "Yikes, that's terrible."

But was it? Susan had made a convincing argument. Yet the idea that the middle-class children were actually the disadvantaged ones because the government showered all its resources on the poor didn't sit quite right with Karen. In her experience, the government wasn't all that generous. Besides, Karen could think of far worse things than middle-class kids whose families could afford after-school enrichment having to go without art or music class during the day. Then again, how would Karen have felt if it was *her* child who was denied the opportunity to make tissue-paper collages?

"It *is* terrible," said Susan. "But I understand it. Mather really is an amazing place. I mean, the kids are basically getting a private-school-quality education for free. Which is why I never feel bad about asking the parent body to contribute their fair due—"

Just then, a square-jawed girl with a light brown pageboy appeared at the top of the steps and yelled, "Ruby doesn't want to leave."

"Charlotte—it's not open to discussion," Susan said sternly. "Her mother is downstairs waiting."

Seconds later, Ruby appeared behind her new friend, sporting a full face of sloppily applied makeup, including a giant red pout that spilled out over her lips, lending her the appearance of a clown who'd joined a punk band. Karen was so relieved that the playdate had apparently gone well that she decided to ignore the makeover. "Hi, sweetie!" she said. "Can you get your shoes on?"

"Do I have to leave?" said Ruby.

"I'm afraid so," said Karen. "But Susan"—she turned back

to her hostess—"thank you again for having Ruby over. And I hope we can return the favor soon!" Karen realized as soon as she'd made the offer that she'd have to rescind it. If she invited Charlotte over to their house, then when Susan came to pick her up, she'd learn that Ruby and Karen didn't actually live in zone. Like other mothers in the neighborhood, Susan likely knew the rough parameters of her school district—or at least that it didn't extend as far west as Karen and Ruby lived.

"I'm sure Char would love that," said Susan.

"Just give us a few weeks," said Karen, thinking fast. "We're actually having some work done on our place right now."

"Oh! What are you doing?"

"Kitchen," said Karen.

"We're doing the kitchen over?" said Ruby, wrinkling her nose.

"Yes!" said Karen.

"Exciting!" said Susan. "We had ours redone two years ago. I never want to live through the dust again, but we're happy we did it now."

"I hear you. Anyway, we should really be leaving you people to get on with your evening," said Karen. She was suddenly desperate to escape before Susan started asking whether they'd considered Caesarstone as an alternative to honed Carrara, which stained so badly. And forget about red wine...Lifting her chin in the direction of the stairs, Karen called out, "Ruby, get down here right now!"

Five minutes after that, they were outside. "Did you have fun, sweetie?" asked Karen, trying to block out the image of Clay pulling her onto the bed that had popped into her head. It happened at random points during the day. The sex drive was so incompatible with daily life, Karen had found—especially family life...

"So much fun," said Ruby. "Charlotte is my best friend."

"That's great," said Karen. Though, of course, it wasn't great at all. "But I'm sure you have *other* friends at school too."

"No," said Ruby, shaking her head. "Just Charlotte."

Lies were also complications, Karen was learning. At work, Joy wanted to know if Clay Phipps might consider joining HK's board of directors and would Karen please find out. Karen promised to inquire. But that meant getting back in touch with him, and she'd promised herself that she'd keep her distance. Meanwhile, the desire to come clean about both her affair and her address had become a drumbeat in Karen's head. Scrolling through her contacts in search of a confidante, she was struck by the number of old friends she'd fallen out of touch with. Karen suspected that location was partly to blame. After marriage and children, Karen's friends, in search of family-size apartments and houses, had spread out—some to other neighborhoods, a few to the suburbs, others to different cities and states and even countries. Money was surely another culprit. In middle age, one's status on the socioeconomic ladder became both more apparent and more fixed. It followed that those who had substantially more or less than you did became harder to relate to—though not impossible, if Karen's friendship with Allison was any indication.

In fact, it was Allison whom Karen ended up texting that afternoon to see if she was free to meet up for an emergency drink after work. For once, Allison's ignorance about the public-school system played in her favor in Karen's mind. Karen figured that, in failing to fully grasp the stark divide that separated neighboring public schools, Allison might be more forgiving of Karen's first transgression. Allison was far more likely to raise her eyebrows at Karen's fling with Clay Phipps—not only because Allison had always been fond of Matt, but because Clay managed a hedge fund. And Karen had always made a show of being the one friend in Allison's privileged world who was true to her ideals.

Whether on account of being a good friend or a voracious gossip, Allison wrote back immediately to say she was free and willing. The two made plans to meet up at a wine bar halfway between their two offices. Karen arrived first and, pretending to have a special fondness for pinot blanc, ordered a ten-dollar glass of it—only because it was the cheapest thing on the menu. Allison showed up ten minutes after that and ordered a fifteen-dollar glass of Sancerre. "You know I love an emergency," she began. "Tell all." She pulled up her chair.

At least she's honest, Karen thought. She closed her eyes and said, "I've made a complete mess out of my life."

"What kind of mess?" asked Allison.

Karen began with Jayyden, then moved on to the stolen utility bill and Ruby's school switch, followed by her daughter's coincidental friendship with Charlotte Bordwell, whose mother now wanted her to help fund-raise. Along the way, she mentioned Matt's undying fury at her. Only at the end did she take a deep breath and say, "Also, I cheated on my husband and can't stop thinking about the other guy even though he's a ridiculous kajillionaire, and I'm even more ridiculous for liking him. That's basically the situation."

Allison's eyes grew large, then larger. Finally, she spoke: "Holy Pan-Seared Mackerel in a Shallot Butter Sauce."

"So, what do I do?" asked Karen. "About the school stuff—first."

"Switch to private?" asked Allison.

Was she being serious? Or was Allison getting back at Karen for having implied she was a hypocrite the last time they met up? "I can't afford it on a single nonprofit salary," Karen replied. "And besides, you know I'm a public-school Nazi." She smiled so Allison would understand the joke was on her.

Allison smiled back and said, "Okay, if I solve your school problem for you, will you tell me who you're having an affair with so I can be scandalized and also live vicariously through you?"

"Oh, please—you and David have a great marriage," said Karen, without really knowing. In truth, Allison barely ever mentioned the guy. For women of Karen and Allison's age, the husbands became conversation-worthy again only when one of them walked out or—God forbid—had a heart attack or got cancer.

"We do?" said Allison.

"Well, even if you don't, I don't recommend my life to anyone. But will you tell me what to do about the address thing?"

"Is there any chance of this woman finding out that you stole her address?"

"Not much."

"Then forget about it."

"That's it?"

"If possible, I'd avoid the whole topic of where you live. But if it ever comes up or the girl comes over, just say you recently moved."

"Okay, but the woman also asked me if I'd fund-raise for the school, the very thought of which makes me want to jump off a bridge. The school is already rolling in dough—I mean, at least by public-school standards. But I feel so guilty around her that I don't know how to say no."

"So don't. Consider it the price of admission. Besides, you can probably fund-raise with one eye closed. If you don't mind me saying so, it seems like you have bigger problems. And on that note, *please* for the love of Christ stop torturing me and tell me who you slept with!"

"I'm too ashamed," said Karen, and it was true, but it was only half the truth. The other half was that she found herself savoring the unique experience of having information that others coveted. "But I will," she added.

"When?" asked Allison.

"Later."

"Why don't you just waterboard me."

"Oh, stop," said Karen, but now she was laughing and, just maybe, enjoying herself. "Order me another drink and maybe I'll tell all."

Allison ordered them another round. "It was the hedge-fund billionaire from college," Karen suddenly blurted out.

"The one who didn't like your nose ring?"

"Yes. And he has four kids and a wife. And a plane. Or at least a share in a plane. But I ended it. I think. I hope. Though I also *don't* hope. Oh, and he also bought me jewelry. Like, real jewelry."

"Wow."

"I have to swear you to secrecy," said Karen, knowing full well that Allison would tell everyone she knew.

"I swear," said Allison. "Now I need details."

"Well, he has these sparkly blue eyes. He's a little on the short side..."

The problem was that talking about Clay only made Karen more desperate to see him.

The next evening, Karen received an e-mail from Susan Bordwell, reiterating what a pleasure it had been to have Ruby over to play. She also asked if, by chance, Karen could attend a PTA executive board the next morning so she could meet everyone and talk about fund-raising and what was next for the school. The meeting was to be held in the school library at seven thirty, so Karen couldn't very well use the excuse of needing to be in the office. Resigned, she wrote back:

Of course! Happy to attend. See you then. Best, Karen

The next day, Karen had the thankless task of trying to get Ruby out of bed a half an hour earlier than usual. Predictably comatose, she lay spread-eagled and with her eyes still shut while Karen tried to fit leggings and a T-shirt onto her body. In exchange for the hardship, she promised to buy Ruby a chocolate croissant on the way to school. But there was a line at the fancy bakery with the fermented bread, so Karen didn't arrive at Mather's school library until seven forty. "Sorry I'm late," she said. Head bowed, she took a seat in the last free Windsor chair at a blond-wood table while Ruby plopped down in a beanbag chair and began to doze off.

"Karen! Welcome!" said Susan, who sat at the head of the table. She was dressed that morning in a slightly more corporate version of the Indian-top-and-frayed-jeans uniform favored by so many of the mothers at Mather—the jeans stiff, the embellished tunic more Tory Burch than Ravi Shankar. Karen's eyes traveled from Susan to the library itself. The walls were painted lime green. The shelves were well stocked and tidily arranged, with banker-style brass sconces illuminating the volumes below. There were also two rows of spanking-white Apple computers, while spanking-white women—and they were all women and all white except for one who was equally pale but who appeared to be of Asian descent—smiled back at her from across the table. "Let me introduce you to everyone," Susan went on. She turned to the others. "Karen is a new parent at the school, and she's a fund-raising professional. And I've already guilted her into helping us!" The other women laughed affably while Karen marveled at the irony; if only Susan knew how guilty she'd actually made Karen feel. "First, this is Denise, our vice president," Susan continued with a nod at a petite woman wearing a mustard-and-brown chain-link-patterned dress of the type that sported a fair-trade label promising the garment had been hand-batiked in Ghana by women named Charity and Esther.

"Nice to meet you," said Karen, nodding.

"And this is Amy, our volunteer coordinator," Susan went on. "And Deirdre, our member-at-large; Liz, our secretary and interim treasurer; Leigh, our chair of the after-school enrichment program; Kim, our fifth-grade committee chair; Janine, our STEM chair; and Meredith, chair of our arts committee."

"Great to meet you all," she said, nodding some more.

"Let me give you a copy of today's agenda, and here are the minutes from our last meeting." Susan handed Karen a short stack of white paper. "But before we get to fund-raising"— she turned back to the others—"I want to say a few words about the Olive Oil Initiative, especially for those who missed last month's general PTA meeting. By all accounts, it's been a huge success so far. Thanks to PTA funds, the lunchroom now has on reserve two thousand bottles of cold-pressed, extra-virgin Trader Giotto. And our new Culinary Institute of America–trained cooking consultant, Olivier, is busy teaching the old lunchroom staff to cook without Crisco."

There were murmurs of approval.

"Though let me just say that, from what I understand, it's been a fairly steep learning curve." Susan smiled knowingly.

Quiet laughter followed.

"Now, moving on to other topics—I want to propose that we dedicate some emergency funds for lice prevention. This has been a very bad spring for it. I would go so far as to call it a full-scale crisis. And I'd really like to bring in a lice expert to do a presentation about prevention and removal. I'd also like to earmark some PTA money for purchasing some of those large, heavy-duty, self-sealing plastic bags for all of our classrooms so students can place their personal effects inside them before storing in their cubbies or the coat closet. Is this something the rest of you can get behind?"

"Sounds like a great idea to me," said Leigh, the after-school chair. "The situation is *really* out of control in Harper's class."

"Same deal in Hudson's," said Janine, who headed up STEM.

"Well, I'm sorry to rain on everyone's parade," began Denise, the vice president, with a pained expression on her face. "But I just have to say—I feel really uncomfortable directing PTA money to the plastics industry. I mean, do we as a school really want to support them? And do we even have proof that plastic bags prevent lice contagion?"

"Denise, as much as I sympathize with what you're saying," said Susan, "the lice specialist I spoke with said they were *essential* for preventing student-to-student transmission. And I think that's enough to go on. But if others share Denise's concern, please speak up."

No one spoke. But Denise wasn't ready to let it go. "Well, I just think it's a little hypocritical of us to be launching our fourth-grade green-and-healthy newsletter—never mind our school-lunch recycling campaign and our new food-justice committee—at the same moment we're sending money to the Ziploc people."

"Okay, but Denise"—Karen could tell Susan was getting the tiniest bit impatient—"we're literally talking about seven hundred bags. It's not like we're going to affect their business one way or the other or make a dent in our own budget."

"Fine." Denise pressed her lips together and grimaced. Then she opened them again. "It's just—I try really hard to raise my kids in a natural environment. And I just feel like this sends the exact wrong message. I mean, human beings have been getting lice since ancient times. I just don't see why we can't try an ancient cure before we resort to zip-lock bags."

"You mean like leeches?" cut in Liz, the secretary and interim treasurer.

There were snickers. Even Karen found herself suppressing a smile. But Denise remained unamused, shooting Liz a look of wounded fury.

"Ladies, please," said Susan, clearly the conciliator of the group. "If Denise feels that strongly, why don't we put the topic of plastic bags away till our next meeting. In the meantime, does everyone approve of bringing in the lice expert for a parent workshop on lice prevention and elimination? All who do, please raise their hands." Reluctantly, and just as the crown of her head began to itch—paranoia or contagion?—Karen lifted her right hand, as did the rest of the group. Even Denise could be seen halfheartedly raising her arm and opening her palm. "Okay, it's unanimous," said Susan. "Now, if anyone else would like to propose some additional spending priorities, please speak. I should add that, legally, and as weird as this might sound, we're actually *required* to spend eighty-six thousand before the end of the school year."

"Well, since we're on the topic of workshops, I'd love to see the school bring someone in to teach meditation," began Kim, the fifth-grade committee chair. "The upper-school kids are *so* stressed out about the upcoming state tests. I think it would really benefit them."

"Interesting idea," said Susan. "But forgive me for asking—aren't most of our fourth- and fifth-graders opting out of the state tests this year?"

"Well, yeah—some of them are," said Kim, sounding the tiniest bit defensive. "But even the ones who are opting out are freaking out about middle-school admissions."

"Tell me about it," said Meredith, chair of the arts committee. "I went on the Middle School for Innovative Inquiries tour last week, and there were literally nine hundred families there for, like, seventy-five spots. It's harder to get into these places than it is to get into Harvard!"

"Ladies, can we get back to business?" asked Susan, turning to the wider group. "Anyone else like to comment?" She scanned the room.

"Well, just to play devil's advocate, I just kind of wonder if we're not *over*coached," said Leigh. "I mean, we're already paying for a math coach, a recess coach, a debating coach, and a chess coach. And I guess I'm also wondering if there's even *room* for a meditation coach to do his or her thing. I mean, I'm assuming he or she would have to find a quiet space to do it in, and I don't have to tell you guys that there is literally not one empty broom closet left in the school building. My daughter just told me that kids are now getting occupational therapy in one of the old maintenance-supply rooms."

"I know—it's ridiculous," cut in Amy, the volunteer coordinator. "But if someone actually went door-to-door and outed all the people who were *lying* about where they lived, we'd have, like, a normal-size school again. Seriously, have you noticed how many kids head to the train station straight from pickup? It's so infuriating." Amy grimaced while Karen swallowed hard.

"People, can we stay on topic?" asked Susan. The room fell quiet. "Anyone else like to comment on Kim's proposal?" But no one did. "Well, a meditation coach is definitely something to consider," she went on. "But since we're talking about a staff hire that possibly requires board of education approval, I suspect it would have to be something we looked into for next year, not this. And we really need to spend the money this spring. Any other proposals for immediate spending?"

Another hand shot up—this one belonging to Deirdre, the member-at-large, who, Karen now noticed, was quite large herself. "Well, I don't know how many people realize this, but the fifth grade has at least one trans student in it. It's actually my friend Kristen's son, Liam, who used to be her daughter *Lia*. Anyway, Liam has *really* not had an easy time of it this year. And honestly, some of the problems have been on the teacher side. Liam's teachers have been refusing to call him by the name he wants to be called and also continue to refer to him as a *she*. On that note, I really think the school could benefit from some guidance on the issue. I actually know someone from the Glockenberg Institute for Child and Adolescent Studies who specializes in this stuff. In addition to sponsoring a trans-sensitivity-training workshop for the teachers, I thought we could do an evening discussion for parents and maybe an assembly for all the upper-school kids."

"Hm," said Susan. "Do you know how much it would cost?"

"I'm guessing ten to fifteen grand for all of it?"

"I like the idea. I just wonder if it's the kind of thing that would make more sense on the middle- or high-school level. I'm not up on the current science, but to my mind, ten and even eleven years old seems a little *young* for kids to be identifying themselves that way. Though I'm sure it does happen."

"Well, there might be only one kid in the school right now who's come out as a trans person, but I'm sure there are others dealing with the same feelings. And even if there aren't, it's an issue that affects the whole school. Apparently, there was an incident last week in which some fourth-graders objected to Liam using the boys' bathroom, and the teacher—I'm not going to name names—basically sided with the objectors, which I thought was totally outrageous. But whatever."

"Okay, but doesn't Lia-I-mean-Liam still have a vagina?" cut in Leigh. "I mean—sorry if this isn't PC—but my son was one of the kids who didn't feel comfortable, and honestly, I can't really blame him."

There was mumbling and grumbling.

"Ladies, why don't we wait to see a proposal before we make any decisions," said Susan. "Deirdre, can you get us something to look at by the end of the week?"

"I'll do my best," she answered.

"Any other proposals?" asked Susan.

"More technology in the classroom?" asked Meredith.

"Well, we already have iMacs, iPads, patch panels, and ceiling-mounted video projectors in every classroom," said Janine, the STEM chair. "And the library—as you can see looking around you—is pretty teched up too."

Once again, Denise's hand popped up. Karen could have sworn she saw certain members of the Embellished Tunic Brigade roll their eyes in anticipation. "I have a proposal," began the vice president. "I'd really love to see the school commit to using recycled toilet paper." The interim treasurer made a face expressing revulsion, prompting a new round of half-stifled giggles. It was becoming increasingly clear to Karen that Denise was the April Fishbach of Mather—that is, the mother whom all the other ones loved to complain about—and Liz was her chief antagonist. "I'm sorry," Denise went on, "but it literally breaks my heart thinking about forests getting destroyed so our kids can wipe."

"So you want the kids to use secondhand toilet paper?" asked Liz, sounding mock incredulous.

"It's not *secondhand toilet paper*," scoffed Denise. "It's recycled paper that's turned into toilet paper."

"Well, that's a relief."

There were still more giggles. Denise grimaced again. "Anyway, it seems to me that if this school is committed to preserving the environment, we should begin using sustainable paper products. If that makes me an ogre or a laughingstock, so be it."

"Well, let's give some thought to all these ideas in the next two weeks," said Susan. "Anyone with a proposal, please submit it by Friday. In the meantime, let's talk fund-raising!" She turned back to Karen. "The school year ends in two months, I realize. And traditionally, fall and winter are our biggest moneymaking seasons. But I think the rest of you know how disappointed I was with the results of the spring auction. We netted just over six hundred thousand." Karen coughed to disguise her shock. "Which might sound like a lot," Susan went on. "But the year before, we made over seven. And we had similarly disappointing results from last fall's Harvest Dance. On that note, Karen, I was wondering if you might have time to mastermind a kind of last-ditch spring fund-raising event. Like maybe a picnic or something? I was thinking we could call it Fund in the Sun. Too corny?" She surveyed the group.

"No, I think it's—cute," Karen replied with as much enthusiasm as she could muster, even as she wondered, *Why raise more money when you can't spend the money you already have?*

"Glad you like it," said Susan, smiling. "And since you're going to be working the money angle, how about becoming our treasurer for the duration of the school year? Liz has kindly been filling in, but—as you can see—she's due any day now with baby number three."

Silently groaning at the prospect of devoting even more time to a cause she didn't support, Karen glanced over at the Mather PTA interim treasurer and realized that her embellished tunic was in fact inflated to capacity. "Wow—congratulations," she muttered.

"Thanks," Liz answered morosely.

"I never made it past baby number one," Karen felt somehow compelled to add, if only as a distraction from her own mounting obligations.

"That's probably because you're sane. Apparently, I have a deep masochistic streak."

Karen smiled, then turned back to Susan and said, "Anyway, I'm very flattered to have been asked. But—"

"But you're busy, I know," said Susan. "I promise that being treasurer is not a time-consuming position. Liz can show you where we keep the books, so to speak, and how to get into the account. And I assume you're familiar with Excel?" Before Karen had time to answer, she turned to the rest of the group and said, "All those in favor of electing Karen our new interim treasurer, please raise your hands!"

Nine hands went up. It was suddenly clear to Karen that no one else wanted the job—moreover, that they'd already tagged her for it. Allison was right, Karen thought. This was her punishment for lying about her address. Even so, her heart sank.

"So it's settled," said Susan. "Karen, congrats. You are officially on the executive board now."

"I'm honored," Karen said miserably.

"Now, moving right along to arts committee business," Susan said, turning to her left. "Meredith, can you tell us what arts enrichment you've lined up for the month? I understand Pilobolus was a big hit."

"Yes, it was. And this month, the fourth grade is going to see *La Bohème,* and the experimental puppeteering troupe Stringtheory is performing a kid-friendly version of *Schindler's List* for the third grade. We also have a West African drumming troupe coming next week to perform for the lower school, thanks in part to the multicultural committee."

"Thank you, Meredith. Sounds fabulous," said Susan.

The others nodded in agreement—even Denise, who apparently found nothing ecologically objectionable about men with dark skin striking animal skins with sticks.

*   *   *

Ruby came home from school scratching. And when Karen lifted up Ruby's hair, she found a row of tiny red bumps on the back of her neck. By then, Karen was madly clawing at herself as well and in a state of barely controlled panic at the thought of bloodsucking insects running rampant on her scalp. It seemed particularly ironic that she had picked them up at a school that looked as clean cut as Mather did. But then, bloodsucking parasites apparently didn't select for socioeconomic status. In any case, Karen knew she had to act. After dinner that night, she sat Ruby down on the toilet seat with a *Highlights* magazine to distract her, while, comb in hand, Karen began dividing Ruby's hair into sections the way she'd seen someone do it on a YouTube video. Ruby was reading her a knock-knock joke that had been sent in by a reader—"'Knock, knock. Who's there? Isolate. Isolate who? I-so-late to the party'"—when a tiny black insect resembling a mosquito only without the wings appeared in her part line. "Oh my *God!*" Karen cried before she dropped the comb on the floor and ran into her bedroom. She'd always considered herself competent, but this task was possibly beyond her.

"Mooommm!" Ruby called to her in a whine.

"I'm sorry, sweetie," Karen called back. She counted to three on the inhale, then three on the exhale. Then she did it again. Feeling calmer, she walked back into the bathroom and announced, "Mommy can't handle this. We're going to see a specialist."

That was how, an hour later, she and Ruby ended up in the vinyl-sided home of an Orthodox Jewish nitpicker and mother of ten. When Karen and Ruby arrived, at least seven of the ten were visible under the dining-room table, playing with plastic toys. Bathsheba sat Ruby down in a chair facing a wall of gold-framed photographs of white-bearded rabbis who appeared to be as old as Methuselah and went to work with a metal comb. Then it was Karen's turn. "You have a bad case, even worse than your daughter," said Bathsheba.

"And you've got quite a brood!" declared Karen, keen to change the subject. "Are you going to have any more?"

"It's not up to me," said Bathsheba, shrugging. "It's God's will."

"Right," said Karen, nodding.

"Please stop moving."

"Oh, sorry."

"So, why do you have only one?"

"One *what?*" asked Karen.

"Child," said Bathsheba, wiping her comb on a Kleenex.

"Oh, right," said Karen, surprised by a question that few dared ask but many likely wondered about. "Well, I got married on the late side and didn't have my first kid till I was thirty-seven. And then, sadly, time got away from me." It was true and not true. In fact, Matt had been iffy on the idea of a second, fearing they'd be unable to travel, even though neither of them ever went anywhere. And Karen had bowed to his wish, even though it was a source of secret hurt. She'd always wanted a big family—or at least, she'd once thought she did. "And now I'm too old, so it's too late to have another," she added.

"How old are you?" asked Bathsheba.

"Forty-five, almost forty-six."

"Nonsense, it's not too late. My mother had her thirteenth at forty-seven."

"Oh—wow!" said Karen, horrified at the very idea.

Afterward, it pained Karen to have to write the woman a check for three hundred dollars for forty-five minutes' work. Then again, Karen would have paid nearly any amount for the ability to think about something other than lice. And Bathsheba apparently supported the family. "He studies the Torah," had been her answer to Karen's question about what Bathsheba's husband did for a living...

"Where have you guys been?" asked Matt when Karen and Ruby walked in the door at ten of eight.

"The lice lady," Karen told him.

"Oh—shit," he said.

"You should probably get checked too. Though according to Bathsheba the nitpicker, they usually stay away from men."

"Unlike some people I know," Matt muttered cryptically before he walked away.

"Excuse me?" Karen said, flinching. For a panicked moment, she wondered if he knew more than he was letting on. But he didn't answer or explain.

That night, she began the first of seven loads of laundry.

At work the next morning, despite misgivings, she began a formal letter to Clay on foundation letterhead that made no mention of their personal relationship. Considering that the document would become part of the charity's archives, it seemed imperative that she play it straight. *Dear Mr. Phipps,* she wrote. *On behalf of Hungry Kids, I would like to officially invite you to join our board of directors. We feel that your experience and involvement would be an asset to our organization, and we hope that you will consider accepting our offer...* She signed it *Gratefully yours, Karen Kipple.* When she finished, she printed it out and sent it via overnight mail.

Clay sent a one-line e-mail the next afternoon. When Karen

saw his name in her in-box, her heart thumped. The subject line read *Your Letter.* The body read:

I'm honored. Now will you do me the honor of seeing me one more time? Pretty please?

It took every ounce of Karen's mental strength not to write back *Yes.*

Two days later, Karen met up with the interim treasurer, Liz, in the Mather PTA office, which turned out to be a hole in the wall next to the music room. Liz, by now so pregnant that she could barely lean over far enough to open the desk and show Karen where the PTA checkbook and ledger were kept, nonetheless managed to teach Karen how and where to manually record deposits and withdrawals. No less essentially, she showed Karen how to electronically access the PTA account that was kept at Citibank. Owing to a sluggish Wi-Fi connection, the page took forever to load. Finally, the numbers became visible. But Karen had trouble believing her eyes. To her astonishment, the account currently contained $955,000.86, not a penny of which appeared to be spoken for. "Jesus, that's a lot of money," Karen muttered.

"Yeah, well, I guess compared to the other public schools around here we're a bunch of rich motherfuckers," said Liz. "Though it's really not that much when you compare it to the endowment of, like, Eastbrook Lab. Then we look like paupers." She shrugged. "I guess it's all relative."

"True enough," said Karen, noting that Liz must have regarded private schools the way Betts parents like Karen had once regarded Mather—as winning lottery tickets being dangled in their faces. "Well, thanks for showing me the ropes," Karen continued. "I think I can take over from here."

"Great," said Liz, "because either my water just broke or I just peed in my pants. In any case, I think I need some of Denise's recycled toilet paper."

"Oh no!" Karen laughed, feeling an unexpected kinship with the Mather PTA's secretary and former interim treasurer—or, at least, enough intimacy to say, "Hey, can I ask you a weird question before you take off?"

"Sure," said Liz. "So long as you don't want to know if I'm excited to have another baby."

"I promise not to go there," said Karen. "I'm just wondering: Has anyone on the PTA ever thought about—how do I put this?—throwing a little extra cash at one of the schools in the area that can't afford to fund-raise? By which I mean, donating some of the donations?"

"Are you kidding?" Liz said drily. "Parents at this school would go ape shit if they thought a dime of their money was going someplace else. Sad to say, but they only care about their own kids getting ahead. And I'm probably no better. Or maybe I'm worse. I wish I gave *more* of a fuck about my kids getting ahead. As it is, all I seem to care about these days is canned pineapple and not missing *True Detective*. Meanwhile, my kids' screen-time allocations are up to six hours a day."

"Hey, you're forty weeks pregnant, you get a pass," said Karen.

"It's actually been forty-one. They're inducing me on Saturday if nothing happens before."

"Oh my God! Good luck."

"Thanks—also for taking the shit job no one on the PTA wanted. I got suckered into it the first half of the year. And now I'm sorry to say it's your turn. When I'm recovered from Newborn-Land, let's go out to lunch and charge it to the PTA as compensation for our hardship. What do you say?"

"It's a deal," said Karen, who felt strangely gratified by the encounter—was it possible that she, too, was starting to make friends at Ruby's new school?—even as she continued to feel horrified by the money hoarding she'd seen on display.

Karen was horrified at the state of her marriage as well. She and Matt were down to about ten words a day, and Karen was at a loss as to how to up the number even to twenty. It was as if they were strangers all over again or, worse, roommates who had found each other on some bulletin board—the kind who respectfully kept their milk and cottage cheese on different sides of the fridge. Sitting alone on her bed that night, staring at the familiar scenery—the unread novels on her side table, the wedding photo on her dresser in its fancy sterling-silver frame, the Roman shade with its now-tedious brown-and-purple-chevron stripes that had seemed so chic at the time she'd bought it—she felt as if she were not in a marriage so much as in a museum of one.

And so, despite still being angry about things that Matt had said, and having too much pride, and dreading conflict, and continuing to fantasize about Clay and checking her phone every five minutes just in case he'd texted, she walked into the living room, where her husband sat simultaneously typing on his laptop and watching some game—there was always one on—and forced herself to say, "Do you want to talk?"

"Not really," he answered with a glance in her direction. "But I will."

"We can't go on like this forever," said Karen.

"No, we can't," said Matt. But he didn't offer any solutions.

"Well, maybe we should book a date night," said Karen. "Try to have fun or something. I don't know."

"Sure," he said.

"All right, well, would you want to see a movie?"

"What is there to see?"

"I don't know—there's always something."

Matt paused, grimaced. Then he blurted out, "It still bugs me that Ruby is going to that school under false pretenses and because you decided it was better. Every day she goes there, I'm reminded of that. Maybe I'm having trouble moving on. It still just feels really wrong to me."

"Well, I don't know what to say except I'm sorry, and I've already said that," said Karen.

"Well, thanks for saying it again, but—"

"But you're never going to get over it?"

"I didn't say that, but I'm not over it *yet,*" said Matt. "And I guess I need to know that, in the future, you're going to include me in decisions that affect our family."

"I promise to include you," she told him.

"But it's also—I don't know—you seem so secretive these days. You're always huddled over your phone, and you're so vague about everything."

Karen felt her chest tightening. "I could say the same for you. Half the time, I don't even know where you are. And it's kind of hard to include you in my life when you're not here to tell stuff to."

"I know, and I'm sorry I've been working so much," said Matt. "It's just been crunch time with Poor-coran, as you like to call it. But starting tomorrow, I'm going to try and get home earlier in the evenings. And maybe we can do more stuff together as a family on the weekend."

"Great—organize it," said Karen, encouraged.

"You're better at that stuff."

"I'm not better. I'm just a woman. And women are expected to manage everything on the home front. But once in a while, it would be great if you could organize something. Maybe we could go play miniature golf some weekend. Or maybe you could look into summer vacations. I think we could all use a vacation."

"I agree," said Matt.

Karen felt even more sanguine when, the next day, Matt surprised her by researching beach rentals, then e-mailing her the top contenders with the subject heading *These Ones Look Decent.*

She e-mailed him back immediately. *Number two looks nice. Want to find out if it's available the third or fourth week of August?*

But in the back of her mind she was wondering if Clay was still planning to invite her to his beach house one of those same weeks, like he'd promised to do—and, if so, how she'd respond.

Meanwhile, to Karen's relief, Ruby seemed to be further settling into Mather. And Karen had received promising signs from several family foundations that, with any luck, might be persuaded to make up at least part of the funds that could no longer be expected from Jesse James. In her few spare hours, and despite the nagging sensation that her expertise was better utilized elsewhere, Karen helped plan the Mather PTA Fund in the Sun picnic at a local park. In the plus column, her volunteer efforts at the school made her feel less paranoid. In the minus one, she was filled with a particular kind of self-loathing.

It was around the same time that Karen's dreams of her dead mother returned on a near-nightly basis. They were always variations on the same melody, and they were simultaneously welcome and unwelcome. *Mom! What are you doing here?* Karen would ask as Ruth Kipple appeared at the top of the stairs in her favorite light blue polyester nightgown and said, *What took you so long? I've been waiting for you for hours.* Her mother was always exaggerating, Karen would think. But she *was* waiting—night after night after night—until Karen woke up, and Ruth Kipple wouldn't be there after all, causing Karen to feel both exasperated and bereft. It was just like her mother to keep guilting her, even from the grave, Karen thought. Yet it was clearly Karen who had summoned her. So, really, what right did she have to complain—about any of it? Karen was one of the lucky ones on this earth.

If only it felt that way.

And then Charlotte blew off Ruby. The only reason Karen knew about it was that, finding her daughter unexpectedly glum at pickup on Friday, she proposed that Ruby invite over one of her new friends for a playdate. It seemed to Karen that enough time had passed that it was safe to reveal where they actually lived. Following Allison's advice, Karen could always say they'd just moved. By city decree, a child who changed addresses didn't need to change schools as well.

"I don't have any friends," Ruby told her.

"What?" said Karen, a twinge in her stomach. "But what about Charlotte?"

"She only talks to Finley now."

"Who's Finley?"

"A girl in my class."

"But why can't she be friends with you *and* Finley?"

"You don't understand." Ruby shook her head.

"I don't understand *what?*" said Karen.

"Everyone has a best friend but me."

"Well, I didn't have a best friend when I was in third grade."

"You grew up in the olden days."

"Are you sure you're not just being oversensitive?"

"I'm *not* being oversensible," insisted Ruby, mispronouncing the word. Karen decided to let it go. "When I tried to sit down next to Charlotte in the cafeteria, she said, 'This seat is taken.' So I sat across the table. And then *Finley* sat down next to her, and they didn't talk to me once the whole lunch period."

Was it something about her daughter that caused other girls to push her away? Karen found herself wondering. Was she too clingy? Too bossy? Or were girls her age just mean? Karen had read in one of her parenting books that elementary-school-age children and especially girls were constantly changing friends. It was part of the developmental process and had something to do with identity formation and was therefore not a cause for concern. But then, why wasn't Ruby sometimes doing the leaving instead of always being left? In any case, Charlotte Bordwell, like Mia, was too young for Karen to be angry at and, at the same time, too old to be considered an appendage of her mother. So Karen couldn't very well hold Susan responsible. Moreover, in Karen's experience, children came out of the womb with their personalities more or less already formed.

And yet…she found she *was* angry. Angry and hurt. It was intolerable to Karen that someone should have made her daughter feel so excluded and so unloved. It made Karen feel those things too. "Well, if Charlotte's going to be rude, why don't you sit with someone else?" she said.

"Like who?" said Ruby.

"What about Maeve?"

"I never see her. And when I do, she doesn't talk to me anyway."

"Well, then you'll make new friends," insisted Karen.

But would she? That was the question that nagged at Karen for the rest of the afternoon and evening.

The next morning, Karen turned on her phone and discovered a group e-mail from Principal Chambers. The administrative office of Betts must not have realized that Ruby had left, Karen thought. *Dear Betts Families,* it began. The e-mail concerned an emergency meeting that was being held in the school auditorium that night. It seemed that the city's board of education had not only approved Winners Circle's co-location inside the Betts building but had granted the WC network permission to begin immediate renovations on their portion of the school building, even though the charter was not planning to move in until the fall. This meant that Betts students would likely be spending their last two months of the school year breathing in construction dust and shouting to be heard over jackhammers. According to Principal Chambers's e-mail, the CEO of Winners Circle was a close personal friend of the mayor, and this wasn't the first time that the mayor had gone out of his way to accommodate her. To add insult to injury, due to budget cuts, Betts had no choice but to let its librarian go at the end of June. Since the library space would therefore be off-limits to Betts students, the city was allowing Winners Circle to take it over as their new robotics room.

As Karen read through the e-mail, she felt angry and frustrated, but also relieved that Ruby wouldn't be personally affected. Those emotions, in turn, were followed by amazement at the randomness of life. Were it not for Nathaniel Bordwell having tossed out his gas bill and Karen having walked by the particular bag of trash in which he'd tossed it while she was in a particularly upset mood, Ruby would likely still be at Betts. But he had, and so had Karen—and now Ruby wasn't. And so Karen gave herself permission not to dwell.

But as the day progressed, she found she couldn't stop feeling outraged at Clay and his ilk for what she considered to be their misguided munificence. It was above all the impulse to punish and shame, not seduce and be seduced, that made Karen break down and e-mail Clay that afternoon—or, really, forward Principal Chambers's e-mail to him without comment. Though as soon as she'd done so, she realized that her e-mail was bound to elicit a response, the thought of which filled her with excitement and trepidation.

In the meantime, arrangements for the fund-raising picnic needed to be finalized. Karen had planned on joining Susan in the school library the next morning to go over the details, but Susan e-mailed that night to say she had a plumber coming to deal with some kind of pipe leak and she didn't want to miss the guy—would Karen mind swinging by her house after drop-off instead? Having already made a decision not to involve herself or Susan in the Ruby-Charlotte schism, Karen promptly replied that it would be no problem at all, though secretly she wondered why Nathaniel couldn't handle it. Hadn't Susan said her husband worked from home? In any case, the

Bordwells lived only a block from the school, so, for Karen, the change of location presented no particular inconvenience.

There was a certain type of woman who always carried a good umbrella, the kind with a smooth wooden handle, a wide span, and a bright-colored block print or stripe. Not Karen, who had never bought a nice umbrella in her life, having always assumed she'd lose it as soon as she acquired it. Instead, she regularly purchased the semi-disposable made-in-China versions that were sold in outdoor kiosks by train stations. After three weeks, she inevitably either lost them or found that the spokes had become detached from the canopy, in which case she threw the whole business in a trash can and bought a new one the next day. But the truth was the plastic handle never felt solid in her hand, especially when she gripped it too tightly. That was what she found herself doing the next morning while standing in a light drizzle at Susan's front door.

It wasn't Susan's fault that Charlotte had blown off Ruby, Karen reasoned. And yet, here she was, devoting her precious free hours to the PTA; it hardly seemed fair that her reward should be the ostracism of her daughter by the president's daughter. Was it any wonder Karen was feeling surly and standoffish when Susan opened the door?

"Karen! I'm so sorry to make you travel in this weather," said Susan, pleasant as ever. Per usual, she was dressed in upscale athletic wear.

"It's fine," Karen said with a tight smile, following her inside.

"I hear our girls have a sub today."

"I didn't know that."

"I try and support the teachers' union," Susan went on, unprompted, "but considering they work only nine months of the year and get to go home at three, I think they get way too many days off!"

"Yeah, well, it's a pretty grueling job," said Karen, thinking that it was somewhat rich of Susan to be complaining that teachers didn't work hard enough when she appeared not to work *at all*. Judging from her outfit, she was probably en route to some "important" kettleball class. Or was Karen, in shortchanging the essential if unbillable work that Susan performed on behalf of both her family and her local public school, being the worst kind of sexist? She followed Susan into the living room.

"Karen—this is my husband, Nate," she said.

Karen looked up and then down. To her astonishment, her eyes landed on a clean-shaven, square-jawed, middle-aged Caucasian man seated in a wheelchair with padded grips. His large biceps were straining against the sleeves of a bright red polo shirt. The lack of a cast on either leg suggested to Karen that whatever ailed him must be permanent. Suddenly, it all made sense—the elevator at the back of the living room, the half marathon for a paraplegia charity she'd read about on the web. He must have completed it in his chair. "Oh, hi!" she said, trying to mask her shock and embarrassment with verbosity. "It's so nice to meet you! I'm Karen and I'm a new parent at the school, and I'm also helping Susan plan a fund-raising picnic for the PTA. Our daughters are friends, which is how I met Susan. She was actually the first parent to invite my daughter over for a playdate, so I'm indebted to her forever…" Karen rambled on and on. It was exactly the opposite of how she'd intended to act. But when she got flustered, she had a tendency to talk too much. Besides, under this new and unforeseen set of facts, how could she justify being a bitch?

"Well, it's nice to meet you" was all Nathaniel said, but he was eyeing her strangely. Or maybe Karen was imagining it; maybe he simply had an odd facial expression on account of whatever condition he'd fallen victim to. In any case, guilt flooded her body, not only due to her original theft, but because she'd dared to pass judgment on this family and their work habits. That she'd piggybacked on the life of a man who couldn't even walk was another issue. Nathaniel Bordwell's paralysis reminded Karen that money was not everything, not even close. Even the affluent suffered. And because their expectations for what constituted a successful life were so much higher, they were sometimes the unhappiest of all. Nothing was as simple as, well, black and white.

Except when it was.

"If you'll excuse me, I'm going to go get some breakfast," he announced while wheeling himself out of the room.

"It was great meeting you!" said Karen.

"Well, you probably have things to do," said Susan, turning to Karen. "So should we get started?"

"Sounds good," said Karen.

"Oh, and if you're wondering about my husband—and most people do when they meet him for the first time—he has a spinal cord injury from a boating accident he was in twenty years ago."

"Oh my gosh," said Karen. "That must be very— challenging for all of you."

"We're both used to it. But, yes, it has its challenging aspects."

"I'm sure."

"We're very lucky that Nathaniel's parents left us the house.

Otherwise we wouldn't be living like this. And we have tenants downstairs who help cover our expenses."

The Bordwells already had tenants? "Right," said Karen, nodding. "And do the tenants have kids too?" The question flew out of her mouth before she had time to realize how odd it would sound.

"The tenants?" said Susan, squinting at her.

"I was just curious," Karen said quickly.

"Oh! Well—not that I've heard about! I mean, not yet. They're still in their early twenties, I believe."

"Right."

"Anyway, back to more urgent matters—were you able to get a permit from the city for the event? I just don't want there to be any beef with the parks people when we get there."

"Yes, it's all done."

"Fabulous. And what about the balloon sculptor?"

"Already booked."

"And the bouncy castle?"

"Same. Though the bouncy-house guy insisted on a three-hundred-dollar deposit up-front," said Karen, "and I couldn't be bothered to argue. So I wrote him a personal check."

"Oh! Well, that's fine," said Susan. "I'm just sorry for you! I'll have to order you a PTA charge card one of these days. In the meantime, make sure to reimburse yourself out of the PTA account. And if you could itemize your expenses in the ledger, it would be much appreciated."

"Of course. I'm happy to," Karen told her.

"You don't have to get really specific, like *paper towels—ten dollars*. But if you could list the category, at least, that would be great. And if it can't be categorized, just write *supplies* or *miscellaneous*."

"Not a problem."

"Terrific. Well, I think that's all my questions. Sounds like we're good to go!"

"Now we all just have to pray for sun."

"Very true," said Susan, with a quick laugh. "What was the name of the Egyptian sun god?"

"Ra, I think," said Karen.

"Well, then, let's both pray to Ra on Friday night."

"It's a deal."

On Friday, the day before Fund in the Sun, Karen still hadn't reimbursed herself for any expenses connected to the picnic. But she'd kept a fairly detailed list of everything she'd purchased out of her own pocket. After dropping Ruby in her classroom, she continued down the hall and let herself into the PTA office with a duplicate key that Susan had given her. She was about to get out the ledger when she decided on a whim to log into the PTA bank account first. Some part of Karen needed to see for herself, one more time, how much money was actually in there. As she waited for the page to load, the nasal honks of a group recorder lesson wafted un-mellifluously from the adjacent music room.

Owing to the lice expert's workshop and other incidentals, the balance was down to $953,000.41. Even so, it seemed like an unfathomable sum for a midsize public elementary school to have accumulated in private donations. And Karen couldn't help but fantasize about what Betts would do with even a quarter of it. To start, they could rehire the librarian, she thought. And with the roughly nine hundred thousand dollars left, they could probably also renovate the library itself, and maybe even outfit it with MacBook Airs, like Mather had, as well as beanbag chairs and a new collection of early-grade books—and still have three-quarters of a million dollars left over. (From what Karen could tell from the titles Ruby had brought home during the previous year, Betts's book collection was at least thirty years old. The covers were sticky and frayed, and no one wanted to open them anyway. Instead of *Ivy and Bean,* the library had multiple copies of *Winnie-the-Pooh.*) After taking these steps, Betts would no doubt begin to attract more affluent families from the community, who would lift enrollment, flooding the school with more money from the city and state, potentially pushing out Winners Circle and, in the process, building their own base of private donations.

After signing out of the account, Karen removed the ledger from the file cabinet and recorded her picnic expenses under the rubric Miscellaneous/Supplies, just as Susan had instructed her to do. Then she got out the PTA checkbook and was about to write herself a check for the amount she was owed— $483.00—when, pen poised over the desk, a tantalizing question lodged itself in her brain and refused to vacate it: Would anyone notice if she added another zero to the amount and sent the surplus over to the PTA of Constance C. Betts?

To Karen's knowledge, that organization—to the extent it even existed as a separate entity from April Fishbach—had made a total of six hundred dollars the year before. And all of it had been from the vanilla cupcakes and sugar cookies sold before and during the intermission of the talent show, a vaguely pornographic affair in which two children played the piano and, to Karen's quiet horror, the rest lip-synched and dirty-danced to that year's pop and hip-hop hits. But that was a separate issue. To Karen's mind, the students at Betts were no less worthy of meditation coaches, lice workshops, and ceiling-mounted video projectors than the Mather kids were. Nor would any of the students at Mather be affected negatively if deprived of roughly .05 percent of a money pile that no one on the PTA could even figure out how to spend. In fact, it seemed increasingly clear to Karen that the fund-raising game at Mather was as much about achieving a number as it was about fulfilling any tangible goals. And the Fund in the Sun picnic was on target to raise at least twenty-five thousand dollars more, since two hundred fifty families had already promised to pay a hundred dollars apiece for the privilege of attending.

And were Karen's inclinations all that different from what her accountant father had done during his lifetime? A closet Lefty, Herb Kipple had once admitted to Karen that, with wealthy clients, he sometimes refrained from employing the aggressive tactics that would have saved them money at tax time, believing that they owed the U.S. government a fair share of their hefty incomes. And who could blame him? Not Karen. And if her motives were not purely altruistic— even if, say, she was seeking to assuage her guilt and atone for her own elitism by throwing a few bread crumbs at the masses she'd already spurned and abandoned—money was still money.

Karen thought of the fixer-upper she'd gone to see on a whim a year earlier in a marginal neighborhood close to her own increasingly affluent one. *Prewar town house! Well below market value; needs work, great potential,* read the ad, and Karen had wondered if maybe she, Ruby, and Matt should get a proper house and yard—if that was what they lacked and what would elevate their lives from good to great. The price was right. And Karen figured that she and Matt could sell their own condo for a profit and get a home-equity loan to renovate. She'd e-mailed the real estate agent: *I'm very interested!*

They'd made a date to meet.

The house had potential, all right—the potential to make Karen run screaming. Not only had it been barely standing, with enormous clear plastic sheets tacked to the ceiling to prevent the elements from coming in, but it had been occupied by at least two dozen people. On the first floor, four of them had been seated on a single twin mattress watching TV while a barely clothed woman had lain half asleep behind them with a newborn in her arms. Shower curtains featuring Mickey Mouse and Donald Duck motifs had separated the various mattresses distributed around the area. "So sorry to bother you," Karen had said, creeping through the tiny sunken rooms, the floors buckling, the walls covered with mold, the inhabitants surely illegal immigrants from foreign lands.

"De nada," one man had answered, smiling, gracious, desperate.

On other floors, the inhabitants had stared wide-eyed at her but didn't appear to understand English or Spanish, so Karen hadn't been able to apologize. Even the basement, with its not-quite-six-foot-high ceiling and concrete floor, had been occupied. There had been a twin mattress parked on either side of the boiler. Karen had felt sick as she'd thanked the agent and explained that it was too big a job for her.

But there were smaller jobs she could take on, she now thought—smaller and more direct ways of creating equity that were far less daunting to contemplate and potentially more effective than writing newspaper op-eds that would probably never be published anyway or convincing financial bigwigs to make tax-deductible donations, thereby starving the government of revenue.

For a few moments, Karen stood staring at the sum she'd written in the ledger. As the recorders honked on the other side of the wall, she wondered how walls had even come into being. They must have arisen in conjunction with the concept of privacy, which itself must have emerged around the sexual act. Or was there something primal about the desire to hide things from others?

Her breath held, Karen carefully added a 0 to the end of the figure, followed by a comma between the 4 and the 8. So the $483 that she'd just recorded as having spent on picnic supplies was now $4,830. Then she held the ledger at arm's length and tried to determine if the figure would look believable to an outside set of eyes. After deciding that it would, she placed the ledger back in the drawer, then quickly wrote a check to herself on the PTA checkbook for the same amount. She put the check in her wallet, then put the checkbook in the drawer next to the ledger. Then she left the PTA office. As she locked the door behind her, her heart was beating madly.

But as she strode down the hall toward the double doors, she felt powerful and righteous. She also found herself thinking of her erstwhile friend Lou and wondering what Lou would think if she could see Karen now. Karen hadn't spoken to her since their awkward encounter by the train station a few weeks before. But in the days since then, Lou had somehow become the face of Karen's remorse—Lou's beautiful, long-lashed brown eyes reminding Karen of the ideals she'd abandoned in the interest of Ruby and herself...

*　　*　　*

All morning at work, every time someone approached her desk, Karen half jumped out of her seat, somehow imagining that he or she could see into her purse. Lunchtime couldn't come soon enough. Karen went straight to the bank, took the check to the window, and asked the teller to cash it. She was concerned that her request might raise the teller's eyebrows. But the woman said nothing, merely methodically counted out the sum in hundreds, counted them again, then slid the bills beneath the Plexiglas.

At the check-writing table, Karen took the roughly five hundred dollars she was owed and stuck it in her wallet. She stuck the other forty-three hundred-dollar bills in a plain white envelope that she'd taken from the supply room at her office. She addressed the envelope to the Parent Teacher Association of the Constance C. Betts School and affixed a stamp to the top right-hand corner. She left the top left corner blank.

She must have stood in front of the mailbox for five minutes before she finally let the envelope drop from her fingers into its maw. As it rattled down the chute with a *ka-thunk,* Karen flinched and shut her eyes in anticipation of biblical punishments. But the skies didn't open. Nor did God strike her down with lightning. When she opened her eyes again, it was sunny and mild. And she was still standing on a busy street corner next to a guy selling pretzels.

Just as promised, Matt was home early that evening. Over takeout, he announced that Poor-coran was almost ready to launch. "That's so exciting!" said Karen, her buoyant mood growing more so.

"What about you?" he asked. "What's the news?"

"Well, I may have found an important new source of funds," she said. "But I don't want to jinx it, so I won't say any more."

"Fair enough," he said.

"Guess what I learned in school today," said Ruby. "How to Charleston!" She stood up from the table and began twisting and torquing her hips, her arms against her sides, her wrists pointing north.

"Awesome!" said Karen, before realizing that she must have sounded exactly like Miss Tammy.

"Also," said Ruby, sitting down again, "Ivy gave me her gummy bears at lunch."

"Well, that's a ridiculous amount of good news for one day," said Karen, who had no idea who Ivy was but assumed it was a new friend. "I say we celebrate."

"Yay!" said Ruby. "Can we go out for ice cream?"

"Sure," said Karen, whose worries had grown larger than how many calories her daughter consumed per day.

"You're in a good mood," said Matt, turning to Karen— almost accusatorily, it seemed to her.

"And what's wrong with that?" she asked.

"Nothing!" he said, shrugging. "Nothing at all."

After dinner, as promised, they went out as a family for ice cream. Karen suggested the artisanal place with the weird flavors. But Matt and Ruby lobbied hard for Baskin-Robbins. Keen to avoid further conflict, Karen gave in. And while she and Matt didn't directly hold hands on the way there—Ruby was in the middle—they were at least connected through her. At least they *looked* like a happy family.

And then they connected some more. After Ruby went to sleep, Karen and Matt split a bottle of wine and watched the last few innings of a baseball game—or, really, Matt watched and Karen let her mind wander. Then Karen forced herself to initiate sex, even though she had little desire to. But once it was under way, biology took charge. And afterward, she was glad that she had. It was neither the greatest sex of Karen's life, nor the worst. And if the encounter didn't quite erase the memory of her and Clay, it pushed him farther into the past tense.

If only she hadn't forwarded him the e-mail about Winners Circle…Karen heard her phone ping just as she was washing up for bed. Matt was already half asleep. She grabbed her phone off the windowsill. Without her reading glasses on, Karen was almost blind. But she held the phone away from her, and eventually she made out the words.

What if I say you're right? WC sucks and so do I. Then will you see me? Please don't be mad. I'm just the idiot who writes checks. And I miss you. Badly. CP

I miss you. Badly. As Karen repeated the words in her head, she felt her heart quivering in her chest. Maybe it was just that Clay had the guts to state what Matt never did or had. While Matt had always been a skilled lover, he was also maddeningly silent, finding overt displays of romanticism to be sentimental, indulgent, and insincere. He was especially critical of couples who said "I love you" to each other at the end of every phone call and before every separation, even if it only involved a trip to the supermarket or the bank. But he took the objection to an extreme. He never told Karen he loved her, not even in bed. He never told her he missed her either. But then, they were rarely separated for long periods. At his most emotive, he'd say, "Did I ever tell you how much I like your meat sauce?" It was an old joke, meant to allude to a night early in their courtship, before they made love for the first time.

And yet…a part of her believed that actions spoke louder than words, and that the l-word had become as meaningless as the word *friend* had on Facebook. Karen also appreciated the fact that Matt gave her space. In her late twenties, she'd had a boyfriend who exuded neediness. Alcohol abuse, overeating, and unemployment were just a few of his many issues. Karen had resented having to take care of the guy. But the role she'd played in their relationship had also felt familiar and therefore comfortable, and she'd struggled to leave him. She'd felt too guilty to do so. Then she'd met Matt. Strong and independent, he'd made her feel strong and independent herself.

But at times he struck her as too independent. Karen had always suspected that, were she to walk out on Matt, apart from his bruised ego, he'd be absolutely fine. Assuming that Karen had custody, he might miss Ruby. Except he'd see her every Wednesday and Saturday, and, quite possibly, that would be enough for him. Or was she being unfair? Maybe his failure to be more emotive was just an excuse for her attraction to Clay—and Karen was simply restless, like everyone else who'd been married for a decade or more.

As she stared at the screen, she wondered if there was a way of letting Clay know that she felt the same things he felt without inviting another encounter. Or was it too late for that? Karen had lived long enough to know that no enduring kind of love could compete with the fascination of a new partner. She was trembling as she wrote,

I miss you too.

Thirty seconds later, her phone pinged again. Karen lifted it to her eyes. Clay had written,

Make up an excuse for the weekend of the 28th. Need to see you.

Not *Are you free the weekend of the 28th?* Just *Make up an excuse*. That was Clay. He didn't ask; he told. As it happened, Karen had no particular obligations that weekend. But what if she had? Or did his kind of money negate such considerations? It was so presumptuous of him, so entitled, and so blind to the reality of other people's complicated lives, she thought—and yet so compelling. For once, Karen wouldn't be in charge of the arrangements or the schedule. So often, her life and motherhood in particular felt like an extended air traffic control shift. And she doubted she was the only woman for whom this was true. In fact, she didn't know a single husband who landed the planes. Most of them didn't even know what days the sitter worked or when gymnastics class started or even what time school got out. The job of keeping track of all those beeping dots on the screen, from permission slips to pediatric dentistry checkups, still fell to women. And while the arrangement admittedly suited the controlling side of Karen, the other side longed for backup and resented its nonexistence.

Another part realized how ridiculous, absurd, and risky the very idea of sneaking off for the weekend with Clay Phipps was. Or could she keep this time—a time that promised to be far longer than the single evening they'd already spent together—a secret as well? And was it his money that made him attractive to her, or was it Clay himself? And could the two even be disentangled? And how could she have fallen for her political enemy? Karen also worried that he'd lose interest in her if she said no—and that this was her last chance before he grew frustrated and then bored by his own frustration and then forgot about her for another twenty-four years. After all these decades, it seemed she was still fretting about disappointing the opposite sex. Her heart was at full gallop as she typed:

Why—where are you/we going?

Karen realized after she wrote it that she might just as well have written *Okay.*

It's a surprise, but sweaters unnecessary, Clay wrote back.

She hadn't been on a tropical vacation since her honeymoon, ten years ago.

Karen spent the next several days alternating between nervous excitement and abject fear—that either her husband would find out about Clay or someone at Mather would find out about her theft of PTA funds. Every time she opened her in-box—or dropped Ruby at school—she half expected one of the PTA board members to ask if she could talk to her for a second, head cocked quizzically. But, in fact, at the Fund in the Sun picnic that Saturday, at least four members of the PTA executive board—Kim, Leigh, Susan, and even Denise—individually came over to congratulate Karen on doing such a great job before returning to their organic cotton, diamond-patterned ikat blankets and rattan picnic baskets containing Rainforest Alliance–certified grapes. Even Liz made an appearance, her newborn in a sling. "Hey, mastermind," she said.

"Oh my God, I can't believe you came!" cried Karen, kissing her hello. "What—did you have the baby last night or something? And who is this?" Karen peeked into the sling, where a tiny lump of pale flesh lay asleep, eyes squeezed tight and fingers outstretched as if reaching for God. The sight of babies still stirred something inside her. But these days there was also relief in the knowledge that they were other people's precious burdens.

"Say hi to Archie, my new slave driver," said Liz.

"Hi, Archie—you be nice to your mom," said Karen, stroking the baby's velvety cheek with the back of her index finger.

It was gorgeous out—they'd gotten lucky with the weather—and everyone seemed to be in a good mood. Even Karen felt moderately contented—that is, until she noticed Charlotte Bordwell and Maeve Collier-Shaw throwing water balloons at each other and laughing uproariously, both of them perfectly outfitted for the event in patterned rompers with drawstring waists and metallic sandals. Maeve's were silver, Charlotte's gold. The image of Ruby's two estranged BFFs joining in merriment while Ruby herself stood in the near distance with a group of younger children trying to pop a relentless stream of bubbles that were being emitted by a large plastic gun filled Karen's mouth with a sour taste. She knew that, in all likelihood, Maeve and Charlotte's burgeoning friendship had absolutely nothing to do with her daughter. There was no reason even to suspect that either one of them had ever mentioned knowing Ruby. But Karen couldn't help but feel that somehow their mutual jettisoning of Ruby had brought them, if not together, then closer.

Karen turned away and was further jarred by the sight of Maeve's mother seated on an ikat blanket of her own with her face partially hidden behind a pair of aviator shades. Karen thought back and realized that she hadn't seen Laura Collier in what was now going on six months. She also realized that there was nothing to be gained by saying hello. But somehow, in that moment, it seemed necessary that pleasantries be exchanged. Or maybe Karen was still holding out hope that Ruby would be reintegrated into Maeve's inner sanctum. "Laura!" she said, walking over to the edge of her blanket.

"Oh, hey," said Laura, but she didn't remove her glasses, which struck Karen as the tiniest bit rude. She didn't get up either. Even so, Karen leaned over and attempted to greet her with a kiss to the cheek. But as Laura remained seated, and Karen was standing, incorrect body parts bumped together.

Afterward, Karen felt even more awkward. "I haven't seen you in a million years—" she said, trying to mask her unease with chatter.

"I know, it's been forever," said Laura. "Is it true you organized this whole thing?"

Karen wondered how she even knew. "If you mean was I *guilted* into organizing this whole event, the answer is yes." She laughed, then wondered why she always revealed more than she needed to.

"That's so good of you. I wish I had time for stuff like that," said Laura. "But between work and helping Maeve edit her animated short, things have been so crazy lately."

"Maeve is making an animated short?" asked Karen.

Laura cocked her head. "Oh! You didn't know that? We're getting ready to submit it to festivals."

"Wow! And no, I didn't know that. Well, I don't actually have time either," said Karen. "But I try to do my part." *Unlike you* was the obvious subtext. Karen knew she was being provocative. But she'd finally lost patience with Laura and Evan faux complaining about how busy they were—and, by extension, how important—while also implying they were superior parents, despite the limited time they spent with their children, because wasn't that the subtext?

But if Laura was wounded by Karen's dig, she didn't let on. "Well, you're a better man than me!" she declared in an ever-so-slightly mocking tone.

"I don't know about that," said Karen, retreating.

"So, have you guys been happy at Mather?" said Laura, changing gears.

"Really happy," Karen told her.

"I actually ran into someone from our old class last weekend—do you remember Bram's mom, Annika?"

"Of course. The Dutch woman with the six-foot legs."

"Right—her. Well, Annika said Jayyden is gone from Betts."

"*What?* You're kidding! Where did he go?" said Karen, trying to mask her dismay. If only she'd waited two more weeks, she thought bitterly. Or had it never really been about Jayyden?

"I guess he sent one too many kids to the ER," said Laura, shrugging.

"Yeah, I guess," said Karen, still marveling at the news. "Wow, I can't believe that. Maybe we should all go back."

"That's not going to happen for us. But maybe *you* should

go back." Laura smiled cuttingly, while a single eyebrow appeared above the lens of her left shade.

Karen knew she'd set herself up for it. But Laura's suggestion, which felt more like a request, stung. It seemed suddenly clear to Karen that Laura not only didn't want Maeve to be friends with Ruby but also didn't want Ruby to attend Mather. Maybe the school had felt like Laura's winning lottery ticket, and she didn't like others sharing in the pot. Or maybe, not unlike Karen, she was embarrassed about the circumstances under which her daughter had matriculated there— circumstances about which, quite possibly, only Karen knew. In any case, Karen felt heat climbing up the back of her neck, then fanning across her cheeks. "Well, maybe you should piss off," she blurted out, "and then go piss on your husband while you're at it."

"*Excccuuusssse me?*" said Laura. But by then, Karen was already striding back to her own blanket. There, she got out her phone and pretended to be engaged in urgent textual communication, but inside she was a quivering tangle of neurons. Had she really just said that? It had felt so good to finally tell the woman off. Only now that she'd done so, she felt embarrassed and uncomfortable. It was hardly the time to be making enemies of Mather parents. Pretending not to feel well, Karen yanked Ruby away from the bubble gun. Together, albeit with Ruby protesting, they left the picnic early.

A new e-mail came in that evening from another neighborhood organization that Karen had never heard of. This one was called Concerned Parents and Citizens of Cortland Hill. The subject line was *Emergency Meeting on Redistricting.*

Dear Mather Parents,

It has come to our attention that the city's board of education, noting overcrowding issues at Edward G. Mather, is floating a proposal to rezone the eastern section of Cortland Hill between Moreland and Cherry. As a result, many families who purchased or rented homes in the neighborhood with the understanding that they would be able to send their children to Mather will no longer be able to do so. Instead, they will be assigned seats at the Millicent Grover school, an underenrolled, underperforming elementary school on the other side of a major thoroughfare.

While we believe that standardized testing scores do not represent the true measure of a child's potential—and that integration is a valid pursuit in a multicultural city such as ours—we are concerned that only 12 percent of Grover's third-, fourth-, and fifth-graders received passing grades last year on the state's English-language and math exams. What's more, for those living on the west side of Cortland Avenue, having their children attend Grover will mean traversing a busy intersection every morning and afternoon, inconveniencing families and endangering lives.

Rather than sacrificing the next generation to a failing school that lacks the commitment to education that has long defined Edward G. Mather, we are proposing that Mather instead transfer its two special-education classes to a facility that is better equipped to deal with high-needs children. This would free up at least two classrooms, where additional kindergarten and first-grade classes could be placed.

If you support this alternate proposal, please attend a community forum in the Millicent Grover school auditorium this

Monday night at seven. Your voice is urgently needed! The meeting is open to the public, but representatives from the board of education will be in attendance.

Thank you,
Concerned Parents and Citizens of Cortland Hill

Karen felt newly unsettled. On the surface of it, the letter's call to arms sounded reasonable enough. But it seemed to Karen as if there were another letter hiding behind the one she'd just read, and the former was filled with quiet hate. She found the suggestion that Mather's special-ed children be kicked out of the building to make way for the regular ones especially galling. At the same time, she was aware that Ruby's matriculation at the school was at least partly to blame for the overcrowding that had led to the board of education's proposal. Also, would Karen have willingly enrolled her own daughter at a school that had posted as low scores on the state tests as Millicent Grover apparently had? Above all, she feared that the fracas over the possible rezoning might lead to a witch-hunt of the kind that had been suggested by the volunteer coordinator at the PTA executive board meeting, in which those families who were found not to be living in the correct catchment area were outed as interlopers, their children expelled from the school. Making a note of the meeting time, Karen closed out of the e-mail.

Meanwhile, to the great joy of the Mather PTA and to Karen's commingled pride and disgust, Fund in the Sun raised far more than anyone had expected—close to forty thousand dollars in one afternoon. Yet again, Karen was on the receiving end of multiple accolades. In the aftermath of such success, and even despite the upset that her run-in with Laura Collier had caused her—or maybe because of it; maybe because it secretly pained her to think she was enhancing the education of a certain small blond child with a hyphenated name—Karen felt newly emboldened.

But it wasn't just about punishing Maeve. It seemed so unjust that the quality of a child's education should be predicated on how much money his or her parents made. Why should rich kids get to attend fancy private schools with swimming pools and small classes and no one interrupting—or public schools that had the same amenities, thanks to property taxes and/or the prohibitive price of the real estate in their catchments—while the poor were left to fester in overcrowded, chaotic classrooms with not enough books and too many problem kids? Shouldn't it have been the other way around? And didn't underprivileged children stand to benefit the most from the extra attention? Moreover, who had decided that, with a few exceptions, the light-skinned people of the planet should rule over the dark ones? Racism was so random, really, when you thought about it. It was as if people one day had decided that attached earlobes were superior to unattached ones, and those with the former should reap the riches of this world.

Or maybe race was only part of the equation. Maybe it was class that mattered the most, Karen thought as she unlocked the door to the PTA office on Monday morning—class and the lifestyle preferences that went with it. That is, the taste for Pellegrino over Pepsi, clapboard over aluminum siding, community-supported agriculture over community college, imported Parmigiano-Reggiano over Kraft Reduced-Fat Parmesan-Style Grated Topping, and beach yoga at an eco-resort in Tulum over daiquiris in the wet bar at the Grand Bahía

Príncipe Coba with a crowd of two hundred overweight, sun-poisoned binge drinkers, at least one of whom could be heard yelling, "Is my wife built or what?" (Also, in a certain echelon of society, you had to know how to nod slowly and say, "Wow, that's so funny," without seeming to find it even remotely amusing after the person seated to your left at some boring dinner party said, "My roommate at Choate was her best friend on the Vineyard.")

But if the government wasn't prepared to divide the riches up more equitably, why shouldn't Karen try to do her part? And was it even stealing if you didn't pocket the money yourself? Besides, by organizing the picnic, she'd more or less earned the dough herself; hadn't she therefore earned the right to decide how to spend it? These questions in mind, Karen wrote another check to herself in the amount of four thousand dollars, then recorded the deduction in the ledger as Portfolio Expenses. It was a phrase she'd learned from her father. She never entirely understood what it meant—she'd always envisioned oversize black-fronted albums filled with modeling shots from glossy magazines—but to her ear, it had the ring of a well-run business.

Just as before, Karen cashed the check on her lunch hour, then placed the bills in an envelope that she sent to the Parent Teacher Association of the Constance C. Betts School, again with no explanation or return address. The only difference was that, this time, as the envelope tumbled down the chute, she felt determination, not trepidation.

That evening, Karen asked Matt to put Ruby to bed so she could attend the community meeting about the proposed re-zoning of the western portion of Cortland Hill. Although doubtful that Ruby would be personally affected if the re-zoning went through, Karen wanted to be prepared. She was curious too. Car keys in hand, she set off in a light drizzle.

Millicent Grover turned out to be only a five-minute drive from Karen's home. But somehow she'd never noticed it be-fore, even though the building looked uncannily like Mather, at least from the outside and at night; it was another story inside the school auditorium. To Karen's surprise, the crowd in the audience was roughly three-quarters African American and about one-quarter white and Asian. Was this because the latter had already decided they wouldn't be caught dead send-ing their children there, so there was nothing to discuss? Or maybe the white families had been too frightened—both of entering the school and of being shouted down—to show up. If and when the next meeting was held in Mather's own au-ditorium, they would no doubt come out in droves. In the meantime, a reverse ratio was visible on the stage, where a handful of beleaguered-looking city officials were seated at a metal table dotted with plastic water bottles. Her head bowed with the hope of not being recognized, Karen took a seat in the back row. The meeting was already under way.

"Mr. Erun Dasgupta," one of the female bureaucrats read off a note card, "please come to the podium."

An expensively suited thirty-five-ish man with a com-plexion the color of caramelized sugar approached the mi-crophone. "Good evening," he began. "I am a resident of Cortland Hill. And I would like to say this: I would never have purchased our condominium were it not for the ex-pectation that we would be able to send our son to Edward Mather. Now all our plans are up in the air. But one thing we will definitely not be doing is sending our child to a failing school where the students are more interested in rap music than arithmetic."

There were hisses and boos from the audience, along with a lone cry of "Racist."

"Peeeeeople! Please," bellowed another of the city officials, this one a balding white man in a brown suit, "we ask that you refrain from expressing your opinion of the speakers. This is a community forum, and everyone has the right to speak here. Please be respectful."

"*He's* the one who needs to show some respect," a woman yelled from the audience. Eventually, the boos and cries died down. But at the sight of the next speaker—a certain Reverend Jeremiah Reed—the crowd again erupted, this time in whoops and cheers. Reverend Jeremiah, for his part, appeared to have been lifted from a time-travel machine that had stopped for gas in the 1970s. A feathered fedora sat on his tightly curled hair, a handlebar mustache framed his lips, and an ascot decorated with fleurs-de-lis filled the triangle at the top of his wide-collared maroon polyester button-down. "My name is Reverend Jeremiah," he began. "Some know me from my God job at the Church of Our Lord the Savior, others from my day job as the parent-teacher coordinator of Millicent Grover." There were more cheers. "Some from outside the community may believe it is their duty to show up here and accuse our school of being in poor shape." He paused. "We know we are poor. But we believe our shape is beautiful already. And so is the color of our skin."

"Amen" came a voice from the front of the audience.

"It took our people three hundred years to achieve emancipation in this country. Make no mistake, Board of Education," Reverend Jeremiah continued, turning to the seated bureaucrats with a raised index finger. "We do not intend to relinquish that freedom any more than we intend to relinquish the leadership of Millicent Grover. This is our school, and if the rich white folks of Cortland Hill send their children here, they need to understand that and play by *our* rules, not theirs." Thunderous applause followed.

Karen was sympathetic to Reverend Jeremiah's argument. She was also disheartened by the divisive rhetoric on display.

Next up was a Grover parent named Lashondra Green who expressed the fear that an influx of wealthy families from Cortland Hill would cause the school to eventually lose its federal Title I funding, which currently enabled it to offer a wide array of enrichment programs, including Mandarin language, playwriting, and African dance. Did poor minority schools actually stand to suffer from the influx of wealthy whites? Karen was thrown off balance by the woman's remarks, which seemed to echo what Susan Bordwell had complained about. Then again, if Susan and Lashondra were both right, why was the blue wall paint in Millicent Grover's auditorium peeling off in giant trapezoid-shaped flakes while Mather's walls were smooth and pristine? Whatever the case, Karen felt she'd heard enough. She also felt uncomfortable. When the next speaker finished, she slipped out of the auditorium as quietly as she'd slipped in.

On Wednesday morning after school drop-off, Karen was waiting in line at Dunkin' Donuts—Karen assumed there was less chance of running into anyone she knew there, plus the coffee turned out not to be bad—when to her amazement April Fishbach suddenly appeared. She had a copy of Karl

Marx's *Capital* in one hand and a raisin bagel in the other. "I didn't realize this was where the ruling-class moms hung out" was the first thing out of her mouth.

"Hi, April," said Karen, embarrassed but also strangely excited by the sight of her. With any luck, April might supply Karen with the information she so desperately wanted.

"How's the new school? Enjoying hobnobbing with the elite?" April went on. "Also, thanks for all the fund-raising help. Not!"

"You're right—I suck," replied Karen, who realized she'd become a legitimate target for April's fusillades. "How's Ezra?"

"Very well! You know, busy living the multicultural dream while others retreat into their velvet cages."

"Fair enough," said Karen. "Hey, I actually have a question for you. Is it true that the Winners Circle charter school is moving into Betts in September?"

"I prefer the term *hostile takeover,*" she replied. "But yes, and my comrades and I on the front lines are already planning our first guerrilla attack."

"Cool," said Karen, wondering precisely who these *comrades* were. Had April Fishbach finally made mom-friends at school? "But I thought you were into the whole nonviolent-slash-civil-disobedience approach to warfare."

April cleared her throat. "I was, but I changed my mind. Sometimes a nation or a group of people is called upon to defend itself."

"I see. So where and when will this insurrection take place? For the record, I'm happy to do anything I can to help."

"Unfortunately, I'm not at liberty to go into any more details about the operation. But I will say it's motivated a lot of people who were previously apathetic to get behind the school."

"Well, *that's* something."

"We've even gained a secret financial backer. Last week, the PTA received an envelope stuffed with a large amount of cash, if you can believe it. Or, actually, we received two envelopes. Two in ten days."

"Wow, really?" said Karen, her heart dancing in her chest. "How strange."

"As you well know, I don't believe in asking for money," said April. "But when it appears in one's lap to finance one's campaigns, one can hardly be expected to refuse it."

"Of course not," said Karen, marveling at the thought that she'd finally won April's approval, albeit without April knowing it, which somehow made it all the sweeter.

"So, that's the update. Meanwhile, how are all the Mather moms in their fauxhemian Indian apparel and fair-trade frocks?"

"Well!" said Karen, smiling despite herself. It seemed she was not the only one who'd noticed the dress code at Ruby's new school. And was it possible that, after all these years, she was starting to *like* April Fishbach? "Anyway, it was nice running into you. I know you probably won't believe me, but I actually miss Betts."

"So why'd you leave?"

Karen sighed. "It's a long story. And I can't say I've made peace with it. I'll tell you some time if you're really interested."

"I have all the time in the world," said April. "In case you didn't know, I'm a middle-aged perpetual graduate student. We don't have deadlines."

"Fair enough."

"Also, for the record, and although we never got along, I was sorry to see you go."

"Well, that's nice of you to say," said Karen. "Maybe we can meet for coffee next month, and I can fill you in."

"Sure."

"In the meantime, can I ask you one more question before you go?"

"What's the question?"

"I heard Jayyden left Betts. Is that true?"

April sighed. "He didn't leave just the school—he left the city. Apparently, there was a fire in his aunt's apartment, and Jayyden was blamed. Since he'd just turned ten, there was legal justification for shipping him off to some kind of juvenile detention facility a few hours north of here."

"You're kidding," said Karen, shocked and horrified by the news. "But how do they know it wasn't an accident? What if he was just trying to light the stove or something?"

"I told you all I know," said April. "In any case, I'm probably alone among the parents in Miss Tammy's class in saying that I was actually sorry to see *him* go too. Maybe I'd feel differently if he'd ever bothered Ezra, but I always had a soft spot for Jayyden. He's had a shitty life, which appears to be getting even shittier. And for the record, I thought he was more or less justified in punching out that little bitch Maeve."

"I secretly did too," mumbled Karen. "But please don't tell anyone."

"My lips are sealed."

And that was how the two parted—Karen feeling unexpectedly well disposed to her former foe and, what's more, tickled by the news that her donation had apparently meant so much. At the same time, she despaired to think of Jayyden, whether or not he was guilty of arson, being pushed to the even more distant margins of society. She imagined him in a tiny gray room with no windows and a metal bed that had been nailed to the ground so there was no chance of using any part of it as a weapon. She wondered if he ever thought about Ruby—and if she or Ruby would ever see him again.

She also felt newly angered about Winners Circle's upcoming co-location and couldn't resist sending a quick message to Clay.

FYI—Ruby's school planning guerrilla attack on Winners Circle co-locators. Needless to say, I've volunteered my services!

Clay immediately wrote back:

So if a stink bomb is found in the robotics room, I will blame you. Greetings from Malaysia. xoxoxo

That he was so consistently good-natured about Karen's disapproval of the main charity he supported was almost unnerving to Karen. She wrote back,

I beg to differ! You will have only yourself to blame.

Clay wrote back:

The only thing I blame myself for is not holding you hostage at the Mandarin.

Karen felt her knees buckling beneath his imagined weight. How would she ever make the feeling go away? Was she really disappearing with him for the weekend? And how long could she keep it all a secret from Matt?

That evening, Ruby announced that Charlotte Bordwell hadn't invited her to her ninth birthday party. Ruby had learned about the snub when she heard other girls in her class talking about how excited they were to be going to the American Girl Place Café to celebrate.

"I'm sorry, sweetie," said Karen, trying to sound stolid. "That's disappointing. But it's almost the end of third grade. You'll have all new kids in your class next year—and new friends too, I'm sure."

But she was no longer sure of anything. Having temporarily relinquished any hostile feelings toward the Bordwells in favor of sympathy for Nathaniel's disability, Karen once again felt mounting fury at the family. Even if Charlotte didn't consider Ruby among her nearest and dearest, Susan could have insisted that her daughter invite Ruby anyway, if only as a courtesy to Karen and because Ruby was the new girl. But Susan had apparently insisted on nothing of the kind.

"I hate my new school," said Ruby. "I want to go back to Betts."

"Oh, sweetie," said Karen, as a tiny sliver of her heart broke off and fell to the ground. At least, that was how it felt.

On Monday morning, after dropping Ruby in her classroom, Karen once again let herself into the PTA office. She placed a chair in front of the door to prevent anyone from walking in and surprising her. Then she pulled out the PTA checkbook.

The baby-blue background looked so anodyne compared to the rage and recklessness that simmered inside her. *Fuck all of them,* she thought. Karen's anger had come to her late in life. But now that it had arrived, it showed no signs of abating. In her most elegant cursive, she wrote another check, this time for five grand. It was a slightly larger sum than she'd withdrawn before, yet, to her mind, it was still not large enough to provoke any raised eyebrows. Even so, this time it seemed safest to make no mention of it in the PTA ledger. If someone noticed the discrepancy, Karen figured she could always chalk it up to an accounting error. To give the check an air of officialdom, she took special care with her signature, producing a deeply slanted autograph worthy of the Declaration of Independence. She put the check in her wallet and the checkbook back in the drawer.

On her way out of the office, her eyes momentarily locked with the school's music teacher's, who was known as Mr. Z. (Like many schoolteachers with long Greek or Polish last names, he'd shortened his to a single letter.) But if he harbored any suspicions about how frequently Karen had been visiting the PTA office, he didn't show it. Instead, he smiled broadly, as if in recognition of her selfless contributions to the school. And Karen smiled back, for a brief moment entertaining the idea that her appropriation of Mather PTA funds was the most selfless act of her entire nonprofit career.

Once again, her theft was met with silence. Little wonder that Karen had begun to feel as if she could get away with anything—even running off for the weekend with a man who wasn't her husband.

On Wednesday evening, she told Matt she had to travel

again for work that weekend and would he mind covering on the home front?

"Oh, wow—I wish you'd told me earlier," he said.

"Sorry," she said, trying to sound blasé. "It's this stupid donor conference in Miami. Molly can't make it suddenly, and she wants me to fill in. I would have told you earlier, but I didn't know I was going. Anyway, I need to leave on Friday afternoon. Oh, and I'm staying at the Ritz-Carlton in Key Biscayne if you need to reach me for any reason." Karen marveled at how easily the lies spilled out of her these days...

But Matt sounded less than convinced. Before he spoke, she saw him search her face. Karen's heart began to beat so fast that she wondered if Matt could hear it too. "All right, well." He paused, grimaced. "I was supposed to see Rick and those other guys on Friday night. But if your attendance is really necessary at this *suddenly announced, urgently important* conference," he said mockingly, "I guess I'll have to reschedule." Rick was one of Matt's friends from Tacoma.

"Well, if I hadn't been going, were you going to tell me about your weekend plans?" Karen snapped back. "Or was I just supposed to be there on the weekend to watch Ruby like I always am?" Despite the skein of lies she was in the process of weaving, she felt irritated again. It was the principle of it—the way Matt felt free to come and go without consulting her first and always with the assumption that she would be there. As if she were a sofa or some other heavy and immovable piece of furniture. Or maybe Karen was only picking a fight to create more distance between them so she could further justify her betrayal.

"Karen—you're getting mad at *me* and you're the one announcing, with one day's notice, that you're leaving town?" Matt said incredulously.

"I'm sorry I didn't tell you earlier," said Karen, trying to regain her composure. "I would have if I'd known."

Matt didn't speak for a few moments. Then he said, pointedly, "So when exactly are you leaving again for your weekend away in Miami?"

"Friday after lunch. So you'll have to pick Rubes up from school, if you don't mind. Or I can get in touch with Ashley and see if she can do it. Whatever you prefer. I should be home by Sunday night."

"Fine," he said bitterly as he walked away.

"I appreciate you covering," Karen called after him.

"It's fine," he muttered again. But it didn't seem fine at all.

On Thursday morning, thirty hours before Karen was due to jet off with Clay Phipps for a romantic weekend in an unknown location, Ruby woke up with a cold. It wasn't a particularly dramatic cold, but Ruby made a big production out of being "ill," as she called it, and she had a temperature of 99.9. Karen didn't consider it a real fever, but Ruby did and begged to stay home from school. And Karen eventually relented, even though it meant her missing a day of work. But Karen figured she could make up for her absence by going into the office on Friday morning instead.

Besides, a part of her welcomed the opportunity to play nursemaid. It was a role that, while mindless, was also clearcut. And there was pleasure to be had in knowing what was expected and then fulfilling those expectations. There was also no denying that motherhood, even if it wasn't necessarily enjoyable on a moment-by-moment basis, could make a woman feel necessary and therefore important and powerful in her own right. Plus, Karen and Ruby's day together, with each in her assigned role, promised to absolve Karen of at least some of the guilt she felt about abandoning her sick child for the weekend so she could spend time with a man who wasn't her daughter's father.

But it's only a cold, Karen attempted to assure herself as she lay sleepless in her bed that night, wondering what to do. And didn't she deserve the occasional respite from the grind? Earlier that evening, Clay had sent Karen another text saying that his driver would be waiting outside her office at two o'clock the following day—and that he couldn't wait to see her, couldn't wait to kiss her all over.

She'd replied, *Me 2, you dirty old man.* As if it were all fun and games. But was she really prepared to play along?

Glancing at Matt, who lay next to her, lightly snoring and oblivious, Karen tried to feel guilty about lying to him. Never mind cheating on him. Yet she found she couldn't summon the appropriate emotion. Her resentment at what she perceived to be his fundamental selfishness overrode it. Or was she lying to herself?

To Karen's relief, the next morning, Ruby announced that she was feeling a little better. While she slurped away at a bowl of Cheerios and Matt slept, Karen went to pack. Staring into her closet in search of clothes for her tropical getaway, she again felt like Cinderella, only this time *before* the royal ball and as if thwarted in her destiny by her failure to own a ball gown and slippers—or, in Karen's case, any halfway-decent-looking sundresses, sandals, tank tops, skirts, or shorts. Not having to obsess about her appearance had once seemed to Karen to be among the great perks of marriage. Now she wondered what she'd been missing. She also wondered if she'd have time on her lunch hour to sneak out and go clothes shopping. But then she risked Matt seeing the credit card bill and growing suspicious of the timing and peeved by the outlay. They were supposed to be saving for their own vacation.

They were supposed to be a happy family too. And they were—sort of. At school drop-off that morning, Karen hugged Ruby extra tight.

"When are you coming home?" Ruby asked her just inside the front doors.

"I'll be back in a few days—I promise," said Karen.

"Where are you going? I forget."

"Miami," she heard herself lying yet again. "Will you be a good girl for Daddy while I'm away?"

"Yes," said Ruby. "But I don't want you to go."

As Karen pulled her daughter toward her, her heart lurched. "Me too," she said with a gulp and wet eyes. And a part of her meant it.

Another part felt inexorably drawn to the abyss. Besides, it was only three days. "I'll be back soon," she told her again.

"You promise?" asked Ruby.

"I promise," said Karen. "I love you so so so so so so so much." After kissing Ruby a final time, she turned her around and sent her down the hall toward her classroom.

Karen was about to exit the building when a new idea popped into her head. Maybe she could take a short-term loan from the petty-cash box in the PTA office—just enough to buy a new pair of sandals and a cute top. Surely a working mother deserved a new outfit every now and then. And if there was some money left over for a new bathing suit whose nylon bottom wasn't sagging nearly down to her knees, like her old black maillot's was, so much the better. She didn't even need five hundred dollars;

four would probably do the trick. To her knowledge, no one even kept track of how much cash was in there.

Karen turned around and, at a brisk clip, started back down the hall. With the key she now kept on her regular chain, she let herself into the PTA office and closed the door. The last she'd seen it, the petty-cash box was in the second drawer down. Karen pulled it open.

At first, she saw nothing but the ledger, checkbook, and a few boxes of ballpoint pens. After ten seconds of rapid sifting, she found the petty-cash box obscured behind a couple of old announcements about a pie sale. She removed its dark wooden lid and quickly counted out three hundred and fifty dollars. It wasn't as much as she'd hoped for. But it was still money. She was transferring the cash into her wallet and preparing to leave when a pair of brand-new taupe-and-white-snakeskin stilettos in an open white shoe box perched on top of the file cabinet caught her eye.

Given the fact that the shoes were still attached to each other with a plastic string, Karen assumed they were unsold goods left over from the school auction. She wondered what would happen to them and who, if anyone, they belonged to. She also found herself wondering if they'd fit and if she could even walk in heels that high. She didn't see the harm in trying. It wasn't as if they were doing anyone any good sitting up there. Karen took the box down from the top of the file cabinet, removed the stilettos, and ran her hand across their rough stippled leather. Had they really been constructed from the remains of a snake—a python even? The thought both fascinated and repulsed her. After she noted the number 38 printed on the inside of one shoe—it was her size too; a happy coincidence?—it seemed like fate that she should have them.

After slipping off her own shoes, Karen sank her feet into the new ones. They were a little snug around the toes, but otherwise fit perfectly. If she and Clay ended up at dinner somewhere fancy, it would be nice to have some equally elegant footwear to put on, she thought. At present, her only dress shoes were a pair of boring black pumps that were best described as "business attire." Karen quickly stuffed the heels in her tote bag. Then she returned the box to the top of the file cabinet, this time with the lid on. If someone asked what happened to them, she figured she could feign ignorance.

Once again, Karen prepared to leave the PTA office, but this time her mind returned to the Easter lunch she'd helped organize a few weekends before at the First Baptist Church of Christ Almighty. She pictured Jayyden in his baseball cap, then Aunt Carla in her sweatpants and shower shoes, both of them waiting patiently in line for their gravy and meat. Then she imagined Aunt Carla examining the charred remains of her apartment. On a whim, Karen reopened the second drawer of the desk, pulled out the checkbook, and wrote a check to herself for ten thousand dollars. She would send five thousand to the PTA of Betts, she decided, and five thousand to Carla Price, care of Fairview Gardens. Maybe Carla could use the money to replace some of the furnishings that had been damaged in the fire that Jayyden had or hadn't set. Karen locked the door behind her and then walked back down the hall and out the front entrance of the school.

It had been a long time since Karen had been in the Hungry Kids office on a Friday. She found it nearly empty. A good number of her colleagues must have petitioned to work from home on Fridays too, she thought. The exception to the rule was Molly herself. She immediately came over to Karen's desk. "I've been meaning to ask you," she began, "did you hear anything back from Clayton Phipps about joining the board?"

"I'm planning to speak to him this afternoon," Karen told her. "We're actually meeting up."

"Oh!" said Molly. "Well, that sounds promising."

"Promising and possibly foolish, but we'll see." *At least I'm not lying,* Karen thought.

The morning dragged on. Karen went through the motions of doing her job, but she was counting the minutes until two o'clock. At one o'clock, she went to the bank and cashed her latest check. She dropped two envelopes in the mailbox outside. Then she walked into a nearby department store. It had been so long since she'd gone clothes shopping for herself that she wasn't even sure what department to look in. Women's? Contemporary? Studio? Eventually settling on Contemporary— she suspected the prices there might be lower than in Women's—she picked out a new skirt, top, and matching bra and underwear. The total came to three hundred and eighty-nine dollars. The bathing suit would have to wait. While paying, she checked her watch and discovered that Clay's car was due to arrive in ten minutes. Karen hurried back to the office.

His white Range Rover SUV was already out front, a driver at the wheel.

"Hello, world traveler," said Clay, kissing Karen hello as she slid into the seat next to him. He was wearing the same pilled fleece pullover he had on the day they first met for lunch.

"I'm not talking to you until you tell me where we're going," she announced as the car sped off down the avenue.

"Don't you trust me?" he asked.

"Why should I trust you?" said Karen.

"Why *shouldn't* you trust me?" said Clay.

"Because," said Karen, swallowing hard.

"Because nothing," said Clay, pulling her toward him and nuzzling her neck. That was when Karen noticed the bottle chillers, then the individual climate controls. It was amazing how quickly one grew accustomed to luxury and even began to find it normal. Indeed, within minutes of climbing into Clay's SUV, Karen couldn't imagine how she'd ever been content driving around in her beat-up old Honda Civic with its vinyl seats and plastic dashboard. And how was it that the seeming entitlement of the Embellished Tunic Moms at Mather should so irk Karen while Clay's unfathomable wealth met no resistance from her conscience? "I've missed you," he murmured in her ear. "Kiss me."

And she did. Wasn't that why she was there? And then she did it some more. At Clay's touch, Clay's smell, Clay's very proximity, Karen felt her insides growing soft and warm...

They took a private plane to a five-star resort on the tiny Caribbean island of Mustique. Clay had reserved them a sprawling villa with a terra-cotta floor, a thatched roof, and its own pool, chef, butler, and white sand beach. The first night, while dining on a patio overlooking the sea and under the stars, Karen wore the snakeskin heels that hadn't sold at the Mather PTA benefit auction, along with her new outfit. "I have an idea," he said, taking her hand under the table. "What about you and I moving down here and starting our own pizza boat like Scooter. I'm serious."

"I'll give it some thought," Karen promised him. And for a second or two, she actually did...

Later that night, they got incredibly drunk and had incredible sex—at least from what she remembered the next day.

In the morning, they slept in, then went snorkeling and saw neon fish in shades of blue and orange. After lunch, they lounged around the pool. In the late afternoon, drunk on the sun, they collapsed on the bed. They'd just begun to make love again when Clay paused, crinkled up his eyes, and said, "Do you ever just think for a moment that the crazy people might actually be right, and the world is about to end or something? Like all that hokey stuff about the Messiah showing up and passing judgment is actually going to happen. And that God really *is* some old white guy with a long white beard. Wouldn't that be hilarious?"

"To be honest, I don't spend that much time worrying about it," said Karen, laughing. "But I do worry I'm one of the crazy people."

"Well, then, come here, Crazy Karen Kipple from College," said Clay, pulling her on top of him. He was laughing too.

At that same moment Karen saw her phone vibrating across the room. In her attempt to block out real life, Karen had turned off the ringer before she'd even gotten on the plane. At first, she tried to ignore it. Then it happened again. It was clear that someone was trying to reach her. But whatever it was, couldn't it wait?

Clay was sliding down her bathing suit when, across the room, Karen saw her phone shimmying yet again. By then, she was deep in the throes of her own internal vibrations and able to block out the sight. Another ten minutes must have gone by. Or maybe it was twenty. Finally, she collapsed in a heap, and then so did Clay. Then she remembered again, slid off the bed. "Where are you going?" he murmured.

"One second," she said.

It turned out there were seven missed calls from Matt's cell, and he'd left four messages. Karen stood frozen as she listened to the first one, a constricted feeling in her chest. "Please call me," he said. That message was followed by "Can you please call me, wherever you are?" And then "Jesus Karen, I don't know where you are but please for the love of Mary, call home—it's an emergency." And finally, "This is fucking ridiculous. Where the *fuck* are you? I'm so sick of this bullshit. Do you even care that your daughter is in the emergency room? Yes, that's right. She had an accident on the monkey bars this morning and got taken away in an ambulance, and you're completely AWOL."

Karen felt as if her head had become detached from her body. "Oh my God—this can't be happening," she said.

"*What* can't be happening?" asked Clay from across the room, his eyes still mostly closed.

"Ruby—my daughter—she's had some kind of accident in the playground, and she's in the ER." Karen grabbed her clothes off the floor and began struggling frantically to fit her arms and legs into the appropriate holes.

"Oh—shit," he said, lifting himself up onto his elbows and half opening his eyes. "What happened?"

"She fell off the play structure or something. I don't know."

"What's a play structure?" said Clay.

"You know—a jungle gym," said Karen, swallowing her words. Socially conscious parents didn't use the term anymore; it was considered retro, if not vaguely racist, though Karen wasn't entirely sure why. But Clay probably wasn't up on stuff like that.

"Kar—I'm sure it's not that bad," he said.

"Why are you so sure?" she said, shimmying her skirt over her hips.

"Kids fall all the time. That's, like, the whole point of being a kid."

"Clay, she got taken away in an ambulance!" said Karen, fitting her feet into her sandals while she tried and repeatedly failed to button the top of her skirt. "I've got to go back to the airport."

"Karen—wait—you're panicking for no reason," he said.

"Of course I'm panicking!"

"But, I mean, isn't your—husband there to deal with it?"

"Yeah, but I'm her mother!"

"Okay but—"

"But what?" Karen paused to search his face.

Clay grimaced, looked away, sighed. "It's just—we have a whole day and night left."

Did he really expect her to fit in a last day of kite-surfing or beachcombing before she left? "Clay, I'm really sorry," she said. "I'm disappointed too. But I can't stay."

"Well, what am I supposed to do here all alone?" he said, sitting upright and sounding almost—was it possible?—peeved. As if she were letting him down, ruining the weekend. It was all about Clay, even when it was about someone else. And this was apparently Clay in a crisis, looking out for his own interests.

Or maybe those were the only interests he was able to recognize. "I don't know—pick up one of those tiki-bar waitresses at the other end of the beach," Karen shot back.

"Gee—thanks for the permission," Clay replied, his tone sarcastic.

But Karen had more pressing concerns than her married lover having to fend for himself for twenty-four whole hours.

She dialed Matt from the side of the pool, her heart thumping so hard it hurt. The phone rang. *Please let Ruby be okay,* she prayed to an old man with a white beard, just in case he turned out to be real.

Matt picked up on the third ring. *"Where the hell are you?"* he said. She hadn't even said hello, and he was already screaming at her.

Karen couldn't entirely blame him. "I'll explain in a second," she said. "But please tell me about Ruby first."

"She swung off the monkey bars and landed on a fucking bike rack—don't ask me how. But she's in horrible pain and asking for Mommy."

"Oh my God, my poor baby," said Karen. She started to choke up. "I'm going to get the next flight out of here. I just don't know when that will be. There aren't that many flights." A mosquito landed on her arm, and she swatted it away.

"Out of Miami? You can't get a *fucking* plane out of *Miami?"* cried Matt. "Or are you even in Miami? I called you like six times and you never answered. I even called the Ritz-Carlton in Key Biscayne, and they said no one with that name ever checked in."

Her time was up. Karen saw that now. Matt would hate her forever, but at least she'd be telling the truth. She took a deep breath and found that she felt strangely undaunted by the task ahead. Maybe it was because, in that moment, her husband knew so little about what was actually going on in her life that he might as well have been a stranger. He wasn't the only one she'd pushed away. When your whole life was a lie, you had no choice but to keep others at bay, lest they get too close and learn the truth. Karen saw that now too— that she'd become an island unto herself. "I'm—I'm actually in the Grenadines," she told him. "I never went to any conference in Miami."

There was silence. In the distance, she could hear the ocean swelling, then receding. "You're having an affair," Matt said. When Karen didn't deny it, he burst out laughing. And Karen experienced the honking guffaws that came out of his mouth as more excruciating than any amount of yelling could ever be. He laughed as if her very existence were a joke and therefore not even worthy of anger. Maybe he was right.

"Yes," Karen finally answered and gulped out, "with Clay Phipps, the hedge-fund guy." Clay himself was only fifty yards from her, but their association had already begun to seem unreal. "He invited me away for the weekend and I accepted. Before this weekend, we'd slept together only one other time. I tried to put a stop to it after that night. But then at some point I stopped trying...If you want to leave me, I understand. Though I hope you don't."

He was laughing again. Then he let loose an exaggerated sigh and announced, "Classy, KK. A really classy conclusion to our decade of marriage. In the meantime, while you're busy sucking off your billionaire friend in Tahiti, or wherever you are, our daughter had a bad accident. So can you please come home and comfort her?"

Karen cringed at Matt's crudity. But she deserved it, didn't she? "Of course. I'm packing right now," she told him in a whisper.

There was never even a discussion about whether Clay would take Karen back to the city a day early in his own Jetstream. He never even offered. He didn't offer to help pay for her return flight either. Apparently, they didn't have that kind of relationship. And the revelation—both of Clay's stinginess and his selfishness—came as a shocking corrective to the fantasies of domestic harmony that Karen had been busy weaving for the previous twenty-four hours. Angry and worried, she packed her bags and, with a forced smile, said, "Thanks" and "It was fun."

"I hope your daughter is all right," Clay told her on her way out, his hands in the pockets of his shorts. But even as he wished her well, he continued to sound hurt. As if Karen were walking out on him. Maybe she was.

Karen took a taxi to the island's tiny airport and paid an astronomical sum for a one-way ticket on a hopper to Barbados. Fittingly, it was the most nauseating flight of her life. As the plane shook and bounced up and down and from side to side, Karen gripped the seat in front of her, half convinced that she was about to fall out of the sky. When they landed, she felt lucky to be alive.

In Barbados she bought another exorbitantly priced one-way ticket—this one to home. The flight wasn't due to leave for another two hours. But at least it was a proper plane with an aisle and seats on either side of it…

It was close to midnight when Karen finally landed in the city. She took a taxi straight to the hospital. She found her daughter still awake and lying prostrate on a bed watching her favorite vaguely inappropriate tween Nickelodeon sitcom, her leg elevated and bandaged all the way up to the thigh. There was a giant laceration on the side of her face. "Mommy," Ruby murmured in a slurred voice.

"My poor baby!" cried Karen, throwing her arms around her daughter. Matt was in a chair at the side of Ruby's bed, looking at his phone. He didn't say hello when Karen walked in. Karen didn't say hello to him either. But after five minutes, she turned to him and said, "Thank you for taking care of Ruby. If you want to go home and get some sleep, I can handle things from here."

"What a kind offer," he answered in a deadpan voice. But he accepted it. He buckled his messenger bag, gave Ruby a kiss good-bye on the forehead, told her he loved her, and walked out.

Not feeling that she could abandon her daughter again, not even to go to the hospital commissary, Karen had a candy bar from a nearby vending machine for dinner. Under any other circumstances, the very idea would have nauseated her. But in that moment, high-fructose corn syrup seemed like the least of her problems. Besides, she hadn't eaten since lunch.

As it turned out, Ruby had broken her leg in two places—one quite badly. Karen felt as if it were all her fault. Obviously, an accident of the same nature could have happened on her watch. But it hadn't. And the fact that it had happened while Karen was sleeping with a man who wasn't Ruby's father filled Karen with a bottomless pit of guilt and remorse. She felt she'd lost sight of what mattered. It somehow followed that all her lies of the past month, including her theft of money from the Mather PTA, suddenly became an intolerable burden to her. For the relief of airing them, she decided she was willing to suffer whatever consequences awaited her, even if it meant humiliation, ostracism, and criminal charges.

In the meantime, Ruby needed a metal rod placed through the middle of her femur. She went in for surgery late the next morning. All went as expected and, two hours later, she came out groggy and with a giant cast on her leg and thigh. Four hours after that, Karen, feeling half alive herself, was able to bring her home.

It was almost evening by then, and Matt was unwinding on the sofa. On the TV screen, a ball was being passed between men wearing bright-colored jerseys. Matt addressed all his words to Ruby and glared at Karen, who did her best to avoid eye contact. In short, it was just like it always was. Except, somehow, everything had changed.

After Karen put Ruby to sleep, she went into her bedroom to finally unpack her weekend bag. Mustique already seemed a million miles away. In fact, were it not for the jarring sight of her new skirt and top, both of them now wrinkled and soiled, she could almost have convinced herself that she'd never been there. Karen quickly stuffed them in a dry-cleaning bag, which she placed in the back of her closet along with the snakeskin stilettos. Then she e-mailed her boss, Molly, to apologize in advance for not coming to work the next day and explaining that she'd had a family emergency. Molly wrote back immediately and, possibly because she loved nothing more than others' hardship, urged Karen to take all the time she needed. Karen was relieved and grateful. But the far more difficult task of apologizing to Susan Bordwell still lay ahead.

Dear Susan, began the e-mail Karen composed that evening. *Hope all is well on your end. I was wondering if we could get together to talk. It's kind of important. Please let me know when you're available. I'm out of the office this week, so I can work around your schedule. Thank you.—Karen.*

As agreeable as ever, Susan wrote back ten minutes later.

Of course! Any time. How's Monday after drop-off?

A text from Clay arrived at the same moment. It read,

Just got back to the gritty city. A tad lonely in paradise—despite the hot French maids. Ha-ha. Dinner? xo CP

As Karen stood staring at the words—Clay's words—regret coexisted with astonishment. Had he really not noticed how furious she was when she left? Or did he think that was all in the past now? She also couldn't help but notice that he hadn't even asked about Ruby. Maybe that was why, despite having been in his arms thirty hours earlier, Karen experienced his latest invitation as, above all, an imposition. As if it—and he—were one more thing on her to-do list that needed checking off.

Karen didn't blame Clay for their affair—far from it. She was a grown woman; no one had seduced her without her full consent. But at some point in the past day and a half, she'd ceased to find him amusing or charming. It wasn't just that he'd shown a paucity of concern for her daughter. It was the realization that he didn't really care about anyone or anything. Because of it, he seemed as hollow as the conch shell she'd found on their private beach. If you held Clay close, you could almost convince yourself you heard the magnificent roar of the ocean itself.

Almost—but not quite.

The next morning, Ashley came over to watch Ruby, and Karen went to meet Susan at Café Beggar, the new coffee shop that held the current distinction of being the Mather Moms' post-school-drop-off café of choice. Predictably, it had unfinished floors, Edison bulbs dangling from a vintage tin ceiling, a menu written on a chalkboard, and a variety of four-dollar anemic-looking gluten-free muffins in faux-healthy flavors like blueberry-yogurt-flax. Before it was Café Beggar, it had been a check-cashing place that took some predatory commission against the paychecks of poor people who couldn't afford to maintain actual checking accounts at real banks.

To Karen's surprise, Susan arrived in what appeared to be pajama bottoms and an old T-shirt with no bra, her hair falling out of a ponytail, her teeth looking a tad yellow. It seemed she wasn't always the model of an orderly life (or wife). "Hello there!" she called.

"Hi!" said Karen, realizing how much harder it would be to confess her misdeeds to Susan's face, especially now that she appeared half human after all.

"If you don't mind, I'd love to hit the smoothie station before I sit down," she said. "I haven't had breakfast yet. It's been one of those mornings."

"Of course." While Karen waited for Susan, she contemplated her opening. Should she preface her remarks with political rhetoric or just get straight to the point? Bjork's latest album was playing on the sound system, and Karen felt as if the singer's atonal ululating were drilling a hole in each of her temples. Finally, Susan returned with a large clear-plastic cup filled with a pasty, violet-colored liquid. *Probably Berry Blast,* thought Karen.

"Sorry about the wait," said Susan, taking her seat.

"No need to apologize," said Karen. "I mean, I'm the one who's here to apologize."

Susan cocked her head and blinked. "For what?"

Karen fixated on the mortar between two exposed antique bricks. "For not being straight with you," she began, her shoulders shrinking into her chest, "or really with anyone at the school. Ruby doesn't actually belong at Mather. What happened is that"—Karen took a deep breath—"I sort of walked by your house one night earlier this spring and saw a gas and electric bill that you or your husband had tossed out. And I used it to register Ruby at Mather. I never thought I'd end up meeting you." Although still fixated on the bricks, Karen looked quickly over at Susan, whose mouth was now ajar, revealing a hint of purple tongue. "And then, by a total coincidence in the universe," Karen said, refocusing on the bricks and forcing herself to go on, "you e-mailed to invite Ruby over. And then you asked me to help fund-raise. And I already felt so indebted that I didn't know how to say no. But once I looked at the numbers and saw how much money the PTA had raised—to be honest, it kind of shocked me. I know you guys don't get Title One funding. But I just couldn't quite believe that a school like Mather, where everybody is basically upper middle class or above, wasn't sharing the wealth at all. Ruby's old school just had to close their library because they couldn't afford a librarian. And it seemed like you guys had so much money that you didn't even know how to spend it." Karen paused to sneak another glance at Susan, whose lips had now tightened into a fish-pucker. "Anyway," said Karen, her gaze falling to her lap, "after I organized Fund in the Sun, I was paying myself back for various expenses when I suddenly had the idea of anonymously sending a small amount of money to Ruby's old school. In retrospect, I realize I should have run it by the executive board first. In total, I—"

"In *total?*" said Susan. "There was more than one time?"

"Yes. In total, I diverted—"

"You mean *stole.*"

"Okay, stole," said Karen, swallowing, "not quite twenty-five grand of Mather PTA money and sent it to Betts Elementary and also to this one poor family who live in the projects and whose kid used to be in Ruby's class. I'm just hoping that, if I promise to get all of the money to you by Friday, you will keep this between us. Of course I'll resign from all PTA duties as well." In search of a shard of sympathy or understanding, Karen tried to make eye contact with Susan. Although humiliated by her confession, she was relieved to have gotten out the truth—or at least most of it. Cutting herself some slack, Karen had decided to omit mention of both the three hundred and fifty dollars in petty cash and the snakeskin heels.

But Susan seemed to have little compassion to offer. "So, you're trying to tell me you've been siphoning off money from the Mather PTA the entire spring?"

"Well, not the entire—"

"I really don't know what to say, Karen," Susan said, shaking her head, "except I'm shocked and disappointed. As for keeping this between us, given the circumstances, I'm loath to make any promises right now."

"I understand," said Karen, shivering on the inside.

"But if you return every last cent by Friday," she went on, "and if my vice president agrees, I will recommend that we *not* press charges. However, I need to look into the legal ramifications of the whole matter first." A lawyer once, a lawyer forever, it seemed.

"I appreciate it—thank you," mumbled Karen, head now hanging and horrified at the thought of a public scandal, her name a punch line in a tabloid story, her job prospects decimated.

"Please have a check for me waiting in the PTA office by

three p.m. tomorrow," Susan continued. "I will also need you to surrender your keys to me within the next six hours."

"That's all doable," said Karen. "In fact, it's doable now. I actually have the key on me, so here you go." She unhooked the PTA office key from her chain and slid it across the tabletop. Susan promptly scooped it up and deposited it in her monogrammed canvas tote. "And here's a check." Karen removed a blank one from her wallet and, as painful as it was to write the number, made it out for $24,187. The sum represented about a sixth of her and Matt's life savings. "But I'd appreciate it if you waited until tomorrow to deposit it," she said as she handed it over. "I have to transfer some funds."

"That's fine," Susan said sharply. "And now, if you have no more crimes to confess to, I'd like to leave." As she stood up to go, her breasts, which turned out to be surprisingly large, flopped to and fro.

But a little fire had begun to burn inside Karen—an underground conflagration that was still seeking oxygen and that didn't feel right about ceding the entire expanse of high ground to Susan Bordwell. "Susan, can I say one more thing?" Karen asked.

"What?" she said.

"I'm sorry to bring this up, but since I'm getting everything out—I have to say that I thought it was really unkind of Charlotte not to invite Ruby to her birthday party last weekend at the American Girl Café. Ruby was really hurt."

There was silence, during which time Susan helped herself to a final swig of her smoothie. The cup empty, she set it back on the tabletop. Finally, she spoke. "To be perfectly frank, Charlotte cooled her friendship with Ruby because Ruby is a loudmouth who yells in her ear and won't let her play with her other friends, and Charlotte couldn't take it anymore."

As chilling as Susan's response to Karen's confession had been, it barely registered compared to the criticism Susan had just voiced of her daughter. "Interesting reading of the situation," Karen replied, "because Ruby's version is that Charlotte lures in new friends, then turns on them to make herself feel important." Ruby hadn't actually said this, but no matter.

"Thank you for sharing that," said Susan.

"My pleasure," said Karen, unable to stop herself. "Oh, and for the record, I regret transferring my daughter to Mather. The computers may be nicer. And her old school may have had more troubled kids in the classroom. But at least the place wasn't filled with stuck-up mean girls like your daughter." Had she really said that?

"Well, then, it sounds like your family ought to transfer back to your old school as soon as possible," said Susan, smiling tightly.

Karen knew she'd set herself up for it. But now that it had been said, it was clear to her that this was exactly what she intended. "I'm planning to do that very thing for the fall," she told her.

"Neither you nor your daughter will be missed," Susan declared as she walked away from the table.

"Same here!" Karen called after her. Though it was unclear whether Susan heard her or not. By then, the president of the Parent Teacher Association of Edward G. Mather Elementary was nearing the front door, her tote hooked snugly over her right shoulder.

* * *

As it happened, Ruby was at home for two full weeks recovering. By the time she was ready to return to third grade, there was less than a month left of school. But that was still almost thirty days, and Karen realized she couldn't stomach even a single encounter with the Embroidered Tunic Moms. Surely Susan Bordwell had told all eight members of the Mather PTA executive board what Karen had done. Among Karen's intimates, it was now only Matt—who was sleeping on the sofa until further notice—who didn't know that part of the story. But she didn't know how much longer she could stall.

When Matt got home from work one evening, Karen told him a version of the same tale she'd told Susan, admittedly playing up the redistribution angle. They were on opposite sides of the kitchen island. Matt had a bottle opener in hand and was busy prying off the top of a Corona Light. Ruby was in the other room doing the homework that, at Karen's request, Ms. Millburn had e-mailed her. When Karen finished speaking, Matt was silent. Then he said, "So you're telling me that, in addition to being a liar and a cheater, you're also a thief."

"If that's how you want to put it," mumbled Karen.

"If you've murdered someone too, now is the time to tell me," said Matt.

"I've murdered no one."

"Well, that's something—I guess."

"I was thinking that, maybe instead of sending Ruby back to Mather," Karen went on, "she could start again at Betts. I'm not sure the administration even realizes she left."

"Fine with me," said Matt, shrugging. "But you better run it by Ruby."

"I will," she said.

And she did.

"Sweetie—there's something I have to tell you," Karen said as she was tucking in Ruby that night. "Daddy and I changed our minds and decided you'd get a better education at your old school."

To Karen's relief, Ruby seemed more perplexed than pissed. "I'm going back to Betts?" she asked, nose wrinkled.

"Yes," said Karen.

"But why? I thought you said I'd get a better education at Mather."

"I did," said Karen, improvising, "but the truth is that I let fear steer us down a road we didn't need to go down. But now we're pointed in the right direction again."

"But where were we going?" asked Ruby, her brow knit.

"That's a very good question," said Karen. "I haven't quite figured that out myself. Until I do, I just want to say that I'm really proud of how you've handled everything. I know you haven't had the easiest third grade."

"Oh—thanks," said Ruby, pausing as if she were trying to make sense of her mother's words. But when she spoke again, it was on a new topic. "Well, I just hope that when Chahrazad sees my cast, she doesn't try to write *sexy* on it," she went on. "It's her favorite word. That would be so embarrassing."

"I agree, and I hope so too," said Karen, thankful for Ruby's digression.

If anyone at Betts should ask about Ruby's absence, Karen had decided, she'd simply point to Ruby's cast and say she'd had a bad accident. It wouldn't even be a lie.

The only person whom Karen felt compelled to contact before Ruby reappeared in Room 303 was Lou. After Ruby was asleep, Karen called her on the phone. "It's Karen," she said.

"Oh—hey," said Lou, neither warm nor cold.

"I just wanted to let you know that Ruby is coming back to Betts," Karen said quickly. "It's a long story, but the short version is that I realized I made a mistake."

"So, it's both long and short?" said Lou, still sounding the tiniest bit prickly. But at least the channels had been reopened.

"Something like that," said Karen, who hoped that, over time, they could rebuild their friendship.

She sent an e-mail along the same lines to April Fishbach.

Welcome back to the front lines, Comrade Kipple, April responded.

An involuntary giggle escaped from Karen, who realized it was the first time she'd laughed in a week.

To Karen's joy and relief, Ruby hadn't been back at Betts for two days before she had a new best friend—Fatima, the Egyptian girl who'd arrived the same week that Maeve left. To Karen's further joy, although she would never have admitted it out loud, Fatima's parents turned out to be educated professionals. Fatima's mother was a sociologist who had a fellowship at a state university branch nearby. Her father was some kind of engineer.

Meanwhile, it emerged in the subsequent weeks that Winners Circle hadn't received as many applications as they'd expected. The result was that two projected kindergarten classrooms had been consolidated into one. After all that, it seemed that Betts's school library would be left as is. What's more, thanks to several anonymous donations made to the PTA, there was suddenly enough cash to purchase new books and even beanbag chairs. But there was still no money in the budget for a librarian, which seemed like a terrible shame to Karen, since the school couldn't keep the library open without one.

Over the next month, Karen and her own NBF, April, hatched a plan to reopen the space with parent volunteers. April did the scheduling, and Karen wrote the e-mails asking for help—and was pleasantly surprised by the number of parents of all colors and creeds (though nearly all of them were female) who came forward to offer their time. A local construction company promised to do a free paint job over the summer. For once, Karen felt as if she was really making a difference. Though she continued to believe there was a place for the kind of fund-raising work she did at Hungry Kids. Maybe it wasn't a pure form of philanthropy, but really, was there a pure form of anything?

The very last Friday in June, Karen was walking down the hall en route to the library, where she planned to help unpack and then shelve some of the new titles that had come in—she'd decided to donate her Friday mornings to Betts, after all—when she ran into Principal Chambers. In Karen's nearly four years at the school, she'd never spoken to the woman directly. In fact, until that moment, Karen very much doubted that Regina Chambers even knew who she was or that her daughter had left and come back. "It's Karen, isn't it?" she said, stopping and pivoting.

Karen could have fallen over. "Yes, it is!" she said, stopping too.

"We're happy to have you and your daughter back at the school," said Principal Chambers.

"Oh, thank you!" said Karen. "We're really happy to be here."

"I understand you ran into a little trouble over at Mather Elementary?"

Karen blanched with embarrassment. Was it possible that

Regina Chambers knew her secret? "Well, yes, a little," Karen mumbled, then chuckled.

"Well, on behalf of the Constance C. Betts School, let me just say thank you for your generous donation. It was very much appreciated." Principal Chambers offered Karen a toothy grin.

"Oh!" said Karen, both gratified and horrified. "Well, it was my pleasure. But how do you—"

"My daughter babysits for a family you might know—the mother's name is Liz Chang. Just had her third kid. She said you were a genius of subterfuge." She laughed lightly.

"Oh, right—I do know her," said Karen, dying on the inside.

"Apparently some of the PTA ladies pushed hard to go to the police, but Liz told me she was the one who advocated letting it drop. Got to hand it to her there!"

"I didn't know—wow—that was so...nice of her."

"Not to worry—it's all between us." Principal Chambers smiled again.

Karen smiled back even as her stomach was busy twisting itself into a poison pretzel. "I appreciate you keeping it that way. Some people might not—understand."

"Well, I get it," she replied.

And that was how Karen Kipple and Regina Chambers became, if not friends, then friendly enough that, by the following fall, Karen felt justified in calling her Regina, just as Lou did.

On occasion, it still made Karen uncomfortable over how few white kids there were in Ruby's fourth-grade class—at last count, just six. When it came time to apply to middle school, Karen found herself worrying, would it hurt or hinder

Ruby to be graduating from such a "marginal" school? But an informal survey of the parents of the new kindergartners suggested that more families from the community were beginning to use the school. And on most days that Karen walked into Betts, she felt proud to be doing her part in pursuit of a more perfect, more unified world. She never felt it more than on the evening of the fourth-grade choral concert. Karen had always considered Whitney Houston's songs to be saccharine and overwrought. But that evening, at the sight and sound of her daughter and her mostly brown- and black-skinned classmates belting out "'Who knows what miracles you can achieve / When you believe,'" Karen felt her eyes tearing up and her lower lip beginning to quiver. Whitney suddenly emerged in her mind as a veritable goddess of all things righteous and inspiring. After nearly five years at Betts, it seemed, Karen was finally getting used to being in the minority. She was also starting to see that race was really just a fantasy, like any other.

Like running away in middle age with a hedge-fund billionaire.

Karen never really spoke to Clay again. Nor did he wind up joining HK's board of directors. Though his LLC did donate another fifty grand at the end of the year. And the two made loaded eye contact across a crowded ballroom during their twenty-fifth college reunion the following June. Karen still found him alluring. But she had no desire to renew their liaison. She couldn't think what to say to him either. She wondered if he felt the same. Several times throughout the evening, she saw him looking over at her table. Though it was hard to tell if he was looking at Karen or checking out

Lydia Glenn, his long-lost crush/red herring (it was never clear which). In any case, Karen had a great time catching up with her old roommate, who—it turned out—was about to direct her first off-Broadway play.

Karen had come to the reunion unaccompanied. But Clay was with his wife, Verdun. There was also a small crowd of people waiting to talk to him at all moments throughout the evening. Even if Karen had hoped to have a private chat, it was unlikely there would have been an opportunity for one. Apparently, all of Karen's former classmates wanted to be near the Class of '91's most successful graduate. In fact, Clay had recently promised to endow his alma mater with a new student center. Karen had read about it in her monthly alumni magazine.

A week after the reunion, Karen had a similarly wordless if far more uncomfortable encounter with her erstwhile Mather friend Liz Chang. By coincidence, they were both in the fruit aisle of Whole Foods, examining organic white peaches—Liz with her adorable toddler in the front seat of her shopping cart, Karen alone. Liz shot Karen a quizzical look and opened her mouth, apparently about to speak. Panicking, Karen fled down the aisle and disappeared into the next one, her heart in her throat.

Karen knew she was lucky not to have been prosecuted for siphoning off PTA funds, and if Regina was to be believed, some of the credit was due to Liz. But ever since a neighborhood mommy blog had published an anonymous account, four months after the fact, of a certain "wannabe Mather Mommy/impostor/swine" who had "lied about where her trough was" and then "helped herself to the PTA teat to the tune of twenty-five thousand dollars," Karen's embarrassment over the circumstances surrounding Ruby's departure from the school had only grown. The final indignity: the article quoted one Mather parent, identified simply as Laura, as saying that it was "past time the school investigate families who don't belong there and who are ruining it for everyone else." That line in particular had made Karen's entire body smart and suffer. What's more, according to the article, on account of both the overcrowding issue and the embezzlement scandal, Mather administrators had recently introduced "far more stringent address-verifying measures" and were now considering "door-to-door checks for the incoming kindergarten class." Little wonder that Karen lived in terror of running into anyone from that tumultuous two-month period of her life—anyone except for Ruby and, more recently, Matt.

In the first month or two after her affair with Clay came to light, Karen had felt ambivalent about her marriage. She was tired of saying she was sorry, tired of being on the receiving end of Matt's hostile and contemptuous gaze. And when Matt moved out of their condo and into his friend Rick's spare room—at the time, it had seemed, for good—a part of her had felt relieved. She hadn't missed coming home from work to find dirty socks and empty coffee cups scattered around the house. She didn't miss Matt passing judgment on her career either.

But over time, she came to miss even the ubiquitous sound of the game, whichever one he happened to be watching. The apartment felt empty without him. Ruby seemed so forlorn about his departure. And Karen felt so helpless in the face of her daughter's melancholy. If only for Ruby's sake, Karen wanted them to be a happy family again—or at least *happy enough,* the way they'd once been. Karen also found she missed having someone to talk to about her day and discuss Ruby with and also complain about her friends and job to. She even found herself pining for Matt's bad puns. And divorce loomed in the back of her mind as, above all, a financial disaster. Plus, the thought of dating again filled her with dread.

Karen reached out to Matt and suggested couples counseling as a precondition to any separation agreement. At first, he refused to go, claiming to find the very concept onerously "middle class," as he put it, in its treatment of relationships as skills that, like tennis or cooking, could be improved. But eventually she talked him into a few sessions. It was there— on the beige, wool-bouclé sofa of a certain Dr. Krantz—that he'd confessed to a platonic flirtation he'd been carrying on with a college intern named Kiley who'd been hired to help with Poor-coran. This, it turned out, partly explained his long workdays the year before. Though as he was fond of pointing out, unlike Karen, he hadn't acted on the attraction. Nonetheless, Karen had been disappointed to hear that, in the end, her tirelessly upstanding, ethical-to-a-fault husband was just another middle-aged cliché. But, really, what right did she have to object? At least everything was out in the open now—or at least, almost everything.

Karen still hadn't told Matt how relieved she'd been to see a telltale dumpster outside Miguel's apartment a few months before.

But she'd told Matt that she wished he'd come back—it was true, more or less—and he'd finally admitted that he missed her too. Slowly, he began to transfer himself and then his possessions back to Macaroni-Land. And now Karen and Matt were officially trying to make it work again. With the encouragement of Dr. Krantz, they'd also decided to take a proper family vacation for the first time in five years. Karen had found a package deal on the Internet to a boutique resort on a relatively undeveloped part of the Dominican Republic. The only question was how to pay for it. Their savings had taken a serious hit after Karen repaid the Mather PTA, and the one-way tickets back from Mustique hadn't helped. Their checking account was lower than ever. And the cost of therapy was only adding to the problem. Karen had only 50 percent reimbursement after a high deductible.

And then, one day at work, while searching for paper clips in the top drawer of her desk, Karen came across the diamond studs that Clay had given her at the beginning of their affair. Realizing she'd never feel right about wearing them and also suspecting that their worth would more than equal the cost of a vacation, she slipped them in her purse and, on her lunch hour, took them to a diamond dealer near her office. The dealer's first offer was on the low side. But when Karen began to walk away, he raised it by two grand. Having now learned the game, she balked again. The dealer's third and final offer was one she felt she couldn't refuse.

Back at the office, she bought the vacation with her new points card, then e-mailed Matt to tell him the good news. She explained that she'd sold a piece of jewelry she'd never liked, so it hadn't really cost them anything. It wasn't the whole truth, but it wasn't a lie either, she reasoned.

Cool, Matt wrote back. For her chronically underemotive husband, Karen had learned, that qualified as a ringing endorsement.

Ruby was especially excited when she heard that there was not one, not two, but *three* swimming pools at the resort.

She was even more thrilled to learn that they were all going together—all three of them—which, in turn, thrilled Karen. She only hoped the weather was good. In the weeks leading up to their vacation, Karen began to obsessively check the forecast in Las Terrenas, each time praying for a little army of sun icons to appear in a row on the screen.

In other news, Karen had just about finished her op-ed about nutrition, poverty, and educational outcomes. Though over time the essay had become less about nutrition and more about inequality. Lately, she'd begun to entertain the radical notion that, as long as there was enough to eat, it didn't matter all that much what you ate. Or rather, it mattered—but only to a point. Having a loving and supportive family mattered more. Now she just had to get up the confidence to send it out.

As for Karen's friends...April finally finished her dissertation, Lou began selling her hand-knit ponchos at a local boutique, and Allison decided to take a leave of absence from her magazine and devote herself full-time to raising her kids after her thirteen-year-old son, Lucien, was caught shoplifting earbuds and selling Adderall to his friends. The police had let him go with a warning, but Allison had gotten scared. Five years after that, he was recruited for squash at Princeton. But that's another story.

As for Jayyden...Karen never heard another word about what happened to him after he was sent upstate. At one point when Ruby was in fourth grade, Karen thought of asking Regina Chambers if she knew anything. But she couldn't think of a pretext for doing so and feared she would only come off sounding like one of those well-meaning, college-educated white liberals who fetishize the deprivations of the underclass.

At another point—years later—Karen tried Googling his

name, thinking that the distinct spelling of Jayyden might yield results. But nothing came up—no evidence of his life, but no evidence of his death either. By then, true to Matt's prediction, Ruby was attending a selective public high school filled with kids from backgrounds similar to her own. One day, out of the blue, while they were shopping for back-to-school outfits, Karen asked her if she remembered Jayyden—"the kid who punched out your friend Maeve for calling his firehouse stupid," as Karen put it—but Ruby seemed barely to recall either one of them. It was like he'd never existed.

Except Karen could never get him out of her head.

ACKNOWLEDGMENTS

Special thanks to Judy Clain and Maria Massie for guiding me through this project; to Amy Davidson and Sophie Rosenfeld for reading and critiquing earlier drafts; to my parent-friends, of whom there are too many to name here, who provided me with stories and perspective. And to my family—BC, TC, and especially JC—for making everything possible.

About the Author

Lucinda Rosenfeld is the author of the novels *The Pretty One, What She Saw…, Why She Went Home,* and *I'm So Happy for You.* Her fiction and essays have appeared in the *New York Times, The New Yorker, Slate,* the *Wall Street Journal,* Oprah.com, and other publications. She lives in Brooklyn, New York, with her husband and two daughters.